QUEST

22 STORIES OF THE HERO'S JOURNEY

B. R. TURNAGE, EDITOR   NYKI BLATCHLEY

ANDY CLARK   SUZANNE DRIGGS   G. J. DUNN

MALAK A. ELTAHTAWY   SUHAIL HABIB

MATTHEW HANSEN   JENS HIEBER   MATT KRIZAN

JOHN NICOL   CATHERINE LO   L. M. PRICE

DAVID STAIGER   ORUWARI IBIAPUYE TOM

INGRID THORNQUEST   OWEN A. WILKIE

FOREWORD BY
DANIEL AUSEMA

Starry Night
MEDIA

DISCLAIMER

This is a work of fiction. Names, characters, businesses, places, events, and incidents are either the product of the authors' imaginations or used in a fictitious manner. Any resemblance to actual persons, living or dead, or actual events is purely coincidental.

Print ISBN: 978-0-9863609-2-3

CONTENTS

Preface   v

Introduction   vii

Foreword   xi

1. Geeks From Space   1
The Ordinary World

2. The Dockers   16
The Ordinary World

3. Nile's Curse   36
The Call to Adventure

4. The Twelve Step Hero's Program   69
Denial of the Call

5. Balor the Spearsman   88
Meeting the Mentor

6. One Good Fight   97
Meeting the Mentor

7. Valley of Wolves and Witches   107
Crossing the Threshold

8. The Shape of a Legend   129
Test, Allies, and Enemies

9. Hero's Retreat   152
Retreat to the Innermost Cave

10. Scepter, Prismscope, and Atelier   169
Approach to the Innermost Cave

11. The Dragonfly Dish   177
The Ordeal

12. The Scales of Fate   187
The Ordeal

13. Soul Music   215
The Reward

14. It Waits For Us All   238
The Reward

15. Fished and Orbed   250
    The Road Back

16. The Princess of Prophecy   270
    The Road Back

17. Wyrmbane   291
    Resurrection

18. The Last Virtue   301
    Resurrection

19. Dead is Dead   332
    Return With The Elixir

20. Doing Scribe Things   356
    Return With the Elixir

21. All That's Left   375
    Return With the Elixir

22. A Hero's Work   384
    All Stages

    About the Author   409

PREFACE

by

B. R. Turnage

Do you remember when you were a kid and played street basketball, your buddy with the basketball was the captain of your neighborhood team? Yeah, that sort of happened with this anthology. I am the editor by virtue of possessing the programs to pull together this tome into a book. That and the fact that no one else wanted the job. I know this because NO one objected when I suggested it.

Kidding aside, assembling this anthology of the Hero's Quest is a team effort crafted in committee. This makes this book an outstanding effort—rendered by the Fantasy Writer's dot org members, with all participants having an equal voice.

We began by presenting various avenues for participation. One was to enter two specific monthly challenges that we regularly hold. The other was a direct declaration that the member wanted to include the story after posting it in the protected members-only section. We excluded no one who wanted to put a story in the anthology, though a couple of members, by their choice, dropped their submissions.

Randomly assigned FWO members also edited the stories of our FWO members. The author and their editor polished the stories, but the author had the final say on an edit. Furthermore, early on, we decided that since we are an international group, we wouldn't force one grammar style on the other members. You'll find US and UK grammar and spelling. Please don't review us as having "lots of typos" because we bucked convention by not having one house style.

That said, none of our stories are perfect, and I would welcome you to review them with a critical eye. Writing a portion of the Hero's Quest as a fully formed story turned out to be harder than we imagined. But we managed it and hopefully illustrated each phase of the hero's journey to bring you this unique anthology.

We hope you enjoy the Hero's Journey.

INTRODUCTION

by

Nyki Blatchley

Back in 2004, I Googled "fantasy writing groups" one day. I'd been writing for many years, and I wanted to find out if there were any online groups specially geared towards fantasy writers.

I got a long list, and the first link I tried out was something called Fantasy-Writers.org. I looked around, joined and never tried anything else on the list.

At that point, Fantasy-Writers.org had been going for about six months and had a handful of members, but I could already see that it was a friendly, helpful and stimulating community. A lot has changed over the past twenty-one years—a completely new website, members dropping off and far more arriving to take their place—but those are still its main qualities.

The heart of FWO (as we call it affectionately) is the story section. Safely behind a password-protected wall, it's a place where we can post rough drafts of stories (everything from a few hundred words to chapter-by-chapter novels) and get constructive, well-informed feedback from other writers that helps us polish stories to publishable standards. I've lost count of the stories I've posted on FWO over the years, and dozens have been published—thanks to the input from my fellow members.

It isn't all work and no play, though. We have challenges, formal and less formal, a fortnightly Zoom chat, and sometimes gloriously silly games. It's a community where we can feel safe.

In 2014, we published our first anthology, Light of the Last Day, and it's only taken eleven years to get the second one out. We wanted a theme this time, and we found one in a process we use all the time, deliberately or unconsciously —the Hero's Journey.

The Hero's Journey was first proposed by Joseph Campbell, in his book The Hero with a Thousand Faces (1949), as a "monomyth"—a template for the structure of stories ranging from heroic tales of mythology to Dickensian life-stories. Although Campbell intended this to be an analysis of existing stories, it's been widely used since as a prescriptive model for creating stories.

Campbell's structure of the Hero's Journey involves seventeen stages, but we decided to go with a simpler structure, proposed by Christopher Vogler in his book The Writer's Journey: Mythic Structure for Writers, which has twelve:

1.Ordinary World—the Hero in their own world, usually restless and longing to leave.

2.The Call to Adventure—events force the Hero to face the possibility of change.

3.Refusal of the Call—the Hero attempts to turn back to safely, though unsuccessfully.

4.Meeting with the Mentor—the Hero meets someone with the ability to prepare them for the quest.

5.Crossing the First Threshold—the Hero leaves the ordinary world for unfamiliar places and situations.

6.Tests, Allies and Enemies—the Hero is tested and has to work out who to trust and who to treat with suspicion.

7.Approach to the Inmost Cave—the Hero and their allies prepare for the most significant challenges.

8.The Ordeal—the Hero confronts death or faces their greatest fear, leading to a new life emerging.

9.The Reward—the Hero obtains the treasure sought for as a result of the confrontation.

10.The Road Back—the Hero sets off to bring the treasure back, though the danger isn't over yet.

11.The Resurrection—in a final test, the Hero goes through death and rebirth, either literally or metaphorically.

12.Return with the Elixir—the Hero returns home, with a treasure that has the power of transformation.

Authors were invited to write a story that focused specifically on one stage of the Hero's Journey. This could be anything from a literal portrayal of that stage in an ongoing story to a play on the name of the stage. Beyond that, each person could write what they wanted (ancient or modern, tragic, moving or comic) and the stories aren't intended to form any single narrative.

In the end, seventeen authors submitted a total of twenty-two stories, with each stage covered at least once. We have everything from a loss-haunted warrior returning home with the reward he's won to a group of heroes trying to beat their addiction to heroism, and from a mediaeval pageant gone wrong to an enigmatic world on a journey through space.

Some of the authors represented here are right at the beginning of their writing journey. Others have novels published, as well as dozens of short stories in highly regarded publications. Some even make their living as writers. Regardless of their experience, though, all have brought something fresh and unique to the mix.

The stories have been edited by a group of ten volunteers. Ultimately, though, we've tried to avoid anything that destroys the character of the writing. Sometimes, the idiosyncrasies of an author's style provide a large part of its charm.

I'd like to particularly thank B. R. Turnage for taking on the mammoth task of formatting and organising the anthology, as well as producing the beautiful cover. I'd also like to thank Nathan Clouse, our own hero, who built our site and defends it valiantly against the monsters of the cyber-world.

So here are the twenty-two stories of Quest: The Hero's Journey, showcasing the talent that's on offer in Fantasy-Writers.org. I hope you enjoy them—and, if you want to join us at www.fantasy-writers.org, you can be sure of as great a welcome as I got twenty-one years ago.

Nyki Blatchley

FOREWORD

by

Daniel Ausema

Writing is so often a solitary thing. You sit down at a computer or with pen and paper and create your wondrous worlds and exciting narratives. If everything falls into place, someone else reads what you wrote in a magazine or off the bookshelf. And maybe, just maybe, you hear from them, hear that your story works, that it touched them somehow. By then, you're probably off creating something new—on your own.

Or you've given up.

This is why writing communities are so important. They bridge the divide between writer and reader and guide writers through the parts of a writing life that are confusing or distressing or simply too much.

Almost twenty years ago, I'd been plugging away at the solitary writing thing for a few years. I had one short story and one poem published (in non-speculative, non-paying markets), a couple of novel drafts on my computer, and a growing folder of rejections. That's when I stumbled across Fantasy-Writers.org.

I began to realize how much I didn't know. About inspiration and getting published, about revising and fine-tuning all the weird and lyrical tales spilling out of my head.

I jumped right into the monthly writing contests as a way to be involved. I cautiously offered up a few earlier stories for critique. I took out some of those novel drafts to get feedback.

We came from a wide variety of backgrounds and brought very different preferences and experiences to our understanding of the genre. We got into wide-ranging discussions about worldbuilding and diversity, about seeing beyond our assumptions and drawing respectful inspiration from many cultures and traditions. To be fair, we also had many silly conversations, as well, many jokes about cookies and dragons, lots of blowing off steam, and lots of encouraging each other.

When I felt ready, I started writing a new novel, and this one I shared with my new friends as I wrote it. It would be another decade before The Silk Betrayal was published by Guardbridge Books, but those early critiques helped shape the story and improve the writing so it would be ready to submit those years later.

Around the same time, I started selling short stories. Many of them began with a contest prompt at FWO.org or were simply sparked by our discussions. The markets themselves were magazines and anthologies I would never have known about without learning from the other writers in the forum.

When I started working on the Spire City series, I was

playing around with episodic storytelling and how serial-izing a work changes its perceptions. I experienced the results directly as I posted the episodes for critique. Other writers—long-time friends and people I didn't know yet—were eager to know what would happen next to my ragtag bunch of orphans and misfits as they faced off against the powerful and corrupt in their fantastical city.

I also had a chance to read many great stories and the starts of various novels and series. Being at FWO.org allowed me to help shape those stories, to figure out what worked and why something else wasn't working, and to cheer them on. We published a couple of anthologies of stories that started here. We saw many other stories go on to various magazines and publishers.

Here, then, are more great stories. While I was not involved in the critiques and revisions of these, but like those earlier stories I read over the years, these have been carefully crafted and cover a spectrum of what fantasy has been, what fantasy is, and what fantasy will be, seeds of the genre in all its wide-ranging possibilities.

If you are a writer or dream of being one, find a commu-nity to join. It may be FWO.org or someplace else, but find a place to participate in the flourishing of many stories and approaches. Read these stories, enjoying the wondrous and the grim, the escapism and the real world told at a slant. They may give you a glimpse and an echo of all the stories you strive to create.

If you're a reader, simply enjoy this smorgasbord of what's on offer. There are flavor combinations you may have never dreamed of and wonders to delight any tastes.

When you're done, share the stories with others! (And consider telling the author how much you enjoyed this or that story—even with the support of writing communities, we writers long to hear from those who read and enjoyed our work!)

———

Daniel Ausema is a stay-at-home dad and educator. His short stories and poems have appeared in Strange Horizons, Fantasy Magazine, and Diabolical Plots, among others. His high fantasy trilogy The Arcist Chronicles is published by Guardbridge Books, and he is the creator of the steampunk-fantasy Spire City series. He lives in Colorado at the foot of the Rockies and can be found online at https://danielausema.com.

CHAPTER I

GEEKS FROM SPACE
THE ORDINARY WORLD

by

B.R. Turnage

J ron ignored the insistent beeping of his communications device and the headache pounding in his temples as he walked from the semester's last class toward his sleeping quarters. He knew what message was waiting for him to answer.

But the awful screeching of his com device seeped into his brain like a siren's call, causing his head to pound further, and he couldn't let it continue. When he whipped out his e-pad, Jron discovered he had not one but two messages. One was from the bursar's office. The other was from the harbor master, who claimed Jron's spaceship slip fees were overdue. If he didn't pay within the next standard day, the ship would be padlocked and held for auction.

His headache increased exponentially.

Fat and overripe yellow qualla berries littered the walkway, and he had to dance around them to avoid stepping into a pile of mush. One purple-leafed branch hung so low it whipped him in the face. Jron dodged the blow but failed to spot a qualla berry and slipped on the pulpy mess.

"Frack!" he swore as he skidded. Jron recovered himself, but not before he heard laughter wafting from the shadows.

"Frack you, Kadek!" he swore, but his friend only grinned a white-fanged smile from the stand of qualla trees, and his yellow eyes floated like lamps in the dark.

"Ha! I caught you acting less than royal for the first time in your life!

"I'm going to show you how impressive my fist is," growled Jron.

Stepping out of the underbrush, Kadek studied his friend's boots, now drenched in the slick qualla berry juice. Jron growled again and wiped them on the yellow ground cover on the side of the walkway.

"For what they charge in tuition for this university, you'd think they'd keep the pathways cleared."

"You are in a foul mood," observed Kadek.

"And why aren't you? You have the same message in your comm unit demanding tuition payments."

"We've got until the start of next semester to pay that," said Kadek brightly.

"But we won't get our grades this semester unless we pay."

"What are you worried about? You're the second smartest guy in our class."

"Second!" snorted Jron.

"Next to me, of course," said Kadek, laughing.

"You quaddock, I carry you through your courses."

"Come on. I'm taking your royal crankiness to the

tavern. A few stiff drinks will straighten out that head of yours. Besides, the girls will be there."

"Girls?"

"Yes, do you not remember? Ilicy and Jenra."

Jron did remember. Kadek had been trying to get a date with Ilicy for the past month. Ilicy came from a very social species in which poly relationships were the norm. While they might go on a date with only one person, they considered it rude to leave friends behind. She would only agree if Kadek got a date for her roommate, Jenra.

"You," said Kadek, "spoiled our double date last weekend because you declared you had to study."

"I've got one more final to study for now," groused Jron.

"Ha, ha. No, you don't. You've been so immersed in work that you don't realize you just took your last final. The last piece for the semester was our joint paper, and I submitted that an hour ago."

Kadek never finished a paper on his own, which made Jron suspicious.

"What are you up to?" said Jron.

"Come on," he said, hooking his arm into Jron's. "We're meeting Fldor. He's got something to talk to us about."

"What?" said Jron. His eyes narrowed.

"Relax! We discovered a way to pay for next semester's tuition."

No amount of prodding could get Kadek to reveal this plan to Jron. At the tavern, Fldor greeted them with enthusiasm. The Silik bore the nut-brown skin, white hair, and very angular features of his people, though today his hair stood in unruly, ungroomed spikes.

The three friends, from different races, suffered the same problem. Each one of them was unusually tall and muscle-bound for their species. In the thinking of their multi-culture, this indicated that they were throwbacks to more primitive and less intelligent forms of their species. It didn't matter that they all drew top marks in their respective majors. In a Universe where small, academic-looking men were considered extremely attractive, they were the odd men in nearly every social gathering.

This common cause bound the three in a tight-knit friendship, and they did nearly everything together.

"Come, come," said Fldor. He poured beer from the pitcher he purchased into their flagons.

"So, what is it?" said Jron. "What is this lucrative plan of yours?"

"Have you heard about the Intergalactic Scavenger Hunt?"

Everyone with a pocket e-pad knew about the ISH. The event, sponsored by the largest galactic merchandise reseller, was a publicity stunt touting Kridex Corp's inventory completeness. The prize was a quarter-billion-credit spaceship outfitted with the latest intergalactic space drive. The problem was that no one had found the spaceship to date, despite all the clues being revealed within a year of the contest's start.

"What? That thing sponsored by the Kridex Corporation?"

"Yes," said Fldor. Excitement shone in his eyes.

"This is your plan? Compete against thousands of people to find one prize hidden in the galaxy? Fldor, that contest has been running for two standard years, and no one has a clue where that ship is."

"Exactly! Because they are looking in the wrong places. Look at this." Fldor whipped an e-pad from his jacket pocket and handed it to Jron. "I've followed this contest and marked out all the areas the registered contestants searched. There are only small sections left unsearched."

"But what about the unregistered contestants?"

"Well, if someone found the prize, we'd have heard about it. For two years, Kridex Corporation has repeatedly broadcast the image of that ship. There is no way that it wouldn't be recognized if it had been found."

Jron couldn't argue with that logic, though it seemed like a far-fetched plan.

"What makes you think we can find this ship when thousands of people haven't?"

"We have a secret weapon," Fldor said earnestly.

"Yeah, right," Jron snorted. "A secret weapon." He resisted rolling his eyes.

"It's true!" said Kadek. "Show him, Fldor."

Fldor brought out another e-pad, held it out, and pulled it back when Jron reached for it.

"This is top secret, Jron. You aren't to tell anyone! I got this from a former employee of the Kridex Corp."

"Are you telling me a former employee sold you proprietary information?" Jron was shocked. That breach could land that employee before the justice bench.

"Sold? No. I can't help it if my uncle, may he rest in peace, used to work for them and kept all his mileage expense reports in a file on his e-net."

"I don't remember you having an uncle," Jron said. He scratched the back of his head, suspicious of Fldor. His roommate was his closest friend, but half his stories were colorful, to put it kindly.

"Well, I did. We didn't talk often because of his work travel schedule. And because I was his closest living relative, I inherited all of his stuff. I compared his expense report to one of the galaxy's uncivilized sectors. Now, why would Kridex Corp. go there? There can only be one answer. That's where they hid that ship!"

"Then go find it," rumbled Jron. He flipped open his com device to stare at his messages again.

"Well, we can't, you quaddock," said Kadek. "To get there, we need a spaceship. And since you are the only one among us that owns one, that would be you."

Jron told Fldor "no" several times, and Fldor smiled while refilling his flask. Jron had no wish to spend his school break wasting his ship's fuel. Nor did he wish to risk damage to the craft, as he was unlikely to get another one for a long time. His father, the ruler of Shibliz, the one moon that orbited this planet, was firm on that score. Because Jron's father indulged his twenty wives with lavish abandon, royal money was tight on Shibliz. The king was both busy and financially drained due to his indulgence in his twenty wives and the fifty-odd children he had sired.

His father's overabundance of marriages was the reason that Jron resolved never to marry. In his royal line, there was no need for more princes or princesses.

As the third son, Jron was not expected to inherit the throne. He worked to earn top grades at school to secure a management position in a galactic corporation. Jron was far from being the only prince in the galaxy with no hope of sitting on the throne his father occupied, and who sought a safe harbor from the politics and finances of home.

As if the devil had been called forth, his phone rang, revealing his father's face.

Jron was tempted not to answer, but that would only result in a lengthy lecture later, so he flicked his finger over the screen.

"Hello, your Highness," said Jron.

"Don't Your Highness me! What is this message I got that your slip fees are due? I just paid for those!"

"I beg your pardon, honored father, but the last time they were paid was at the beginning of the school year. The quarterly payment, ah, never made it to the dockmaster."

"Ridiculous! I'll have Warko look into this right away. In the meantime, you tell that quaddock dockmaster that if he sends one more threatening message to me, he will find out what diplomatic immunity means! Good day, Jron."

His father's image faded, and Jron gave a wry chuckle. He knew his father lied when he insisted he had paid the dockmaster because he always failed to pay Jron's expenses. As the third child of the king's first wife, he was less noticeable to his father than to his other siblings. To preserve his royal dignity, the king only blustered.

No. Shiblez's third prince would blaze his destiny without his father's help. He earned money through board and card game contests, where his large size lent an aura of stupidity, which Jron played to his advantage. There were many weekends when he took first or second prizes.

But the real money came in when Kadek placed side bets. This wasn't legal here on Micklin, but it worked well for both of them until Kadek bet too much on Jron's last set of games, and their association was discovered. Kadek spent the night in jail, but Jron did not, thanks to his diplomatic immunity. But the episode cost Jron his meager savings to bail Kadek out of jail and a stern reprimand from his father, enough to force Jron to give an honor promise to stay away from the gaming tables. As a result, Jron was flat broke.

He would not be paying for any of tonight's beer. And he did not have the slip fees. Jron needed to whip up a solution fast or lose his ship.

But chasing after a ship that no one has found in two years? That sounded like a waste of expensive fuel.

Jron relaxed under the beer's influence while Kadek and Fldor continued talking. The school administrators were quaddocks who didn't care about the students. The dockmaster was a double quaddock for giving him such a difficult time. His father was, well, his father. There was no changing the man.

"Come on, Jron," cajoled Kadek. "It's only a short trip through the Flennen Wormhole. We can take a quick look around, and if it doesn't work out, we'll come home."

"Yes," said Fldor. "If it doesn't, my brother can get us jobs on the farm he works at on Stradex Moon. They like big guys there to help manage the livestock."

"Great," said Jron sarcastically. "Working on a farm. How exciting."

"Do you have a better idea? It's either search for the ship or that."

"Fine, fine," agreed Jron. "We'll go look. But you must help me get my ship out of the dock."

"Does this require anything illegal?" said Fldor.

"Well, maybe a little."

Fldor scoffed. "There is no such thing as a 'little illegal.'"

"You always worry too much," said Kadek. "It's Jron's ship. It's not like we'd be stealing anything. Wait, look. Here are the girls."

Icily, the girl Kadek had been hounding for a date, slipped next to him and gave him a peck on the cheek.

"Hey." Icily's eyes zeroed in on Kadek, though they did wander to Fldor.

"Glad you could come," Kadek said. "We're celebrating the end of the semester."

"Oh! You're already finished? I have one more final at the end of the week."

"Here, have a beer and relax. Where's your friend?"

"Here," said a deep voice.

Jron turned to see a Hylon female slipping onto the stool beside Fldor. The female next to him towered over Jron, though she was short for a female, only seven feet tall. He decided he liked her height. For once, he didn't feel like an overbuilt freak. Her skin was a mottled purple, which Hylons considered very attractive.

"Hello," she said in a sexy, low voice. "I'm Jenra."

Jron smiled. Things were looking up.

Jron motioned for the barman to bring another flagon, and he poured Jenra a drink from their shared pitcher. She sat on a stool at the bar, easing the height difference between them, and Jron noticed her pretty face.

Kadek and Ilicy were getting along well, and his friend regaled her with how he disturbed a nest of jindle bugs and ended up with at least a hundred little red itchy bites. Ilicy laughed, but she might not have known it was during Kadek's attempted seduction of another co-ed in the park that disturbed the jindle bug nest. Jron knew Kadek would steer Icily to the park when they all had a few drinks. Jron considered the same move, too.

He glanced at Jenra. Jron was particularly fond of Jenra's dark eyes and the round globes of her breasts, which were provocatively protruding through the wide neckline of her shirt. Soon, they found themselves pressing their legs against each other. The flowing beer helped Jron feel comfortable and relaxed, and he began to think that Jenra's mottled skin was very sexy. When her hand wandered to the inside of his thigh, he got the inkling that the feeling was mutual.

"Let's take a walk," suggested Kadek with his arm around Ilicy.

"Sounds good," replied Jron.

As they walked away from the bar, Icily looked back at F'ldor sitting alone, drinking. "Isn't he coming?" she said.

Kadek laughed. "Him? No, he's part of some weird cult that insists on celibacy until marriage."

"Oh," said Icily with disappointment.

"Yes," said Jron. "I went home with him one time during a school break. We spent all of our time drinking. They have an excessive number of bars there."

Kadek pulled Icily into him with his arm. "Don't worry, honey. You don't need two men with me in your arms."

Jron was in a good mood due to the beer and the sudden realization that he had completed the school year, likely with outstanding grades. It was a pleasure to have a female interested in him for once. And now that they were out of the noisy bar, they could converse.

"So, Jenra, are you dating anyone at home?"

"Dating? Ah, dating, Icily explained this. No. We don't date. We arrange our marriages from birth."

"Marriages?"

"Yes, after my fourth year here, I will marry a fourth-level electronics system technician. He has excellent advancement prospects. My skills in computer programming will make us a formidable economic unit."

"So, you are engaged," he said with some disappointment.

"Not in the manner you perceive. There is no impediment for us to pursue our pleasures as we see fit. And what of you? Do you have a mate-in-waiting? I don't mind, but I understand such things cause difficulties for you."

"Me? No. There is no mate-in-waiting."

"Delectable," Jenra rumbled.

They entered the park, where the only illumination in the evening gloom was round yellow globes on tall poles. The hazy glow of the light bathed the walkways, but darkness enveloped the little trails that strayed from the main paths. The park was a favorite spot for university students to enjoy privacy from prying eyes. Kadek and Ilicy had already wandered up one trail into a stand of trees.

As they walked through the park, Jron and Jenra let the darkness gather around them. Jenra's hand cupped Jron's backside, which he didn't mind. They heard the rolling sound of water running over rocks before they saw the stream glinting in the moonlight. In the dark, a thicket of bushes on either side of the path thinned to a carpet of yellow-gray grass. The scent of Jula flowers enveloped them.

"This is lovely," said Jenra.

"I see something more lovely," said Jron.

He crushed his lips onto hers. Jenra moaned in enthusiastic enjoyment, and Jron deepened the kiss. Jron decided that Hylon women were his favorite interspecies mating experience.

"Yes," said Jenra. "Give me more."

Jron sought her lips at Jenra's eager encouragement. He gripped her back, running his fingers along her spine, and she arched it.

"You've please me mightily, Jron."

He kissed her on the cheek.

"And you please me."

"Good," she rumbled. "You will make an excellent pleasure mate."

Jron pulled away and gave her a sharp glance. "Excuse me?"

"I'm surprised myself. Usually, we take longer to choose, but I think you'll do nicely. Congratulations, I've chosen you as my pleasure mate. It is a tremendous honor. And Xendix, my marriage bond, will be pleased I made such an excellent choice."

"Um, that's very nice, but I wasn't looking for anything permanent."

"It matters not, Jron. I have chosen you. However, I anticipate that you will require additional training. I will arrange it."

Growing alarmed, Jron scrambled to his feet.

"I say it matters very much, Jendra. You are a sexy girl, and I enjoy your company, but a few kisses do not make a relationship."

"On my planet, it certainly does. Do you not understand? I have chosen you. It's true, I did not expect to make such a choice so soon. And, unfortunately, I have only a few domestic duties for you to attend, but this will give us plenty of time to attend your training before Xendix and I have children for you to care for."

"Listen," said Jron more forcibly. "I don't know what you expect here, but I have plans. They do not include domestic duties or caring for children."

"Sit down, Jron," ordered Jenra authoritatively. "I'm not ready to leave here."

Jron decided that Hylon women were not his favorite interspecies mating experience. They had very strange expectations.

"Well, I am." Jron took a few steps, and then, his feet flew out from under him. He landed face-first in bushes that scraped his face and felt himself pulled backward. He struggled, but the Hylon female had an iron grip on his ankles.

"Stop struggling," Jenra said.

"Let go of me!" he spat. He didn't want to hit a woman, but she was rapidly leaving him no choice.

She yanked him upright and smiled at him as if she had just caught her prey.

"Playing difficult to get? Good. I like that game."

"I'm not playing," Jron said. He jerked his body to break free from her iron grasp.

She sighed. "You will learn to obey. You should learn this now." With that, she smacked him hard in the face.

Jron flew back from the attack force into another set of bushes. However, this time, he heard frantic buzzing and felt the sharp sting of insect bites. He sprang up, and the enraged jindles followed him. Soon, they attacked Jendra, too. As she swatted away the stinging flies, Jron ran. His feet hit the park's path hard, and he fled from Jenra and the bugs. Jindles followed, stinging Jron relentlessly until he exited the park.

He ran back to his dorm, his shirt flapping and his chest heaving from his exertions.

But Jron had forgotten about the qualla berries, and as he neared his dorm, his feet flew out from under him. He landed hard on his back, and his head hit the pavement. As he lay in a haze with the jindle bugs who followed him stinging, unable to move, he wondered what would happen if that crazed Hylon woman found him here. Would she drag him off somewhere to begin a life as a pleasure mate, complete with attendant domestic duties? The idea made him shudder.

Footsteps sounded on the pathway, and Jron desperately tried to raise his body off the ground, not relishing the idea that Jenra had found him.

The footsteps stopped, and he looked up to find both Fldor and Kadek standing over him.

Kadek smirked. "Jron, why are you lying on the ground? Jenra is looking for you."

"Help me up, you quaddock."

"Sure, sure," said Fldor. Both men hauled Jron to his feet. "You fell hard for that Hylon female," laughed Fldor.

"You knew what Hylon women were like," Jron accused.

Kadek grinned widely, and Jron wanted to smash that look off his face.

"I might have heard some stories that they like things a little rough," said Kadek.

"A little rough?" said Jron. "Whatever you heard is far worse. Jendra wants to make me her domestic slave."

"What?" hooted Kadek.

"She's serious."

"Oh, come on," said Fldor with skepticism.

"Jron? Jron?" He heard his name called from a distance away. "You can't hide from me long."

"See?"

Fldor took his communication device from his pocket and typed into it. His eyes widened.

"By the gods. This is serious. Jron's right. If her focus is on him, she will relentlessly pursue him until she locates him and brings him back to her planet."

In the dark, he heard shrilly, "Jron!"

"Let's go," said Fldor.

"Where?" Jron didn't see how he'd escape the determined Hylon woman.

"Your spaceship. It's time to liberate it from the dockmaster."

THE END

BIO: Born into a less progressive era than her brain is wired, Beth makes her living through activities some find dubious. One of these professions is ghostwriting, in which she pens stories for other authors in exchange for money. Shocking! She has also published romance for Bryant Street Publishing under a pen name. Her science fiction MM romance, *Ostakis,* is published under Nine Star Press (how dare she!), and she self-pubbed that story's prequel, *Segun,* both available on Amazon. Her current work in progress is the SF story *Master's License,* though if she doesn't finish the book version of *Geeks in Space,* her sister will keep nagging her about it. She's been a member of Fantasy-Writers.org since October 2013. You can find her at: https://bethtur nage.com/, https://bsky.app/profile/bethturnage.bsky. social, & https://x.com/beth_turnage

CHAPTER 2
THE DOCKERS
THE ORDINARY WORLD

by

Matt Hansen

Balog woke, each muscle in his back protesting. He'd overdone it a bit the day before, but as it was said, the wind and tides wait on no one. Yesterday, he and his boys had rowed until they couldn't manage another sweep, and seeing as he could already smell the fish from Codswell Square, he figured another long day was imminent.

Shoulders and back screaming, Balog rose on unsteady feet. Something about the solid ground made him sick. He reached for the small, oil wick lantern on his bedside table and tried to bring it to life, only to find it was empty. Making a mental note to get more oil from the market, he moved to the hearth to stoke the remnants of the previous night's fire until the coals glowed and beat back some of the pre-dawn's chill. He reached deep into his barrel of fresh water and filled a pot, throwing in a handful of coffee to boil over the embers.

Once ready, he took a sip and sighed. Nothing like a warm brew to raise the sails on a cold morn. Donning his fresh wool pants and cloak and pinning the official Dock-master Crest on his shoulder, he walked down to the water, always keeping an eye out for the night's chamber pots being tossed out of second story windows. The early crowd already shuffled about Codswell's market, setting up booths of the night's fresh catch.

Finding Glintern dozing in his usual spot, with his maroon oil merchant badge pinned to the gray wool cloak wrapped about him, Balog said, "Mornin' Glint. Need a small barrel if ya—"

"Can't do it," interrupted Glint, opening one eye. "Lampers Guild already bought up my whole stock. Look at 'em.," He gestured to a man in a white cloak scrambling from street lamp to street lamp along the wharf extinguishing each glowing wick. "Sunrise's still an hour off and already they're putting 'em out to save on the stuff. Haven't seen a whaler in almost two seasons. Northern passage is still closed up tighter'n one of your own bowlines."

Balog frowned. "That bad?"

"Aye, and a sight worse. Hanrathy's due to send two more ships out to see what's causing it."

Sighing, Balog nodded. "I know. Me'n the boys get to spend the day rowing 'em out, what with the wind onshore. Could smell you from my house."

Glint smiled. "Best get to it, then."

Balog nodded again and continued down the wood

planks to the docker's hut where Kralmer sat with his feet up watching the quiet morning waters.

"Master," nodded Kralmer.

"All quiet for the mornin' watch?" Balog grumbled. He gave the kid the extra cup of coffee he'd brought down from his place as a thick yawn stretched from the boy's mouth. Man, Balog reflected. Seemed he'd grown a foot in the last year alone, even if he still had that youthful rosiness about his sun-darkened cheeks. Balog wrung his hands together, easing some of the age from his joints.

"Yes, master. Thank you," Kralmer said to the coffee, taking a careful sip. "The *Sea Hammer* and *Hero's Kiss* are making preparations to sail."

Balog nodded, and the two of them stood in companionable silence as gentle waves lapped the granite boulders that had been blasted and hauled down from the mountains to create the calm harbor. Crews swarmed the decks of the two ships under flickering lantern light as the night sky gave way to coastal gray and the sun rose behind the thick marine layer.

Once all dozen of Balog's boys had arrived, each blinking the sleep from his eyes and stretching thick shoulders in preparation for the day, Balog addressed them. "Tide's crawling today and the wind is only slightly onshore."

Kralmer waved him down with a half-sleeping nod. "Yea, yea, yea, we know."

Smiling, Balog continued. "We've got another day of hauling here before us. Rememb-"

"Well if it isn't Balog's little docker club."

Balog turned. A young man in full, shining armor, with a helmet under one arm and his other hand resting upon a jeweled hilt, sat upon a magnificent horse. It was jet black with a chest like a pair of barrels. Balog kept mostly to shore and ships these days, but he remembered enough of his youth and had loaded enough animals to know that this one would charge down a dragon without flinching.

"Hero Destream," Balog said, inclining his head to the man. Balog admitted he couldn't use the word boy with this one, regardless of his smooth chin, full flowing hair, and lack of a single line of age on his face. He definitely looked the part of Hero. "We humbly wish you luck on your journey."

"Luck," Destream scoffed. "The ordinary man's elixir. I'm trained by Hanrathy himself. My skills will propel me to victory. Not any such tripe as luck."

"Well, we wish you skill and-"

"Enough, peasants," he said, bowling the boys aside.

Iranol the cadence drummer, Balog's youngest at around thirteen, grumbled at him.

"The *Hero's Kiss* awaits," Destream continued. "I shall see you before the first snows of autumn. And with me shall be the head of Goldiathrax the—"

"Enough, Dessy," said another voice from behind Balog. He turned and Bryce Broadarm, named for the arms that seemed to stretch his mail to its limit, stood behind him. This Hero was more the boulder-type of human and less that lean and clean type of Destream. "We don't even know if Goldiathrax is behind the attacks. Now this man wished you luck on your journey. Thank him and begone."

"Hmph. Not an ounce of class, Bryce, to interrupt a declaration such as mine. Upon my triumphant return, you and I shall have an accord, if you make it back alive, that is." Balog flinched as Destream removed his gauntlet.

All eyes watched the clanging metal strike the cobbles at Bryce's boots.

Without taking his eyes from Destream, Bryce said, "Dessy, we're to be allies in the coming battle. And our enemies are strong. Over a dozen Heroes we've already thrown at them, and their widows will tell you how they fared. Now pick it up yourself. I'll not enter this fight as enemies."

"Fine then, coward," said Destream. "When we meet the monsters in the field, do not get—"

Everyone paused as Kralmer, one hand holding the now-empty mug, reached down and picked up the gauntlet. Destream hesitated as the young man held it out to the knight.

Balog smirked. Anyone would hesitate to challenge Kralmer, even a trained soldier. Though Balog still thought of him as a boy, he couldn't deny that few, including Destream, were a match for Kralmer's new found height. And Balog knew for certain Kralmer could hoist a ten-butt dinghy on his shoulders. The only reason he wasn't in the Hero's Guild was because his family couldn't afford Hanrathy's ridiculous fees. Balog was lucky to have the boy. It cut his own rowing nearly in half.

"I'll not take challenge from a peasant boy." The knight swallowed. "Dockmaster, I shall have this docker flogged as soon as I return for such an affront." He snatched the gauntlet back. With a steady spine and without looking back, Destream rode down the docks, his horse's hooves clomping across the timber.

"Sorry about that," said Bryce. "He's good, but he can be an ass about it."

"It's no matter," said Balog. "But you're right, Hero Bryce. In the last season, we rowed out thirteen ships, each with a hero and an entire squad of soldiers." Balog shook his head, the weight of the loss settling on him. "Whatever's keeping the northern passage closed is a fierce beast. A full-grown male dragon at the least."

"I know," said Bryce as his gray eyes looked towards the open sea.

"Just watch yourself," said Balog. "And keep an eye on Hero Destream, too. I'd rather the city not lose another one."

Holding out his hand, Bryce said, "I will, Dockmaster."

Balog shook it in earnest.

Grinning through a wince as Balog released him, Bryce said, "These many years of rowing have given you a boar's strength. I think if we put maces or axes in the hands of you and your boys, we'd be unbeatable as a nation."

Balog smiled. "Not in these hands. Nothing but sweeps and ropes for me. Good fortune favor you on your journey, Hero."

Inclining his head, Bryce stomped towards his waiting ship with all the impetus of a boulder rolling downhill.

"All right, boys," growled Balog. "Tides turning. Let's get to it."

They all lumbered into the row boat. Calling cadence from the bow, little Iranol fell into rhythmic pounding on his drum while Balog took his place at the rearmost oars. They rowed first towards the *Hero's Kiss*.

"Anchor down," shouted the ship's mate from the capstan, once they were in position near the bow.

As the creak of the chain rattled, Kralmer hooked it with his gaff and eased the iron anchor—heavy enough that one wrong move with the thing could capsize and kill them all —into the boat while the rest of the boys kept it steady. Even having trained them to do it, Balog marveled at the efficiency and precision of the team before telling Iranol to start up on the drum. They rowed out a distance and then

Kralmer heaved the anchor over the side with a splash. Balog signaled, and the *Hero's Kiss* inched forward as the capstan winched the line back in.

Leaving the *Kiss* to its business, Balog's crew struck up a new cadence and practically flew over the water towards the *Sea Hammer* to do the same with them.

Alternating between vessels, they inched both ships out of the harbor, one anchor chain length at a time.

When the long day of kedging was through, Balog sat on the dock with his bare feet dangling over the water and attempted to rub the feeling back into his scarred and calloused hands. He watched both ships catch favorable northbound winds and disappear over the horizon into the setting sun.

Dock planks groaning under his bulk, Kralmer walked up with a steaming bowl of broth. "Do you think Bryce will make it?" he asked.

Balog sighed. "I hope so. As much of a posh as Destream is, I hope he makes it, too. I don't know what's riled the beasts up, but I don't like losing the city's Heroes. I just wonder what Hanrathy's doing with them for them to be so ineffective. They should be prepared for a dragon or two. And I can't imagine what's clogging up the passage. Glint said we haven't had so much as a fishmonger make it through in two seasons."

"Well," said Kralmer, "I hope Bryce clears it for us. Or the whole city's in for another lean winter, and my family's rations'll be the first to go. Me'n all the others."

Swatting Kralmer's shoulder, Balog said, "Best not to worry. Leave the Heroes to their business. For now, join the others at Ordy's for a pint. I've got somewhere to be."

Kralmer nodded, tipped the bowl of broth back, and then left.

Sitting for a while after Kralmer had gone, Balog decided he couldn't put off a visit any longer.

Winding his way through the dockside alleys, his legs, tired from rowing all day, protested as he began the rise uphill towards the Arches District, so named for the grape vine arch that one had to pass through to reach the sprawling estates of the wealthiest families of the city.

The guard posted at the portal nodded at Balog's crest as he walked by.

Past the orchard owner estates and the city council housing, Balog saw the sprawling compound of Hanrathy the Hydra Slayer, Heromaster of the City of Bellenfall and the surrounding countryside. The place glowed with lantern light in the soft dusk of evening, clearly pulling extra rations from the city's dwindling oil supply. Gold leaf trimmed the marble walls of the gaudy palace, and the white sand pathway wove through sculpted topiary. Creatures of all shapes and sizes surrounded the well-lit, hundred-headed hydra centerpiece.

Balog scoffed as he walked up to the entrance of the main house.

The guard, a hulking figure in full plate armor with both a mace and a sword at his waist, held out his hand. "Guild-master Balog," he said. "I shall send a servant to announce you."

Inclining his head, Balog waited while a boy, no older than ten, scrambled into the house to find Hanrathy.

When the boy returned, out of breath and sweating, he nodded at the guard, who in turn waved Balog forward. The interior of Hanrathy's mansion was just as opulent as the exterior, but compared to Balog's dockside hut, it seemed a drafty cavern of cold stone and an even colder welcome.

The boy led Balog into a dining room that could've

housed an entire ship, with a massive table around which sat at least a half-hundred chairs. Only one, however, was occupied.

At the head of the table with a roast boar, a plate of grapes and cheese, and a goblet of gold before him, sat Hanrathy.

"Balog." The man's voice boomed as his jowls shook under what used to be a prominent chin. Spittle flew over the table, and Balog swallowed his disgust.

"Hanrathy," he said, inclining his head.

"Please, please old friend." Hanrathy gestured at the seat to his right.

Balog sat.

"Some wine? I insist." Snapping his fingers, Hanrathy didn't even look up as a servant shuffled forward with a second golden goblet full of a rich maroon drink.

Balog took a polite sip, almost choking on the dryness as it slid down his parched throat.

"Finest of the Balfrances' western fields. A bit softer than last years', but the richness..." Grinning, Hanrathy took another sip.

The intricacies of wineries and vintages were lost upon Balog, so he placed his cup back on the table and said, "We need to talk. I just saw off Bryce and Destream. Both headed to the northern passage."

Hanrathy slowly put his own goblet down and swallowed. "Both fine boys. Success is sure to—"

"Save it," said Balog. "I'm not some lordling you have to sell on your classes. I just want to know why more than a dozen Heroes haven't returned from this fight. What're you teaching them?"

With each word, Hanrathy's face fell and his eyes hardened. He looked up at the servants standing in the shadows ready to refill anything he asked for. "Away with all of you. Out."

Waiting until they all scurried from the room, Balog continued. "We need the lanes open. What's sinking the ships and why can't the Heroes take care of it?"

"You think I know what's sinking them? I've sent out scouts and ships both. They either disappear or come back reporting clear skies and not a trace of beast on the land. You think I'm not saddened by the losses? Brendan. Lasheen. Pritori. I knew them all from children. How dare you come here and question me?"

"Just stop sending the city's promising youths to their deaths. Sail out and find out what it is."

"I don't see you readying your own ship to go," said Hanrathy.

Balog's face fell. "It's not my job."

"Exactly," growled Hanrathy. "You could've trained them. You killed the Hydra and chose to give me the credit because you couldn't hack the attention. So go back to your fish-rank, salt-rotted planks and leave my business to me."

"Bah," Balog grumbled again and stood to leave.

"Always a pleasure," said Hanrathy, voice dripping with venom. "You're welcome anytime."

Fuming all the way home, Balog opened his door and slammed it. The timber groaned against the abuse. He grabbed his lantern, forgetting that he had no oil left and instead stumbled through the darkness to relight the hearth. He cursed as he stubbed a toe on a chair leg. Sinking into the seat, he sat in silence, staring at nothing until he could keep his eyes open no longer. He dreaded the early morning hour that already crept up on him and hoped he'd wake with enough time for morning coffee.

GRAIN from the northern farmlands and oil from the whalers became a scarce commodity in Bellenfall. And still Balog waited every day for any sign of the Heroes' ships or any news of them. But there was none until one day so deep into autumn that the city had already seen a few nights of snow, and when Balog was sure the ice must have closed off the northern passage until spring, the silhouette of a sail appeared on the horizon before a dying sun. It was tattered, strips like ribbons flailing in the wind.

Squinting, Balog sat up.

"Master, what shift have I—"

"Shush," Balog told Kralmer. And the man stepped up next to him.

"What ship?"

"I'm unsure," said Balog.

"Scurbanol," cursed Kralmer. "That's the *Hero's Kiss*."

Ice gripped Balog's chest. "Are you sure?"

"Absolutely. Square-rigged schooner. Two masts and a puckered lady's figurehead. Yes, it's the *Kiss*."

"Go," said Balog. "Ring the bells and get Hanrathy down here. She's limping and something looks to be cutting the water a hundred or so paces behind."

Kralmer ran off, and before long, the warning bells boomed in the coming night.

The ship sailed into the harbor, blessed as it was on the outset of its journey by a favorable wind. The trailing ripples submerged somewhere outside of the breakwater.

Standing at the prow with his armor dented and torn, Destream threw out a rope to one of Balog's waiting boys. As his boots clanged on the planks, Destream dipped in exhaustion, and Balog was there to catch him. Wincing

26

against the foul, spoiled-fish smell emanating from the knight, Balog helped lower Destream to a bench.

"What happened?" Balog asked. "The *Sea Hammer*?"

"Kraken," cried Destream. "It was a kraken."

Feeling all the blood drain from his face, Balog paused. He grabbed Destream by the shoulders, gently shaking focus back into the man's eyes. "Bryce?"

Destream didn't say a word, and Balog's heart fell further.

"He saved us," Destream whispered before anybody could hear. "The beast had me in its clutches. Was squeezing the life out of the *Kiss*. Bryce sailed straight into its maw so we could get away. I've never seen—" Destream hesitated.

"A Hero to the end," said Balog.

"The truest Hero," agreed Destream. "Him and his crew. Lit their damn ship aflame first, but the beast's thousand arms tore it apart, swatting it to the depths. Gave us just enough time—" Destream stopped again. He didn't need to say anything further.

Stepping forward from the gathering crowd, Hanrathy grabbed Destream, elbowing Balog out of the way. "What happened? Did you kill it?" A smile split Hanrathy's face as he yelled so the surrounding citizens could hear. "I knew it'd be Destream the Destroyer who finally vanquish—"

"No," yelled Destream over him. "We didn't kill the kraken." The bustling crowd quieted. The only sound was the word kraken rippling through to those who hadn't heard Destream's pronouncement. "It harried us all the way home. Even now it's out there somewhere."

Eyes grew wide in the deepening darkness of the night.

Hanrathy's face glowed white like the full moon shining overhead. "Kraken," he croaked. "In our harbor?"

Panicked yells started from the back of the crowd, and Balog sensed fear gripping the mob. They began to surge away until Kralmer stepped atop a pile of rope and yelled above their heads. "Enough! We will not panic!"

Everyone quieted, staring at Kralmer. Gesturing towards Hanrathy, he said, "Heromaster is here. What is a kraken compared to a hydra? He'll know what to do."

Every eye turned towards Hanrathy, and he wilted like a man three weeks in the desert.

"I...I..." he stammered. "We...We can't beat a kraken. My boys are warriors. Trained with firm wood or solid earth beneath their feet. What am I supposed to do about a kraken?"

Rumblings echoed through the crowd.

Watching all of the ashen faces glance around looking for someone to lead them, Balog swallowed his own rising panic. He'd faced beasts in his youth, armies and dragons and even the hydra, but to place the entire city's fate in his hands was something he'd spent his whole life avoiding, preferring to just lead his little dockers. All his boys were watching him. Balog looked at his tired hands to avoid their beseeching eyes. Rope burns crossed his palms, and his knuckles were thick and red from decades of abuse. Clenching them into fists, he growled. "Bah. Begone then, Hanrathy. Run back to your gilded home and your false trophies." Turning his back on the Heromaster, Balog looked to the captain of the wall guard. "Scorpions. As many as we got mounted bayside. If a limb breaks the surface, spear it."

The man nodded and ran off bellowing orders to his men.

Turning towards the lamplighter's guildmaster, Balog continued. "And oil. I know we're low, but bring whatever the city's got left to the catapults. And then set the harbor afire."

As the lamplighter scrambled away, the crowd grumbled until Destream yelled out. "The rest of you, be gone. A kraken's useless on land, but I've seen the tentacles' reach. Anyone harborside of Arches'll be in danger."

No one really moved until Kralmer, still atop the ropes and a head and shoulders above everyone, yelled, "Hop to! You heard the warrior."

The people scattered.

Balog and his boys raced towards their boat.

"Load up," said Balog. "Kralmer?"

The man looked at him.

"The harbor's gonna burn like a bonfire. Soak the boat so we don't go up with it."

Nodding, Kralmer grabbed the nearest bucket and began dumping water on their row boat's wooden planks.

Watching the dark water as the bells throbbed in earnest throughout the city, Balog trembled. The center of the harbor exploded in a huge rushing wave. The kraken broke the surface. In two tentacles, it held aloft giant, blasted-granite boulders from the breakwater. It hurled them through the air.

Balog watched as the rocks arched high overhead, one coming down with a thump on the fish stalls of Codswell Square, the other decimating the *Hero's Kiss*. Wood splinters flew like a swarm of wasps, forcing Balog and the others to cover their faces. The entire dock trembled.

As another tentacle wound up to release a third boulder, the scorpions thrummed from around the walls. Javelins speared the tentacle, and the boulder fell from its grasp while the wounded appendage slipped beneath the surface.

"Let's go," shouted Balog to his dockers.

They scrambled into the boat with a stack of spears. Just as Balog was kicking them away from the dock, Destream, with sword drawn, jumped in with what remained of his armor.

Looking at Balog, determination lining a face that before had never held a worry in the world, he said, "I know what I've been my whole life. Let me make recompense now. Let Bryce's sacrifice for me not be for nothing."

Balog nodded.

"Sit here," said Kralmer, moving Destream to the bench just behind the barrels and out of the way of the sweeping oars. "And try not to move until you're needed. You'll knock us out of time."

Nodding, Destream settled into the boat.

"Sound us off, Iranol," said Kralmer.

The boy beat out a cadence on his small drum, and the boat rocketed forward just as a bulbous head, like an octopus the size of an entire ship, breached the surface. It was armored like a crab with two eyes glowing above a giant mouth that roared so loud a ripple, like wind blowing across the otherwise still waters of the harbor, pushed their boat back a dozen oar lengths. Yellow teeth as long as swords were speckled with the leftover meat of past meals, and a splinter, unmistakably from the prow of the *Sea Hammer*, pierced its bleeding gums.

And still the dockers rowed forward.

The creature flinched as scorpions from the walls harassed it. But more tentacles with more boulders broke the surface, sending the missiles towards the city's defenders.

At least it distracted the creature from their little boat.

Looking at the sweat-lined faces of his boys pulling at

the oars, Balog's stomach soured. He might lose some tonight.

A different thud—this one of a catapult instead of the scorpions—sounded, and Balog turned in time to see a barrel explode against the side of the creature's head, coating it in the thick slime of lamp oil.

A flaming arrow arced high over the harbor next, but the shaft hit short, fizzling out in the water.

"Kralmer," Balog shouted. "Wet the wood some more. It's about to get hot."

As Kralmer set to work, Balog watched the shore. He could see Hanrathy unloading a wagon full of barrels. Smiling, Balog hoped that Hanrathy had refound his backbone.

Another thud and another barrel.

"Steady," said Balog. They were under the flailing limbs now. Ten ton rocks, stolen from the seawall, flew overhead. They were in the heart of what felt like a maelstrom trying to suck them all to depths and pressures that would grind their bones to dust.

Another barrel and more oil. And a swarm of flaming arrows. This time, they lit. And the fire slid across the surface of the water like a charging cavalry.

The beast roared.

"Row!" Balog screamed. And his boys didn't flinch, not even little Iranol on the prow. Grabbing his spear, Balog continued. "Kralmer, we've got to get close. Straight into the maw!"

Balog watched as another thrum of the catapult sounded. This barrel flew straight at the kraken's face, but the creature plucked it out of midair with a flailing tentacle. Whether out of reflex or anger, it shoved the barrel into its mouth.

The next rock it threw slammed into the wall, and Balog had to look away. He couldn't worry about that now.

They were fifty oar lengths away, and the kraken's eyes, like deep coals burning white and hot, fixed on their boat. A tentacle, wider than four Kralmers, stormed out of the water next to them and dove back into the water on the other side, threatening to encircle the entire craft and drag them all under.

The grip tightened, and Balog thought only of his boys. Grabbing one of his half dozen spears, he turned towards the tentacle, but Kralmer stole the weapon from him and said, "Kill the thing. I'll keep us floating."

Destream drew his sword.

Drawing thick globules of lime green blood, both men struck either side of the phalange. The kraken roared. As quickly as it had arrived, the limb released them, disappearing beneath the dark waters.

The wood of their hull singed as the flames caressed them, casting Destream in orange, flickering light. Standing on the rocking boat, sword and armor stained green in the monster's blood, he growled back at it.

Balog had to admit it was the most heroic thing he'd ever seen.

Kralmer nodded at Destream just before five more tentacles erupted from the water.

"Twenty out!" screamed Balog, and he gripped the spear, focusing on his own task. It would be difficult to throw on the rocking vessel, especially as Kralmer and Dessy moved back and forth hacking at the beast's limbs. And they all were covered in gore, hands slick on the oars as his own were on the shaft of the spear.

But still his boys rowed into the danger, bolstering his own courage.

At fifteen oar lengths out, Balog rolled the tip of his first spear in the flaming oil sitting on the surface of the sea. It lit. The creature's face was a man's height above the roiling water, and in its mouth, Balog could see the leaking barrel of lamp oil. Steadying himself, Balog hurled the weapon. It arced out but glanced harmlessly off the beast's carapace.

Black smoke billowed in the air all around them. Balog's eyes stung, tears threatening to blur his aim.

The creature roared again and flailed its limbs.

Crouching down, Balog steadied himself on the sides of the boat as another tentacle, thick as a dolphin, slammed into the side of it. Balog's spears rolled, and he lunged for them, singeing his hand but managing to grab a single one before the rest plummeted into the burning bay.

No more barrels flew.

No more javelins.

It was just Destream, Balog, and his dockers.

Cursing as another limb struck the hull, Balog watched Kralmer stumble off balance. His arms spun like a mill wheel, and just as it looked like he'd land inside the boat, another tentacle slammed into Kralmer's chest, propelling him out and into the water.

Balog almost jumped after him, but a tongue of flame made him flinch. Before he could recover, Destream, in his broken armor, leapt from the bulkhead sword first, splashing into the turmoil of the harbor. The flames curled around him as he went under.

Balog, with smoking tears in his eyes, focused on his final shot.

He lit the tip of the spear. The only one left.

Hefting it, he watched as the kraken opened its mouth in a bellow that rattled inside Balog's skull. Through the spittle and rotting debris, Balog threw.

33

The weapon pierced the barrel of oil between the beast's teeth. It exploded, blasting the barrel apart and painting the side of the kraken's face in fire. The carapace blackened and cracked, and the flesh beneath charred like a baking fish.

With a final, keening cry, it keeled over, limbs falling limp in a series of splashes around Balog's boat.

The creature slipped beneath the surface, and the blazing waters stilled.

Collapsing in exhaustion, Balog watched his boys slump forward, oars hanging limp in the air.

Balog's heart was heavy.

Kralmer. Destream.

"There," shouted Iranal. And a head broke the surface of the bay in a spot not burning.

Kralmer, hugging the still form of Destream, side-swam towards the boat.

Tossing a rope, Balog's boys managed to haul them in.

They floated there as Destream's eyes slowly blinked open.

The moon still shone overhead, and the water danced on fire. Flickering city lights sparkled like the star-strewn sky behind a crumbled section of the wall. And in a boat, a hero sat with ordinary dockers, having saved their city.

THE END

BIO: Matt Hansen is a passionate storyteller and fantasy enthusiast who draws inspiration from the breathtaking landscapes of Southern California. With a love for the ocean and snorkeling, as well as a knack for mountain trekking, Matt crafts immersive worlds hoping to transport readers to otherworldly realms. He shares his life with his talented musician wife, whose encouragement has helped him turn his dreams into reality. Together, they embrace the magic of creativity and adventure, inspiring others to explore their own imaginations. Matt has been a member of FWO for over 7 years.

...

CHAPTER 3
NILE'S CURSE
THE CALL TO ADVENTURE

by

Malak A. Eltahtawy

C leo's feet hit the cobblestones as she stomped away from the headmaster's office. She exhaled, recalling her conversation with the old beast.

"Miss Cleodora, to what do I owe the pleasure?" he had asked, pinching his nose.

"Sir, it's been four days. Four whole days! Where's Friddy?"

"I told you, he'll be back soon."

"It is unusual for him to leave without notice. Are you sure he's not in danger?"

"May I remind you that you are responsible as a vice president to lead other students by example and not cause unnecessary disturbance? It's best you apply yourself to your studies and let us adults handle this."

"But sir–"

"Trust me, Mister Fridolf will be back soon. Now, if you'll excuse me," the headmaster said, kicking her out politely.

Cleo had bowed her head before she left his office. With how far his promises went, she knew she would have to take this matter into her own hands. She would not risk her friend's safety because of neglect.

The golden rays of the early spring sunset weren't enough to warm her insides. It had been like this for the past four days. She constantly had bags under her blue eyes, her wavy brown hair was as frizzy as possible, and her muscles ached. But she wasn't the only one affected. Her friends were in similar states.

Cinda was always in some sort of daze. The heat had faded from her cheeks, and her colorful fae wings had withered. Nadia's red eyes had sunken and faded, while her vampire appetite had vanished. Nick's pitch black hair was sticking at every angle, and his fangs poked out, seeking the nutrients he neglected to take.

Cleo's body protested every move and thought as she made her way to her room. Once inside, she threw herself on the bed, wanting nothing more than to nap. Nick wouldn't consider lying on the mattress in uniform to be sanitary, but she couldn't care less. Searching all night with her friends and attending classes all day had left her with no time to sleep.

The second her eyes closed, her thoughts roared back to life like an engine switched on. Friddy was an only child like her. He knew her struggles firsthand. So, when Cinda would fight with her many siblings and sulk off, or the twins would give each other the silent treatment, Friddy and Cleo would hang out together. They often felt jealous of the sibling bonds they lacked in their lives.

They had made a pact back when they were fifteen that they would be siblings, too. He was eleven months younger than her. So, technically, Cleo was his older sister. Ever since then, she felt oddly protective of the boy.

Her mind listed everything she knew so far. Fridolf had been missing since Sunday. The boarding school's security guard was the last person who saw Friddy. The guard was stationed at the main gate when Friddy had left for his early morning run. No guard had seen Fridolf returning. It was Wednesday now, and still, no one knew where Friddy was.

Cleo had to think harder. Surely there was something she had missed. Her mind raced, replaying all her recent memories with Friddy. Everything was as normal as could be...except, perhaps, for his new interest in marine life. Now that she thought about it, there was something weird about him ever since he had returned to school from the winter holidays.

Unlike before, Friddy would now come back from his weekend runs flushed and absent-minded. He would be away for too long. He would even come back smelling of salt and fish. Once, over breakfast, Nick had asked Friddy about his new interests, but Friddy said nothing and rushed out of the hall. This behavior wouldn't be odd for a magical water creature, but for a werewolf, it sure was.

Friddy had even asked her many questions about sirens, seeing as she was the only one at school. But Cleo didn't know the answers to any of his questions. She had no family besides her parents, and her mother was the only siren she knew. They weren't a social species. All her friends knew that. But she was only a siren by name. She had a colorful tail and golden griffin wings, making her a water-air creature. That was it. She knew nothing else.

Her hands dragged across her face as she sighed. The stress wouldn't let her body relax. Her eyes burned with the lack of sleep. A hard knock shook her out of her miserable state. Her friends must be back from dinner. Huffing, she went to open the door.

The century-old door screeched open, and she barely had the energy to care about the noise. Met with the heavy breathing of her friends, Cleo stepped aside and allowed her friends to enter. "What happened? Have you guys been running?"

Nadia threw herself on the bed, just like Cleo had a few minutes ago. Cinda sat on the edge of the bed, her gaze fixed on the ground. Nick placed a covered plate on her desk, then sat in the chair.

Nadia raised a leaf in one hand. "This. This happened."

"A leaf ... happened?" She didn't understand how a leaf could make her friends run until they were out of breath.

"It's a note," Cinda said, barely audible.

"A note? What do you mean?" Cleo's eyes searched her friends. Nick was the only one who looked at her. Her eyebrows furrowed at him.

"Eat first." He nudged the plate towards her.

"You want me to eat when all of you look like you have just seen a human?"

Nick stood and led Cleo by the shoulders, moving her towards the plate of food. "You haven't been eating well. We'll talk after you eat."

"But—"

"The note can wait."

Cleo sat as Nick uncovered the plate, revealing a tower

of sandwiches. She could smell the cheese and turkey. Maybe it was better to talk on a full stomach.

"I'll eat if you guys tell me what happened. I won't talk, Nick. I'll just listen."

Nadia spoke first. "We couldn't eat in the hall with everyone, not with how they all look at us as if it was our fault. So, we bought some sandwiches and went to our room."

"I went to put my plate on my desk, then found this note," Cinda said, her gaze still fixed on the floor. "We don't know how it got in or who sent it, but we think it has something to do with Friddy."

Cleo choked on her bite, coughing until she saw stars. Nick gave her a cup of water as he patted her back. "Easy. That's why I told you to eat first."

Cleo ignored him. "What do you mean it has something to do with Friddy?"

"You'll know when you read it," he replied.

Discarding the sandwich, Cleo stood and snatched the note from Nadia against Nick's protests. The note was made of a single, huge, green oak leaf. Scrawled on it, barely legible, was something grayish. With how it was smudged in some areas, it was probably charcoal.

'*Amidst the shadows of the old oak tree, a message waits for those who dare to see. Follow in the footsteps of the past to where the river bends, and there you'll find the key to unlocking the end.*'

Cleo felt goosebumps all over her body. "What's that?" she whispered to herself. She and her friends were no masters. The said masters weren't doing anything. So, how were a bunch of seventeen-year-old students supposed to understand this?

"Technically speaking," Nick said, "no one, not even a

40

staff member, can enter Cinda's and Nadia's room unless they allow it."

"Except ... a certain type of fae," Cinda said, as her dark skin paled.

"Wait. How is that even a problem?" Nadia asked.

Cleo recalled from her fae creatures' research last year that fae magic allowed certain species to enter any room they wanted under certain conditions. "You would've sensed their residue anyway, right?"

"Not if they were a dependent fae," Cinda said as she bit her lip.

Cleo's mind struggled to keep up with the amount of information. These types of fae could only stick to water bodies, trees, graves, and such. They couldn't leave their homes for too long, or they died. They also didn't have residue because they only went to places where faes were already present.

"So you're telling me, the fae sensed Cinda's magic, which allowed them to enter the room undetected and leave the note?" Cleo asked.

"Exactly." Nick nodded. "I think someone is trying to communicate with us from outside."

The sunset's fading light dimmed the room as it lowered. Just what did Friddy get himself into? That guy genuinely couldn't keep himself out of trouble. As if being the school's number one athlete for the third year in a row hadn't gained him enough enemies already.

Cleo scanned her friends. They had been best friends for almost three years now. It was crazy to think that the only reason the group had formed was because they were helping her. Other magical water students avoided Cleo because of an old family feud she barely understood. She had heard the rumors, but she couldn't care less. Her parents would never hide anything from her.

Cinda and Nadia had approached her first. They had said she looked too cool to be spending meal times alone. Cinda had that ear-to-ear smile and those shiny caramel eyes. Her wings had fluttered and tangled with her dark curls when Cleo smiled back at her. Nadia's playful grin had shown her fangs as she winked at Cleo that day. Unlike Nick's pitch black, her silky silver hair was braided and propped on one shoulder. Then, through the two girls, Cleo spent time with Nick, Nadia's twin, and his roommate, Fridolf.

The rumors about her parents always scared students away, which left Cleo with no roommate every year. But she didn't mind, since she would turn her room into the group's warehouse. She joined her beds into a queen-size for sleepovers and used one wardrobe for clothes and another for the group's collections: a chess set and board games for Nick, workout tools for Friddy, paints and canvas for Cinda, and astronomy books for Nadia.

Cleo remembered one time when Friddy had mounted one of Nadia's early-version science rockets and had nearly broken the window. He'd lost control and hit his head against the glass. He ended up with a big bruise on his forehead and a broken canine. It happened just earlier this year, but now it felt like it was ages ago. Was that the side-effect of growing up?

"By the way," Nick said. "What did the headmaster say? Anything that could help us?"

"Oh, don't remind me. Not a single word. I seriously had to keep reminding myself not to kill him."

He scoffed. "Well, the man can't tell you anything if he knows nothing."

Frantic, Nadia's eyes grew wide. "What now?"

"We need to decipher the note first," Cinda said while patting Nadia's back.

Cleo nodded. They needed to form a plan. Nick paced the room, reading the note over and over, studying it from every angle as if it were hiding something.

"Stop it, for God's sake!" Nadia hissed. "You'll give me a headache."

Nick rolled his eyes, too tired to argue back.

The curfew's second bell rang. Cleo hadn't even heard the first one. The school had an extremely punctual schedule with strict punishments for rule-breakers, and she wasn't in the mood for another lecture from the headmaster. Another word about upholding her image or something about how she should be a model student would surely make her explode.

"Library tomorrow after classes?" Cleo asked. Her answer was a round of yawns, stretches, and nods.

CLEO HAD A RESTLESS NIGHT. She kept thinking of all the situations in which Fridolf might disappear. She tuned out all of her lessons, thinking until it physically hurt. Her day went by in a blur with only one goal: going to the library to solve the note's puzzle.

"So, we all agree Friddy has been acting weird lately?" Nadia said right away as they sat around a study table towards the back shelves.

"Nick, you spend time with him the most," Cleo said. "Did something happen in the last month?"

"Besides getting into making jewelry of the seashells piled up everywhere in the room, trying to style his untam-

43

able hair, and receiving lots of coral trinkets from his fans, no, nothing's new."

But Cleo already knew that much. And with the headmaster's attitude, the responsibility of finding Friddy was left to them. It wouldn't be easy, but they would have to do it. She would not give in to doubt or the fear of letting her friends down. She promised herself that they would bring Friddy back.

Cleo stood and started looking through the books, reading everything she could find about deciphering a note from a fae, but it wasn't fruitful. Apparently, no one had ever had a friend go missing, which was patently ridiculous, or no one felt the need to write a book about it. Perhaps she would write one after finding Friddy.

The school was also far away from human civilization, which meant no computers and no internet. It wouldn't be smart to go anywhere near humans, either. Even if she could fit in, the twins and Cinda would never. So, she collected all the books she could find.

Everyone was busy doing something. Nadia, who had criticized her brother for reading the note from every angle yesterday, started doing just that. Nick rolled his eyes at his sister before he left to go to the back shelves. Cinda was surely somewhere within the library looking for answers.

An hour passed, and everyone had piles of books scattered across the table. Except for Cinda, who was still nowhere to be found. However, just as Cleo was wondering if Cinda had disappeared the same way Friddy had, a book was slammed down in front of her. She looked up to see Cinda grinning. The noise earned them a few looks. Cleo looked at the librarian and bowed her head, muttering an apology.

"Cinda!" Nadia hissed.

"Found it!" Cinda said, ignoring her.

"Found what?" Nick's head emerged from the book stacks around him as he spoke.

"Come closer." Cinda sat down and leaned into the table, with the rest mirroring her. "Did any of you notice what the note was written on?"

"... A leaf?" Nadia said, looking at Cleo for help. Her gaze was filled with concern.

"Tsk, not just any leaf. It's a white swamp oak leaf. The forest near the main gates has some of them. If Friddy had never come back and stayed outside, something or someone could be guiding us to where he is."

With a gasp, Cleo said, "It could be a dryad!"

"What?" Nadia asked, looking at Cleo just like she had looked at Cinda earlier.

"If Friddy sent us a message with a fae, it could be a dryad. You know, tree spirits that have speech limitations, are very shy, can't leave their trees for too long, blah blah blah." Cleo moved her hands in circles as if that would explain things to Nadia. But she was a lost cause.

Nadia only excelled at astronomy and astrology, not that it would help them much right now. Cinda, on the other hand, excelled in anything related to art, nature, and her folk. Nick was a mind games master, the observer of the group. He spoke only when he had to speak. Otherwise, he was off analyzing everything and anything.

"The note also clearly mentions a river. I think there's one in the forest, right, Cinda?" Nick said as he moved his books aside, and Cinda started looking through hers.

"It's not a river per se," she said, "but there's a small stream in that vicinity. There'll be plenty of white swamp oak trees on the banks, too."

45

Nadia looked over the page Cinda had opened and said, "That's around fifteen miles. Not bad!"

As the curfew crept closer, the group agreed to travel right after dinner tomorrow to reach their destination, get Friddy, and come back, all before next Monday. Cleo was charged with getting them in and out of the castle. Nadia was assigned to the trip's supplies. Cinda was to study the place they were going, while Nick would devise a rough plan.

"But if Fridolf was really in trouble, why would he tell us and not someone in charge?" Nadia asked as she got up.

She had a valid point. Cleo thought of her conversations with the headmaster over the past few days. If the one in charge was like that, no wonder Friddy didn't want to ask for his help. It overwhelmed her, but she had to pull herself together. She had a duty to do, rescue her stupid friend, and get all her other friends back to the castle safely.

"Maybe he doesn't want anyone besides us to know," Nick suggested.

He had to be thinking the same thing as her. Maybe she wasn't the only one feeling the same. She sighed as the thought comforted her.

Cinda nodded as she stifled a yawn.

"You guys go ahead," Cleo said. "I'll return the books before I go to my room."

All her friends looked tired, and they needed rest. She was tired, too. But if she worked some more and deemed herself useful, maybe she could sleep and prepare for tomorrow.

"I'll help," Nick offered.

Nadia raised a single eyebrow, having a silent conversation with her brother. They did it often, but Cleo caught up on the language. Nadia gave him the *What do you think you're doing?* glare. Nick glared back at her, yet pleading at the same time. *Leave me alone, will you?* Nadia rolled her eyes. Cinda and Cleo exchanged looks. In the end, Nadia and Cinda bid their *goodbyes* and *goodnights* before they left.

Instead of asking Nick what had just happened, Cleo went for the books. As she piled one stack, he began another.

Cleo felt like something was missing. It was Nadia's call to go look for Friddy. Nick had said they needed to do more research. However, even Cinda had agreed with Nadia. Something about a hunch was telling her they had to get moving.

So Cleo agreed, too. Yet, she couldn't stop feeling that she and her friends weren't thinking about this as thoroughly as they should have.

Cleo chewed her lip, glancing at her friends asleep beside her. What if Friddy hadn't sent the note? What if this was more dangerous than they realized? Would she be able to protect her friends? Her thoughts spiraled. Her gut told her not to take the risk. But if she didn't, would Friddy ever come back?

As Cleo went to stack her last pile of books, her arms screamed to be put out of their misery. She stood on her tiptoes, struggling to return the last book to its place. It belonged to Cinda, who was a few centimeters taller, so she had access to books Cleo couldn't even see. Jumping to push the book into place, another one fell right onto her head.

"Ow!"

Cleo glared at the book, rubbing her head. The book had fallen open and landed on its face. *The Ancient Aqua*

Clans and Their Myths. Why would a book like that be in the maps section?

As she picked it up off the floor, her eyes landed on a random page. The chapter headline read *Nile's Curses.* Curiosity got the best of her, and she began reading. Among all the myths about life, death, fertility, and gods, one curse had knocked the breath out of her lungs. Cleo gulped before reading the text again.

'Thousands of years ago, the ancient Egyptians were believed to have sacrificed young women into the Nile as offerings to Renenutet, the goddess of nourishment and harvest. The exact reason for this practice is unclear, though many speculate it was to gain blessings for a successful harvest.

According to legend, the spirits of these women became trapped in the river, unable to move on to the afterlife. Over time, these spirits transformed into vengeful water nymphs, who targeted men specifically. There were no records of women being harmed by these cursed entities, which led to the belief that their anger was directed only at men, particularly those who served as priests during their lives.

It was said that these nymphs would silently drag men under the water, leaving no sign of struggle. The bodies would disappear, hidden in places no one could find, and it could take days before someone realized the man was missing. The only way to recover the body was if a female relative—like a mother, sister, or grandmother—called the man's name over the river. When that happened, the body would surface, usually covered in claw marks.

Other magical water creatures were also known to perform similar rituals, using the same curse to abduct their victims. Whether the men were killed or simply held captive was up to the creature's choice.

This curse was known to be incredibly powerful and difficult to perform, and it was eventually banned by the river gods, the Potamoi, and their sisters, the Oceanids, who wished to stop further abuses of the river.'

Cleo heard a quiet titter from behind her. Warm air brushed her back, raising the hairs on her skin. The book slipped from her hands. Frozen in place, she turned her head slowly, only to be met with a mass of black hair.

"Boo!"

"Nick, what the heck? You scared me, you idiot!"

Nick shrugged as he picked the book up. His eyebrows furrowed as his eyes roamed the page.

Cleo should've heard him sneaking up. She always did. With her supposedly super hearing, no less. She could only blame her sleep deprivation. But there was no place for such mistakes tomorrow. The forest was vast and magic–draining. She'd have to rest well tonight.

"That's bad, bad," Nick said once he finished reading. His jaw locked, and his throat tightened. He was as disturbed, and possibly disgusted, as she was.

Was it wrong to be a little proud of her people? Sure, it was evil, but it was clever evil. An opportunity to get back at him opened its door for her.

"It can't be that bad. I mean, I am safe," she chuckled.

"You're safe because you're a woman!" His red eyes twitched, and his voice grew louder with each word.

"And you're not, but that's okay. I'll call you even if your sister doesn't." Her right hand was on his shoulder as she looked at him through her eyelashes.

The dim lights of the library helped set the effect she wanted. Cleo winked at him and smiled innocently. His eyes widened. Nick was frightened. That was what he got for almost giving her a heart attack a minute ago.

Cleo took the book with her and went to the front desk

to sign it out. Nick was trailing behind, ranting about how Nadia wouldn't abandon him like that. Cleo didn't notice how comforted she felt by his voice until she reached her dorm. Standing before the door, she didn't feel time pass.

"I don't think what we read is important, right?" Cleo asked, not wanting to get into the room just yet and be left alone with her thoughts.

"If Friddy was the one who sent us the note with the dryad, I suppose not."

"Right. What would even put him in such a situation in the first place?"

Nick hummed, agreeing with her.

"So, we're going after the dryad for now?"

"Yup."

Cleo's eyes found the floor. She had nothing more to say, and it would be very awkward if she just stood there silent.

"You should go to sleep. You look tired."

He stifled a yawn as he nodded. "Goodnight, Cleo. Sleep tight."

"Goodnight, Nick."

She offered him a smile and a hand wave before creeping into the darkness of her room. It was going to be a long night. Cleo hoped she could keep her thoughts and adrenaline away. She had to sleep properly. There was a mission awaiting her tomorrow.

THE USUALLY CLEAR early March skies were cloudy, and the fading sun rays didn't reach the group as they made their way to the main gates. They had rushed to leave right after dinner so they could get on the road in daylight, but it was already navy blue outside. Cleo and her friends stood before the huge, worn wooden doors, waiting.

The ghoul guard limped to them, raising his hands in objection, but Cleo just gave him an envelope. After struggling to open it with his long nails, he read the letter inside. With narrowed eyes, he pushed the gates open. Cleo bowed her head, took the letter back from him, and left, her friends following closely.

"What's that?" Nick peeked over Cleo's shoulder.

"The power of being the vice president." Cleo flipped her hair, hitting Nick in the face. She put the slip back in her bag.

"Ouch!"

"Come on. We are heading north," Cinda said as she lit her torch and turned right. "The compass says it's this way."

"Do you smell anything, Nadia?" Cleo asked.

Nadia closed her eyes, sniffed the air, and gagged. "Well, Friddy's smell is all over the place. Damn werewolves, they spread their scent so thickly."

"What about you, Cinda? Feel anything weird?"

"More than knowing where to head, I'm sensing nothing."

Cleo sighed. They were already off to a poor start.

"It's getting darker. I don't assume you and Cinda can keep going," Nadia said.

"Thanks for the reminder," Cinda replied with an eye roll as she led the walk. She never liked how her powers were so limited.

"Cleo," Nick called. "Why don't you just fly above the canopy for a quick look?"

"And leave you guys? No."

"He's right. You gotta do it. Cinda can't fly or we'll get lost," Nadia replied.

"Just go straight ahead and return. Don't go too far. You can have a better look tomorrow during the day," Nick said.

"But how am I going to find you? I can't see well in the dark."

"You fly faster and higher, stop whining," Nadia said.

"I'll give you ten minutes, then point my torch upwards. You better be quick, though. We don't want other creatures to notice us," Cinda replied.

Worry was filling Cleo's body and prickling under her skin. She closed her eyes and directed her energy to conjure her griffin wings. Bones stretched out of her back and cut through her shirt. Golden feathers built themselves on top of one another. The weight of the wings was familiar, but now her shirt was ruined. Good thing she packed another one.

Cleo opened her eyes as she ruffled her wings.

"I can never get used to that," Nadia said as if she couldn't fully change into a bat on demand.

Nick stood still. His red eyes were wide and glowing. His mouth was slightly gaped.

"What?" Cleo asked. "They're ugly, right?"

"No, just huge," Nick replied.

"They're lovely," Cinda said as she stroked the feather.

"Hey! They're ticklish," Cleo chuckled.

"Alright, get going," Nadia said.

Cleo rose off the ground as her wings lifted her. Her feet dangled, and the chill bit her cheeks. The wind played with her hair, and she relished the feeling. She was so high that all she saw were treetops.

Nothing seemed unusual as she flew, but vision was

difficult, so she also relied on hearing, too. The forest was tranquil, and no matter how much Cleo tuned in, she heard nothing besides the rustle of leaves and breezy wind.

Ten minutes passed, and the night grew darker. The moon was out, and the constellation painted the horizon. She looked behind and a beam of light pierced its way out of the trees into the sky. Just before she made her way back, she found a gap among the trees.

As she descended, leaves and dirt flew everywhere. Muttering an apology, she tucked her wings back in.

"Did you find anything?" Nick asked.

"No, but I noticed a gap between the trees further away. I couldn't go that far. It was too dark, and I had to come back."

"It should be the stream Cinda found on the maps," Nadia said.

"I still think we shouldn't fly there. What if we miss any clues?" Cinda spoke.

Cleo got the impression they had started this conversation while she was away.

"We also gotta find the dryad's tree. We need to stick to the ground." Nick said.

"What do you think?" Nadia asked Cleo. She had her hands clasped as she mouthed fly.

"I agree with Cinda and Nick. It won't be wise to keep traveling at night, either. Too dangerous."

Nadia grumbled, which earned her an ear-twist from Cinda.

It was around midnight when the group camped at Nadia's request. The huge leaves and crowded trees made it impossible for the moon's light to reach them. And even though they had torches, the forest was too dark and silent. The vampire twins helped set up their temporary camp, and Cleo couldn't be more envious of their night vision.

As everyone settled, Nadia went rummaging about in the supplies, stuffing her face with snacks. Cinda opened her maps on the ground. "We're now about seven miles in. So, three to four more hours and we reach the stream."

Nick was making sure the place was safe. His eyes roamed around the camp. He was moving like a madman, inspecting every tree, leaf, log, and even the ground.

"Wait, no one move," Nick said. "Do you guys hear that?"

"What do you mean? I hear nothing," Cleo replied.

"I heard a branch breaking," Nick said.

"Stop with the paranoia. You're in a forest. Of course, there'll be sounds," Nadia spoke with a full mouth.

"I don't feel any energy shifts, either," Cinda said.

"Fine! Just keep your voices down. Don't want to attract any attention," Nick whispered with his eyes closed. He was leaning on a tree, one knee propped up.

Nadia lay on the ground, resting her head on her bag as if it were a pillow. Cinda sat with her back to a tree, her eyes shifting between Cleo and the sleeping Nadia.

"Go to sleep, Cinda. I'll wake you up at dawn," Cleo said. Yet, Cinda made no move.

"I'll be fine. Sleep."

With one last look, Cinda turned towards Nadia. She crept close, put her bag on the ground, and laid her wings carefully before she slept beside Nadia.

Cleo was sitting cross-legged, facing her friends, who all slept soundly. She took out the book she had borrowed yesterday from the library from her bag. She didn't feel the hours pass as she kept reading more about these ancient, magical aquatic creatures. Her people.

A shadow moved out of the corner of her eye. Cleo turned around anxiously, looking in every direction, but saw nothing. She cursed her vision for not being as good as the vampires. A branch breaking turned her head to the left. Her heart sank in her stomach when a ghostly figure floated towards her.

The creature grew into focus the closer it got. As her eyes adapted, Cleo saw a woman, twice her height, standing before her. Her body was made of wood and lots of leaves. Her face was adorned with patterns, and she had a nest on top of her head.

Craning her neck, Cleo was met with huge, black eyes. She took a few steps backward carefully. The wooden figure extended her hands to Cleo, palms open, facing the sky. Her dark eyes gleamed, and her half-smirk felt more menacing than friendly.

Cleo gulped as her insides twisted. She spared her friends a glance. She had put them in danger, and they hadn't even been a full day out in the wild. Just how did she not hear that creature approaching? If Nick had been awake, he would've noticed early on and done something.

Her eyes wildly searched for ways to wake her friends and escape before something nasty happened. Cleo should at least alert them. But her voice was stuck in her mouth.

The creature huffed, sending some leaves from the ground flying. "Take note," she rasped. Her bitter voice and sharp, rotten teeth sent a chill up Cleo's spine. The woman nodded towards her palm, and Cleo saw another leaf.

"... What are you?"

"Dryad."

Cleo inhaled sharply. She was unsure if the creature was dangerous. The dryad didn't look friendly at all. One swing of her hand would be enough to throw Cleo meters away.

Could the dryad have kidnapped Friddy? But why? What did he ever do to her?

"Where's Friddy?"

"Can't say."

"Why? Did you kidnap him?"

"I not foe."

"Then where is he?"

"Take. Damn. Note."

"What? I can't trust you!"

"I now leave," the dryad said, grunting, placing the note on the ground. She backed away, and her ghostly figure became more transparent with each step.

"Hey! Where are you going? What's this?"

"Work it out, halfwit," she spat before vanishing completely from sight.

Cleo was right. There was a dryad in the equation. A scary and rude dryad. But how did she know where Friddy was?

BIRDS CHIRPED AS DAWN CAME. Sun rays sneaked between the leaves and branches. Cleo inhaled the fresh air of a new day. After the dryad had left, Cleo thought perhaps sleep had overcome her and that she had been dreaming. No way all that had happened without her friends waking up. But the note in her hand proved otherwise. It was not a dream. The dryad was real. Maybe she had put a sleeping spell on them.

Cleo sighed as she read the note again. How were they going to decipher the note here? There was no library lying around in the wild. Biting her lips, she tasted sulfur. She wiped the blood off. If the headmaster had seen her, he would've lectured her ear off. Bad habits, bad choices, bad lifestyle. Tsk tsk tsk. She grimaced at how well her mind conjured the image.

Nick rustled from where he slept. He slowly opened his eyes, taking in his surroundings. The girls were waking up too. Cleo's gaze fell to the ground. Her whole nervous system was tense. There was this feeling in her chest, and it felt so wrong. Nick was right. They hadn't done enough research. Cleo closed her eyes as she breathed in. She would tell them what happened, no matter what they thought.

So, after everyone had eaten something for breakfast, Cleo brought them closer and told them everything. "I am sorry. I couldn't make her reveal more."

"Hey, it's okay," Cinda said as she put her arms around Cleo's shoulder. "I am pretty sure you handled this better than any of us would."

"But—"

"You definitely handled it better than Nadia would have," Nick said, smirking.

"Even I know that's true. But come on, dude, I am your sister." Nadia nudged Nick in the stomach.

"But we have to decipher this now, and I don't know what to do," Cleo said.

Cinda took the note and started reading it aloud. The twins stopped fighting immediately and focused on her.

"*Where the river sings its tale,*" Cinda read, "*through the whispering forest veil. Moonlit shadows dance with leaves, ancient trees, and their secrets breathe. In this enchanted, shadowed glen, a clue awaits both bold and keen.*"

"That's it? It can't be." Nadia snatched the note and read it again. "Is everyone confused, too? Please tell me I am not the only one."

Cinda replied as she helped Nadia strap her bag. "You're not the only one."

"We'll think as we walk. We still have at least three hours left to reach the river," Cleo said, motioning for Cinda to lead. She wouldn't trust anything in her life more than the fairy's intuition.

Nick had his lips pressed as he looked into the distance. He often did that when playing his games. He had told her before that he would envision his opponent's moves so that he could counter-attack them before they happened. The question was, who the hell was their opponent? It couldn't be Friddy. What about the dryad? She looked like she could kidnap someone.

"Something feels missing," Cinda said.

"Right? That's what I thought, too," Cleo replied.

"All I can tell is that walking to the river and the appearance of the dryad confirm we are on the right path," Nick said. He looked at Cleo with narrowed eyes. She raised her eyebrows at him as she mouthed, *What?*

"The 'sings its tale' and 'Moonlit shadows dance' are new," Nadia said.

"Does that mean that whoever captured Friddy is ruled by the moon and could sing?" Nick asked, making everyone stop in their tracks.

"Is Friddy kidnapped?" Nadia said.

"That makes so much sense!" Cinda gasped. "Maybe when Friddy left on Sunday to run, he was kidnapped. And now they're dragging us out to pay them. Like a ransom."

Cleo turned the thoughts around in her head. What Cinda said was the most probable scenario. "But the notes never mentioned payment. Plus, we didn't bring any money with us."

"If that's the situation, we'll just sneak him out," Nick said. "We're not returning empty-handed."

"You're right," Nadia said as she looped her arms around Cinda's shoulders and stalked forward.

THE SUN WAS at the center of the sky when the group reached the stream. Sweat stuck to Cleo's forehead, and a sense of unease settled in her stomach the more she walked. The gentle babble of water did nothing to soothe her nerves.

Cleo didn't know what to do next, as usual. Their goal was to find the stream, and there it was. But that couldn't possibly be it. They even had asked Cinda for a hunch, but she had none. All she said was that she felt like something was going to happen. Nadia and Nick hid under the trees' shade to cool off while Cinda went around studying the plants.

Cleo crouched down by the narrow river and looked at her reflection. Her hair was wild, and the bags under her eyes darker. Folding her pants up to her knees, she waded into the current. The cold water should cool her off.

As Cleo leaned down to wash her face, something cold slithered around her ankles. Her breath got stuck in her throat. Before she could run, a gray, horse-like figure emerged from the water.

She fell back with a scream as her friends rushed to the bank. The figure shape-shifted into a man with dark gray hair and pale skin. His red eyes, cold and predatory, pinned Cleo where she fell.

"You're trespassing, miss."

Cinda gasped and put her hands over her mouth. "Are you a kelpie horse?"

"Yeah, why?" His eyes held a strange glint, somewhere between curiosity and hunger.

Cinda tilted her head, and her eyes shone as she hummed. Nadia dragged her away by the elbow, glaring at the man.

"How is she trespassing?" Nick asked the Kelpie as he helped Cleo out of the river. She held his forearm as she stepped onto the banks.

"The river belongs to the siren clan. I am just a guard."

"Siren clan?" Cleo asked.

"Yes, the siren clan farther down the river. At the bay."

"Cleo, give me the note," Nick said, holding his hand out for her. Cleo looked at him with narrowed eyes as she opened her bag and took out the note. Before handing it to him, she leaned in and whispered.

"What are you doing?"

"Getting answers. Watch."

Nick held the note to the man. "We are here because a dryad gave us this."

"A swamp white oak leaf," the kelpie said as he inspected the note. "You can find their trees on the bay's shore."

Cleo's back straightened. Maybe that dangerous creature knew something after all.

Nick spoke again. "We don't understand the message. Can you please help us?"

The kelpie read the note and eyed the group. "I don't know the context, but a siren is trying to contact you for sure. There's a problem, it seems."

Cleo felt the blood rush away from her face, and she was sure she had gone pale, judging by the man's reaction.

"Are you alright, miss?" The man asked unnervingly. "I hope I didn't scare you much." His voice was cold in contrast to the nice words he uttered. It was as if he were replaying sentences he learned but would never mean.

"She's fine," Nick replied. "Thanks for the help. We have to go find that dryad, though."

The kelpie gave a curt nod before shapeshifting into a horse and disappearing into the water.

Her senses had malfunctioned again. Another creature had sneaked up on her and she hadn't heard a thing or seen them coming. What use were her heightened senses if they weren't working properly?

Nick held Cleo by the shoulders, guiding her to the two girls. "Cinda, Nadia, let's go."

On the verge of having a full-on panic attack, Cleo fought for each breath. Her skin tingled as her mind produced a million thoughts per second. Nick must have connected the dots, too.

"He smelled of fish and salt for a while before disappearing," Cleo hissed to Nick.

"You think what I'm thinking?" Nick asked.

"You think the sirens kidnapped him, too?"

"I also think they used the Nile's curse on him."

"No, they couldn't have."

"I wouldn't have thought that if the second note didn't mention a song or a tale. This is the only curse both of us know. It's our best prediction."

"You realize what you're saying? He could be dead!" Cleo shut her mouth so quickly.

"Dead?" Cinda asked, stopping in her tracks.

Cleo covered her mouth. She had accidentally shouted the last part. The last thing she wanted was to put negative ideas in her friends' heads.

"Cleo. Who's dead?" Nadia raised her voice.

"N-no. Um ... no one's dead. I was just-"

"We think the sirens kidnapped Friddy," Nick said. "We don't know why. But that's our best guess with all his recent interests and the note."

"Oh," Cinda said, her wings withering and the coloring fading from them.

"Still doesn't explain why I heard the word dead." Nadia crossed her arms.

Cinda mirrored Nadia's pose and looked at Cleo. Cleo shook her head sideways and pointed at Nick. The two girls shifted their glares to him.

Nick coughed before speaking. "Cleo and I found a text about a curse that we," Cleo nudged him, "that *I* think was used on Friddy. I'm unsure, but we must keep this possibility in mind."

Cleo took the book from her bag and gave it to Cinda before she walked away. It was afternoon, and they still had one more hour of walking. She already felt suffocated, and the heat didn't help.

Almost thirty minutes later, Nadia was the first to speak. "Is he dead-"

"No. No, he's not. He can't be," Cleo replied.

"B-but what if ..." Cinda's tears were flowing non-stop.

"He's fine!" Nick said. "We are going to get him. We'll go back to school and we will all start next week. Together."

Nadia nodded aggressively, and Cinda wiped her tears.

They shouldn't be losing hope now. Not after they had come all this way. Cleo forced her body not to shake as she wished with all her might that Fridolf had nothing to do with these sirens. He had to be alright. Everything would be just fine, and they would get him back at all costs.

❧

THE SOUND of the waves and the fine sand particles underfoot gave way to the shore. Two green mountains enclosed the bay at both ends. The forest line ended a couple of meters away from the beach. It was full of oak trees, the ones they were looking for. If she wasn't looking for Friddy, Cleo would've enjoyed this as a nice hangout.

"About time. Was waiting." The dryad greeted them in her raspy voice as she separated from a gigantic tree. That explained why she was so tall. Startled, Nick fell on his back. Nadia and Cinda shrieked before running to hide behind Cleo.

"You! You made it really hard to come here, you know," Cleo snapped, pointing.

Nick stood up and brushed the sand off his clothes. "Who sent you?"

"I did." A girl about the same age as the group replied instead. She had emerged from the water, her lower form changing to human feet the moment she stepped on the sand. She was a siren. "I'm Unda. I take it you're Friddy's friends?"

"Where is he?" Nadia asked at the same time as Cinda asked, "You know Friddy?"

"I need one of you girls to call his name and tell him to come out," Unda said.

From the side of her eye, Cleo saw Nick clenching his fists. Cinda covered her mouth, and Nadia gasped.

"How dare you use that curse on him?" Cleo shouted. Her breaths came in short as she struggled to breathe.

"I'm not saying anything before you call him."

Cleo was left with no choice. She didn't like that. But she had to put her worries and rage aside to rescue Friddy.

She would deal with this Unda girl later. The siren had serious attitude issues.

Cleo looked at Nadia and Cinda. She could see that they were as scared as she was. They still needed to get him out. Dead or alive.

"We'll call him together," Cleo said as she guided the two girls closer to the water, wrapping her arms around her friends' shoulders.

"On the count of three?" Nadia asked.

Cinda sniffed and replied, "... one ... two ... three."

The three girls yelled together. "Fridolf, come out!"

Drenched, Friddy emerged from the waters. His hair stuck to his forehead, and his brown eyes shone. He smiled and waved with both hands. "Hi guys, what's up?"

"Oh, my gods! You're alive," Nadia said as she sprinted to hug him.

He returned Nadia's embrace. "Why wouldn't I be?" Friddy replied sheepishly

After overcoming their shock, Nick, Cleo, and Cinda ran towards their friends to join the hug. Cinda was crying happy tears, while Nick was tickling Friddy. Squeezed in the cluster, Cleo could barely manage to ask, "What were you doing there?"

"I think it's time I announced," Friddy replied. "I have a girlfriend. Surprise!" He was struggling to keep his voice even, partially from being choked by the hug and partially because of Nick's tickling.

"And?" Nadia inched away, looking Fridolf in the eye.

"She's a siren."

Cinda sniffed. "How does that have anything to do with you going missing?"

"Her mom invited me over to their place!" Friddy said, grinning.

Cleo blinked. He said that like he hadn't been missing for days. Like this whole thing had been... casual.

"Mom kidnapped him," Unda confessed. Her cheeks turned red as she avoided eye contact and stood near the dryad. "Sorry about that."

"No, she didn't." Friddy furrowed his eyebrows. "She said she wanted to know me better." Cleo and the rest broke off the hug and faced Unda.

"She kidnapped him because she didn't think he would be up to her standards. She had lost a sister to a similar situation. So, she would've killed him if she didn't like him." The siren explained the motives behind her mother's actions, tucking a strand of hair behind her ear. Fridolf's jaw fell open.

"Only a monster would do something like that," Nadia said.

"Well, she's not the head of the clan for no reason," the siren replied, looking Nadia in the eye.

Cinda laid a protective arm around Friddy's shoulders. Nick was glaring daggers at Unda. With how sleep-deprived Cleo was, she felt like she needed subtitles for the conversations. All she thought of was that Friddy was alive. Their mission was successful, and they could return to school safe and sound.

Rubbing her temples didn't ward off the headache, though. She knew she would have to sit with this girlfriend of Friddy's and see for herself. Friddy was too trusting to be a good judge of character.

"How did you even get this far, dude?" Nick asked, gesturing wildly as he threw his arms up in the air.

Friddy shrugged. "Weekend training. I would run in my wolf form up to the beach and go back."

Nick blinked. "So this whole search party was just us catching up to your cardio?"

Friddy then told them all about how he met his girlfriend for the first time. It happened last year when he got his clothes dirty and went in the water to clean them. Unda had scared him by telling him he was trespassing. Cleo tried not to react to the memory it triggered. Seriously, what was it with these people and trespassing? Water bodies were all a part of the free nature.

Friddy continued talking about how this silly prank was the beginning of their friendship. He had only asked Unda out last Christmas. That explained the seashell jewelry and the coral trinkets.

"One of my guards saw us and reported back to my mother," said Unda. "So she invited Friddy for lunch and used the curse on him without his knowledge, or mine. She didn't have faith he would make it out alive," Unda admitted, filling in points her boyfriend apparently didn't know.

She went on about how Friddy had gained her mother's approval, but she still needed his friends to come pick him up. The old woman had talked with the school, telling them she was his aunt and that she had to take him for a couple of days. Then she sent for the dryad to contact us to come and get him.

Cleo internally screamed at that old woman, shouting the most vile words she knew. She thanked the gods and the skies that the headmaster wasn't neglecting the case, but keeping it confidential. It wasn't permissible to speak about a student's business to anyone unless they were a teacher or the headmaster. Still, very poor security. They didn't even check if she was his real aunt.

"Long story short, I just met my future mother-in-law, and she loves me!"

Cleo resisted the urge to throw him back in the water.

"What?" Unda's mouth fell open as she glowered at her boyfriend. As Friddy wiggled his eyebrows back at Unda, who punched his shoulders, Cleo got the impression that it was the first time Unda had heard such a thing.

"But Friddy, the woman kidnapped and even planned to kill you," Nick said.

"If she had meant ill, she wouldn't have notified the headmaster, Nick," Friddy replied, never taking his eyes off of Unda, whose face was alarmingly turning redder as time passed.

"Sap," Nick murmured with an eye roll.

"I still have so many questions," Cleo said. The fading adrenaline left her hyper-aware of every fiber in her body and, dammit, she was exhausted. Still, she was happy that they had retrieved their friend safe and sound. That was all that mattered.

"Promise I'll tell everything once we're back," Fridolf replied and went to bid Unda goodbye.

After walking and chatting for some time, they spotted the very top of the castle miles away. It shimmered in the orange glow of the setting sun. Fridolf exchanged wicked glances with everyone. They all knew what he was going to pull right at that moment.

Cleo quickly got her golden wings out. The twins transformed into their bat forms, and Cinda ruffled her wings, preparing them.

"Whoever gets to the school's gate last will do all my missed homework!" Friddy shouted before turning into his werewolf form and running. The rest of the group flew above as Friddy raced them below through the familiar woods.

The End

BIO: Malak Eltahtawy hails from Egypt, where she attends medical school. As if she didn't have enough to do, she jumped headfirst into fiction writing and just discovered Fantasy Writers. Org in March 2024 to help her on her quest to bring Egypt's rich mythological traditions into modern fiction.

CHAPTER 4

THE TWELVE STEP HERO'S PROGRAM
DENIAL OF THE CALL

by

Andy Clark

F riar Barach entered the room, willing calmness, holding back the envy nipping at his soul. He sat with the three heroes, uncertain how the words he must utter would land with these bred and reared warriors, ready to fight any monster, matching strength with strength, speed with speed, and wits... Well, sometimes the wits didn't match up, but each of them possessed a courageous heart eager to accept any challenge.

Except the ferocious boredom resulting from their victories.

Nolan was the tallest, so muscular many would assume there were rocks buried under his skin, and not pebbles, indeed his chest could pass for a boulder. He had all but required long, blond hair and numerous scars. Three dragons, a vampire and two werewolves had fallen under Nolan's mighty sword, as had the fifty village huts Nolan had invaded, certain they hid diabolical menaces rather than countless mice.

Niamh was the woman, with ebony skin, armor clinging to her body in a way that would entrance an attacker. Even Barach could not help identifying places his blade could impale her. Curly blonde hair cascaded down her back. She struck lethally, slaying the winged snakes of the Skellig Islands and many other vipers as well. With those threats cleared, she moved onto lesser menaces, including overly expressive dogs and cats. Her rampages through howling pets terrified parents of vociferous children. Niamh viewed Nolan as if expecting him to drop to the floor and slither at any moment.

Finally, there was Cillian, as much a thief as a hero. A small, thin man, better built for stealth than brute force, but appearances deceived. Cillian had strangled a Golem and his sly ways spelled the end for many an unfortunate wizard, freeing Hibernia from the cabal of Necromancers who had seized Oriel. Now, Cillian used his skills to break into town meetings, crying, 'aha! I have you!' during discussions of sinister topics such as fertilizer distribution.

Barach would lead them on a new voyage, beginning by coaxing from them the honesty required to admit that their old life was no longer beneficial, instructing them, guiding them, redirecting them, until the journey arrived at the day where they accepted a different form of service as their path forward. Each step in this path would run counter to everything they had learned. The barriers to the faith they would require to complete this program would be the greatest enemy they would ever face. As it had been for Barach's own ten-year pilgrimage.

And so he began. "I know you do not believe you belong here–"

Nolan slapped his palm on the table, cracking the three-inch-thick oak. "Truth."

Clearly, his reputation for brevity was well founded. "Yes, the truth is where we begin," Barach said. "The truth is that you've delivered great service. For many years, your heroism was the land's greatest asset, but now you've become its greatest scourges."

"Ungrateful weasels," Cillian said. "I should have let the Necromancers steal their souls. Now the evil men are more crafty, concealing their plotting and scheming in devious ways."

"Like snakes feeding on the souls of the unwary," Niamh said.

"Precisely!" Cillian said. "We must hunt harder to ferret out the villains, but do not be mistaken. We will find them everywhere."

This was getting out of hand. "Silence," Barach said. "The king ordered you here because you are doing more harm than good. You are heroes, trained to kill monsters with strength, speed and brute determination. But the monsters are gone now, and you help no one by looking for them in every decrepit shack and hay loft throughout the land."

Nolan sprang up. "Of course! I should check the lofts. Who knows what devilry they hide?"

"I do," Niamh said.

"Stop it!" Barach said. "This is not a time for chasing imagined enemies. You will either wind up dead or living in a desert of corpses. Your only hope is to start by admitting to yourself that you need to change. That will begin the most arduous journey of your lives, a constant struggle with your most implacable enemies: yourselves."

The understanding dawning on their faces was dimmer than a drowned fire. He'd have to be direct and fight them with the one foe that would bow any hero, humiliation. "Niamh, tell me about your last fight."

"I came into a village and no one was moving."

"Was it in the middle of the night?"

"Yes! That is the time when evil is afoot, and that is what I found. Little demons scurrying through the streets. They were all but impossible to catch. Had I not had my bow, they would have all escaped, but I hunted down every one of them."

She actually looked proud. Did she not know what was coming? "Indeed. You've fought demons before – correct? I mean the thick-skinned types carrying axes and scimitars and breathing fire or ice."

Sunset whispered across her face as she said, "Yes, but they can also be shapeshifters."

Barach nodded and said, "Yes, that is true. But in my experience, a single arrow does not slay them. Tell me, how many arrows did you fire that day?"

"Forty."

"And how many demons did you slay?"

Pride returned to her bearing. She was an incomparable archer. "Thirty-eight!"

"Did any of them transform after being shot? Return to their natural form, pluck the arrow out and continue fighting? Demons are notoriously bellicose. Did any of them attack you at all?"

She answered with silence.

"And did you stay until the next morning to accept the gratitude of the villagers? Or did you leave rather than face heartbroken children and their parents after you had slain almost every family pet?"

"I left," she whimpered as Nolan and Cillian guffawed. Barach turned on them. "You will be quiet. Your stories are both as bad and I will get to them, but for now, I'm talking to Niamh." He refocused on the Nordic Nubian. "Niamh, how long since you killed the last monster that showed a monster's form in its corpse?"

Her head sunk into her hands. There were no tears. She wasn't ready to shed any yet, but there was moisture in her eyes. "Two years."

"And how many fights have you had with things you thought were monsters in those two years?"

"Seventy-three."

An exact count was a good sign. "You know, don't you?"

Now she was ready for tears. "Yes, I know. Lord, help me, I know, but I can't stop myself. You don't know how it is! The fight, the joy of the combat is there constantly, calling to me, begging me to strike. Everywhere I turn, danger calls. God help me, I just can't prevent myself from answering. It feels too good."

This was a start, but he needed more. "Have you tried to stop?"

"YES! I've done everything I can think of. I've buried my weapons, but found my bare hands and feet to be sufficiently lethal. I've tried drinking myself into oblivion, and all that does is give me less control over my desire. I even once had a sheriff tie me to a tree, directing him to spend an hour making the most intricate knots imaginable. It took me less than thirty minutes to unravel them and start searching the hospital for ghouls. I can't control myself!"

There was the admission he required. He hugged her. "Niamh, I do understand. Your story is my story. I must

73

have destroyed a dozen taverns, certain that sorcerers had poisoned the local brew to create zombies. I stopped a wedding before the sixteen-year-old bride could transform into a Medusa. I stole a baby because I was sure its parents were devouring it when they were changing its diapers."

His three potential wards looked at him with amazement, restrained laughter bulging their cheeks. He disengaged from Niamh.

"Go ahead. Understanding how ridiculous it can be is part of learning to be honest about what you have become. You have acted with foolish awfulness because you can't stop being heroes. And Niamh, you are correct. You can't fight this battle on your own. The good news is that you don't have to. There are more of us and we'll stand with you, helping you to find the faith that you must have to control the urge to see monsters everywhere and attack them without mercy. The bad news is that you will have to fight the urges every day for the rest of your life. But stay with me, and you will never be alone."

Barach let that sit for a moment before continuing. "Niamh, there will be good days and bad days. You will stumble and fall. Are you willing to commit to this fight?"

"This wrong," Nolan said. "We kill all monsters in Ireland. Maybe. All monsters in many lands. Now we punished. Not right."

"It's not only right," Barach said. "It's to your benefit. A better life awaits you–"

"Wait a minute," Cillian said. "The lummox has a point here."

"Me no lummox," Nolan said.

"My apologies," Cillian said. "The key point is—how do we know all the monsters are gone? The island was crawling with them. What if they are in hiding, waiting for us to retire so they can strike?"

That was when the messenger appeared at the door. "Friar Barach, my apologies for interrupting, but there's a werewolf loose in Limerick."

In unison, the three heroes rose and reached where their swords would be had they not given them to the sheriff and had them locked them up the previous night. He'd kept the key lest the sheriff face an enraged hero. Or three.

"Barach, you must unlock our blades!" Cillian said.

"Oh, never mind," said Niamh. "It's not like any of us can't break into the prison, dig through the floor and pick the lock."

"No need blade for one little puppy," said Nolan.

Barach had to take control of this catastrophe. "Exactly!"

All turned to him with confused looks.

"One werewolf is not a problem," Barach said. "The town guards and residents of Limerick can win this battle. There will be more threats in the future. Today, you need to let others handle these. You are more of a problem than a single werewolf, an addled spellcaster or leprechaun."

Though it would be good if werewolves only responded to full moons, as they had in days of legend. But perhaps that had never been the case, for the slightest sliver of moonlight awakened the monster.

"I'd forgotten about the leprechauns," Cillian said. "They're the worst. We'll never be free of them. They draw people in with promises of gold and make them do weird dances."

"Stop it!" The friar said. "Dancing the occasional jig is in no way as bad as having your house torn down or sheep dog killed because some hero needs the thrill of a fight. Get ahold of yourselves!"

Something new appeared on Nolan's face, an expression of insight. "Idiot! One werewolf not a problem? For us, no, but only heroes resist bites. Limerick filled with wolves soon. Must go."

By all the saints and martyrs, Barach hated to admit it, but brains in his biceps had a point.

Niamh came to him, stroking the side of his head, eyes full of a promise no friar could accept, yet no man could ignore. "Barach, just let us go. This is real."

He closed his eyes, took her arms in his hands, and pushed her away. "Very well, but I have a condition."

"Anything," she said at the same time as Cillian said, "What?" and Nolan grunted.

"I will come with you, and once we've addressed Limerick's werewolf problem, you're going to sit down with me and start the essential work required to control your heroism."

He listened to their assurances, knowing they were lying, but smiled with satisfaction when he opened the chest and saw their confusion at the presence of a fourth blade. The blade Barach stared at for a moment as his hands trembled around the scabbard. He should leave it, but what if he needed a weapon to defend the townsfolk from these three? He tied it to his waist, ignoring the sensual feel of the blade, and the desire for blood that washed through his body, as the Limerick quest began.

THREE DAYS LATER, an hour before sunset, they walked into Limerick. There had been no guards at the gate, either a very good sign or a very bad one. With a werewolf on the loose, militia should control traffic into and out of the walled city, imprisoning any particularly hairy people, holding them until night had come and gone, and exposure to the moon's beams proved their innocence. Or not.

"I say we spread out to cover the city," said Cillian.

"Absolutely not," said Barach. "If the lycanthropy has spread, they will attack as a pack and you will need all three swords."

"Three?" said Nolan.

It flashed on the friar, the fight he'd had with the dragon queen, a contest hanging in the balance until the end as he dodged flames, teeth, claws and tail. Barach had been fortunate to 'corner' the beast in its lair. That had led to a fight like no other, requiring every grain of his skill as he moved and dodged, nicking the fell beast through the holes in its scales. Not one hero in a hundred could have fought as he did, and yet it was almost not enough. The cuts irritated without injuring the dragon. When its tail finally struck him, his bones crunched and his sword went flying. Still, he grabbed the tail, clawing his way up the back until he reached the eyes and put his dagger to work. Exultation flowed through him as the queen died. At that moment, he was the king of heroes.

He could go back. Be that man again. But a hundred heroic fights took his toll on him. More and more often, his battles faded into fields of raw red and he emerged with no memories. Then came the day when he looked down on the young bride after he'd charged between her and her beloved, hurling her to the ground, naming her a she-devil, followed by the scream of pain when he grabbed her cascading raven hair, pulling it to find snakes. He'd left her bald and bloody. Lord, give me strength. I cannot go back.

"I am not here to fight monsters. I'm here to protect Limerick from you."

In series Niamh, Cillian and Nolan opened their mouths to object, then closed them. Good, there was some understanding in all of them. He prayed it would be enough.

An older man waddled up to them as they entered the gate. "I am Cathal Flannigan, the mayor. I don't know what your business is here, but you'd best find an inn." He gazed at each of them. "You're heroes, aren't you? And they say you're never around when needed. We're in a desperate spot. All our guards have been turned and there are a hundred werewolves in Limerick. I thought we were going to have to evacuate, but to where?"

"You be fine now," Nolan said. "We kill."

"Do you know where they are?" Cillian asked. "It's much easier to take care of them in human form."

"No, they hide from us during the day."

And with all the guards turned, there was no one to go looking.

"Right," said Niamh. "We'll start going from house to house."

Visions of children roused, and bearded fathers cut down, roiled through the friar's mind. Fortunately, this was a simple idea to push off track. "No, there are three of you. Where is the glory in picking them off one at a time? Why not go to the town center and wait for their attack tonight?"

Niamh and Cillian looked at him suspiciously, while Nolan said, "Yes, fight worth remembering," as he thrust his hero's sword, laced with silver for just such a fight, into the air, pointed toward where the moon would rise. Two other silver-tinged blades rose with his as Barach caressed his hilt.

On the way through town, Barach stopped at a baker's shop and purchased three loaves of bread that he wrapped in herb bags. They found the town square, a wide-open spot, which they left with dispatch to find a nice corner where they would be blocked in on two sides. There was no such opportunity in the square itself, and as their search expanded to other buildings, Cillian twitched. "That must be one," and he sprinted across the square, tackling an old woman with a mustache that teenage boys would look on admiringly. The others ran after him, catching up as he knocked the woman to the ground, grinning as he held her down with his right hand and cocked his blade, ready to strike. "I have you. Tell us where the rest of your pack is."

Nolan and Niamh came beside him, swords raised in white-knuckled hands, backing up their comrade.

"Please, sir, I don't know anything. The sun is setting and I'm trying to get home."

"Sure, you need to get home and come back with reinforcements!" Cillian said as his blade pricked the woman's neck and she whimpered. "See how she fears my silver?"

"I dare say she fears the steel every bit as much," Barach said as he arrived where the woman lay face down under a window with a golden candlestick in the wall of a large house. The candlestick itself would be a good month's pay for a mason.

"Grammy," cried a young girl as she charged onto the street. "Don't hurt my Grammy!"

"Who are you?" Niamh said to the little girl as she moved toward the child. "Did this one turn you?"

The girl, likely only six, went to the old woman and

hugged her, holding her tight. "This my Grammy. Grammy good. She makes good soup and plays with me."

"What sort of games does your Grammy play?" asked Cillian. "Fetch?"

"Enough!" said Barach. "Child, would you please eat this?" The friar pulled a piece of bread that he'd packed next to wolfsbane, which the child took a bite out of as he offered more to Grammy.

"Yuck, I don't like this," the child said as she dutifully ate all she was given, as did the old woman.

The flush on the heroes' faces surpassed the noon sun in brilliance.

"Please get indoors," Barach said. "Tonight, it will be very dangerous out here. Even more so than it is now."

The heroes continued their search for an acceptable battleground. Not a word was said among them until they located a corner with no windows above. A space where they would be protected on two sides. Their best position, given that a horde of ravenous lycanthropes would soon arrive from every direction. Nolan stood between Niamh and Cillian as the good friar backed into the corner.

As they waited, his hands began to sweat. He could take the sword and stand with them. Surely, the glory of one last fight wouldn't ruin him. And it wouldn't be for glory. This was a necessary fight, the type of combat every hero sought. His heart accelerated as he imagined himself striking down foes by the dozen, showing these three who the greater hero really was.

But he'd made a promise, to himself, to his bishop, to his God, and to an almost bald bride fifteen leagues from here. He was no longer a hero. Barach said a silent prayer to find the strength to make it through the night with his honor intact. He would not return to being the man who terrified grandmothers and little girls.

As the moon rose, glowing above the city, howling rolled in from every direction. Soon, the battle would be upon him.

IT STARTED WITH AN INITIAL CHARGE. Twelve wolves, each the size of a pony, raced in, teeth bared, eyes wide, driving at the heroes with the speed of falcons. The beasts' rampage met eagle-swift swords. Cillian, Niamh and Nolan each decapitated a foe in a heartbeat's shadow as they joined the howling with screams of joy: heroic battle cries. Yet, even as they struck down their first foes, others fell on them. Teeth tore into flesh, wounds that should infect with lycanthropy, but the deadly poison had no effect on the blood of those bred for valor.

The swords re-cocked, each falling seven times, cutting through their enemies. The victors laughed in exultation, though the laughter slowed as the corpses before them reverted to human form: six with heads separated from their bodies, three halved through their abdomens, three cleaved into multiple pieces, one diced into ten parts.

Barach sank into the corner, covering his eyes with his hands, praying for deliverance and wishing that the sweet aroma of slaughter did not beckon to every cell in his body. He should have kept his eyes closed and covered, but he could not. Barach watched the mayhem between quaking fingers. Praying he would not sink back into the dark pit he'd clawed away from ten years ago.

Werewolves were not stupid, and the heroes weren't uninjured. True, none of them would turn, but each of them bore the marks of multiple bites and scratches. They would recover from these wounds, but it would take time. The demonic dogs began taunting them, moving in and out, too quick to be cut, but keeping the heroes active, daring them to break formation. Which they naturally did.

"Enough of this," Nolan said. "I say we attack!"

"No," Niamh said. "We hold our ground and wait for them to grow impatient or for the sun to capture them. Once the first light comes, they will become human and easy prey for us. Time is on our side."

"Yes, if we break our ranks, they will overwhelm us. Besides," Cillian said, gesturing toward Barach, "we need to defend our 'heroic' protector."

The laughter stung the friar as much as the imprint of his weapon along his leg. Suddenly, a weight hit his back and teeth sunk into his shoulder.

"One's coming off the roof," Nolan said, whirling around. "Close ranks behind me." But there was no need for him to intervene.

Anger roiled through Barach as he rose, all his prayers forgotten as he hurled the wolf off. Red washed across his vision as he looked down at the beast and his body reacted. The lycanthropes teeth marks healed as every muscle in his body tightened. Barach stood on the edge and he gripped and drew his sword. This was battle, what he was made for, what his body longed for as a baby sought its mother.

This couldn't happen. He couldn't go back to the lunacy of his former life. He'd taught himself to deny this. Surely, he had the strength to hold back here. But as the grip on his sword loosened and his vision cleared, the monster threw itself at him.

He sliced through the beast with the ease of an axe cutting butter. Now, everything went red. Perhaps he could stop at one. He stood over the dead wolf, trembling, as his muscles fought the battle between friar and berserker. Barach had to pull back right now, or his world would be lost.

He took a deep breath, started to sheath his sword, fighting for self control. Then two more wolves fell from the roof.

Barach's mind receded and his body took over, doing what it naturally did, and he dispatched both in a single strike. He screamed and ran past his three potential proteges, throwing himself into the wolf pack, a whirling blade unleashing a waterfall of blood as all consciousness left him. None of these puppies would survive his wrath.

But would Limerick?

Barach remembered none of his battle madness, and one day, he might count that as a blessing. Reality came back into focus, with Nolan, Niamh and Cillian holding him to the ground.

"Get a hold of yourself, man," Cillian said. "Calm down. You've killed all the wolves and taken down a dozen houses."

"The town's evacuating," Niamh said. "They're more afraid of you, of us, than they were of any werewolf. So, they're braving the night and any lingering monsters to escape. You've got to get back under control."

"We too," Nolan said. "We kill buildings too."

Barach rolled onto his face and cried. How could he have done this? He had slain nothing in ten years. How could his God have abandoned him? Or was it the other way around? He'd put himself in a position to fail, all but begging the battle lust to return as he pretended to reject it. Unworthiness filled his soul.

"I've failed you."

Niamh leaned down and stroked his hair. "You tried. I've seen no one fight like you did. I can't imagine being as good as you and giving it up." As she scanned the ruins, she continued. "But I think you've convinced me. We have gotten dangerous, and people are too used to relying on us. This should never have gotten this far—Limerick should have handled a single werewolf. But you, Barach, they will never be ready for something like you."

There was a moment of silence before Cillian answered. "I think I agree with her. Our time is done. I'm willing to become something else, or at least try. If you're willing to teach me."

What was going on here? Who was he to teach anyone about walking away from heroism? Everything he'd worked for was gone. Ten years of discipline evaporated. Was it really discipline or had he been a coward, afraid to accept what he should be? Should he just accept his heroism and be done? Barach didn't have any answers.

Among these thoughts lay confusion at the reactions of these three. He pulled into a seated position. "After what you've just seen me do, you'd trust me to teach you about peace? Are you crazy?"

"*Especially* because of what we've seen you do," Niamh said. "Are you still willing to try?"

This was a cruel mockery. Now, with his years of devotion scattered in ruins around him, did God seek to torment him, laughing as his soul shrank into oblivion and all that he'd once thought good failed before his impulse for violence? Or was there another truth here? For ten years, he'd denied his natural skills. Perhaps his destiny lay in conquest, destruction of evil, even when it came in the form of old ladies and young boys, as surely all bore the seeds of sin. Perhaps the lesson was that his struggle was hopeless and he should accept the proper role of avenging angel.

And yet... He had known joy as a hero, but never peace, never contentment that lasted longer than the swish of a blade. Barach, the hero, had moments of hollow exultation that left his heart tired. He had a choice here, claw his way back to the life that had brought him fulfillment, or accept the role of the angel of death. He had no idea which path was right.

"You idiots. I no give up," Nolan said as he walked away, shaking his head and mumbling.

Nolan was right, but he was also wrong. Barach had fought his nature for ten years, and the fight had always been difficult, but it was the only thing that brought him any peace at all. He was not fit to be anyone's teacher, but he had to restart his own journey from the beginning.

Barach stood, pulled his friar's robe off and tossed it to the ground, leaving himself in his faded shift. "I'm sorry, but I can't lead you down this path. I've got to find my own way back – who am I to lead you?"

"Our best hope," Niamh said. "Now we know you are one of us. Let us find our way through this together. What you've taught us today is that we'll always be heroes, and that's a burden. Show us how to become heroes who don't destroy, and that if we fail, we can get back up and move forward."

The warrioress picked up his friar's robe and held it out to him.

Cillian drew his sword and tossed it down the street. Then he grabbed Barach's sword and threw it, while Niamh hurled hers. "It seems to me that you should have done that long ago."

"Probably," Barach said. "But it's more complicated than that. The sword discouraged people from attacking me. It's not like we need blades to break people's necks."

"Sounds like you're telling yourself a story," Cillian said. "Maybe you didn't try hard enough, always left yourself a way back. Come on, the three of us can work this out."

Yes, he should have gotten rid of the sword years ago. Had he really changed at all, or did he just spend ten years denying himself? Barach needed to get back to Boyle Abbey and get some answers.

And he was still in no condition to help these two.

He shook his head, turned north, and began walking. Cillian and Niamh followed him. Barach thought to chase them away, but decided against it. If they followed him to the Abbey, they would get help. A half a league from Limerick, he became aware of Nolan following far to the rear, but closing the gap. Their devotion was as heartwarming as it was annoying. He had nothing to give them.

No longer could he offer guidance, no longer could he pretend to be wiser than any other hero. All Barach could do was to claw his own way back to sobriety.

It occurred to him as he walked the road that fellow travelers might not be a bad thing. So, an hour outside Limerick, he wordlessly accepted his robes as Nolan pulled even with them.

No, he would not be anyone's mentor. But maybe, just maybe, he might be someone's friend.

THE END

BIO: Andy has previously published short stories on Moon Drenched Fables, Black Ink Press, Black Hare Press,

Nordic Press, and Bullet Points. He lives in Richmond, Virginia, with his wife, son, and grand-dachshund and is a moderator for fantasy-writers.org. Andy also produces the Frenchie Frier's Story Land YouTube channel.

CHAPTER 5
BALOR THE SPEARSMAN
MEETING THE MENTOR

by

Catherine Lo

N obody in Balor's town could remember a time when they had not been at war. Generation after generation of young men and women joined the City Guards, training to protect the population from their traditional enemies, the Hungry Hordes.

Every class of graduating students pledged to do their duty. The City Guard Commander assigned all of Balor's friends to mentors for guards' positions, leaving Balor to the last. Jase had been the first one, assigned to the sword master. That wasn't surprising. His father was a senior Guardsman. Balor's father had been a spear holder. He had fallen repelling the first onslaught of the Horde. Balor had inherited his father's tall body and strong arms and shoulders. Balor's mother had named him after the war god, but that had not made the Commander take him seriously. The list of available mentors had dwindled down to near zero. Now the Commander called him.

"Balor, Madam Shuma will be your mentor."

"No!"

Balor was appalled. Madam Shuma was the garrison's head chef.

The Commander looked displeased.

"You don't understand the honor. Madam Shuma asked for you herself. She said you had the highest test scores in your class and could master the complex recipes quickly. The Garrison's health and strength depend on nourishing meals. You will also learn to make potions to ward off infection."

"I want to be a fighter. Let one of the girls learn to make potions."

"All the positions in the Guards are valuable. Stop arguing. Madam Shuma expects you tomorrow morning at dawn."

Balor sulked all evening till his mother lost her temper.

"A soldier's first duty is to obey orders. You will never be accepted as a fighter if you are insubordinate."

BALOR REPORTED to Madam Shuma in a black humor. She looked at him with a faint smile and led him to a huge cauldron.

"This must be kept boiling all day," she said. "I will add different ingredients. Your task is to stir them in slowly at a consistent speed. This is tiring work, but essential."

She handed him a giant wooden paddle with several holes punctured in it at random intervals.

Balor had to stand on a bench to reach into the

bubbling mixture. After a few turns of the paddle his arms began to ache. Half an hour later, his shoulders throbbed and his biceps cramped till he could have screamed with the pain. He saw Jase and his friends mocking him and bit his lip. He would not give them the satisfaction of seeing him cry. So Madam Shuma had asked for him, had she. All she wanted was his strong arms and back.

There was no respite till three hours after sundown. Madam Shuma showed Balor the mixture. It was smooth. She tasted it and nodded.

"Here, try it." She handed him a spoonful.

The stuff was bitter, with a hint of an exotic honey flavor. A few minutes after swallowing it, the aches and pains in his upper body vanished and Balor felt as refreshed as though he had just woken from a long night's deep sleep.

"Do you see now why it is important for our Guardsmen to have this?"

"Yeah."

Mrs Shuma finally pronounced the brew ready. She told Balor to bring out a cart stocked with hundreds of tiny vials.

"The vials are filled and distributed to the Guardsmen," she told Balor. "That is a chore for my other assistants. Now it's time for you to learn more advanced procedures."

She led him to a small room and unlocked the sturdy door.

"This is the recipe room. I also store some of the more valuable ingredients here. No one is allowed in here but you and me. You must not ever divulge what you see here."

She walked to a low cabinet and took out a sheet of parchment.

"This is the ingredient list. Read it aloud."

"Shouldn't I close the door first?"

"No. It is very difficult for anyone to eavesdrop when standing in an open doorway. Keep your voice down."

Balor was impressed. He looked at the list and gasped.

"One freshly laid dragon's egg?"

"Yes. It must still be liquid so it can be beaten into the soup."

"Where do you get a dragon's egg?"

"Ah. Did you imagine I only needed your strength to stir the pot? You must find an egg."

Balor gulped. "Where?"

"Dragons nest in the barren rocks along the northern cliffs."

"Who got you the last egg?"

"A brave young Guardsman. Unfortunately he was gored to death when he went after a wild boar. The recipe calls for a wild boar: sides, head and trotters. After you've got the dragon's egg, the next task will be to spear a wild boar. Your father was a gifted spearsman. You have his arms and shoulders."

"But I have never been trained to use a spear."

Mrs Shuma nodded. "You will start tomorrow morning. I have asked the Guards Commander to send his Spear Master here."

THE SPEAR MASTER was a middle-aged Guardsman with a ragged scar running down the right side of his neck and a no-nonsense attitude.

"Your mentor says you must learn how to spear a wild boar," he said.

"Yes, sir."

"Watch me, then imitate my movements."

He handed Balor a training spear and proceeded to go

through a series of attack and defense moves. Balor imitated the moves correctly, tentative at first, then faster as he gained

confidence. After an hour, the SpearMaster stopped for a water break and said,

"You pick up the moves quickly. Have you ever seen someone spear a boar?"

"No, sir. But my father was a spearsman. I have his arms and shoulders."

"Oh? You are the widow's son?"

"Yes, sir."

"Too bad he was clumsy at the wrong moment. As was I."

He fingered his scar.

"I did not keep my eyes on the boar I was trying to spear and it grabbed the spear in its jaws and bent the head towards me. If you want to come out the winner in a contest with any wild beast, never let down your guard."

After a week of lessons, the Master declared Balor competent to hunt his boar. Jase and his buddies were incredulous.

"Potions Boy," they jeered, "You think you can spear a boar?"

"He will do it better than any of you," the Spear Master said. "None of you have the focus. And if you don't show some respect for a fellow guardsman, your commanding officer will hear from me."

At the end of the last lesson, Balor asked the question that had been foremost on his mind.

"Master, would these same moves serve me in fending off a dragon?"

"A dragon. Male or female?"

"A mother dragon who will protect her egg."

The Spear Master swore.

"Madam Shuma deceived me. She needs you to steal a dragon's egg for her brew."

"I could not tell you this."

"A mother dragon is much more dangerous than a grown wild boar. She will be ruthless and dragons are smarter than boars. She will be able to read your mind, anticipate your moves. The only way you can hope to spear a dragon is to get the tip of your spear between the scales, then drive it in with all your strength. You will have one chance."

"I don't want to kill the mother. She needs to stay alive to keep on laying eggs. How big is a dragon egg? I will have to carry it somehow, but I need both hands for my spear."

The Spear Master shook his head. "I don't know. Come. We must ask the Lore Master."

THE LORE MASTER was a bent old man in a long, dirty, brown robe. He lacked two front teeth which made his breath whistle oddly when he spoke.

"Most dragon eggs are the size of a large honey dew melon, only egg shaped, not round. The eggs have a tough, leathery skin instead of a hard shell like a hen's egg. A dragon's egg will not crack if you drop it, but it might bounce. You won't be able to retrieve it if it bounces away from you. The mother dragon will kill you first. Get a strong fisherman's net with a drawstring at the top. As soon as you put the egg into the net, tie it securely."

"What color are the eggs?"

"The same color as the mother's scales. The dragons that nest on the cliff closest to your village are gray, so their eggs will be gray too. A little lighter, perhaps."

The Lore Master stopped to wheeze and cough.

"If a dragon has royal blood, its egg will have an iridescent pattern," he added. "You will not see such an egg. Royal dragons seldom conceive to lay a viable egg. A pity. With no acknowledged heir to control them, the lesser dragons run wild and encroach on human territory."

BALOR TIED a strong rope around his waist and looped the net's drawstring over the improvised belt. He carried an eight foot long spear in his right hand. The spear head had been blunted so the narrow tip was smooth. The barren cliffs where the dragons nested were a day's hike from the village. By evening he was close enough to smell the acrid scent of the dragons' breath. Three dragons flew past, hunting their supper of rodents and unwary birds. When they settled down for the night, Balor crept closer. The dragon slept. The egg was large and surprisingly heavy. Balor wrestled it into the net and hurried to a hidden hollow in the rock he had identified as a safe place to wait out the night. He lit a stub of candle to look at his trophy. The large egg was light gray. A swirl of iridescent colors decorated the surface. Balor's heart sank. A royal egg.

MADAM SHUMA WILL BE VERY pleased to have this. Then he recalled the Lore Master's words. If I destroy this royal egg, we will soon have all the gray dragons eating our sheep and goats. I should return it.

How to do that and avoid being burnt to a crisp was a problem that occupied Balor's mind all the way back to the royal nest.

. . .

QUEST

THE DRAGON QUEEN lay curled around her empty nest. Dim flashes of fire puffed from her nostrils. Balor could hear a sad, low keening. He stuck his spear between two knee high rocks and untied the draw string so the patterned egg was exposed.

With a heartfelt prayer to all the gods for protection, he called,

"Your Majesty, I have returned your egg. It is unharmed."

The queen raised her head and met his eye. There was a frightening, shrewd intelligence in her glowing golden orbs. She slithered forward and a three-foot long crimson tongue shot out between razor sharp teeth. Balor imagined the feel of those teeth closing on his spine. The dragon rolled her egg over and over, inspecting it inch by inch. When she was satisfied, she stood up on her hind legs and bowed to him in a regal manner before grasping the egg in her claws and flying off.

BALOR DECIDED he had had enough adventure for one day and returned to the Guards' base. What Mrs Shuma didn't know wouldn't hurt her.

He reckoned without his mentor's psychic vision.

Mrs Shuma held his eye for a long moment.

"What are you not telling me?" she asked.

"I found a r-royal d-d-dragon's egg, but I returned it," he stammered.

"You returned it? Why?"

Balor repeated the Lore Master's words. Mrs Shuma folded her lips tightly, obviously having trouble keeping her temper.

95

"You are an apprentice. You do not have the authority to make such a decision."

Balor shuffled his feet.

"I couldn't leave the dragons without an heir. I will pack my gear and go home," he said.

"I did not give you permission to leave. I still need a fresh dragon's egg and a newly slaughtered wild boar for the potion, and I still need you to stir the boiling pot. Go eat now, rest, and go back at first light tomorrow for an egg and a wild boar."

THE END

BIO: I write fantasy stories for amusement. After finding the Fantasy Writers' website, I was happy to learn of so many others with the same interest. I enjoy reading their stories and receiving critiques on my own. I have been a member of Fantasy-Writer's.org since March 2015.

CHAPTER 6

ONE GOOD FIGHT

MEETING THE MENTOR

by

L. M. Price

His first ten-day and guarding the throne room! Mofi stood still and straight and proud, like Heron hunting. *Do just like me,* Bedu had told him. *Nothing will happen. We will stand by this door, you on that side and me on this side, and guard nothing from nothing until the sun goes down. Hold your spear like this. Keep your head high. Even a stupid boy from the mountains can do it right.*

Mofi had grinned and thought about fighting him. He could put him down, he thought. Probably. Maybe. But maybe not, and Gida had said no. Gida. Mofi shook his head in admiration. Gida was old. His hair was grey instead of black. He was fat. But hoo! He could move! If Gida said it, Mofi would do it.

He checked the high windows. Probably nobody could

get through them. He couldn't. He looked at the ceiling. Face after face, round and black with golden eyes, looked back. The gods, painted there to watch over the king. It would be interesting if some of the eyes were really holes and men were hiding behind them. He checked every face, but all the eyes were the same. He sighed. It was a little boring, guarding nothing.

He spent a while imagining himself in the paintings on the walls. Men in knee-length white shema, just like his, threw spears or shot arrows at elephants and lions. A lady-smith, her fires coiling through her hair, crept up behind a giant snake. Surreptitiously, Mofi moved his foot on the polished floor. The sole of his sandal whispered against the stone, and Bedu glared at him. Mofi froze. It would be hard to sneak up behind anyone on this kind of floor. Not in these sandals. Maybe barefoot. He was better at being quiet barefoot.

Another painting was of a battle. Two men in the middle hurled spears at a man wearing a head-dress of ostrich feathers. Mofi changed his grip on his spear, trying to match theirs. Then he changed it back. There was another giant snake in this painting. Maybe it was the same snake, even. He leaned forward to see better. Bedu hissed, and he jerked back to standing heron-straight.

Then he stood even straighter, because the king had come in the other door, the one at the far end of the hall with gold and ivory pillars. Mofi's door was only some sort of black wood. There were other guards on that gold door— men who'd been in the palace for many years. Stupid boys from mountains guarded side doors. Ah well. He was lucky to be in the throne room at all. And the king had come! Bedu hadn't thought he'd be here today. Mofi's heart swelled with joy.

The king walked like a lion. No, like the cheetah whose spotted pelt he wore slung around his shoulders with the paws hanging down in front. Its claws curved like it had just pounced and slid them out, mid-air, to crack the neck of its prey. The king walked like that. Mofi wondered which of the men scattering around him was the antelope. That one, maybe, with the sour face and eyes that hid secrets.

"Great King," that man was saying as they walked past. "You must send word to Inyaga. When the queen arrives—"

"I must?" growled the king.

The sour-faced man persisted, "When the queen arrives, the Rasa may resent her. You know how many wanted a daughter of their own to catch your eye. That you chose a stranger, and a foreigner—" He shook his head.

"Enough!" snapped the king.

Mofi sucked in his breath and didn't move. He wasn't stupid enough to catch the eye of a hunting cheetah! Besides, if he so much as twitched on duty, he would be running around the yards until he was old and wrinkled. Gida had said so. The king went up the steps to his throne on the balls of his feet, fast like a springing cat. Mofi flexed the muscles of his calves, imagining how he would bound up stairs like that. The king was a great warrior, Gida had said. Not a man who sat on his throne and forgot how to live.

The king wore armor, even in his own throne room. Mofi looked at it critically. It was just like what he wore over his tunic, only the king's was gold with red knobs. Mofi's was plain brown. He pictured arrows hitting those red knobs and skittering away. Probably, under the paint, it was rhinoceros hide. Probably, the king had killed it himself. He looked closer. Yes, there was an honor ring in his ear. The king didn't have a spear, though, only a short, curved sword on his belt. Mofi looked fondly at his own spear. A single blue-grey feather hung from its shaft. That was for the time when—

"You! Boy! Guard!"

Bedu hissed, and Mofi jerked his attention back. "Sir," he said, remembering, and thumped the butt of his spear. A hard-faced man was striding towards him. Bedu was making little flapping motions with his free hand, out of sight of the throne. "Bow," he muttered without moving a muscle in his face.

Mofi tried to keep his face that smooth, but he wanted to scowl. He shouldn't have to bow to anyone who wasn't the king.

"Bow!" Bedu said again, urgently.

Mofi bent himself at the waist. He was a heron, stabbing down. That man was the snake. Mofi imagined him writhing helpless in the water. When he straightened, the hard-faced man was glaring at him.

"Who let this untrained child loose in the throne room?" he demanded.

Untrained! Mofi's hand clenched on his spear. Let that man come out to the yards and see what untrained was!

The man was still talking. "Go. Tell the guard captain to send someone fit for the king's presence."

"What?" Mofi blurted. "I didn't - "

"Untrained and insolent." The man sounded pleased.

Bedu's hand clamped around Mofi's arm and dragged him out into the narrow hallway before he could say anything more.

Mofi wrenched himself free, glaring at Bedu. "I didn't do anything wrong! How dare he—"

"Shut up, boy," Bedu said. "That was Sindu. And next time, when I say bow, bow!"

"He wasn't even a lord," Mofi protested.

"How do you know? Save me from stupid boys who think they know everything. In that room, you bow to everyone, lord or not, hear me? And Sindu! Do you want him to decide he is your enemy? Go tell Gida exactly what he told you to."

"But—" Mofi began again.

Bedu's hand snaked out, grabbing his shoulder and shaking him, faster than Mofi had imagined he could move. His *za'ar* must be Mamba. That snake was even faster than a heron. Maybe Mofi wouldn't be able to take him down after all. "I thought you were smart. Go find Gida, and be quick about it."

Bedu shoved him down the hallway and strode back inside the little door. It shut behind him. Mofi stared at the elephants carved into the black wood while sick humiliation rose up in his stomach. Finally, he turned and left.

"WHAT ON EARTH did you do, boy?"

Mofi reminded himself of herons and stood perfectly still. "Nothing," he answered. "I watched Bedu and did all the same things. I watched the king—he walks like a cheetah, and I wanted to see how— and I watched that sour-faced man with the secrets in his eyes. I didn't do anything."

Gida looked at Mofi for a long time, then sighed. "Is he trying to make my life difficult? Of course, you're untrained. Standing guard is how you get trained. What does he expect?"

"Who is that, anyway?"

"Didn't Bedu tell you? Sindu is the second most

powerful man in the kingdom. He is the king's right hand. His foster brother. The king trusts him above everyone." Gida shook his head admiringly. "I saw him save the king's life, myself. He's not a man with a quick temper, either. You must have done something—no, don't argue. Send Mesifa to the throne room and tell Betga I said to give you some job that isn't guarding. Digging out the latrines for a ten-day or something."

"What?!" Mofi said, outraged. "I came to be a guard, not a—"

"Don't argue with me, boy. The likes of us can't go against the likes of him, not unless we want to spend the rest of our very short and painful lives feeding termites. Now go."

Mofi went.

He sulked his way down the long, snaking corridors that led out to the training grounds. Woven stripes of sunlight fell through lattice shutters along the top of each wall, and marble floors changed to wood and then to woven reeds. Mofi trudged across them all, not even bothering to practice walking silently. He took gloomy pride in how loud the slap of his sandals echoed down the halls. The sound was different on stone than on mats, but what did that matter now? Latrines! For a ten-day!

He, Mofi, had come across the mountains to join the king's guards and fight many battles. He had not come to dig dung pits. He brooded on the wrongs done him while he saluted Betga. Maybe he should go home again. There were many caravans going that way. Every day, probably. He could get a place, easy.

Betga sighed. "All right. You're on latrine duty this ten-day. Dig them all out."

"All of them?" Mofi repeated, aghast.

"All of them. Get going."

NINE MORE DAYS, Mofi told himself, hurling a shovel-full of muck over his shoulder. It splattered on landing, spraying stinking filth all over him.

Eight more days, he thought, patting his spears sadly as he passed them. We miss you, Mofi, they said to him. Come play with us. Come fight. What do you want to be grunting in holes for?

Five more days. "What did I do?" Mofi asked the pitiless skies as he climbed out of the pit and went to dunk himself in the river. There was no answer. The god of all warriors had clearly decided Mofi was none of his. Mofi slunk back to the barracks and buried his head under his blanket.

"The dung beetle's back," said someone nearby.

"A whole ten-day! The worst I've ever gotten was half. He's not old enough to have done anything that bad."

"Go away, boy," jeered someone else. "This is the place for men to sleep. Fighting men, like us."

"Shut up," Mofi mumbled into his mat. Even yesterday, a taunt like that would have brought him off the floor, fists at the ready. The day before yesterday, a taunt like that had brought him up fighting. He had a black eye and bruises on his ribs to prove it. Today, he didn't move. He was a beetle in truth. A ground worm. He was turning into a farmer. No! He hurled himself up and dove at the closest guardsman without even looking to see who it was.

Half a breath later, flat on his back with his head ringing, Mofi was staring up at the hard-faced lord who had kicked him out of the throne room.

"You!" he said bitterly and picked himself up. "What are

you doing in this place? It isn't enough that you ruin my life? Now you follow me around and beat on me here in my own bed?"

This was not the way to speak to great lords. Mofi knew that. He didn't need the shocked hisses to tell him so. He crossed his arms and glowered defiantly at the second most powerful man in the kingdom.

"You," Sindu pointed out, "attacked me." He looked around the room at the other guards, and jerked his head towards the door.

"Out."

Mofi scowled at him and stalked outside. Sindu followed him. Mofi heard the rustles and thumps as everyone else did too. A whisper of air alerted him. He dropped, twisting mid-air, and landed rolling. He sprang to his feet and flung himself at Sindu's legs, suddenly cheerful. This was better. This was much better. Anything was better than digging out dung pits! But a good fight, that was best.

Except, Mofi realized, as he stared up at the sky, ears ringing again, it wasn't going to be much of a fight.

"Well?" taunted Sindu's voice. "Just going to lie there?"

Mofi sat up and blinked. Then he leaped up, hitting with both fists as fast as he could. His knuckles stung, and he shouted gleefully. A hit!

Two strong arms locked themselves around his chest and squeezed. Mofi stared into Sindu's hard, black face from a hand's-width away as the air wheezed out of his lungs. Hoo, he was strong! But not gold eyes, he thought, and almost giggled. Not a god.

Softly, Sindu said, "You've got guts. I thought you might. Do you have stamina, boy? Can you keep going on and on when the Sun King has turned his face away and there's no victory to be had, not even death?"

Death wasn't victory. Mofi didn't have enough breath to say so, but he nodded anyways, because whatever the man meant, he, Mofi, was not giving up. He tried to kick Sindu in the groin.

Sindu chuckled and squeezed harder. "You don't know what I mean, do you?" Mofi felt his eyes start to pop out of his head.

"Listen, boy," Sindu said, lowering his voice still further. "I need someone. Someone nobody knows is on my side. You're new here. That's good. Gida said you saw that Ras Sosa is keeping secrets. That's good, too. I can use that. I'll get you better training with that spear of yours—you hold it like a plow! Training in other things, too. If you're up for it."

He flung Mofi over his head, whirled, and dropped, pinning Mofi's arms and jamming his knee into his back.

"What do you say?" Sindu asked as if he were teaching a child how to wrestle.

All the hot shame of the last days spilled away like nothing. A rush of excitement filled Mofi's chest. Training! A secret mission! But Bedu had scolded him for thinking he knew everything without asking. He should know what kind of mission this was before he accepted. He thought fast. This man wouldn't want him to ask in front of everyone. He would be impressed if Mofi showed he knew that. He should say it so everyone would think he meant something else.

"What are you doing?" he demanded, as rudely as he could with dirt in his teeth.

He gasped as Sindu yanked his arms up behind him. "Giving you a lesson in respect. When you're defeated, what do you say?" Under his breath, Mofi heard him add, "Keeping the new queen safe."

That was a job! A man could be proud of that job. The new queen, Mofi thought joyously. I will guard the new queen. And learn more ways to fight. "Yes," he whispered. "Yes." And aloud, sullenly, "I yield."

The pressure on his back vanished. He sat up, shaking his arms out. Sindu stood over him, glowering. "Let that teach you proper behavior to your betters."

Mofi bowed to hide his face. When he straightened, Sindu was gone. Mofi hadn't even heard him go. What he could learn from a man like that! He made his face blank like Bedu's and went back to his sleeping mat, ignoring the other men.

"You all right, boy?" One of the other guards dropped down beside him. "Don't let it get to you. Sindu's not that bad, mostly. You're lucky he didn't beat you harder for talking to him like that, but he won't hold it against you. Over is over, with Sindu! And latrine punishment, we all get that. It's only five more days. They'll be gone before you know it."

"Yes," Mofi said, trying to sound glum. It was hard. He wanted to race circles around the palace and shout. What was five days? Nothing! He was a lion. He was a cheetah, running like the wind. He was Heron stalking, striking down the queen's enemies.

THE END

BIO: L. M. Price travels around Montana and Wyoming and writes poetry and fantasy. In between other projects, she writes collaborative Lord of the Rings fanfiction. She has been a member of Fantasy-Writers.org since 2010.

CHAPTER 7
VALLEY OF WOLVES AND WITCHES

CROSSING THE THRESHOLD

by

Jens Hieber

The icy whiteness of the valley floor was still in morning shadow, but the first rays of the sun had fallen over the mountain tops and bathed her cabin porch in their glow. Kciyta sat perfectly still so the old chair would not creak and gazed across the solitary expanse below her. The snow-laden pines shielded this cabin on the hillside from view yet also gave her the beautiful vista.

She would miss this place now that spring had come. Her Winter of Isolation completed, she could return through the mountain cleft called the Threshold, back to the Queendom in the lowlands beyond. The rite was required of all young witches as they finished their second decade of life, before they could fight their way up the social hierarchy. Kciyta knew she was better prepared than some, but she did not relish the idea of the amount of strife it would take to carve out even a small niche for herself. She inhaled the biting air one final time before standing and putting on her carefully assembled pack. She rechecked the straps, ensured the wooden door was locked, and placed the key in the hidden nook under the cross beam above her head. Fitting herself into the snowshoes, she took one last look before breaking the blanket of snow.

The crunching as she walked temporarily silenced the morning twitter, but as she threaded her way through the trees, it started back up. Many witches dreaded the Winter of Isolation, yet she had sought it eagerly; so much time away from the others, honing her skills, had been refreshing. Witches were supposed to be self-reliant, so Kciyta had never understood why the others at the training school in the capital spent so much time around each other, stirring dramatic interpersonal conflagrations and betrayals. They strove outwardly for independence and still flocked to each other without noting the inconsistency. And the way they idolized the celebrity witches like the flashy Weraine, the mysterious, merciless Teryn, or even the Witch Queen herself was nothing short of sycophantic.

Spring came late in the north. Likely, the remaining young witches who had spent their Winter of Isolation in other regions of the Queendom had long since returned. Kciyta pushed her senses outward, even while she held close the warmth of her inner fire, protecting her from the morning chill. She had chosen her cabin carefully despite the risk of wolves in this valley; generations of previous witches had established a perimeter of safety. Now, stepping beyond a row of pines and into a large clearing, she knew she would have to rely on her senses and wits. There shouldn't be any wolves left this far south; they usually retreated into the deep mountain valleys as soon as possible to avoid any confrontation. She knew she could take care of herself, having honed several magical skills, including several ice maneuvers that few witches would know. Nevertheless, Kciyta liked to be careful.

She sensed the new life, the straining bulbs under the white covering, the bright green buds on several trees, and the furry creatures in their warm nests. She had never understood the callous contempt most witches displayed for their surroundings. Many saw the wilds only as places to tame or destroy with their training. Many had assumed that in choosing this valley beyond the Threshold, she hoped to capture a wolf pup as a familiar. She had seen the wolves thus bonded and how little life of their own they retained and had no desire to tie such a creature to herself.

The next patch of trees was low enough that some had already sprouted beyond their buds. In truth, she could have returned several weeks ago but had been loathe to leave this tranquility. The wet pine needles beneath her feet were no longer covered, green stalks pushing up between them. Stepping out from under a row of eaves, she came into the valley proper, the same view as from her porch though much closer. To her left in the south, she could see the cleft through the mountains, the Threshold that would lead her back to the chaotic struggle of her real life. Did she really want that?

Her senses brought her to a halt.

Someone had been nearby recently. Far below, a row of footsteps, recognizable by the clear pattern of snowshoes even from here, broke the expanse. Someone had walked through her valley in the night, and she had not sensed them.

TASO WOKE when the sun hit his face. The heat from above against the cold beneath shocked him into awareness. He tried to lift his head, but his fur was stuck fast, requiring more effort than he had. Spatters of dark blood among the blinding reflections of snow brought the attack back to him.

He jerked up, tearing himself loose from the ice below. A stab of pain raced through his hind leg as he saw the bodies of his pack members. Jahra lay on her side, unbreathing, gashed open from shoulder to tail while the youngster, Ungal, had been practically decapitated, his fierce snarl frozen in place. The deep loss sucked the air from his lungs again—his pack was gone.

At least Taso's mother had not lived to see this, their entire pack slaughtered. He had led them for less than half a winter, and already he had failed. Frantically he counted wolf bodies—seven, eight...someone was missing. He listened for their voices in his mind, but was met with only silence. He remembered that when the attack had begun, he had heard only their growling and yelps of pain, not their voices in his mind. And his orders had gone unheeded as though his pack had not heard him. He ran from body to body, knowing his search for signs of life would be futile yet unable to keep himself from hoping.

Forcing himself to ignore the pain and to hold still, he raised his head and filled his nostrils with morning air. The smell of cold, dried blood overwhelmed him, and yet underneath it, the freshness of spring in its multitudes spread as well. And beneath that, the faint but unmistakable scent of the witch.

How had she remained undetected, hiding behind a

tree while their entire pack had passed her by? Ten wolves should have noticed her from afar, yet none of them had scented her in time. Taso, as pack leader, knew it had been his responsibility—his failure. His mother would not have let this happen.

The wave of grief, threatening as he padded again to each fallen pack member, remained at bay. The faint scent of the dark woman lingered and kindled deep in his being something more powerful. They had been so careful all winter, never crossing through the Threshold as other packs did, choosing the meager, yet safer, hunting grounds of these low valleys. And now, just when they were about to retreat into the mountains, the witch with her black hair flowing and her merciless eyes had taken everything.

Hangara. That's who was missing, the young pup not yet a year old. Her three siblings lay slain near Jahra. The witch had taken her, the worst fate he could imagine for a young pup.

The witch, thinking them all dead, had not bothered to cover her tracks. Not that it would have made much difference as Taso could follow her scent anywhere. Steeling himself to the pain, he loped off along the depressions in the snow towards the Threshold. He had to catch them before they crossed into the terrible lands beyond. If he did nothing else, he would save Hangara.

WHOEVER HAD WALKED through her valley must have been a witch as well. Kciyta had a sense of the presence of others, especially witches, and knew their proximity without fail. Her years at the training school had been overwhelming because of this awareness, especially around some of the more lax witches. Occasionally, she even sensed impressions and whole thoughts..

But she had been blind to whoever had walked through here, dragging a young wolf pup, by the looks of the prints. That was unsettling, though perhaps it opened an opportunity to travel back to the Queendom with another person, to slowly re-acclimatize herself to the society of others before being thrust back into the maelstrom of activity in the capital. As much as she detested the idea of a bound wolf pup, this was not an opportunity to spurn, particularly if the other witch could be convinced to divulge how she kept her presence hidden.

Kciyta followed the prints from a ways off, keeping her senses trained carefully so she could detect when she came upon the other witch and her captive wolf. It would not do to surprise her, unlikely as that was, but Kciyta also didn't want to be surprised herself—most witches were territorial, and some downright malicious.

The lone wolf was almost upon her before she noticed its presence. The grizzled beast had raced up from behind, while Kciyta's focus lay purely on dangers ahead. Kciyta whirled and intercepted the charge at the last instant with a hasty gust of air between them, pushing each of them aside. The wolf rolled in the snow, scrambling to face her, and charged again.

This time, she had longer and funneled compact air at the wolf's feet, tripping it up again. Kicking herself for her stupidity, Kciyta cast her senses outward for the rest of the pack. Why had this wolf attacked by itself? And it seemed injured, a large gash down its hind leg. She sensed no other wolves nearby, which only unsettled her the more. First the witch, now the wolf—had her abilities diminished over the winter?

The bag on her back had come somewhat undone in the initial skirmish; as she started to right it, the wolf snarled at her, rage and hate filling its eyes. It rushed again, and she turned aside, not wanting to kill the beast unless necessary. Except if a witch was caught unaware, a solitary wolf could do little against her. The wolf twisted about suddenly, and its jaws slashed through her cloak as it barreled towards her again. With the unbalanced bag and the awkwardness of the snowshoes, she lost her footing, and the wolf was upon her.

Its teeth tore at her shoulder, digging for a hold on her neck. Its weight held her down while its hind legs pushed it closer, the fangs drawing nearer to her lifeblood. Kciyta focused her fire and thrust it upwards into the wolf's chest, launching it across an expanse of trampled snow. She scrambled up quickly, closing the gap to where it lay, trying to regain its bearings.

Then she sensed its pain. Not the physical pain of the leg or her fire, but the anguish, loss, and rage it felt.

Hangara.

She heard the word clearly in her mind though did not know what it meant. The wolf focused on her, awareness of its vulnerable position momentarily showing in the dark eyes. She could not bring herself to kill the wolf, despite its unprovoked attack. Something must have...

The other witch. She had likely killed the rest of his pack and made off with a pup, the sort of needless violence Kciyta abhorred. The wolf had attacked either because he had mistaken her for the other witch, or simply because he had sensed danger in her.

Hangara.

That word again. She sensed the wolf's urgency, and

then it painfully rose and loped off along the other witch's tracks, not looking back.

~

EVEN AS HE had jumped at the young witch, Taso had known he was making a mistake. She was shorter, had lighter hair, and there was no sign of Hangara nearby. No, this was not the witch who had slaughtered his pack. He knew stealth was his only option, but even so, she had sensed him.

Once committed, there was no turning away. Even this young witch had proven too adept for him. Why she let him run he couldn't figure out, but her moment of hesitance made up his mind. He had been at her mercy and she had looked at him as though she could almost understand him. If this young witch, mostly surprised, had almost killed him, what chance did he and Hangara stand against the other, more experienced witch?

He ran on, the ache in his chest from where she had hit him throbbing, tightening, constricting. He pushed it aside and continued, moving as swiftly as he could to his doom. Already he felt himself tiring. Taso knew he would likely die, but he hoped to give Hangara the opportunity to escape while he did so. A copse of small trees allowed him to catch his breath and drink from an icy puddle. He padded back out to the footprints where Hangara had briefly resisted, then raced on. If he could catch them before they reached the Threshold, it would be possible for Hangara to disappear if she escaped.

The warm sun melted the snow ever faster. As the two sides of the cleft loomed over him, his hope of catching the witch on this side diminished. If they got down into the lowlands, he would have even the land itself against him. He had heard the stories of human-made fences, of villagers on the hunt, the temptations of the domesticated animals, and the cruel pogroms against wolves. Even if Hangara managed to escape the witch, she was unlikely to find her way back to the mountains unscathed by herself.

Soon, too soon, the cleft rose directly ahead. The massive slates of gray climbed into the blue sky, leaving a narrow, winding gap that slid downward to danger. Taso came to a stop at the head and peered down. There was no snow here anymore, yet the witch had dragged Hangara through. He could not see them ahead and so he hesitated, wondering how far they had traveled. Surely they would need to rest eventually—even the youngest wolf and the strongest witch, could not run forever.

Taso stepped into the Threshold. Seen from here, the narrow path that led through the cleft seemed much wider than from afar. The whole pack could have loped through here side by side, though it narrowed occasionally as the route twisted around rocky outcroppings. The path led down, inevitably down. Finally, he reached a crest of ground and, at its peak, saw the mountains on either side falling away to reveal a breathtaking view.

This was as far as he had ever come. Here he had stood months ago at the start of winter, his mother beside him. She had known her time would come soon and warned him again about the lowlands. Many other wolf packs risked the dangers during the winter—those that returned sleeker and fatter than those who remained in the mountain valleys. So few returned.

And now, Taso would disregard his mother's advice. It had been given to protect that pack, and in that he had already failed. Only Hangara remained. Better to save her than to remain a bitter wolf, forever alone in the mountains.

He took the first, dangerous step and then continued to the lands beyond.

As sad as she was to leave the solitude of her valley, part of Kciyta felt relief at seeing the lights coming on in the village below. Perhaps, she admitted to herself, she did need the company of others at times. She had passed through the village in the late autumn and acquired her provisions there, and a local guide, who escorted her up the pass and through the Threshold to her cabin.

She wondered whether the other witch and her captive wolf were below. She had not caught up with them or the older wolf who had attacked her, nor had she seen any sign of their passing once the obvious prints in the snow had disappeared.

It grew dark early this far north and to continue past the village would not serve her. And, she did still hope to find the other witch. She sensed the presence of the villagers below, though at this distance, they were still a mass of merged identities.

The fringes of the lowlands smelled different, the greenery much further along, and already the landscape teemed with additional life. She passed several villagers along the road, who carefully averted their gaze from the passing witch. Kciyta heard the people, not just through her ears, but in her mind. Their impressions nestled beside her awareness of them, dull feelings of discomfort, a sense of purpose, another of stifled hope. It had not been thus before the Winter; had her isolation and training strengthened her abilities? Yet she had missed the witch passing so close to her cabin.

She still did not sense the other witch. Had she moved on already, choosing to risk the road by night rather than stay here?

In town, Kciyta made for the small Threshold Inn, more a local tavern with a few boarding rooms. She had stayed for two nights on her way up and had been looking forward to the warm fare all day. The homely front with the low eaves was inviting, the glow from the front room spilling out onto the shadows, longing their way down the muddy street.

Tthen she sensed the wolf—a different wolf, younger, distressed. Kciyta turned to a building behind another, nearer to her. It was a stable or barn of sorts, openings between the slatted wood, and likely one of the oldest constructions in the village.

She adjusted the pack again, so it hung mostly from her uninjured shoulder. In a previous moment of rest, she had checked carefully; the wolf had not broken her skin, but the bruising had already begun. She had one shoulder that was bruised and the other aching from carrying most of the pack. Kciyta knew she must appear a curious sight and was aware several villagers were watching her warily through the windows and shutters. Yet, they would not bother her, no matter how suspiciously she acted.

Squeezing around a low hedge, she avoided the low eaves of one house and trudged carefully between two buildings, reaching the rear before pausing. The barn looked even more dilapidated from up close and was in easy sight of the tavern two houses down. Kciyta crouched and closed her eyes, extending herself outward while grounding herself on this patch of earth.

Two people in the house to her right, three to the left, and five in the tavern. And one very frightened wolf in the barn ahead. There was no sign of the witch in her awareness, though she knew that meant nothing. Could she similarly cloak herself? What if the other witch could also accurately sense the location of others? Their intentions?

The scared wolf drew her attention, and Kciyta resolved upon her course of action. This little she could do. She crept forward, finding the side door open, and slid smoothly into the musty interior of the barn. It took a moment for her eyes to adjust; a single bale of hay, a dwindling stack of firewood, and an ancient looking mule tied up in one corner. And there, along the far wall, a cage with a snarling young wolf.

Kciyta extended her sense to the frightened creature and issued an essence of calm and patience. She hummed noiselessly, exuding goodwill and friendship, then risked a word. *Hangara?*

The wolf stopped moving, its glistening eyes bored into her out of the dark.

I am Hangara, she heard–definitely from the wolf.

I help, Kciyta thought in response.

Witch! The curiosity was replaced by fear, stronger than before. How to convince this poor wolf that she was not like that other witch?

Once again, she exuded calm and peace and walked slowly towards the cage, kneeling before the lock. If she could make it seem that the lock had failed, perhaps the other witch would not notice it had been tampered with and her wolf pup released. Would she hunt down an escaped wolf pup?

I help, Kciyta thought again. She conjured an image of

the older, grizzled wolf that had attacked her and emanated it to the frightened pup.

Taso!

Is that the wolf's name? Taso? She thought.

Taso? The name was accompanied by an image of the older wolf running across snow with a snarling visage. Of course the pup would not know what a word like 'help' meant. But she had recognized the other wolf.

Reaching forward, Kciyta inspected the simple mechanism that kept the cage closed—not a lock. The rusty bar was wedged through thoroughly and latched in a complex enough manner that no wolf could open it. Could she make it look like it had bent and thus allowed the wolf to escape? Did it matter so much that the other witch thought it an accident?

She touched the bar and sensed the young wolf tense up, fear shuddering through her.

"What are you doing with my wolf?" a voice asked softly behind her.

Kciyta whirled, still crouched down with the heavy pack on her back. "I..."

"If you want one, little witchling, go and catch your own." The other witch, imperious in her bearing, stood silhouetted against the faint light that came through the slats of the barn. Her long hair spread out an aura of power and majesty as she strode forward.

Who was this mysterious witch?

Kciyta readied to defend herself, then suddenly found it difficult to breathe. Her chest would not move, no air entered her lungs, and all at once it became difficult to see or remain upright, as though the witch was pulling all life and awareness out of her.

"Stay out of my way," the witch threatened, looming

over her. "They may think me merciless, but see how I let you live? If I killed every witchling that crossed my will, the Queendom might become unstable. So I will allow you to live and learn from this."

Before she lost consciousness, Kciyta felt again a deep fear, though whether it was an impression from the young wolf or herself, she could not determine.

It had been good to lie down in the thick hedge through the night, hidden from the bustle of the world. Taso had not dared to risk the large cluster of human dwellings. The strong smells emanating from the village were enough to confuse him, and he knew that being seen by anyone would cause a panic. He had meant to rise early, yet exhaustion had flattened him.

As night had dropped with its coolness upon the village, Taso had slunk around it, trying to note whether the witch and Hangara were still there or not. The roads to the south were clear of any recognizable scent, so he had waited, edging as close as he dared in the hopes of making contact with Hangara if she was being held in the village.

The sun would come up late; already the earth about him stirred with morning and the anticipation of activity. He knew it would be difficult to rise. The stiffness of his hind leg made worse for the cold night spent unmoving, though he felt more rejuvenated after the hours lying here and the plump bird he had devoured before sleeping.

Something stirred just inside the village and then materialized into a horse, pulling something behind it. He saw first the witch seated behind the horse, then a cage. Oddly, he could not sense Hangara, though he clearly saw her cowering inside the cage. Was she dead that he could not feel her presence? No, he saw an ear twitch.

Taso pulled his own being into himself, as he would do on the hunt to keep his prey from sensing his presence. Perhaps that was what the witch had done to avoid their detection; even though he could smell her and see her, otherwise, she was a blank space on the road. He held perfectly still, letting them pass before easing into a crouch and emerging noiselessly from the hedge. At times, he left the track as he skirted open country, and at others, he held back for a time yet always maintained contact.

Rounding a corner after a stand of trees, he finally saw his opening. The rolling wheels that allowed the horse to pull the cart became stuck in the already deep rivets on the road. Taso held perfectly still as the witch swung down, clearly alert for any danger. Then, moments later, when she cursed the contraption, and a wary Hangara cowered low, Taso rushed into action. If he could knock the cage from the cart, it might break and allow Hangara to escape.

This witch was more aware than the last and turned before he could even launch himself at her. Taso changed course so that the blast she effortlessly hurled at him rushed past his shoulder. For an instant, he heard Hangara.

Taso! It was mingled with a sense of relief but also fear and worry. *She will capture us both. Or kill us.*

Taso could not respond, instead raced across the ditch to one side, knowing he could not remain in the open against the attentions of the witch.

The witch spoke, though aside from the snide menace, Taso only understood the word 'dead'. The sounds humans used to communicate made little sense to him, yet he recognized occasional snippets from the hunters that sometimes invaded the mountains.

Hangara, he called. *Escape the cage, I will distract the witch.*

I cannot, the anguished cry. Then, *the other witch comes. She tried to help. She showed me that you were coming.*

This was accompanied by an image of the young witch, though less clear. And then he sensed her, behind him, coming along the road. And the dark witch before him had clearly noted this approach as well, for she strode away from the cart and faced the turn in the road, waiting.

Should he attack, while she was distracted? Or wait for the other witch? Who had ever heard of a witch that helped wolves? But Hangara seemed so sure. Could she be mistaken?

Now, Taso, Hangara called. *Please!*

Taso made up his mind. This was as good an opportunity as any and his old rage had rekindled. This witch had killed, had taken his pack, had bound Hangara. At least the other witch had not killed him after he had attacked her.

He left the cover of the brush and raced to his likely death.

Kciyta knew the witch was waiting for her just around the bend. Kciyta did not attempt to hide her coming, knowing it would make no difference, especially since the other witch did not attempt to hide herself anymore. And she could sense the presence of the two wolves, the frightened pup and the enraged older wolf.

The witch stood in all her menacing glory, staring her down. Kciyta had figured out who this must be, the infamous Terya. She was a legend, stories of her mythical exploits whispered in the halls of the training school by obsessed young witches. Kciyta stood no chance here.

Before she could speak, the older wolf rushed toward the witch and so Kciyta threw her own attack, pushing heat and flame directly at the older witch's center. Whirling in her dark blue robes, eyes flashing, Terya stepped aside and slashed diagonally. Kciyta just managed to deflect the sharpened air.

The wolf hit, toppling the majestic witch into the mud, a mass of tangled cloak and snarling fur. The wolf had only moments remaining and with no easy way to intervene, Kciyta turned her attention to the captured pup, slamming concentrated power into the locking mechanism of the cage, breaking it open. The young wolf shuddered in fear, then pushed forward, ramming against the inside of the damaged cage.

The frightened horse spooked, dragging the cart from where it had stuck in the mud. The witch used the same thrust of air Kciyta had used when the wolf had pinned her; the grizzled beast was flung through the air and Terya rose imperiously.

"This is how you repay my mercy? I should have killed you both when I had the chance," she hissed. "Not too late, I think."

The witch had given Kciyta an idea, something like Terya had done to her in the barn. Kciyta waited until the woman had exhaled, then established a barrier of negation and emptiness. She had to hold it long enough to take effect and hope the other witch could not break free.

The fearsome woman kept fighting, throwing fire, slashing air, and striding towards her. Kciyta backed down the road, evading and blocking as best she could Terya's continued vicious assault. Kciyta briefly registered that the wolf lay where he had fallen, unmoving. She was on her own.

Ice. Notoriously difficult to work with, but she had spent all winter on this pursuit. Even in the spring morning, it should be possible. Kciyta held the air, crouched down, and slammed the ice spikes conjured from the frosty air at the other woman. They were smaller here, and Terya deflected several. One melted through the incoming blast of fire, but three struck her left leg. Terya buckled, one knee in the muck.

Now, the young witch had to finish it.

Terya rose again, murder in her eyes and hurled everything she had, rocks, compressed air, scorching flames. Kciyta sprang side, landing in the ditch beside the muddy track, feeling the pain of several blows on her side.

Still, she held onto the air negation around the other witch.

Kciyta scrambled quickly along the ditch, hoping to remain below the line of sight, yet fearing it was too shallow. She projected her voice to gain time, echoing it against the trees on the other side.

"This is my territory," she proclaimed with more strength than she felt. "Go back and play your games in the capital with the other witches."

Terya did not respond. It took a moment to remember that without air, she would not be able to. Then, Terya exploded into her head.

You little upstart! You know nothing of games.

Of course! Like the wolves! That's how she did it, how she hid herself. And clearly, she thought she alone had this power.

You're not the only one who can do this, Kciyta thought clearly, then stood and hurled another handful of ice spikes.

The witch was not there. Kciyta turned swiftly, expecting to feel the killing blow. Instead, she saw a wolf, younger, skinnier and darker in color hurtling at the witch from behind. Kciyta readied the next blow, and saw that it was unnecessary. Hangara stood upon the other witch's laid out form, snarling. It had taken three of them, but they had done it.

Hangara did not go for the kill, and neither did Kciyta. She knew mercy might be a mistake. Yet, leaving a trail of bodies as so many witches did, was no way to live a life. She released the air negation.

Taso! The young wolf called, running to the limp form. *Alive,* she sent after carefully sniffing the slumped form.

Kciyta turned a final wary look at the fallen witch, then went to see about whether she could help the old wolf.

THE BLURRY FACE of the young witch brought an instant snarl as he woke. Then rising as swiftly as he could, Taso's mind cleared somewhat. Had she helped? Did he have to kill her?

Taso, you're alive. Can you walk? Hangara asked. He had not noticed her right away; she seemed well, her usual lively self. She was panting and walking in circles, occasionally casting hurried glances back to the road.

The witch?

We did it! Hangara said. Excitement had replaced her fear.

Dead? Is she dead? We should kill her.

No, but she can't harm us now, Hangara said. *The other witch helped us.*

Why had the other witch helped? And if the evil one was not dead, then they had to kill her or leave quickly.

Taso found that his rage had been quelled, replaced only by dull grief. He turned to the young witch. As though she sensed his question, she began speaking, though he did not understand her words.

He brought to mind his sense of gratitude, however inexplicable he found her actions after he had attacked her. She nodded and he turned to Hangara. *Come, we must return to the mountains quickly.*

What about her? Hangara asked. *Won't she be in danger when the other witch wakes?*

Let the witches fight and kill each other; that is what they do, he said.

Hangara kept looking back, but followed as he loped across the field, not letting the deep pain in his chest affect him. He knew it would likely never heal, yet his duty, his charge to Hangara remained.

She is still behind us, Hangara said as they came into view of the village. *She is following us.*

Hangara had always been good at sensing, better than Taso. He turned and waited. Sure enough, the witch stepped from behind a group of trees and approached, beginning to speak.

Along with her incomprehensible speech came an image. It was of a deeply peaceful valley, the valley in which his pack had been killed. The sun had just come up above the ridge, the snow sparkled with morning crispness and a profound calmness suffused the image.

She wants to come with us, Hangara interpreted.

How do you know?

It's confusing. I think I can somewhat sense her intent and an idea of her thoughts, Hangara said. *She loves the valley, does not like the witches, seeks companionship as we do, but not with other witches. She wants to come with us, be with us.*

Then let her stay in the village, Taso said. *We cannot trust a witch.*

I trust her, Hangara said.

Who ever heard of wolves and witches together? It's not possible.

I think it is. Ask her. Hangara had gone forward, walking about the young witch, smelling every part of her.

Why? Taso hoped the witch could understand his question.

She sent only an image, like the valley before. It was one of yearning, a pup caught alone in the wild having lost its pack, isolated.

Taso saw that she needed a pack, just as he did, as Hangara did. And she had helped them.

Come, he thought, turning. *We will start a new pack.*

STANDING on the verge of such a change, Kciyta looked back where they had come from. The village slumbered in the distance, the sun having just sunk below the far mountains to her left. The two wolves had already continued up the cleft, but Kciyta took another moment.

Had she really decided to do this? To leave the witches, the Queendom, her previous life?

One look up the cleft reformed her resolve. In the shared care and camaraderie of the two reunited wolves, she had sensed her deepest longing. To know, to be known, and to belong to others. She would not find that around the other witches–perhaps the wolves could teach her.

Kciyta stepped into the cleft, crossing the Threshold once again to her life beyond.

THE END

BIO: Jens Hieber lives cross-culturally with his wife, his cat, and his hope for the future. Currently residing in Malaysia, he teaches HS English, spends a lot of free time reading, and enjoys keeping tropical fish. He aspires to Ray Bradbury's words: "Just write every day of your life. Read intensely. Then see what happens."

CHAPTER 8

THE SHAPE OF A LEGEND

TEST, ALLIES, AND ENEMIES

by

Nyki Blatchley

Queen Shalla's heart was pounding as she slipped out of the postern to find the mount she'd secretly ordered saddled, bridled and waiting for her. Her favourite mare, Blaze, one of the fastest horses in the royal stable. She could reach the northern army by nightfall. Better not to think any further than that.

Swinging up into the saddle, in the way her father always used to call unladylike when she was a child, Shalla settled herself and then handed down a couple of coins to the stable-lad holding the rein. "For your loyalty. And if the King asks, you never saw me."

The boy gaped, and most likely not just because of the small fortune she'd handed him, probably worth three months' wages. King Carrom was universally loved throughout Dunsell, and going against him would be difficult. But she'd chosen this boy—only a few years younger than her, really—because she knew he had a crush on her and would want to please her.

Shalla kept her hood pulled forward as she cantered away from the palace and into the streets of Tassna, hoping no-one would recognise her. Somebody might recognise Blaze, of course, but it wasn't unusual for the young queen to go riding alone. As long as word didn't get back to Carrom before she was well on her way.

She didn't really think it would take Carrom long to work out where she'd gone, but maybe that would be just enough of a lead. What would he think when he realised? Shalla tried not to imagine.

Was she really doing this? A wave of panic flooded over Shalla, and she made a move to turn Blaze around, go home and pretend none of it had happened. But she fought it down and, after a moment, continued riding on, although her hands trembled on the reins.

Until today, it had never occurred to Shalla that she could ever do anything against Carrom. She loved him until she could hardly breathe, and it had always seemed that he felt the same.

Then war had broken out between Jeshi and Bahzel, which both lay to the north.

In reality, she still knew that he loved her, but he was a king, too, and not a tyrant who could ignore the opinions of others. She understood that, but even so she'd never dreamt he could make the decision he had. That his Council had insisted he made.

She couldn't let this happen. Although not entirely sure what she was going to do on reaching Vordan, commander-in-chief of the northern army, she had to do something.

Once clear of Tassna's gates, Shalla couldn't resist cantering Blaze down the broad, well-paved highway for a while, but soon dropped back to a trot. She wasn't entirely sure of how far it was to the camp, but it would take her all day, at least. A worn-out mount would make it even longer.

She bypassed towns on the route, in case anyone recognised her, but she risked stopping at some of the villages to rest and refresh both herself and Blaze. The villagers clearly realised she was noble—her whole demeanour proclaimed that—but if they speculated further, they said nothing.

It wasn't until the sun was already halfway down towards setting that Shalla began to worry seriously. She'd no clear idea of how far she'd gone since leaving Tassna. Although she'd asked the names of the various villages, they'd meant nothing to her. What if night caught her on the road? She hadn't thought, in her hurry, to bring light, and she wondered whether she could be sure of staying on the highway in the dark.

Or could there be more serious threats? The King's highways weren't known for being plagued by robbers, but it still wasn't impossible that she'd be set upon. And what about other terrors? As a child, she'd always loved being frightened by tales of goblins and ghouls that devoured travellers, and the fae-folk who'd lead you off the track, never to be seen again. She still loved such stories, to tell the truth, especially anything about the fae, but it was very different when she was out in the middle of nowhere, facing the night alone.

A flash of movement snapped her from her thoughts, but Blaze had already spooked at the stag dashing across the road. The horse reared up, and Shalla fought to keep her seat, but the world turned upside-down. She hit the ground hard.

Dragging herself up, she saw Blaze vanishing into the distance at full gallop. Trying to move her legs to stand, she winced as pain shot through her ankle.

Shalla stretched down and felt her right ankle gently. Not broken, as far as she could tell, but certainly twisted. She must still be a long way from the army and on foot. If she could even describe it as that.

It was so tempting to sit and cry. It would be a comfort and a distraction, but that wasn't who she was. No-one had seen her cry after her mother died when she was eleven, eight years ago, although she'd surrendered to tears when she was alone. And she wasn't going to cry now.

First of all, she needed to find out whether she could walk, and that meant standing up. Whatever the verdict, it was going to hurt. After a moment to gather her nerve, Shalla curled her good leg under her and put her foot on the ground. Slowly unflexing her knee and pushing up with her hands, she stood, dragging the bad leg up with her.

The first slight weight on it sent a dagger through her ankle, but no further. That was good news, suggesting she hadn't damaged the rest of the leg.

Her foot had instinctively risen at the pain, but she forced herself to put it gingerly down again. The pain wasn't as bad this time, but she clearly wouldn't be able to put enough weight on it to walk.

What about a stick? She could pull down a branch from one of the trees alongside the road. As she glanced around to find the nearest, though, a couple of lights flickered and moved in the corner of her eyes. From off to her right and a little behind her, a voice like wind rustling the leaves murmured, "Seven to three it don't walk away from this place."

～

CARROM CURSED himself for a fool as he trotted his horse along the highway. Why had he assumed Shalla would just accept his decision and do nothing? That wasn't in keeping with the strong, intelligent young woman he adored and admired so much.

As soon as he'd realised what she'd done, he guessed what she was planning—exactly what he'd have probably done in her position. And he knew there was only one person who'd be able to countermand the Queen's orders.

He rode with only two pages and his standard-bearer. The captain of his guard almost had an apoplexy when Carrom had refused to take a full armed escort. Yes, there was some slight danger, though not much on the King's highway, but he wasn't going to lead an armed force against Shalla.

The stable-lad who'd been found returning from the postern and brought before him had refused to say what he'd done. The poor boy had turned red and looked on the point of tears, but it didn't matter that he wouldn't speak. Carrom knew already.

He should have punished the boy, but he couldn't bring himself to do that. The lad hadn't actually flouted any order and had, on the contrary, been obeying his queen. It wouldn't be right to make a servant suffer for being caught in a royal dispute.

Shalla had only been thirteen when he'd first met her. Far too young, in his opinion, to be married at all, let alone to a stranger nearly twice her age. But there'd been compelling political reasons for the match—reasons that had since evaporated—and he'd allowed himself to be persuaded.

Their first meeting had taken his breath away. It wasn't just that she was a stunningly beautiful child on her way to being an even more beautiful woman. Or even the slight other-worldly impression she gave, as if she were a fae child. He was impressed most of all by the fierce resolution with which she almost hid the terror she felt.

Hidden to most people, but not to him. So he'd married her before the people, but had refused to force himself on her. Instead he'd cherished and cared for her, leaving her to grow up in her own time, until, several years later, she'd begged him to take her to his bed.

So what was he going to do with her now? Could he really persuade the nobles and the people that this wasn't treason?

He'd kept the pace to a brisk trot. Early in the journey, young Ludril had pulled up alongside him. It was a breach of etiquette, but Ludril was his cousin and had never taken easily to subservience.

"Shouldn't we be going faster? Sha—the Queen, I mean, must be well over an hour ahead of us."

"Exactly," Carrom had said. "We're not going to get there first, so I want to be there in time to stop whatever's happening. Not to be left on the road with foundered horses."

Now, as twilight was falling, Ludril pulled up alongside him again. "Sire," he said, "look."

Following the child's pointing finger, Carrom made out a horse quietly cropping the grass just off the road up ahead. As the animal turned side on, he saw it was fully saddled and bridled.

Walking his own mount slowly and gently forwards, praying he wouldn't spook the other horse, he got close enough to be sure—this was Blaze, Shalla's favourite mare.

She whinnied slightly—in pleasure at recognising him, perhaps, or else recognising his horse—and came closer. Carrom dismounted and made much of her as he looked her over. She showed no sign of injury, and there was no blood on her saddle.

Before the escort could get close enough to see, he opened the saddlebag and glanced inside. Yes, what she'd stolen was still there. He restrapped the bag quickly and stood back, wondering what on earth had happened to Shalla.

SHALLA WHIRLED around to where the words had come from. Her bad foot gave way, and she sprawled face-first on the grass.

"Told you," murmured the voice.

Pushing herself up with her hands, Shalla looked around. There were two of them looking down at her, and at first she took them for children, or maybe adolescents. Probably no higher than her shoulder, they were either very pretty boys or very figureless girls—and, the longer she stared, the less sure she became.

That was the least strange thing about them, though. Their skimpy tunics, partly covering them, seemed sewn from leaves. Their skin had a distinct green cast, with faces of a slightly deeper green. Thick, tangled hair hanging wildly to their waists was of a colour Shalla couldn't put a name to. Their eyes sparkled silver, making them look like

135

children with a new toy. There was only one explanation—except that it was impossible. Still...

"Are you fae-folk?" she asked.

The two strange figures looked at one another with comically exaggerated expressions of surprise. They were almost identical, except that one seemed slightly taller.

"No idea," said this one, examining Shalla. "Are you?"

"Of course not," she snapped, then wondered why that had made her so angry. She needed to stay in control of herself, in spite of the situation. "I'm Queen Shalla of Dunsell, and I'm on a crucial mission. Can you help me? I'll reward you well."

She felt a little guilty as she made this glib promise. Would she really be in a position to reward anyone, whether she succeeded or failed? It seemed unlikely.

The two strangers looked at one another again and both burst out laughing.

"It's lost its horse," said one.

"And hurt its leg," added the other.

"Can't do its journey."

Shalla's temper threatened to boil over. "I'm not an *it*," she snapped, "I'm a *she*." Partly in an attempt to control herself, she asked, "What about you? Are you male or female?"

They were both silent for a moment, as if she'd asked them a difficult question. Then the shorter one shrugged. "One of those. Probably."

Shalla turned away in disgust. Wasn't it bad enough that her plans were in tatters? She'd betrayed her beloved Carrom in a way she'd never be forgiven for, and she'd have nothing to show for it. Now she was being forced to listen to this childish stupidity. It was more than she could bear.

It was a moment before she realised that the two fae-folk had come up on either side of her and were gently stroking her hair. It felt like a warm breeze playing with it on a summer afternoon.

"Tell us," said one, and it all came pouring out of Shalla: a torrent of words like the torrent of tears she refused to shed.

"I'm Queen of Dunsell. As I said." She paused a moment, unsure if the fae would even know the name of the country they lived in. Neither made a comment, though, so she continued. "But I was born in Jeshi. That's up north. My father's one of the leading nobles. So that's why I was married to Carrom, as a token of friendship between us. He's King of Dunsell, you see."

Their expressions gave no sign of whether they did understand or not.

"Well, I was only thirteen, and I was terrified, but...he was so kind and so beautiful, I wasn't scared any more. He made me feel safe, and he didn't make me do anything I didn't want to do. We talked a lot, and we did things together, but he made sure I always had somewhere to go on my own if being queen got too much.

"We...we were so happy. Until Jeshi went to war with Bahzel."

She stopped, struggling not to cry, and realised the fae were looking at her curiously.

"Why would they want to fight each other?" asked one.

"Well..." Shalla had never thought of the need to explain that. "I don't think they really do, either of them. But there's this stretch of moorland they've both always claimed. It's never really mattered too much before, but there've been storms and bad harvests, so they both need the moorland more. And they each started saying the other was attacking them, and...it just grew from there. I think...

it's really just that both sides think they'll lose face if they back down."

The fae were looking totally baffled now, with their eyes and mouths stretched so comically that she almost gave way to hysterical laughter. "That's just silly," said one.

Maybe it was. Maybe Shalla had even sometimes fleetingly thought that herself, though she'd never admit it. But was not losing face really worth all those lives?

"Anyway," she went on, "both countries appealed to Dunsell for help, as we've always been on friendly terms with both. We have a bigger army than either. It never occurred to me that Carrom wouldn't support Jeshi, but... but today he announced we'd be going to the aid of Bahzel."

If the fae had been human, they'd have made some comment of sympathy or outrage. They just continued gazing at her.

"I do understand," she blurted out quickly, reacting to the criticism no-one had made. "Bahzel could give us so much more than Jeshi. Carrom argued against it, he really tried, but the Council insisted. I suppose he didn't have a choice, but...but..."

"But he's your true love," said one of the fae.

Somehow, that let loose the tears she'd been holding back all day, and she tipped forward, face down on the ground, and sobbed her heart out. She was dimly aware of the fae sitting on either side, gently stroking her.

Eventually, all her tears were gone, and Shalla sat up, wiping the back of her hand across red-raw eyes. "So why are you here?" asked one of her companions.

She took a deep breath. This was the hardest part to think about, let alone explain. Would the fae be shocked? Or would they simply not understand?

"I stole the Royal Seal," she said. "That...well, with it, everyone would think I'm acting with Carrom's authority. Only...I've lost it. When the horse bolted."

"What were you going to do with it?"

This should have been a simple question to answer, but in reality, Shalla had been fluctuating between the two options she seemed to have. "I'm not sure. Perhaps make our army intervene and stop the fighting. Or, if that wasn't possible, to take the field on Jeshi's side. Their army's smaller than Bahzel's, and my father would be fighting. He might be killed."

There was silence, as the vision that had been plaguing Shalla all day swept through her head again. Her father lying, cut to pieces, among the ruins of the army.

"And do you still want to do that?" asked one of the fae at last.

"Well...yes. But it isn't possible any more."

"We'll help."

Her head snapped round at the speaker, then more slowly at the other fae. "You can get me to the army before Carrom reaches it? I can't walk, you know," she added, an instant before remembering that this was what they appeared to have been making a bet about when she'd first heard them.

"Oh yes," said the other. "But you still have a choice to make. There'll be tests on the way, three of them, and what you choose will affect what you do."

The implication sank in. "You mean, if I fail the tests, you won't help me?"

Both the fae burst out laughing. "Not that kind of test, silly. There's no right, no wrong."

"What you decide," the other explained, "will show you what you really want."

Shalla couldn't make any sense of this. Maybe she was distracted by the pain in her ankle. Maybe it was the piled-up emotions of the day. Or maybe the fae actually were talking nonsense. Still, she might as well do what they said, as it seemed the only chance she had.

"Come with us." The fae-folk took her hands and, helping her to her feet, led her into a silver mist. It seemed as if the path they followed twisted in directions she couldn't quite understand.

They'd gone some distance before it occurred to Shalla that she was walking without pain.

SHALLA HAD no idea how far she'd walked when a crossroads loomed before her out of the mist. It was especially surprising, because she hadn't even been aware that she was walking on a road, but it seemed so now. Maybe it was only a road when it needed to be.

Her two companions stopped and looked at her expectantly, their silver eyes sparkling. "Which is the right way?" she asked.

"That's for you to decide."

That was ridiculous. "How am I supposed to know my way here?" she snapped. "I thought you were supposed to be guiding me."

"You can only know the right way," said the other fae, "if you know where you're going. There are three destinations here, and you must decide which is the right one."

This was starting to feel like something out of the fairy tales she'd loved as a child. And still loved, to tell the truth, although she'd had little time for them in recent years. So how would this work?

"I can't see the destinations."

"Look hard. You'll see them."

Taking a deep breath, Shalla stared fixedly at the turning to the left. Slowly, a vision swam into view: her room back at the palace in Tassna. Not the bedroom, nor the parlour, nor the receiving suite, all of which she shared very happily with Carrom. This was her private room, the place he'd insisted on setting apart for her when she first arrived, a scared, uncertain adolescent. The room no-one else ever entered when she was there, where she could be whatever she chose, imagine whatever came into her head, play like a child if she needed to.

Even more than with her mother when she was little, even more than with Carrom until today, this was where she felt absolutely safe.

And she longed now for that safety.

There were two other options, though, and she should see them all. After all, she hadn't risked everything setting out on this journey only to turn back to safety.

She turned to the right and, again, a scene appeared. She guessed this was an army camp, and a vast one, with tents and fires and soldiers drilling or lounging and craftsmen working hard as far as she could see. She was seeing the guard-post, and the guards were receiving Carrom. He seemed to have only two pages and a standard-bearer with him. Where was the rest of his escort?

And she saw, with a lurch of the heart, that one of the pages led Blaze. So Carrom knew something had happened to her.

A soldier was detailed to lead Carrom and his tiny escort through the camp and rouse someone from one of the tents. A man emerged—a man she recognised as the general, Vordan.

It was only Carrom she had eyes for, though, and watching him brought back in a great wave how much she loved him and he'd loved her. How he'd looked after her when she was vulnerable and let her take the lead when she was strong.

She could be with him again, and everything would be all right. She'd forget his decision (which, after all, she understood), he'd forget what she'd done, and it would be the way it was before today.

Then Carrom spoke to Vordan and pointed, and she realised what was going on. They were arranging for the army to march—march against her homeland, her father.

Shalla tore her eyes away and looked at the destination in the central way, a wide stretch of open moorland. It looked very like the moors between Jeshi and Bahzel, although it was many years since she'd been that way. Two armies were drawn up, facing one another, as if the charge could begin at any moment. Their banners flew out in the wind, and she caught a glimpse of the winged serpent of Bahzel, and...Her breath caught in her throat at the sight, above the smaller army, of the so-familiar rearing white horse of Jeshi.

Thoughts of love and safety vanished. She had to stop the army of her homeland being massacred, her father slain on that moor.

"This way," she said, and led her companions forward.

The mist returned as soon as Shalla stepped onto the road ahead, and with it the vagueness about how much time was passing. It was either moments or hours later that something else loomed out of that timeless fog.

Shalla wasn't sure whether to laugh or ask if she was mad. Ahead of her was a shelf, suspended in mid air, and on it stood three books, beautifully bound in engraved leather.

In fact, they looked familiar, and as she drew closer, she became sure. These had been her three favourite books as a child. Her father had arranged for them to be copied and gloriously illuminated for her.

Shalla had read them over and over through her childhood, and she'd brought them with her when she'd come to Tassna to marry Carrom. They were in her private room, back in the palace—so what were they doing here?

Never mind that. These were intensely familiar, comforting things, and that was exactly what she needed, in the midst of all this strangeness. She spent a while leafing through each in turn, connecting back to the words and the colourful illustrations that she knew by heart.

There was the tale of the ancient Queen Passala, who had faithfully served her land and her people, guiding them through dark times, and who had become a byword for the perfect ruler. There was the tale of the knight Ardern, who roamed the world fighting for just causes, until he became a legend of hope for all oppressed people.

And then there was her favourite of all: the book of little tales and songs about the fae playing, celebrating their revelries among the flowers and the small beasts. She'd often, especially when she felt lonely and sad, comforted herself by dreaming that she was playing with them.

"You must choose," said one of the fae.

"I don't understand. What am I choosing between? The books?"

"Between the stories," said the other. "Do you know what a story is?"

"Well, of course. It's..."

She ground to a halt. Obviously she knew what a story was, but she couldn't quite put it into words.

"A story," said the fae, "is how you understand the life you want to live. How do you want to live yours?"

Shalla was beginning to grasp what they were talking about. "You mean, do I want to be a queen, a fae or a hero?"

Her companions both burst out laughing. "You're already a fae, silly. You always have been. You wouldn't have met us, otherwise."

"And you're already a queen, too," said the other. "But what do you want to do with what you are? Be dutiful, be a legend, or play. That's your choice."

"But you don't have to tell us. You've already chosen, even if you don't realise. That will tell you what your third choice needs to be. Come along, you need to make that choice soon."

Feeling she was in a dream, Shalla started walking again through mist, only belatedly realising that the shelf and the books were gone. A time passed, and then the mist cleared for a third time.

This time, three pedestals stood in front of her, each topped by a small, closed chest. They were plain but sturdy, which seemed strange for a product of the fae-folk. Assuming it was theirs.

"What now?" she asked.

"You must choose which you want," said one of her companions.

Shalla stared at each box in turn, but there was no hint of any difference between them. "They're exactly the same. What's in them?"

"Each contains a word of power that will give your voice irresistible persuasion. But only its own kind of persuasion. There's the word that will bring love, the word that will bring hate, and the word that will bring peace. You must choose."

This didn't feel right. "You mean, I'll be able to control what people feel? I'm not sure I like that."

"Oh, you can't make anyone feel anything that isn't already there. The words allow them to find what's inside them—love, hate or peace, as you choose."

She examined each box again, before turning to the fae. "And when I decide, will I know where to find that word?"

The other fae gave a faint smile. "It doesn't work like that. You must pick a box, and what it contains will be the word that's in your heart, whether you know it or not."

"And, as we told you, it'll be connected with the story you chose."

Again, the feeling overwhelmed Shalla that she was in a fairy story. It made no sense, but what alternative did she have but to follow the rules she'd been set?

Approaching the boxes, she examined each minutely, trying to sense what might be inside. Surely she should feel an attraction to what, if the fairy-tale rules held true, would be the one she wanted. Which would that be? One would allow her to win Carrom back to her heart, and surely one would give her the power to send the army of Dunsell against Bahzel. That was what she'd chosen, wasn't it, when she picked the middle way as her destination?

And the story. She realised now that the fae had been right, and she knew deep down which she wanted. Even though she'd loved the stories of the fae more, it was Ardern, the champion of the oppressed, who had always stirred her heart the most. Surely that meant she was destined to lead her army in a just cause...though it seemed wrong that would mean picking the word of hate.

"Have you chosen?" asked one of the fae.

"I'm trying," she snapped, though it was from frustration rather than anger.

Both of them laughed. "Don't try. Just pick one."

It made no sense, but none of this did. Shalla took a deep breath, closed her eyes and whirled herself around. Then she walked forward until she touched the box she was facing, and felt it spring open.

The word from within suffused her, and she knew at once she'd made the right choice.

CARROM STOOD in his stirrups to look down the line that stretched across the width of the moor, Dunsell's army on the left and Bahzel's to the right. It made a fine show, bristling with spears and adorned with brightly coloured banners.

It looked magnificent, but when Carrom looked more closely, most eyes were cast down. The few faces he could see clearly, both from Bahzel's army and his, looked scared rather than heroic. As they should, he had to admit.

Vordan was beside him, staring wordlessly ahead, and his own little escort was just behind. The standard-bearer proudly held the royal insignia high, while the two pages fidgeted, though he wasn't sure whether from excitement or fear. Probably a bit of both.

Following Vordan's gaze, Carrom strained his eyes through the mist that rolled across the moor to make out Jeshi's forces facing them. Compared with the massed armies of the allies, they looked pitifully few.

He'd agreed with Vordan's recommendation to march at first light, though in the end it had been an hour or two after dawn before everything was ready. Vordan's scouts had confirmed the two armies were drawn up just three hours away, and having made the decision to support

Bahzel, there seemed little point in delaying. The army had been battle ready for weeks.

In reality, Carrom had hoped their arrival would put a stop to this war. Jeshi was hopelessly outnumbered, and surely this new blow would persuade them to treat and offer concessions.

As far as he could see, however, nothing had changed. Although the mist deadened sound, he could distantly make out shouts and battle cries from the enemy. It seemed that they were still preparing to fight.

Somewhere among their ranks would be the banner of Shalla's house. It had torn him in two to finally give in to the pressure from his council to take up arms against Jeshi, and he offered up a silent prayer that the day wouldn't end with his father-in-law lying dead.

That brought him back to the other big worry plaguing him—what had happened to Shalla? It had been so hard to stick to his duty, rather than riding back in search of her. As soon as it was light, though, a party had been sent out, detailed to carefully search all along the road for any sign of her.

Carrom wasn't sure whether he dreaded more that she wouldn't be found or that she would. Even if she weren't injured or dead, what was he going to do when they met?

"Sire!"

Carrom's attention snapped back, and he turned to see where Ludril was pointing. A little to one side of where his gaze had been, mist swirled and roiled on the bare moorland between the armies. Soil and stalks rose up, faster and faster, like a whirlpool in the air. A void gradually formed at its centre, a shape that reminded him of something he couldn't quite grasp, and three figures stepped out.

Two were strange-looking creatures: human, more or

less, but small, and they seemed green-tinged—just as the fae-folk were always described. But the central figure, a head and shoulders taller, was both achingly familiar and utterly strange. Dark hair blew free in the wind around a face he knew intimately, but he hardly recognised this Shalla. Light and strength poured from her, and her voice, when she spoke, rang across the moors as clearly as if she stood an arm's length away.

"I am Shalla the Peacebringer," she announced. "Shalla of the fae-folk. There will be no fighting today."

Utter silence fell over both armies, as she continued to speak. Carrom could never quite remember her words afterwards. She spoke of calm and quietness, of days in the sun and games in the snow, of feasting and of families gathered around the fire, of love and friendship and companionship. But that was only the bare bones. The words—they caressed him inside and out, calling on memories of every peaceful time he'd known.

By the time she finished, all Carrom wanted was to lay aside his arms and sit down in peace with the armies on both sides of the moor.

"Let the kings come to me," Shalla said at last, before falling silent.

Feeling that he'd just emerged from bathing in light, Carrom glanced along the line to where he could just make out his ally. He couldn't see the Bahzel king's expression, but the man nodded to him, and both rode forward. Carrom's escort fell in behind him, but he knew he must go alone and waved them back.

The two kings reached Shalla at the same time as their Jeshi counterpart. She smiled at Carrom, but distantly, as if at someone she'd once known. That hurt a little, but it seemed to fit this new person she seemed to have become.

All three dismounted and, for a moment, stared uncertainly at one another. Then Carrom held out his hand, and the other two took it. "Shall we have peace?" he asked.

The Jeshi king looked at him uncertainly. "I want peace," he said, "but what about the lands Bahzel claims?"

"They're ours," said the Bahzel king, though there was no heat in his words. "You attacked our communities here on the moor."

"We were only defending our own communities." The Jeshi king, too, seemed unable to speak angrily, in spite of what he said. "And we need this land. Our people are starving, after the harvest failure, and these are the best pastures in the kingdom."

"Our people need food too. There's iron and copper in the hills north of here that we could mine and sell for supplies. But we can't get at it, if you have farms all over the moors."

There was a slight pause. "We need both of those," said the Jeshi king, "but we don't have the skills to mine."

Could it really be as simple as this? They were clearly both edging towards the ideal solution, but Carrom decided to give them an extra push. "So you need to use the land," and he looked at the Jeshi king, then turned to his counterpart, "and you just need to move through it. You need the food they can produce, and you," turning back to the Jeshi king, "need the metals they can mine. Is there really any need to fight?"

After a brief silence, both kings shook their heads. A warmth of relief and joy surged through Carrom, and he immediately said, "I'll host a feast today, for both of you and your nobles. We'll eat and drink together, and we'll seal this agreement."

When the other two kings had ridden back to their

lines, Carrom turned to Shalla. "I'm...I'm sorry. I should never have put you through the choice you had, but you chose right, after all."

He looked closely at her two companions for the first time. Shalla had proclaimed herself as of the fae-folk, and these looked very like the tales described. What did that mean? His mind slipped back to the first time he'd seen her, when he'd been struck by that air of otherworldliness.

"Will you come back with me?" He held his breath as soon as he'd asked the question, but he suspected deep down what her answer would be. She'd changed so much, changed into a legend.

Shalla smiled sadly and shook her head. "I've discovered who I am, Carrom. I'm of the fae, and I'm the Peacebringer. That means I'm a champion, and my work will take me a long way from here. There's so much war in the world. I still love you, but I'm more than that now."

"So...won't I ever see you again?"

Her eyes turned inward for a moment. "Perhaps. I hope so." She suddenly looked a little more vulnerable, more like the Shalla he'd always known. "Thank you, Carrom. You're a good man and a great king. What you've done for me, how you protected me when I needed it—that's helped make me who I am now."

She kissed him briefly and stepped back. The mist began to roil again around Shalla and her companions, until it covered them. When it cleared, they were gone, but just for a moment Carrom thought he saw a shape of emptiness where Shalla had stood, and he recognised it this time.

It was the shape of a legend.

THE END

. . .

BIO: Nyki Blatchley is a blue dragon, cunningly disguised as an author, poet and copywriter, who lives just outside London. He's been writing fiction since he was four, and his novel *At An Uncertain Hour* was published by StoneGarden. He also has a collection, *Eltava: A Sword for All Ages*, from Gypsy Shadow Publishing, and around ninety shorter pieces published, recently by Smoking Pen Press and Swords and Sorcery magazine. You can find out more about him at https://nykiblatchley.com/

CHAPTER 9

HERO'S RETREAT

RETREAT TO THE INNERMOST CAVE

by

Andy Clark

The militia Nolan, Niamh, Cillian and Barach had trained stood at the top of the hill, a mile from the walls of Galway, watching for the zombies who would advance along the main road leading to the coast. Based on the report of their scouts, the monsters would appear at any time.

Barach watched their army and frowned. The two hundred militia they'd spent the last two weeks training trembled as the snarling mass of monsters stumbled toward them. Perhaps it would have been smarter to wait behind stout city walls, but they did not have the troops for that, and the zombies would surround and climb until they broke through. Once they did, the undead would wreak almost as much damage as four unleashed heroes would. Almost.

Niamh stood next to Barach, pressing against him, likely reveling in the knowledge of how uncomfortable the contact made the defrocked friar, as she whispered, "They'll never hold, but that's not our plan."

Two weeks. They'd only had two weeks to teach the militia the weapons-craft of skilled warriors. All things considered, the soldiers had done well. More time would have helped. But whether it be two weeks, two months or two decades, they'd never have the hearts of heroes. Nor would they have the bodies that resisted wounds and disease like merchants avoiding tax collectors. These two hundred from Galway would never defeat this horde of a thousand flesh eaters surging toward them. They didn't have to.

Niamh's body continued to distract him. "We have a few minutes before they arrive. Perhaps you'd care to..."

"We do not, and why do you keep offering me something I cannot accept?"

"You are no longer a friar. You refuse your robes. Why don't you take comfort from me?" Her smile reminded him of the snakes she was so fond of killing. "I promise I will be gentle."

He shook his head, dropping it as if praying, but he wasn't there yet. Barach knew that to break his addiction to violence, he had to accept his fallibility and turn the problem over to God, but he couldn't. He could pretend faithfulness, giving the appearance of praying, letting loose and handing his passion over to the Lord, but in his heart he knew he still relied too much on himself. Looking back, this had been his problem all along. Too much Barach, too little faith, and that hadn't changed. Yet he had hope, and his hope said faith would come. "Niamh, you know I plan to go back, to reclaim the robes I lost in my rampage of hatred, but it's only been three months. Why do you tempt me?"

"Because I know you, Barach. Right now, your mind is filled with worry. You worry about these townspeople and losing this fight, but most of all, you worry about losing control. You remember the houses you destroyed at Limerick. I also know that you, like I, have killed innocents when battle was finished, but the heroes' rage in your heart wasn't clenched. So you worry we will destroy this entire city. We all have that worry, but it's eating you up. So, I'm trying to distract you a little." Her laughter tinkled. "There is no way you are going to make love to me in the middle of a battlefield, though that would certainly take everyone's mind off the coming fight."

With her sleek ebony body and golden hair, Niamh was exotic and a distraction from his ever-present desire to kill and destroy. Since he had broken his pledge and yielded to his hero's wrath in the slaughter at Limerick, he struggled to rediscover the grace that held his battle lust at bay. Her flirtations were a gift, intended to help him find his balance. Barach wondered what she'd do if he ever said 'yes.' This was a question best left unanswered.

One day, he hoped to reclaim his robes, and he would not increase his betrayal of the mission he'd pursued for ten years. He was a man of many flaws, as he knew all to be, and he had broken his faith in small things many times as all did.But only that one time had he'd turned his heart over to the hatred that fueled his battle fire. In this, he brazenly broke his promise to God. Barach had thrown away years of work where he'd examined his sins, pulled

God into his life, begged forgiveness from the villagers he'd damaged, and walked each of the twelve steps that had controlled his violence for ten years.

Such pride he'd had! In his heart, Barach had believed he had self-control. He wore the robes and said the words, but arrogance ruled his heart. Arrogance melted in the fire of battle.

"What are you thinking about?" Niamh asked.

"Many things. I wonder if you understand the importance of turning your addiction over to God, of releasing self-control to accept peace?"

She stepped away. "Yes, I think I do, but it's hard, almost impossible. Not a natural project for a hero. Do you doubt me? Are you saying that because I flirt with you, I don't take this seriously? Because I do. I pray daily, hourly, to never again look upon the faces of children whose pets or parents I've killed, or houses I've destroyed because the battle madness has come upon me. Or the even worse evil waiting if my heart stays unguarded. There is still something inside me telling me I can control this myself, but I've failed for years on that path. So, yes, I'm ready to try God."

"It needs to be more than that. Much more."

She nodded her head. Barach had had talks with each of them over the past few weeks. Each time explaining it in different words. They had all experienced the failure of their wills, and agreed with him during the calm between fights. But would they hold their faith in battle? He needed to take every chance to remind them who must be in control throughout the afternoon.

"I understand I need to be faithful," Niamh said, "but I don't think faithfulness comes at the expense of laughter. I can commit myself to taking the steps needed to not commit murder, but do not ask me to stop having fun at your expense. Particularly when it's for your own good."

The lady was incorrigible. What would he ever do with her? What would he ever do without her?

Cillian, the slender hero-thief, appeared on their right, with Nolan behind him. Cillian's rat-like face reached the same height as Nolan's right bicep. Roughly the same size, too.

"Niamh," Cillian said. "Make that offer to me and see what happens. I, for one, would appreciate a bit more drill before the battle."

Nolan, a massive man with muscles sufficient for tossing oxen, laughed while Niamh shook her head and bit her lip.

Nolan and Cillian must have finished their trip through the militia, checking the crossbows. Earlier, they'd worked with the soldiers during target practice in the forest. The trees escaped with minor damage, while the two heroes took turns adjusting stances, aims, and even the basics of loading the weapons without dropping bolts. And, occasionally, pointing loaded bows in the right direction.

"I want you all to remember," Barach said. "Why we must not fight. I must not fight because of Limerick, where I tore down buildings hunting for werewolves, and a dozen villages scattered through Normandy, Sussex and Wessex, where I did much worse to men, women, children, and anything else that got in my way after too brief a fight."

"I must not fight," Niamh said, "because of the children whose hearts I broke when I killed their pets, the women and men whose spouses died facing my anger, and the thousands of others I might one day kill."

"I must not fight," Cillian whispered, "because of the

enemies I've made up to feed off my glory. The eight villages that have been left without mothers, fathers and grandparents. And other acts of terror, which I can no longer remember."

"I must not fight," Nolan bellowed, "because I do not know how to stop killing, to stop tearing things apart, until exhaustion overcomes the exhilarating rage that fills my heart. And that takes a long time for me. If I unsheathe my blade here, this entire army could die."

They all understood. If he'd done nothing else, Barach had gotten through to them and they would hold their word. As long as their battle plan worked.

The crossbows would not inflict many casualties on the zombies, but they were a crucial part of the battle plan. Nolan's and Cillian's work on the militia's archery, along with the hours of training on swords, shields and spears, were the only thing that gave this plan any chance of success. Failure would be horrible. Barach wasn't sure what any of the four heroes would do if they reached the point where they had to choose between dying and unleashing the violence within. He hoped they would die. A good hero is always ready to die. It's living a life of peace that's the challenge.

The zombies appeared along the horizon. Barach took Niamh's right hand and lost his hand in Nolan's left as the four formed a circle, bowing their heads in silent prayers for strength in the face of the day's cravings. It lasted only twenty heartbeats. Peace whispered to Barach as the zombies screeched in the distance.

At first, the monsters approached slowly, heads down and arms dangling in front of their emaciated bodies. Once they spotted their quarry, that changed. Within the time of a raven's heartbeat, the decaying heads rose, and they charged forward, snarling and waving hands over their skulls as they came.

Why did they do that? It was not a good way to run. Well, when you are somewhere between dead and alive, posture likely no longer mattered.

"Remember your faith," Barach said. "If you rely entirely on your own self-control, you will fail, and you might take all of us with you." Very little could restrain a hero other than another hero. So the failure of one threatened them all.

Each of his friends nodded their heads as the zombies scrambled closer.

"Archers, let fly," Cillian called, and the Irishmen raised crossbows and fired. This was extreme range and the bolts would kill no zombies, but they would maim them, maybe bring some to the ground, and with the weakness of the undead flesh, a single bolt could pass through ten at a time. A few coordinated volleys could stop a mortal army.

"Reload," Nolan called as he passed along the back of the line, spouting profanities as he went. He ran to the right flank, while Cillian worked on the left and Niamh, the center. Barach stood back, partially to manage the battle for the militia, but mainly to keep an eye on all the heroes, knowing they all did the same for him.

The plan was for the guardsmen to get off five volleys before the zombies approached their lines. Barach saw one soldier drop his bow as he attempted to fit the bolt, and another fell as its wielder attempted to cock and lost her grip. They'd be lucky to get off three volleys. Barach adjusted. "Don't worry about volley fire. Fire at will and get in as many shots as you can." After all, this was not a disciplined army to be shocked by the sudden loss of life. This was a foe with no comprehension of losing.

"Can't we at least take up our bows?" Niamh said.

He could join them. They wouldn't use the slow cross-bows of the militia—rather, they would retrieve the discarded long bows which had proved useless to the lightly trained defenders, and fill the sky with arrows. Where the militia's aim was uncertain, the heroes would target heads and necks, bringing monsters down. As they did this, heroic hearts would fill and they would become the monsters on the field. Lord, defend me from my strengths.

"No," Barach said. "You know this as well as I do. If we start fighting, we won't stop, and we'll be far more dangerous to these brave men and women than the zombies will."

Cillian stood near and grunted, "That's hard to believe."

The zombies were halfway to the line. Most of the guards had released two or three volleys, which had stopped less than forty zombies. The closer shots would have a bigger impact, but it was like drowning a forest fire by shaking the dew off lilac leaves. Still, every one of the loose-fleshed, howling bodies down was one less to tear into their lines.

"We may have to fight," Nolan yelled. "There are too many for these barely trained sentries. We can cut through them."

Here and there, militia looked back with expressions that said they could point their crossbows at their leaders. For all the good that would do.

"Be quiet," Barach called. "Remember our vows." Of course, the four heroes could slice through the zombies, like tornadoes through thatched huts. But what would they slice through once they were done? And if they didn't stop now, then when? How would anyone ever be safe around them when there was always another emergency, another excuse? No, fight now and they accepted violence as their god, killing as their sacrament. Yet, the temptation was there.

Barach felt the weight of the sword, which wasn't mounted on his belt. The sword he'd buried on the road from Limerick three months ago. All four of the heroes cast their blades into that grave. All swore to seek a better life, one of teaching others to defend themselves rather than indulging in wanton destruction. A life that faced its limitations, accepted them, and moved forward, walking the path to freedom.

Yet earlier, their courageous words were spoken without the lure of a fight upon them. Not amid two hundred villagers with swords they could easily borrow. Or take.

Barach breathed a petition as he turned his attention back to the battle. The swarm was almost to the line. "Stow your bows! Shields and swords up!"

As the defenders fumbled with their weapons, the foremost of the attackers stumbled into the first trap, a covered pit as deep as a house, with stakes along the bottom—the work of the entire city for the first week after Barach arrived, and learned of the approaching danger. The pit worked perfectly, with the leading ranks of the zombies falling in, and the stakes ripping them apart. Too much damage for even a zombie to absorb, but eventually the bodies covered each other as the swarm continued moving forward and the undead began clawing their way toward the defenders.

Spears poked the attackers back and held them at bay, but this would not last. "Fall back."

It was not time to make a stand. With luck, the pit, bolts

and spears had taken down two or three hundred of their foes. Not enough to stop the charge. The militia turned and fled except for one woman, a baker who had joined the militia for this battle. Tara had lost almost all the mock scrimmages during her training, but she never accepted defeat. As she did not now.

Barach ran toward her, but Nolan was ahead of him, wordlessly grabbing the woman and throwing her over the shoulder like a bag of wheat.

"PUT ME DOWN AND LET ME FIGHT!" the forty-year-old woman screamed. "Zombies drove my family out of Cork. Let me kill them!"

Could she have some hero in her? No, this was the foolishness without the talent. They'd seen this in the mock battles. Cut Tara, and she bled, and without the near immediate clotting of the disciples of violence.

Barach sprinted the hundred strides to the next line, where Cillian and Niamh were forming the militia into battle lines. Looking over his shoulder, he saw zombies lumbering out of the pit. He pushed through the line yelling, "Bows out, fire at will," hoping they didn't hit Tara as Barach crossed through the lines and jumped into position. No worry there, as Nolan set the enraged woman down twenty paces to Barach's right. "Don't make me save you again," he grunted.

"Next time, let me fight!"

The attackers were dispersed after escaping the trench, and many suffered broken bones and other inconveniences which slowed the assault. They were injured enough that the ragged bolt fire cut down much of their vanguard. Most of the bowman got another bolt or two off before the attackers closed. All progressed according to plan.

The monsters were disarrayed enough for a brief stand.

"Spearmen forward. Bowman target the threats to your spearmen. Do not shoot your spearmen!" Barach yelled, as he and the other heroes ran along the line disentangling the soldiers, who had practiced this many times, but never in the face of an attack. Barach picked up one bowman who tripped, untangled three spearmen who couldn't get around their bowmen, and positioned five other bowmen in correct positions—all the while, he stepped carefully, staying close to the back of the line. Using business to hold hunger at bay. Lord, stay with me.

This was the third most dangerous part of the plan as the undead crashed into spears, pushing themselves along the shafts, even pushing beyond the crossbars, which would have stopped any wild animal from reaching the weapons' wielders. All the while, bowmen targeted zombie heads and spearmen switched to swordsmen as needed. Terrible swordsmen, but this was not a foe which required finesse.

Barach, Nolan, Cillian and Niamh continued running along the line, correcting errors and offering encouragement. All was going as well as could be expected, but they knew this stand would have to be a brief one. Barach prayed the next step would not trip any of them. And so it was that after a hundred heartbeats it came time for the second most dangerous maneuver.

"It's getting too hot," Cillian said. "We need to move to the next step."

The four heroes made a line, and as one yelled, "DISENGAGE!"

The bulk of the militia ran past the four heroes, leaping as soon as they reached them. Again the heroes went along the line, throwing militia who quailed at the cow's length jump. Three of the townsmen didn't clear the hidden trench and slid into it. Ten of them couldn't disengage. These had to be abandoned.

"How many times am I going to have to save you?" Nolan said as he charged toward Tara, who was locked in combat with a zombie. This was very bad.

Nolan reached the woman and threw her back across the mostly hidden trench. As he did this, a zombie bit him and the giant man's face went red as he howled, anger unleashed. "I WILL DESTROY YOU ALL!"

"Call to God and back away," Niamh called as she and Barach sprinted toward Nolan, but it was too late. He waded into the zombies, weaponless, yet beyond lethal. Arms, legs and heads flew as the hero's hatred fell upon the monsters.

Barach started to follow, but Niamh grabbed his arm and said, "Remember who you are and what you must be. We need to form up the militia. We'll deal with Nolan after the battle."

Nolan would die. But if Barach helped him, together they could win. And once they won, once they'd slain every zombie, their remaining rage would fall upon the towns-people. Niamh and Cillian would fight to contain them, and violence would be the day's victor. Lord help me. This is too hard.

Niamh took his hand and pulled him back. By the time he was behind the line, the zombies had formed a giant circle. Barach was certain Nolan was in the middle, where he continued to see a geyser of body parts flying into the air. Even Nolan couldn't keep this up forever; cuts, scrapes, even bites were healed quickly, but not instantly. Heroes were strong, but they could die. If Nolan still had his bastard sword, there would be little danger of this, but this fight was hand-to-hand, bite-to-bite.

"We could order a charge," Cillian said. "The militia would be attacking the rear."

"Until they made contact," Niamh said. "Then they'd be lost."

The circle did seem to be collapsing. Barach felt lost. They couldn't do nothing, but he didn't dare order an attack. All that was left was futility. Sometimes you have to accept feebleness.

"Soldiers of Galway, take up your bows and fire," Barach screamed. Ideally, this would cause some zombies to turn toward them, leaving Nolan with a winnable fight. It would take a few monsters down too. As for the possibility his friend and student would be hit, well, Nolan had bigger problems at the moment.

Again, his tactics worked, just not well enough. Two dozen zombies turned and charged the villagers, all being cut down or falling victim to the trench.

Then a blond head flew into the air, and all the remaining zombies turned toward the militia. Nolan had fought well. There were no more than two hundred left. But he had died a hero, with all the hatred and anger that this entailed. May the Lord have mercy on his soul.

Tara screamed, dropping her crossbow, dragging out a sword and leaping across the trench to close with the undead. Again, Niamh grabbed his arm as he started after her. Within the space of two breaths, Tara was down. Five zombies swarmed around her body, disposing of her remains.

The militia killed the remaining zombies at the second trench, and never had to fall back to the final and most desperate line, where they would have fought behind a short wall, all using the halberds waiting there to cleave their implacable foes' bodies. This last line would not have worked unless the zombies were heavily reduced before reaching it. Barach had calculated that there was an even chance that the successive traps would effectively slow and damage their mindless enemy to where the soldiers would survive the last skirmish. As it turned out, the attrition had occurred much earlier. In the end, twenty-six citizens of Galaway lay with the thousand zombies.

And one hero.

The townspeople came to the battle site, helping gather the zombie bodies together, bringing wood for the night's bonfire. Everyone worked digging the graves, burying Nolan and Tara with the other fallen soldiers from the day.

"You should say some words for Nolan," Cillian said to Barach. Barach shook his head. He'd given up that right. The village priest would do just fine. Then the priest's homily began, saying how all of them, Nolan, Tara and the other fallen, were heroes, giving up their lives for the common good, making the ultimate sacrifice for love of their neighbors and their God.

Did this simple priest appreciate how Nolan and God had failed each other at the end? Doubtful.

The mayor followed, praising all the soldiers, holding them up as examples for everyone to follow. "Remember this day forever. Remember the example of today's dead and take it to heart. They showed how all can be heroes."

This was all Barach could take. He'd heard a dozen of these in his hero days, praising those who fought with him, who frequently died of their own stupidity or the misfortune of standing in his way. The speeches always bothered him. Tonight he threw up in his mouth. He had to stop it.

Barach shoved through the townspeople. With one look, the mayor's mouth fell slack, and the idiocy ended.

The man who wouldn't be a hero looked out at the crowd, then down at Nolan's grave, and let his words flow.

"Don't remember these men as heroes. Remember them for what they have meant to you. Each of you knew one of these, maybe liked them, hated them, loved them. All had relationships that tied them to you. Those of your neighbors who you buried here sacrificed those relationships, and their lives, to protect you. They will be ghosts in your heart. Make them good ghosts, but don't make them heroes.

"Nolan was a hero. For most of his life, he moved alone from village to village, fighting monsters where he found them. He never put down roots. Unlike your friends, courage was not something he struggled to attain. From the time he was born, he was given a body stronger, more durable, more capable than any of you here. And a total lack of fear. What he was not given was the ability to be a member of a community. He had to fight or die.

"Nolan only found friends when he took up the struggle to renounce his heroism." Barach looked up and saw expressions of shock, save for Cillian and Niamh, who nodded. "This was the struggle where he showed true courage as he surrendered himself to going against his instincts at every beat of his heart, during every breath he took. But he knew he had to accept that struggle, the constant fight for God's freedom. The struggle of me and my friends. When we came to Galway, we represented the biggest threat you'd ever faced, but you needed us to prepare for the battle ahead. This was something we could do, but our primary mission is to remake ourselves so that we are not lone warriors attacking all in our way. This day, Nolan won that struggle, and maybe his victory is the only way forward, but my faith tells me there's another."

Now the crowd listened in complete silence, if not complete understanding. Tears entered Cillian's and Niamh's eyes. Had they ever cried for a fallen friend before? Probably not.

"Respect the sacrifices made here, both Nolan's and your friends', and honor all that they gave. Pray for their souls when you think about them." Now fire entered his eyes, and he spoke through clenched teeth as he sought the eyes of parents with young families. "But whatever you do, don't let your children grow up to be heroes."

Nolan had gotten one chance to turn from war to peace, and he'd lost it along with his life. And so, the big man would sleep forever with his anger being his only legacy. It could have been Barach set alight in these flames, had Nolan not been quicker on the field. Where was the justice in this?

Having said his words, Barach walked back to Niamh and Cillian, and the three of them picked up their rucksacks before continuing the remainder of the journey, turning north for no particular reason. When Cillian held out his robe to him, he nodded. Barach was ready to accept the duties of the friar and whatever penance the church demanded, which could not be harsher than the pain he'd suffered this afternoon, when the death of a friend burned his heart to the ground. That death had to make a difference.

With a prayer for fidelity, Barach slipped his robe back on.

If this was what this quest was going to be like, they needed a friar along to bolster their faith. He wasn't much of one, but he was the best they had. And when Niamh took his hand, he squeezed back, ignoring the hint of regret in his soul.

. . .

BIO: Andy has previously published short stories on Moon Drenched Fables, Black Ink Press, Black Hare Press, Nordic Press and Bullet Points. He lives in Richmond, Virginia, with his wife, son, and grand-dachshund and serves as a moderator for Fantasy-Writers.org. Andy also produces the Frenchie Frier's Story Land YouTube channel.

CHAPTER 10

SCEPTER, PRISMSCOPE, AND ATELIER

APPROACH TO THE INNERMOST CAVE

by

Suhail Habib

As I climbed the stairs leading to the Autocrat's atelier, a turbulence crept into my heart.

What if he does not heed my words? I thought, and quickly shunned the thought from my mind. But the turbulence remained, for my mind was not that into which it had crept.

As the captain, I was responsible for guiding our small planet safely through the universe. Thus, when I had apprehended that we were soon to enter a vast openness bombarded by cosmic radiation, I stepped into my teleporter and was in the Autocrat's atrium. From there, it was a matter of climbing the stairs to reach his atelier. Our solar sails must be unbound; our journey delayed. This I had to tell him. Our ageless errand— the nature of which only the Autocrat knew— would have to wait.

I carried with me only my unmaker—small and light-less, a black hole in the palm of my hand. Pray I will have no use for it.

The stairs spiraled high into the tower that housed the atelier. Before I reached the door behind which the Autocrat resided, I passed a round window. I did so without thought at first, but then took a few steps down the stairs to stand beside it again and look outside.

Beneath the House of the Autocrat extended our capital, with its residences of tin and steel, and beyond that were vast purple fields stretching far to tickle the feet of the mountains at the edge of the world. The mountains rose like sharp swords, and vast solar sails danced between their sharp summits. Beyond the mountains was the nothing-ness of the black infinite sea.

I looked up then. Above everything, the pocket sun we had brought along with us still burned. In recent years, it had dimmed.

I shook my head to escape my reverie and climbed the stairs. A few moments later, I stood before the door of the Autocrat's atelier.

Before I could knock, the door opened all on its own, and I felt the space inside the atelier fold and expand to pull me in.

I stood before three women, armored from head to toe. The first had a machine gun at her belt, the second a sword behind her back, with its hilt poking over her shoulder. The last had no weapon. Each bore two round shields—one on each arm—and wore a plumed helmet as if out of antiquity.

Behind them stood the Autocrat, with his back to me,

staring into his prismscope and gazing into the stars, as the Autocrat must.

Our planet had been sailing the vast void for generations unfathomable, and I was closing in on nearly three decades of service. My only superior was the Autocrat. I served loyally, as I had served his three immediate predecessors. Autocrats had a habit of dying merely a few years after inheriting their scepter, their prismscope, and their Autocracy. Still, when he turned to face me, I was taken aback by his youth. His years could not be more than twelve.

"Captain," the Autocrat said in a low, muffled voice. The atelier was narrow and long, but even though he stood at its other end and farthest from me, I could see that his eyes were big and round and innocent, but his face was ashen and gray.

"Grand supreme," I began to bow, but he shook his head, and I stopped. "What brings you to me in this hour?" he said.

"Grave peril, our—" I began and stopped, for I saw something flicker in his eyes.

"Go on," he spoke softly.

"Our planet will soon enter a region of space soaked with radiation. To go through it would mean the death of our fields and the mutation of our sun. A cataclysm on a global scale. Mountains will be toppled; our sails will be torn. The sea under this city will overflow and flood its quarters, killing millions. We are not prepared for this. We must stop and remain here."

For a while, the Autocrat didn't speak. He then turned to look back into his prismscope before addressing me again.

"How long would we have to wait? When will the storm pass?"

I could not help but smile while his back was still turned. This was indeed a young boy and prone to over-valuing years. In the vast openness, the lifespan of a man meant very little, the wise of us knew.

"Millions of years... who is to say? Perhaps more," I answered, very slowly. He turned back to face me again. "We are more likely to have scientific and industrial advancements that can be used to shield our planet before 'the storm' actually passes, and then we could be on our way again."

A SECOND OF happiness curled the edge of his lip into a fleeting smile. He shook his head. "Out of the question. We must brave the storm, captain. I rely on you to make the best of this. Our errand cannot wait."

Can he be so arrogant as to put his godforsaken errand above the lives of his subjects? "You are asking me to kill millions of people. Very few would survive this passage," I tried again. "And those who would, would be altered in ways unimaginable."

Silence, for a minute.

"I understand," he said, and a gleam in his eye told me he might soon cry. Hope... for a brief second, at least.

"But this is my planet, captain. You will do as I say, or you will die. All of you will. All of you must."

"Supreme Autocrat," I felt my fingers loosening their grip over the power in my palm, "your errand, whatever it might be, has been forgotten for aeons uncountable. What-ever it is you are trying to do has been rendered meaning-less by the relentless grind of time. If it is galactic conquest, the civilization you are sent to conquer would have been reduced to a cosmic footnote. If it is a holy search, the artifact first beheld through your prismscope by your nameless predecessors is by now an infinity—and more—away. Your people are impoverished. Our sun progressively dims, our crops fewer by the year. Our fields are slowly eroding, sinking back into the metal beneath. We can sustain ourselves for perhaps a few millennia, no more. Let those who are alive not die in vain."

"You mistake me, captain." There was something in his voice that I could not for the life of me identify. This perhaps was the most alarming thing. During my service, I prided myself on being able to guess accurately the thoughts of any man, something that has allowed me to end any mutiny while it was still being concocted.

Ancient glyphs, symbols, and drawings I had not the patience to try and decipher were drawn on the walls of the atelier, and along them candelabras stood like sentinels. There were no windows. It was an ideal place for a fight.

"You think like a child, for you are one," I said.

"I should have your tongue for that," he answered, and I was alarmed yet again to see that he was very calm.

"I meant no insolence, your grand supremacy. I was merely observing that your years are few, and thus you are prone to overvalue each one," I tried again. I had resolved to speak to him as one might indeed speak to a child, to soothe his nerves and promise him a reward when all was done. "Us old-timers understand that we must not think of ourselves as individual persons, but rather as a species. A person can live to be a hundred years, but species can live for millions. And what are a hundred years compared to a million? Waiting here for a few millennia would to our species be like waiting in your atrium for a few minutes is to one of your subjects. If you do not wait, you will be remembered as a malevolent child—a destroyer. If you wait, they will raise monuments in your honor. I will make sure of it. I will send my sailors throughout the infinite city to let all know that their Autocrat is good and just."

I am not a godly man to believe in a holy watchman. You need naïveté to be godly. During my service, I have beheld sights that have exorcized any faith onto which I might have otherwise been educated to hold. But at that moment, I prayed.

The child seemed relieved, if only briefly, and he said, "I do not have a choice in the matter. I will say this for the last. Our errand cannot wait.

"However, you hold your own choice. Do not think I am ignorant of it. The power of a black hole in the palm of your hand. I have/had/will see/n it. So make your choice. Trust, or treason."

I felt heavy, in foot as well as in thought. There was more at play here than I had initially realized—I, who saw through men's words and knew their hearts. As he said his words, it seemed to me he was many faces overlaid, one on top of the other, all of the same person, speaking in different voices that were one and the same.

The thought of apologizing, bowing, and leaving briefly settled in my mind. But like any faith, I failed to hold on to it. Time, from whose bottomless well a species may drink, had run out for me and this boy, and the choice was indeed mine and had to be made now. Were I to leave, my life would be forfeit, I knew. But it was not concern for my life that sealed our fates.

$$\sim$$

"It is done," I spoke into the device in my ear. My crew would soon join me there in the atelier.

The ordeal of the coup was not as bloody as I had expected, but it took years. It is documented elsewhere. The boy was relieved at its conclusion. As he handed me the scepter only we remained. I reached out to grab it, but he pulled the hand that offered it back saying "Have you ever wondered why we die only a few years after we inherit the scepter and the prismscope, captain?"

When I did not offer a reply he offered the scepter again — poisoned reward. As soon as I took it from his hand, myriad lifetimes seemed to afflict him at once, and where once stood but a child, with a grave and ashen face, now collapsed an old man. I walked past him, eager for an answer. Eager to understand what I had done. I looked into the prismscope. I did not understand what I saw, until I did.

The Beast of All Dimensions, striving at our tail.

No monuments will be raised in my honor. I have taken his burden from him, and now I must myself become a malevolent destroyer.

I looked back. Several members of my crew had appeared. "We must brave the storm," I said to them. Terror flooded the faces of two of them. A tremor went through another's legs, and he dropped to his knees. The last one mustered himself long enough to ask, "Have you lost your mind? What is it you wish to achieve in taking us into this cataclysm?"

I looked at the lifeless body of the Autocrat beneath my feet and then surveyed my men for several long minutes. They must not know, but it will not do to ask for blind obedience. Not from them.

"Haven."

THE END

BIO: Suhail has spent most of his life finding things to tinker with and create. As a child, he took up painting, of which he was fond, and playing the guitar, of which he was less fond. In high school, he wrote his first novella and cringed heavily when he read it decades later. He joined Fantasy-Writers.org in 2008, and after a few years of activity, became enamored with video game development and pixel art, and found work developing algorithms for self-driving cars— but he never stopped writing. In the past few years, he has added Latin dancing and board games to his hobbies, and a wife and a child to his life.

CHAPTER 11

THE DRAGONFLY DISH

THE ORDEAL

by

David Staiger

This was my moment. All the pieces had fallen into place. It had to be now.

Now, or never again.

The Overseers had gone, believing us subdued. I, too, should have been meekly curled upon my mat, content with a single bar of fruited grain and meager swallow of drink, however sweetly flavored. But I could not be content. I would not be, knowing what bounty lay beyond the Great Wall, what promises they kept from us, hoarded for their own greedy desires.

When I'd left the others, I saw Kay Lynn's eyes upon me. She knew where I was going. She understood my intent. She could have called out, could have raised an alarm. That would have ended everything. But she didn't. She stayed quiet beneath her once-white blanket, the one her mother had made and laced with now-fraying flowers, and left me to my own designs. Her face, though, told me I was crazed. With a small blue-eyed look and shake of her head, she said, *Don't go. You're going to get caught.* You're going to fail. But I knew otherwise. I simply nodded once and crept away.

This had to be done. They told me to settle. They commanded us all. They herded us, bent us, stole our light and demanded our dreams. They showed us how and when to grovel. But I knew where to find them. Others had seen. I knew where the sweetest dreams waited. Guarded, untouchable, but not beyond reach. Someone had to do it. I did this for us all.

I almost laughed out loud, just in thinking it. No. This was for me and no one else. This was my test, my challenge to overcome. And when I succeeded where no one else ever had, then I would laugh in earnest. I would laugh at the Overseers and their pretense of supremacy. I would scoff at the Wall of Rules and make my Papa proud. I would lift my eyes with satisfaction to know that I, Thi Cam Hanh, daughter of all daughters, had become legend.

But I needed to move, and so I did. Time did not come in infinite supply, that much I knew, and the Overseers would return soon enough. The lights never remained out for long.

I slunk amid the shadows, feeling the cool slate of the Way upon my bare toes. The walls towered to either side, creating a singular chasm with promise gleaming at the far end, beyond the Wall. If the Beasts came—when they did—there would be no place to hide, no other Ways to turn. Yet I had taken that into account. My plan relied upon it. I needed the Beasts, or at least one of them. Specifically, I required Oslo, his size and his strength. Gideon, I could do without.

Naturally, I didn't go alone. Strider came with me. My dino went everywhere by my side, loping along on two legs and always ready for a fracas. Together we made our stealth down the Way, only pausing when we heard the distant rumbling of the Overseers. They could come at any time, always, but as long as the dark held sway and the quiet calm endured, they often only peeked at us. I don't think they ever counted the lumps beneath the blankets.

When Strider and I reached the end, the Great Wall stood. An imposing barrier, forty feet high if it was four, it crossed the threshold of the Way's end, the bright space beyond waiting with untold bounty and limitless reward. The gaps between the white pillars of its construction had been spaced deliberately too narrow to squeeze through yet wide enough to entice with a view of my destination.

I glanced around and listened. The dragonflies hummed. I could also hear Prowler moving somewhere on the other side, around the corner and blocked from view, lapping at the water from his trough; but his presence was not a concern. Fat and mellow in all ways, Prowler did not pose an obstacle. I had the Ray to deal with him. It dangled from my waist, ready to be used at need. And much like Oslo, Prowler would serve my plans, so I was thankful to hear the creature awake.

The Wall remained. I pressed my hands, made one final vain attempt to slither between the pillars. No use at all. Strider was thinner than me, much more malleable with his form. His limbs contorted easily to place him on the opposite side, but that helped me nothing. From his vantage, he looked back, mournfully. He knew why he'd come. He understood his necessity. Still, I gave him a smile as I helped him back through the gaps. I pressed his forehead to mine, sharing our collective courage for the ordeal ahead. *You've got this*, I thought to him. *You too, Hanh*, he thought back. *We're in this together. Forever and always.*

Then I uncoiled the rope from my shoulder as Strider took a defensive posture at my side. From my pocket, I pulled out the Silent Shrill. Together we stood, ready. I put the slender device to my lips and blew through it. Barely a hiss of my breath emitted. We looked back down the Way, waiting.

Both Beasts arrived, nearly in unison. Oslo walked, a loping mass of muscle and mucus on four legs. He paused briefly as if to study what had called him there, to be certain he should approach further. Beside him, almost trotting in comparison, Gideon surged, a smaller black shadow of wild fur and wicked fangs.

The lesser Beast, but only in size—half the height of Oslo's shoulder still rose above my own waist—Gideon sprang into a charge, bolting between the chasm walls like a feral demon. He lunged, ready to tear my throat with surety, but in the same instant, Strider leapt unfalteringly to my defense.

They clashed, a snapping, growling tumble of teeth and sinew. My heart thumped, and for the moment, I feared most that their noise would rouse the Overseers to investigate. I held fast to Strider's back and tail, keeping his green and brown form between myself and Gideon's red and white maw as much as possible. I tried once to reach forth and rap Gideon on the snout, but that had as little effect as a stern glare, so I did the unthinkable instead. I let my companion handle the matter on his own.

I lost hold of Strider and watched in impotent worry as he and the black Beast rolled away from me. Their ongoing battle carried farther and farther until they vanished around the far end of the Way. At the same time, I was left with the other Beast to contend with on my own. I had to trust Strider to do his part while he trusted me to do mine. And Oslo loomed, closer with each step, heavy claws rattling on the slate. I readied my task.

Hastily, I strung the rope between the gaps and around one of the pillars. Using the knowledge I had gained from observing my Papa prepare for his journey each morning, I secured one end as tightly as possible to the Wall. Then I paused only until I felt the Beast breathing upon my neck and the first drip of spittle on my exposed skin.

I turned as Oslo lashed out with his tongue. Drool and slobber coated my arms, my torso, and hot, rancid breath washed my face. This Beast preferred to taste his prey, to torment them before feasting, so I knew I had that little bit of time remaining. I reached up and slung the rope across his back, pulled it through his legs from the other side. I wrapped the coil around the thing's neck, over its breast and tucked what end was left into the now snug binding at his shoulder. With an almost giddy sense of accomplishment, I fell back, took a few steps down the Way, away from the Wall.

For too long a moment, Oslo just stared at me, his dark eyes pondering. He stepped. *Yes.* He stepped again. *Yes. Yes.* He stopped when the rope came taut.

Somewhere behind, I heard the conflict between Strider and Gideon still raging. Pride and relief on one hand, fear and uncertainty on the other. This task wasn't done yet. My part, this one essential step, had not been achieved. *Come on! Come on you stupid Beast. Come and get me!*

As if hearing my mental shout and understanding every word, Oslo tried to step again, strained to reach me. The rope tightened upon the pillar as much as around his body. He made another step. I heard him grunt, almost a whine, and I feared then that all would come to nothing if the cord itself snapped in two from the tension. But remarkably, miraculously, it held. The rope was stronger than the Beast. And the Beast, as I'd anticipated, was stronger than the Wall.

With two more steps, I watched the Wall shudder, its top beginning to lean forward even as Oslo stretched out his massive tongue. As if taunting him with a torture of my own, I lifted my hand to within a bite of his teeth. He licked my fingers and that was all.

The Great Wall collapsed with a rumble and a roar, a clamor and a clatter. If the Overlords had not taken notice, I would be amazed. I had shortened my timetable instantly. As Oslo stood and looked around, befuddled, the coil of rope still dangling loosely about him, I launched myself forward. I dashed around the Beast's confused mass, clambered over the ruin of the Wall, and leapt into the light beyond.

My eyes scoured the surrounding ledges. The cliff faces glared back, sheer and unscalable, each one taller than the Wall itself had been. But Prowler was there, right where I imagined he'd be. He stood, arching his back and reaching out with massive paws, alerted by the din of the Wall's collapse. He stared at me, eyes wide despite his usual drowsy demeanor as if unready to decide why I was there, what my presence had to do with the sudden racket.

Of course, the Overseers stirred, one of them expressing concern to another. I scanned the cliffs, desperate to locate what I knew would be there, what others before me had said they had seen. There. It had to be. It could be nothing else. The humming echoed over everything.

Balanced high upon one ledge, a gleaming white urn—an enormous crock with a lid—rested where the light fell as if to proclaim its magnificence. Across its porcelain surface, with wings splayed like guardian angels, a swarm of multi-colored dragonflies lingered, each one easily as large as a hand, maybe even as big as one of Prowler's great paws.

They were coming now. I had to move. With both hands I lifted the Ray, not even taking the chain from my belt loop. I aimed. In an instant, a flame erupted on the cliff wall behind Prowler's head. He didn't see it, could not hear the silent magic at work. I lowered my aim. The flame exploded on the floor, moved back and forth to claim attention. Prowler took notice.

Even as the sounds moved along the Way, Oslo still struggling to release himself, I used the Ray to make the flame dance. It flickered toward one cliffside and Prowler dashed after it, claws scraping along the stone. I moved it over and up and watched as Prowler leapt. An Overseer made a call of alarm. My time was coming to a close, but I still had some, still had my opportunity. It all hinged upon Prowler now. I needed his girth in motion.

I moved the flame up and Prowler jumped. Despite his size, he had the legs for it, the power to push his mass as high as need demanded, to pounce upon any prey within his sight. And now he saw the flame as his target, the quarry he could not grasp. I used the Ray to lead the flame along the ledge and Prowler followed dutifully. The Overseers had come to Oslo.

I moved the Ray, moved the flame, moved Prowler. His weight collided with the urn and the dragonflies fluttered, their wings thrumming. I darted the flame from one side of the vessel to the other, making Prowler shimmy back and forth. The urn shifted beside his prodigious bulk. It was taking too long. *Curse you, creature! You have one purpose!*

I heard the screech behind me but did not turn around. Let them take me. I will not fail! I leveled the Ray at the vessel itself, the bright flame jumping off the alabaster surface as the dragonflies whined. Prowler lunged, both great paws slapping forward to strike the ephemeral target. A shadow loomed behind me, talons shrieking down to grasp my wayward form and carry me back where I belonged. But I had won. The urn toppled as I felt the claws take hold, seizing my shoulders to lift me away.

When the urn struck the bottom of the cliff, it shattered, fragments of white stone screaming in every direction. Dragonflies took flight—red, green, purple, yellow—sailing off as if they knew their task had come to an end. And from within the burst container, a tidal flood of magic erupted, seeds of every different color in the world—so many more hues and shades than possessed by even the dragonflies themselves—cascading outward like the gathered dreams of all humankind.

I, Thi Cam Hanh, Daughter of All Daughters, had won.

As I LAY on my back looking up at the pastel blue sky that never dulled, at the clouds that never moved, I could not help but smile. The other children ran about, played their games and had their arguments, giggling or shouting as their moods took them, oblivious to my adventure. Only Kay Lynn looked at me once, her blond curls and pursed lips shaking in disapproval. In the background I could hear Miss Maggie, the Director of the Tender Moments Daycare talking on the phone, most likely to my father.

"Oh no, she's fine, I assure you. Probably just a little

startled. We checked her over thoroughly for any cuts. We just wanted to let you know in case she mentioned anything that might have sounded more dramatic than it was.

"Well, it was the most bizarre set of coincidences, really. Our cat knocked over the jellybean dish and I think that probably scared her more than anything else. No, she should not have been in the kitchen, I agree, but it seems one of the dogs got himself tangled up in a jumprope and managed to pull down the safety gate. I know, right? Of all the things. Right during quiet time, too. Yes. Yes, I know. Tell me about it. But I think she heard the gate fall and got up to check it out. The cat knocking the dish off the counter was just a freak of timing. No, I assure you it wasn't her. I don't think she could reach that high if she tried.

"But, yes, I just wanted to tell you that Hanh is perfectly fine. No worries. No, that won't be necessary. She's back playing with the other kids as if nothing happened. That's okay. No, not at all. This kind of stuff happens. Okay. Yes. Take care. See you at five. Bye."

A moment later, another face interrupted the mural of the sky, the bright yellow, smiling face of the sun replaced by a human one. Miss Jenny crouched down with a long-familiar green-and-brown plush dinosaur in hand.

"Here you go, Hannah," the young assistant teacher said. "Looks like Gideon got ahold of him when no one was looking. But don't worry, Strider's a real scrapper." Jenny wiggled him against me as I collected my trusted companion in both arms. I giggled reflexively. Jenny leaned in, offering a conspiratorial tone. "If you ask me, I'd say Gideon got the worst of it." She smiled with a wink, tousled my hair, and went to stop Brandon from eating his boogers.

I lay back again, grinning contentedly. I had done it. I, Thi Cam Hanh, had done the undoable.

With no one looking, I opened my palm to reveal the golden yellow gem of my victory, the single jellybean quite sticky in my grasp. I popped it in my mouth.

Papa was going to be so proud.

THE END

BIO: Dave lives with his family and assorted dogs in Upstate New York. In addition to writing, he enjoys hiking, mountain biking, rollerblading, and hockey. When he's not in the classroom teaching special needs children, Dave argues with fellow FWOers about what makes a good story. Sometimes, he's right. If he could, he'd make his living writing drabbles, but he's found the scant pay-for-word won't keep the mortgage company happy. While working on his WIPs, he has been published in two anthologies, Festival of Fear by Black Ink Press and Black Hare Press' Fourth Year Anthology. He's been a member of Fantasy-Writer's.Org since March 2017.

CHAPTER 12

THE SCALES OF FATE

THE ORDEAL

by

Malak A. Eltahtawy

T he air was thick with the smell of burnt wood and charred fabric, a stench that clutched Alex's throat. She wrinkled her nose as she walked down Coastal Street to the newspaper stall. A newspaper a day was a must for her profession. She had to monitor the public reactions to the activities of her group, the Exterminators.

Small grey flecks tickled her cheeks, and Alex brushed them off. Winter had just begun, and it was early for snow. She looked to the sky, expecting to see more, but found nothing. Her eyebrows furrowed. Did she imagine that? Blaming her lack of sleep, she shook her head.

As Alex turned right, the wide market street was covered in black. Her eyes fell on the newspaper stall beside the remains of the only flower stall, which had been reduced to black rubble. Another shop burnt down. Her stomach tightened as she made her way to the stall.

That was why business wasn't good. Few customers could buy more than the necessities, as everyone floated on the edge of disaster. So, the most famous market street in Chaska was deserted.

Standing before the newspaper stall, Alex knew a life had been lost recently through the young cashier's body language: hunched over the counter, eyes red and sniffling.

"The young girl?" Alex asked him. She usually began her talks with a greeting, but she couldn't be bothered now.

The boy hadn't noticed her and jumped back in surprise, facial muscles taut. Her question must've made him recall the event.

"She's ... in a better place now."

"How?"

"Apparently, not giving away flowers is a crime," a much older man, sitting at the back of the stall, replied. "I mean, how dare she, when it was just for an anniversary."

Alex had hated the smell of the flowers whenever she came to buy the papers. She would crunch her nose and frown away memories. Emotions weren't her thing, nor was reminiscing, yet even though she could've found another newspaper stall, she kept coming back.

Alex exhaled sharply, pinching her nose. Another soul she had failed to protect. Standing here without the scent of wild roses invading her nostrils felt vile.

"Today's paper, please," Alex said. The cashier had zoned out again. She knocked on the counter, dragging him back to reality.

"Three bics, miss."

"Since when?" It was just one bic yesterday.

"Since today," the owner replied. "Take it or leave it."

They had to have raised the taxes again—by five hundred percent. How were the citizens supposed to cope with this? What about the poor?

With a defeated sigh, Alex took out three bronze coins and set them on the counter before taking the soot-covered newspaper. The burning must've taken place early this morning.

She rubbed the soot off with her sleeve as she walked, but the headline knocked the breath out of her. Heat spread through her as her blood boiled with frustration. She stopped in the middle of the street to read the article.

New Exterminators' Recruit Arrested for Attempted Murder of Chaska City Leader.

Early Saturday morning, Feola Karmin, a 19-year-old law student and a new recruit of the notorious Exterminators, was caught attempting to assassinate Chaska City's beloved leader, Sintah Yasmoor. According to eyewitness reports, Karmin was apprehended by security forces attempting to break into Yasmoor's residence last night.

"Feola Karmin carried the signature dagger of the Exterminators," stated a source from the Chaska Security Guard. After a brief but intense confrontation, backup forces arrived, and our heroic guards subdued Karmin around 1:30 a.m. Though she has refused to confess, the dagger proves her allegiance to the Exterminators. This group, known for their failed efforts to disrupt Chaska's peace, has now resorted to recruiting young, impressionable citizens in their fruitless fight.

Sintah Yasmoor himself addressed the incident, denouncing the Exterminators as "dirty rats" and vowing to eradicate them. "One by one, they will fall." Behind The Scenes will continue to follow this shocking development as more details emerge from this harrowing event and the fight for Chaska City's security.

Reporting by Darius Kain, Behind The Scenes.

This paper was known for being dramatic, but Alex checked it often because it was also the first to spread the news. Still, her limbs tensed, and her grip on the paper tightened. She had warned Keley many times, told him this would happen.

As sweet as Feola was, she was also driven by a hunger for revenge. She had recently left the concentration camp with fresh wounds. Losing a brother and a home could drive anyone insane. Alex had told her that the group wasn't a vessel for revenge. She couldn't indulge her thirst and throw away all the work done before her. But Feola went and did just that.

Alex sighed, and her muscles ached. This day had begun with the worst possible news. She crumpled the newspaper and threw it into a trash can. The knowledge of all the work she would have to put into freeing the girl and sending her somewhere safe prickled her skin. She scratched the scar across her face, running from her nose bridge to her right jaw, dividing her cheek into halves.

Glancing at her wristwatch, Alex cursed and ran down the road. Adam was waiting, and she was fifteen minutes late. The chill wind ruffled her brown leather jacket, resisting her sprint, and surely her sandy hair flew every-where, and her pale skin reddened when she wanted to look her best.

Panting in front of the coffee shop, Alex stopped and tried to fix her clothes and hair. She couldn't be late to her and Adam's monthly coffee meet-up, looking like she was being chased by a Nasachi. Everything worked against her this month, but the hangout would surely be a wonderful change. Curse it all, but Adam felt like home. Was this because he was her childhood best friend—the boy next door—or because he was the last thing that remained from their village?

Her hand went into the pocket where she kept another carefully folded newspaper article. One she'd cut out three years ago, just after meeting with Adam, became a regular part of her life. Maybe the best part.

Captain Instarchi Assassinated!

Captain Instarchi, beloved leader of the People's Inspection Guard, was stabbed in cold blood outside his home on Stretchar Street near midnight. This heroic leader has led his valiant soldiers in the arrests of over 500 rebels, and was just coming from a meeting with our beloved mayor to discuss plans for the increased safety of the citizenry. Adam Georgus was the first policeman on the scene, but he was seconds too late to save Instarchi, or to net the assassin.

"This was the work of a professional," said Officer Georgus, "and I saw nothing, but mark my word, justice will come his way!"

The article went on, but that was the phrase that had given Alex heart for the past three years. Adam had arrived just as she pulled the knife free, and their eyes met before she ran into the night. They never spoke of it afterward, but where she'd started the meeting looking for information on police operations, they became something more. She no longer looked for information from him and had no desire to put him at risk with the Exterminators. Adam was a friend on the other side, and that was precious. However, she did always wonder what justice she would find.

As soon as she opened the door and set foot in the cafe, she was wrapped in the warmth of it. This was the harshest winter of her life. Her forearms trembled, and her nails were purple from the cold as she raised her hand to beckon the server. He returned the gesture from across the room.

At the far right corner of the cafe, Adam waited in their spot. He hadn't noticed her yet, and she felt guilty. He probably thought she wouldn't come. Rushing forward and practicing an apology, the coffee's smell and the chatter relaxed her. Without calling out his name, Alex took off her jacket, hung it on the seat, and sat.

Adam looked at her and pouted. "I thought you weren't gonna come."

"Sorry. I lost track of time reading the paper. Have you waited too long?"

"No, just thirty minutes. Not much for a not-so-busy cop."

"I said I am sorry, dude. Don't get salty."

Adam rolled his blue eyes at her and brushed a hand through his hair. "Was the paper worth it? Are the aliens finally invading us?"

"Adam. Stop your sass or I'll leave."

"Yeah, go ahead, you leave me, too."

Alex was speechless. How could he pull this move on her? Flexing tense hands, she hated how he always knew how to rile her. The history between them gave him too much power.

"You know I would never leave, not after we found each other again. I am sorry I was late. I promise to come fifteen minutes early next time. Fine?"

"Fine."

Alex sighed. Now that the drama was over, she could order. A hot, extra-sweet black coffee for him and an ice, sugar-free coffee with milk for her.

As they waited for their drinks, Adam asked, "Could you at least tell me why you were late?"

"I told you I was buying the newspaper."

"Anything worth making you late?"

"No, nothing new."

"Huh, I could swear I read about this girl who broke into the Head's house this morning."

Adam had a twinkle in his eyes. He knew something he shouldn't. He had that same look when they were young and hid candy from their parents.

Right. Her friend, the cop.

"Yeah, I read that too," she said carefully. "But that's nothing new. An increasing number of Exterminators are being caught these days."

"But you have to admit, this Fiona girl was pretty stupid. Who goes to assassinate the city's head with just a dagger?"

"First off, her name is Feola. Second, you never know what drove her to that."

"I do. It's idiocy! You're a journalist, you know that."

"As a journalist, I'm taught to be objective and not subjective, Adam. I write exactly what's done."

Alex huffed as she clenched her hands under the table. Adam didn't get her frustration, but he should still be mindful of other people's situations. He didn't know that she had to put so much effort now into freeing Feola. The Nasachi's New Order system wasn't hard to infiltrate, but was nearly impossible to escape.

"Speaking of which, do you still work as a professor's assistant?" Adam asked.

"I do, when I've got time."

"Isn't it boring working with—what's his name? Professor Kilton ... uh, Keller ... Professor Kettle-"

"Professor Keley," Alex replied with an eye roll. Adam had serious issues with names. How had he ever gotten a position with the Nasachis? She didn't have a clue.

"Yes, him! Professor Keley. I hear he's good at his job, but is your job fun?"

If only he knew. The reason that Alex became a journalist was because she thought she could change the world with words—with peace. Time proved her wrong, and she was recruited into the Exterminators in her third year of university. Professor Keley, who founded the Exterminators, gave her the position of professor's assistant when she graduated. That protected her and her activities from the death squads.

"Job means purpose, which means commitment, and commitment is a choice. Choices don't have to be fun. They have to be right. Good."

Adam gulped, and his hands fell to his lap. His eyes were wide open as they locked with hers. He had dark circles, and his cheeks were shallow. Adam, who'd always been obsessed with his beauty, looked like a death row convict. Alex shook the thought away. She couldn't lose someone again, not someone this dear to her. Yet there was a feeling in the pit of her stomach of something wrong.

"Adam?"

His eyes darted in panic. For a split second, his expression faltered. His mouth opened, but he quickly shut it again, glancing away. Did he have something to confess?

"Are you alright?"

Shaking his head, he smiled, but it didn't reach his eyes. "I'm perfect. I even got promoted."

"Congrats!"

"Yeah, I'm working in the Nasachi's fortress now. Tada!" Adam spread his hands wide.

"You mean the Chaska Fortress? I'm so proud of you. You deserve the raise." But she had to wonder, what had he done for that? What had her best friend done?

The fortress was a beautiful, ancient castle over-looking the sea. Her grandfather used to tell stories about how their courageous ancestors had fought wars with enemies on these shores. The fortress was visible to everyone in the city, and tomorrow night she had business there. A business she didn't dare share with her best friend.

"... Alex?" Adam asked in a low tone.

"Yeah?"

"Your drinks are here!" The server set the drinks on the table with a soft clink. Alex and Adam thanked him.

Before sipping her iced coffee, Alex asked. "So, you were saying?"

Adam's eyes fell on the steaming mug in his hands. "I was thinking of our village. Call me nostalgic, but I tried recalling one of your mother's recipes to make for dinner yesterday."

Paraptra, their village. Any New Order maps would not have it. Almost fifteen years ago, the Nasachis had visited them, and before leaving, they took everything: lives, homes, childhoods, flower gardens, and peace. Alex was there. She had lived it all, as had Adam. And now, he was one of them. How could this be?

Memories flooded her. Clear skies and chirping birds. Mama's food, Grandpa's garden, Papa's workshop, Aunt Twyla, and Justin the cat. Her home. Gone. Forever. Adam was just like her. He, too, had lost all his family, his home, and almost all his friends. He was her childhood best friend. The boy next door.

"Yeah, she was that good of a cook, wasn't she? But I didn't have the time to learn anything. I was busy playing with you," Alex said, to diffuse the tension. She was totally not in the mental space to have this talk, not in the space to

195

face who he was. Why did it have to happen today of all days?

"No, you mean they took us too young."

"Adam, don't."

"How long are you going to hide from our past?"

Alex slurped on her drink, hoping for the coldness to put out the fire burning in her heart. Whenever she talked with Adam about the past or her fake job, it always felt like her heart was being stabbed by a Nasachi. The solution was to ignore him till he switched up the topic.

"I want to go visit my parents' grave, Alex."

But they both knew that, if he tried to, they would kill him before he even set foot in Paraptra. He might be a Nasachi cop, but he was a peon. Unless he'd done something to change that.

Her eyes focused on the coffee in her hands. It hurt like hell that the Nasachis killed everything. Killed was an understatement. They tied people in their houses, burned them alive, and made the kids watch. Then, they took all the kids under eighteen to concentration camps in Chaska. That was lesson one: If you disobeyed, you died.

Lesson two was that if you showed your magic, you died. Their natural, radiant magic. It wasn't like the superpowers heroes possessed. It was an extension of one's spirit. People walked in beautiful hues, their energy buzzing around them like living paintings.

"Alex, I miss them." His lower lip quivered as he whispered the words.

Her eyes hardened, and words broke away. "You work for the ones who killed them."

Ten-year-old Alex would've never imagined this. Adam was the small boy she fought with another kid for in their martial arts class. Now he was a Nasachi cop. Cute little

Adam, who was forced to learn self-defence by his older brother so he could stand up for himself. The boy who brought her ice cream after she had fought for him. The boy who felt so safe and went everywhere with her. How in the world could that same boy, who grew into the man who protected her, work for these murderers? Had they finally gotten to him?

"I had to join them. Don't you get it? I would've died there." He leaned forward, his eyebrows furrowing and pursing his lips.

Alex wanted to understand. She wanted to forgive him for what he'd done—for choosing survival over everything else. She, of all people, knew what the likes of them had to go through to be treated like humans. It wasn't fair.

"I get it. But I would never work for them. Never."

"You don't know what it's like being one of the smallest boys in the camp. We killed each other to survive. I had to learn to obey to stay alive."

That was where they were different.

It was a miracle that Alex and Adam were still alive. By the age of eighteen, most kids didn't make it out. They either lost their sanity, their life, or both. The Nasachis would throw all those who were a burden to the dogs to eat. That was their way. You breathed too loudly; you died. You laughed; you died. You became a burden; you died. You caused trouble; you died. Even when you were dead, you died again.

"I made it out just fine." She crossed her arms.

"I wasn't the one who went around killing people," he said, staring at her.

Her eyes widened, and her hands brushed her scar.

"Your reputation reached our camp. I even made friends with older boys just 'cause I knew you."

Alex's eyes flicked to the door. A man wearing a navy long coat with the symbol of the Nasachis brushed past outside, boots clicking on the pavement. The symbol of the Nasachis was three overlapping circles formed into a triangle, circles in which she saw pits of despair based on oppression, injustice, and cruelty.

Adam must've seen him, too, because he placed his elbow on the table, raised his shaky forearm, and leaned his cheek on his palm. He was hiding his face. But why? Alex shifted in her seat, lowering her voice and scanning the room. Everything seemed normal...for now.

"I did that to protect others and myself!" She leaned forward. So, what if she had killed a girl or two? It was self-defence. They would've killed her and the other girls if they had lived.

He rolled his eyes. "You had a killing streak. We had bets on who would be next."

Alright, maybe it was more than a girl or two. But Alex still felt a sense of pride when the girls came complaining to her that someone had bullied them. And it was worse than bullying. Some girls beat others to the point where they couldn't do their work, and the victims would be dead the next day. Executed. When this happened, Alex had to act. Each time, the bully would be dead before dawn. She protected others and herself, eliminating danger. Permanently.

Her first year there, at the age of twelve, Alex killed five girls. They'd hurt other girls, threatening their lives, and she got fed up. She took them out, one by one, and whoever dared follow in their footsteps. The scales had dropped on one side. She was restoring balance. She was protecting people.

The only reason she wasn't caught was that the girls

feared her. She was satisfied that the girls in the camp recognized her as someone dangerous, maybe even as dangerous as the Nasachis.

"If you knew all this time, why didn't you say something?"

"I thought you wouldn't like it if I did."

"You're right, I hate it. But if I went back in time, I would do it all over again."

Alex would rather be a predator than a prey. Being a prey once made her lose everyone. The day they took her away was the day she vowed she would no longer be a victim or stay silent. In fact, taking matters into her own hands had been very effective. She was going to continue doing that until this city was set straight again, with all the Nasachis dead. Except for Adam. She would never hurt him.

"You still killed people!"

"Bad people, Adam. They're not the same."

Was he a threat? Was he going to turn her in to the Nasachis? The ones who killed their parents and burnt their village. He hadn't given her away before, but he was still a cop who maintained a faulty order in the name of justice. Alex narrowed her eyes at him. "Why did you do it, Adam? Become a cop."

Adam's eyes darkened, and his jaw tightened. "That's none of your business."

"And just like that, my business isn't yours, either."

It was her fault their friendship was tense. When Alex had approached him in the cafe one day, three years ago, she had her motives. She recognized Adam among the list of all the newest members of the New Order that Professor Keley had given her. She didn't tell Keley about her discovery, still believing that Adam was forcefully swept into this mess.

Alex's initial plan was to gather information from him. Simple questions about how his day was should've been successful. He used to love complaining to her. She could read him. When he was quiet or deliberately lied, she sensed something was off.

Not too long after, and through some deep research, she found out that he had willingly become a Nasachi. Adam was right at the centre of the mess. If she'd confronted him about it, she might have said too much and exposed herself, so she stayed silent. But for weeks, Alex felt sick at the thought. He was her enemy, who protected her.

It wasn't a simple, people-pleasing experience for him in the camp; he allowed them to reprogram his mind. They brainwashed him to do all the dirty work for them. He had studied law before becoming a cop. He knew the New Order's law like the back of his hand. Getting bad people out of trouble was his job. He prevented them from suffering the consequences of their actions.

Yet he hadn't given her away when he might have done. That was the one thing she held onto, the hope that he didn't entirely belong to them.

Adam's chair creaked as he shifted; he had finished his coffee. He drew in a long breath and set his hands on the table. As he politely coughed before he spoke, she knew he had something to say.

"Alex?"

"Yes."

"It's completely hypothetical, alright?"

"Just spill it!"

He gulped, and his eyes fell to the table. "I-if your life was in the hands of one person, who would you trust it to?"

"You. You're the only thing I have left."

"What if I let you down?"

"You're the only person who could kill me, and I would still forgive you."

"You're lying."

"No, I'm not. If it were someone else, I would kill them, sure, but not you."

His eyes swelled with tears.

"What did you do, Adam? What are you hiding?"

He sniffed as he wiped his eyes with his sleeve. "Nothing."

"You don't look good. Did something happen?"

He pursed his lips together and held her hands on the table. His thumb stroked the back of her hand as he shook his head, his fingers trembling. What was he holding back?

"Trust me, I'm better now that I've seen you." He attempted another smile.

Extending one hand across the table, she ruffled his hair. She used to do that a lot when they were kids. The brown mass of silky hair was captivating. Young Adam didn't like people playing with his hair, but he let her. Just like now. She hoped it comforted him as much as it comforted her.

Alex looked into his blue eyes, begging them to tell her what she needed to know. Something must've happened. Had he betrayed someone? Who?

She would check up on him after she got Feola out, but for all the drama, there was warmth here. The cozy cafe, the familiar handhold, the scent of coffee, and the sound of the violent winds outside. She allowed herself to enjoy the moment.

She'd told herself it was the job, told herself she had met up with Adam to gather information, but that wasn't the case. Alex needed him more than he needed her. He was always a constant in her life before everything fell into hell.

And getting back with him after years of separation meant it was fate.

Standing in front of the cafe, Alex looked up at the night sky and its shimmering stars while Adam tied his shoelaces. The coffee shop had closed, and they had to say goodbye. Adam kept recalling all their little adventures from when they were young and reciting their inside jokes.

As she read the 'O'lfa Cafe' sign, a thought crossed her mind. What if she asked him to meet twice a month instead of once? Could she allow herself to come to terms and honestly open up? If she really trusted him, would that mean life or death?

She wished she could give their relationship a serious chance. Drop the ulterior motives, which weren't working. Could she do that? Take that risk? No, not today. It was too tense. Maybe she would ask him next time. Gave herself some time to think before she took that crazy step.

The chilly wind bit her face, and Alex winced. Adam pulled her into a tight hug. She sighed. It felt so close to home. He chuckled when the wind ruffled her hair and tickled him.

"Thanks for letting me pay today, Alex. I know it was your turn, but I just got my paycheck and I had to spend it on something."

She squeezed him tight. "It's alright, I'll pay next time."

Just before they broke away, he whispered in her ears. "Thanks for saving me again."

"Huh? What do you mean? Hey! Come back here."

Instead of replying to her, he turned on his heels and walked away. This was the first time he hadn't listened to her.

A few meters away, he raised his hands to the sky and said, "Get home safe, Alex. See you soon."

As Alex watched him leave, all she could do was shout back. "Take care and get home safe, jerk. See you." She raised her hands and waved, not caring that he didn't see her.

Thanks for saving me again. The words echoed in her mind as she watched him disappear into the night. Saving him from what? From himself? From the system? A knot formed in her stomach. She scratched at her scar as anxiety crept in. What was he hiding from her? How had she saved him? Alex tried to imagine returning to a life where she couldn't save him, but that was unimaginable.

THE NEXT NIGHT, Alex walked to the city's east harbour, ready to pursue Keley's plan. Fighting the snow falling on her face, she pulled the hood of her cloak up. The warmth of her suit was a comfort. She'd still rather be home by the fireplace, but she had to get Feola.

It was almost midnight when she knew the guard shifts changed. Once she entered the Chaska Fortress, she would only have ten minutes to get back out.

As Alex stood in front of its huge wooden doors, she breathed in deeply. The dirty limestone walls were nearly twenty meters high, with a tower at each corner. It had been a pristine work of art, but the Nasachis destroyed everything beautiful.

The gates creaked open, and Alex crept underneath a carriage, holding onto its underside. She made a quick prayer. If they stopped for inspection and she got caught, her mission would fail before it even began.

But the carriage drove on and stopped in the fortress

garden after a minute. The driver knocked on the carriage once. Twice. Thrice.

That was her signal.

Alex dropped and rolled, hiding in the shadows. She motioned to the driver, indicating he should wait outside, as arranged, and leave if she didn't come out in fifteen minutes. With a nod, he drove the carriage away.

Making sure that her hood covered her face, Alex slithered forward. Based on the map she'd studied and according to Keley's intel, Feola was imprisoned on the eastern side of the castle. It was strange, as usually the Nasachis didn't put prisoners there. It overlooked the shore directly, so there was a risk of suicide before they could get the information they wanted.

The waves pounded the walls of the fortress. Alex had never been this close to the sea before, as the Nasachis had all the coast blocked off, and she wasn't happy that her one chance to see it was on a mission.

As she entered the passage that should lead her to Feola, Alex squeezed her eyes and clasped her hands together, muttering another quick prayer.

The passage was narrow, with high, arched ceilings. Her feet kissed the tiles. She wouldn't want to slip, or worse, be heard. Keley said that Feola would be in the seventh room. So Alex began counting the doors to her right.

The first room passed by, and there was no guard. The second room was also clear.

The sound of the sea was her only comfort as she crept through the passage, counting the doors until she reached the seventh. It was worn down and could be easily broken with a kick, but noise was her enemy.

Trying to silence her heartbeats, she closed in and put her ear to the door. There was no movement, no sound. If

Alex knew Feola well, the girl would be thrashing around right now, demanding to be let out. Unless she was asleep or drugged.

The silence was suspicious. The calm before the storm. Someone was trying to be silent. Was this a trap?

Concentrating hard, Alex listened again. There was a shaky breath beside the door. Was Feola trying to run away, having heard Alex? Or what if it was a Nasachi?

Her shoulders cracked as she turned them over. Alex shook her whole body, trying to control her adrenaline rush. *Focus, no space for mistakes.* If it were a guard, a quick punch to the throat would put him down.

Alex stuck herself to the wall outside, nimbly picked the lock, and pushed the door open. There was still no movement. The creaks should have alerted whoever was inside. But no one came.

Alright, Alex would make the first move.

She slid in. Adjusting to the sudden darkness, she stayed close to the wall. She was running out of time. If the room were empty, Keley would be in serious trouble.

Air crept along her left shoulder, freezing her in place. She gulped. Someone was here. Turning her head slowly, her eyes widened. *No, no, no.* That couldn't happen. Glossy blue met her brown.

Why?

How?

"Hey, Alex. I was waiting for you."

Adam's voice cracked near the end. Dark shadows framed his face. He looked like he hadn't slept in days. But he was fine yesterday.

"Adam. What are you doing here?"

Nothing made sense. He hadn't betrayed her, had he?

"Feola was killed at dawn. Sintah came in drunk and finished her off."

Her stomach tied in on itself. Everything trembled around her as if it were an earthquake.

"No, she's supposed to be here."

"I'm sorry."

Alex sought the wall's support with her hand. She couldn't believe it. Feola died because she was late. Another person she'd failed to protect.

"But Keley—"

"I sent that. I had to speak to you."

"Here?"

Brows furrowed and body shaking, Alex felt betrayed. He'd willingly brought her here, to her death. Enraged, she started backing away. "I trusted you, Adam. What have you done?"

"My best. I did my best. I tried to save her!" His eyes fell to the floor.

Alex had to get away. Staying here a second longer meant death. Running for the door, she heard the guards coming behind her.

Dammit!

She sprinted the opposite way. Alex didn't know where she was going. All she saw were passages blocked and rooms closed.

Her path led her to the roof. She ran past a pair of ropes dangling over the back edge of the crenellation, supporting a worker's scaffold before continuing downward toward the snowy ground. Great, these ropes were her way out.

"Not so fast, Alexandra." Adam's voice rang behind her.

Cold chills struck her spine. When had he ever used her full name? What in the world was he doing? Had he warned others of her presence?

"I said we need to talk. You hurt my feelings, running away like that."

"What the hell, Adam!" she hissed. Her nerves yelled at her to run, to jump, and to fight. "Stay away. I don't want to kill you, please."

Blinded with anger and betrayal, Alex knew she would lose control. It was stupid to trust him. He was just like all the Nasachis: a traitor.

"I just need to talk, Exterminator."

The air slapped out of her lungs, and she fought to breathe. "Since when?"

So, he knew all this time. Was he also the one—"You! You kept ruining my plans."

"Yeah, sorry about that." He folded his hands behind his back. His face was granite, emotionless.

"How?"

"Trade tricks aren't meant to be shared, honey."

Trade tricks? That was it. All she did was just tricks?

Alex saw red. Her efforts to save her city's future were ruined by her childhood best friend.

As he stood there smirking, his eyes looking so proud, Alex swore she heard her heart shatter into pieces. No, he was no longer a friend. She had lost her friend that day when their home burned down.

Alex didn't know if it was the snow or the betrayal, but her vision blurred. A sound—closer to a whimper than a growl—escaped her mouth as she dived for Adam's throat.

He blocked her punch. Magic, green and red, exploded at the contact. She kicked his side. He punched her ribs.

As their blows connected, memories flashed through her mind: the sound of his laugh when they played hide-and-seek in the village, the way he used to cling to her when they were scared. How could this be the same person standing before her: a Nasachi, an enemy?

That wasn't the boy she once saved or the man who held her hands in the cafe yesterday. The man who'd only saved her to use her as a source. This was a lowly Nasachi who deserved nothing but death.

Dodging a kick to her side, Alex took a step backward. Recovering quickly, she pulled two daggers from her waist belt.

She planted one foot before the other and held her daggers tight. With a quick shake of her head, she lunged back at him.

The impact of steel on his cheek drew blood. He hissed, stepping away.

Satisfied, she lunged again. Swinging her hands in an unpredictable pattern, she landed cuts on his arm, abdomen, and leg. She punched him square in the face before he could regain his balance.

Adam wasn't quick enough to react. After all, Alex was the killer, not him.

He spat blood on the floor and straightened his back. She saw an opening and kicked him in the chest. He caught her leg, his hands imprisoning her ankle.

Hopping on one leg, she moved her dagger. As she aimed for his neck, he caught her right wrist and twisted her hands. She screamed from the pain as the dagger fell to the floor.

"I hate you!"

Alex jumped and tied her legs around his neck, and flipped them over. The dagger that was still in her left hand pressed against his throat.

She heaved aggressively. "Do you hear me? I hate you, Adam!"

His eyes closed, and he threw his head back on the floor, breathing in.

How dare he take her so lightly? Didn't he care about his life?

"Why aren't you fighting back?"

He knocked her hand away from his face. "Because I'm trying to help you."

"How?"

"It's all your fault, really. You can't help but save me. Every. Damn. Time!"

He was talking nonsense, trying to distract her. She wouldn't let him. Alex placed her dagger at his throat again. Adam flinched and closed his eyes.

Something was wrong. The way his body was relaxed, accepting death. She kicked his leg, forcing him to look at her.

"Tell me honestly. What are you hiding?"

"They'll come for you, Alex," Adam murmured. "But I won't let them. They'll blame me for everything. And they'll never know you were here."

He met her eyes as he said, "Kill me, Alex. I would rather die by your hands."

"Just tell me what you did?"

"I stole, okay?"

"What?"

"I stole...something from them last week. Something that could make all the difference to their enemies. To you."

"What do you mean? You're not making sense."

"I wasn't promoted to stay in the castle, Alex. They suspect me and I'm on lockdown—when they can keep me in, at least." He paused before whispering. "I'm a dead man."

The world stopped.

No, Alex couldn't lose him, too. What was she thinking earlier? How could she attack him? Adam wasn't even fighting back.

A plan weaved instantly, the dots connecting. Feola's hideout was still empty. Alex could follow all her steps, but with a different person. She stood up and pulled Adam from the floor. Clenching his hands, she made up her mind.

"I can help you. Come with me."

"They'll track me..."

"Not if we go now. Please, we can make it out together."

"If you save me one more time, I might as well die of shame."

"Why would you say that?"

Why did he reject her offer?

Putting his hands in his suit jacket, he pulled out a small black box. "Take this." He placed it in her hands.

"Open it when you're somewhere safe, alright?"

As Alex inspected the box in her hands, shaking it and weighing it, the snow formed a layer on top. Right, it was still snowing. Her toes and fingers were freezing as the adrenaline subsided.

A sharp breath came from her right. Adam stood on the eastern roof edge, his eyes filled with tears trickling down his cheeks. The blood staining his cheek where she'd cut him had dried out.

He stretched his arms manically, embracing the snow. Adam looked back at her and smiled.

Realizing what he was doing, Alex ran forward, dropping the box.

"Adam. No!"

"I'm sorry, Alex. But I can't let you kill yourself trying to save me."

He leaped backward, a foot outside the castle wall. Time

stopped as she jumped to catch his hands. Her right hand held his left. Alex landed on the floor at the edge.

His weight pulled her forward. Her arms were numb as she leaned over the edge.

Snow fell on both of them as he dangled over the water. Adam was giggling.

Alex braced her legs against the stone to balance the weight. She tried pulling him, but that only risked them both falling. Her muscles and lungs screamed for relief. The realisation that she wouldn't be able to hold on long sank her heart.

Alex reached down with her other hand. He had to take it.

"Give me your hand, Adam. Please, don't leave me. You're all I have."

Her hand was sweaty, and she could feel him slipping away.

His laughter rang into the night. His face was red, and his dark hair was white from the snow.

Her best friend was going to die, yet he was grinning from ear to ear.

"Oh, Alex. Let me go." Adam blinked softly at her. "My parents and brother are waiting for me. I did my part the best I could. I leave the rest to you. No matter what anyone says, I trust you, Alexandra. So please let me go."

"No. No, I won't. Just give me your hand, you idiot. Please, Adam. I can't lose you, too. Just give me your hand!"

He raised his hands slowly, and her heart skipped a beat. He listened. Their hands were inches apart. Grunting, she dropped her hand lower, seeking his.

Suddenly, he grabbed her right hand and opened her fingers at once. In the blink of an eye, he freed himself from her grasp.

His fingers slipped through hers like water, smooth and inevitable. No matter how hard Alex tried to grab him again, she couldn't. "Please!" she screamed, her voice cracking, but Adam just smiled. That same smile that used to make her feel safe now only shattered her heart into a thousand pieces.

Her heart dropped to her stomach as she met his eyes. He was still smiling. The bastard was laughing as she was up there screaming.

"No. No, no, no...Adam!"

He mouthed, "I forgive you," as he dropped. He broke on the shore. Water splashed from the impact.

Her hands covered her mouth, muffling her screams. The sea was briefly tainted red, but the current swept the colour away. Snow fell more heavily, and so did her tears.

Minutes passed as she stood looking at the water.

Flashbacks of everyone she had lost flooded her brain. Her whole body was on fire. Her skin felt too tight. Her lungs rusted from the lack of oxygen. Her muscles were numb. Her heart ached like it had been stabbed a million times.

Alex fell to her knees. She hadn't felt like this in years. She'd failed to protect him. And Feola. She failed to protect her people. Again.

She would never hear his laugh or embrace him again, and a scream escaped her mouth. No more monthly coffee meetings. No more Adam. No more home.

She'd lost Adam, and she'd never told him how much he meant to her. Her shoulders violently shook as the scene of his death kept replaying in her head. Alex had failed again.

"I-I'm so sorry. I am so sorry, Adam," she muttered through her sobbing.

Resisting the urge to jump after him, Alex covered her face with her hand. All the energy seeped out of her body. If she knew what was going to happen, she wouldn't have come to the fortress today. But how could she not?

Adam was gone, and she didn't know what to do, didn't even know what the time was. Looking around, the small black box caught her eye. Too spent to stand, she crawled to it. Her body ached everywhere as she held it with shaky hands.

When she opened the card box, there was a silver necklace and a note. The necklace had a key dangling from it. What was that?

Alex unfolded the handwritten letter and began reading.

I left you a gift at home. Our home, Paraptra Village. Something that will make a real difference to you.

I know you can do it, Alexandra. I believe in you.

Love,

Adam.

She threw the box on the floor, tears falling on the note. "Coward!"

Her voice echoed back at her, thin and hollow in the night air. There was no answer. Just the box. Just the key. Just her.

Some part of her was still screaming. The rest had already gone quiet. She wiped her face with a trembling hand and picked up the box. With shaking fingers, she slipped the cold metal necklace over her head.

Adam had left this for her. She would keep it safe. Until she figured out how to use it.

She dried the letter with her sleeve and slid it into her pocket. He always believed in her more than she deserved.

Alex didn't know how long she'd stayed up there until

the first rays of sun hit her eyes. Glaring at the sky, the dawn's light felt like an insult. A new day, beginning in a world that no longer had Adam in it.

Alex clutched the necklace and key, feeling the weight of it against her chest. Adam was gone, but the fight wasn't. She grabbed one of the scaffolding ropes and began the long descent. She would carry on. Not for herself, not even for the people. But for him. For the boy who couldn't survive in this messed-up world.

THE END

BIO: Malak is an emerging Egyptian writer who balances her passion for YA fantasy with her studies in medical school. She loves exploring themes of found family, fate, and a little bit of tragedy. She joined Fantasy Writers Org in March 2024 to connect with talented writers and grow her craft.

CHAPTER 13
SOUL MUSIC
THE REWARD

by

Suzanne Driggs

Gliding on the wind currents, the three flyers scanned for the energy signature of the yellow Thera venting out of the fissures below. Flying through the energy column would kill the giant raptor and its rider even at this height.

Zasi eh Bru'u sensed rather than saw movement in the endless beige and windblown scrub, making a trail where it shouldn't be. They curved around and signaled for Setic eh Falu'u's and Jsta eh Cestu'u to spread out so that they came back to the place, lower this time. The disturbance in the sand led toward the main vent.

Walkers, even powerful Thera Masters, avoided the Yellow Wasteland. Jasi squinted hard and urged Bru'u to

215

use his binocular vision as well. The figure that emerged gave off two life vibrations.

Zasi eh Bru'u calculated a route to land out of the way of the deadly energy.

"*Looks like two beings,*" Jasi said to the others in mind-speak.

"*Cloaked,*" Setic agreed. "*You think Szatto a thief?*"

"*No, too much work. They rather steal energy from children,*" Jsta added.

"*There are some healing plants out here,*" Zasi paused, "*The Herbal Master?*"

"WE'LL REST HERE."

Telfrombry heard the soft scratchy voice in his head, louder than his ears, amid the hot wind whipping around them. He lowered the energy keeping the travois above the broken landscape to rest on the ground. Baladre - Herbalist, Yellow Master, and his mentor for many years, lay still as death, his dwindling life force pulsing close to his body.

"*I can feel the vent,*" Baladre thought to him. Telfrombry leaned down and dripped some water and tonic into the ancient's mouth.

A streaky image of the windswept landscape, sparse scrub, and sand-blasted boulders formed before him. As he watched, the focus moved to the horizon with the shadow of the mountains in the distance. The vision morphed into a field of deadly columns of Yellow Thera.

His normal sight returned; Tel looked for the mountain line marking the yellow energy that would carry his mentor to the source.

"*I remember when you were born. Even then, your aura was*

a strong sky blue, not ordinary blue." Baladre's mind often cycled on their story when he acknowledged Tel "hearing," his thought talk. *"I knew the cult would hunt for you as soon as word went out. So tiny, and yet you understood when I showed you how to hide base force."*

The early connection with the Yellow Master shielded Tel from the cult. Untrained Therans caused havoc with the energy. The Color Masters determined it would be safer for everyone to take the children to the Demian mountain stronghold and train them to control their power. Theran children as unusual and gifted as Tel fell victim to the energy thieves.

Tel smiled at the memory of the excitement of seeing the herbalist walk up the road with his bulging backpack. In Telfrombry's twelfth year, Baladre took him as his apprentice. To further mask Tel's energy, the Yellow Master changed his appearance, dressing him in the peddler's combination of cloth and skins, and darkening his long white hair. A travel hat shadowed the boy's pale blue eyes.

They roamed the world following the seasons, collecting rare and wonderful plants and cures. His mentor taught him the power of blue first. As an exceptionally gifted Theran, Tel had mastered all the colors in the ten years since.

"We should go. Someone is following."

Startled, Tel jerked the travois to lift it and flooded Baladre with green energy to soothe Baladre's failing back and joints.

In mind-speak, Baladre protested. "You should save that energy for yourself."

The power of yellow strengthened as they moved closer. Relieved of the uncertainty of the vent's location, Tel's thoughts drifted back to the warnings and fears they encountered in the villages. The villagers scrutinized them with wariness, instead of the anticipation of the past.

The many shades of blue allowed Tel to hear thoughts and see images. With his mentor's guidance, he learned to navigate the complex desires and fears of those around him. The ability to know his energy separate from others proved to be the most powerful tool.

They avoided the Melian color masters and their search for untrained Therans. The exceptions were the few trusted friends. Rumors grew of the Red Master Szatto. She discovered a way to transfer energy from the children to herself. Not only did the stolen color energy strengthen her own, but it also revitalized her, giving the appearance of youth and beauty. Color masters flocked to the mountain to learn her secrets. Her price, complete loyalty. Thus began the Cult of Szatto.

∧*∧

"A walker," chirped Bru'u, Zasi's winged mount, whose keen eyesight confirmed the images. They banked and began the dive to investigate the non-flyer.

THE WIND SHIFTED as if blocked, then returned full force.

Something was coming. Telfrombry stopped and moved the energy to form an invisible protection around himself and Baladre. His heart thumped the seconds in the wait. Then in the sky over the route they had taken, growing larger, the shapes resolved into three flyers. The clans of bonded pairs of Theran and birds of prey were common in the highland mountains far in the distance.

They came on, heading right for them. Tel rechecked the protection energies. They seemed intact. The first giant

218

avian swooped toward them then back winged, stirring a cloud of dust. Tel realized too late; that the sand would coat their protection, making them visible.

Back from the first, the others landed, causing a surge of sand to envelop them. The lead shook the sand from its feathers and shrieked. Turning to them, it curled its great yellow head down to inspect Telfrombry from one eye and then the other. While he and Baladre had traded with several flyer clans, these were unfamiliar.

"Skreee, sahh jeb'bg?" What is your business? The rider demanded from his perch high above them.

Before he could answer, Baladre spoke, barely audible, "Zasi eh Bru'u. Sheee sabb'a Thera jisst."

At this, the flyer trilled, and its mount extended a huge, silver, and dust-feathered wing. He leaped from his seat to slide down the slope into a crouch that unfolded to a tall, thin frame wrapped in leather. The elongated head bent to inspect Telfrombry's face and energy up close. A yellow feather-covered skull cap helmet mimicked the avion's markings. A long, curved nose dominated the features with dark, black-brown eyes blinking away the dust.

He leaned close to Tel's ear and said, "Who are you to the Yellow Master?"

Wide-eyed Tel answered with his lips ruffling the feathered cap, "Apprentice."

Eyeing him skeptically, the flyer demanded, "Do you know the Yellow song?"

"*He knows all the songs.*" Baladre's thought voice intervened. "*Why are you here?*"

The lanky flyer melted to his knees beside the old man. "We need you!" At the panic in his voice, the giant avian let out a high-pitched SCREEE.

"*Stop that!*" Baladre scolded the beast. "*Telfrombry will help you now. It is my time to join the source. You must sing and gain strength with my blessing."*

Tel gauged the intensity of the flyer's aura. His yellow had matched the streaming energy surrounding them. "Can you sing yellow?"

"Yes, and the others." Zasi tilted his head to the two flyers behind him.

Tel nodded and turned to move Baladre through a maze of small dangerous cracks streaming yellow Thera energy. The hum of yellow grew louder as they approached the primary vent. Keeping the travois levitated was easy with the yellow energy. The danger came from the Thera vaporizing anything straying in the path of a crack.

They found an area on the edge of the main vent large enough for Tel to lift Baladre naked from the litter and set him on his feet at the rim with his back to the energy column. The hum surrounded them. The flyers stood facing the ancient color master and began the yellow chant, matching the hum.

Baladre's ecstatic face turned to Telfrombry, the pain and sorrow gone. Tel joined the yellow song and felt the joy enter his heart when he released his hold, letting Baladre drift backward, transforming into the yellow energy.

Standing there, Telfrombry realized it was the first time he felt true happiness without fear.

∧*∧

Zasi regarded the apprentice. His aura moved like a non-Theran's now that the chant was done. It occurred to him that Baladre would have only taken a strong Theran as an apprentice, teaching him to hide his power as he had the flyer Therans. Standing near the yellow vent, they all would appear yellow.

Not knowing any other options except to trust Baladre's

wisdom, Zasi explained, "The Szatto's converts raided the flyer caves looking for Theran children." Sending images of the caves hidden in the high mountains.

"They have used up all the walker children!" The flyer called Jsta burst in with images of pale, frightened children taken from the settlements.

"Will you help?" Zasi pleaded.

TELFROMBRY NODDED ONCE and bent to the travois to pull out the herbalist's backpack. Standing up, he let his natural sky-blue aura flash, implanting his energy connection. The flyers blinked and relaxed.

"*You will know when I am sending thought-talk. We will not meet again.*" With that, he slid the travois into the vent and slung the bulging pack onto his back as if it were empty. As they walked to the waiting avians, Tel pushed the wind to blow away the signs that they had been there.

Zasi climbed Bru'u's wing to the seat on top of the harness. He tried to parse the ancient Yellow Master's answer to their plea. As uncertainty grew, the sky-blue energy washed it away, leaving a new calm. He settled into the harness leg straps and glanced below at the lone figure walking across the wasteland.

WHILE WATCHING the flyers circle above and turn to the mountains, Tel set his protection energy to render himself invisible. He gathered the yellow energy to lift him above the sand and rocks. The wind cooled his face even as it blew away the flyers' and his tracks. He glided along the dry stream bed, heading for the Rift and the next step in Baladre's plan.

Until today, the bliss of joining the Thera had been stories told in the firelight. The image of the Yellow Master diffusing into the yellow energy stream, his face filled with ecstasy, left an emptiness, though Tel could still feel his mentor's joy in his heart. Would that be enough?

The years they traveled building energy threads to connect them to the Therans of the world vibrated with the growing threat that the Red Master, Szatto, trained by the Melian Color Masters, gained knowledge of energy transfer. Luckily, there were no rumors of Baladre's work to end it.

Szatto, like all the trainee Therans whose base energy vibrated at red, arrived at the Red Rift in the belief that being close to the Vent would provide all the power she needed. She, with a long line of others who dreamed of controlling the pure red energy, found disappointment. The vents call the energy back to Thera.

The rare and exceedingly valuable Thera stones, collected from the beaches of islands near underwater vents, enhanced the energy when needed. The sand-sized granules of red, orange, yellow, green, blue, indigo, and violet provided limitless power when combined just right.

Trapped by her obsession for more energy, Szatto seduced the leading masters and when she had beggared their coffers buying Thera stones, she convinced them that draining the Theran children before they could resist was best for all. As time passed, she, and the Master's in her thrall, needed more.

For generations, Szatto and her followers controlled the dreams and beliefs of the villagers of the Red Rift. The surrounding villages under her influence believed that their

Theran children were serving a noble cause and learning the secrets of Thera.

Tel followed the creek to the beginnings of the mountain. The low, spiny plants gave way to bushes and straggly trees. He moved on, following the course to the foothills.

∧*∧

Zasi and the other flyers dreamed in the sky-blue vibration. When they woke, they knew how to communicate with each other and how to hide their Theran vibration. They travelled between the flyer clans connecting the Therans they met to Tel's vibration.

FOR THE PLAN TO WORK, they needed the rare Thera stones. Baladre and Telfrombry sailed the seas scouring the beaches for enough of the stones to make an energy that, when released, would erase the control of Szatto and her minions. They never found the colors together or mixed on the beach. To create the right balance of energy, the stones needed to be in a precise combination held together in a ball of clay. It took several years to gather all the ingredients.

Baladre established their base in a hidden cave on the edge of the Red Rift, large enough for them to store their herbs and treasure, and protected by a careful arrangement of Thera stones.

Tel stood alone at the cave mouth. Not having Baladre's presence physically, and in his head, accentuated the emptiness. He modulated his vibration and moved the blue stone out of alignment to open the energy gate blocking the entrance. On the other side, he replaced it, sealing himself in. The forest sounds dimmed as he glided deeper inside. His rustling passage echoed off the stone roof and walls.

∧*∧

The dreams always started with a sky-blue border. Zasi eh Bru'u circled over the forest, searching for the tree in the dream. Bru'u chirped and dived, snatching the bulky pack from the treetop.

THE ENERGY-DISRUPTING balls were now distributed to the flyer clans, Theran-trained villagers, and Thera Masters who would align the balls in the designated patterns. The plan didn't rely on one call to battle. Instead, the vibration of the high noon sun would activate the hundreds of balls.

Telfrombry stood on the ridge above Red Rift Keep. Built to protect the Red Vent, granite walls surrounded it on three sides. On the ocean side, a towering cathedral served as a watchtower and lighthouse. In his mind, he could see hundreds of candle-like glimmers waiting.

To Tel's mind, Baladre had always been old. He shared his knowledge of plants and minerals and drilled the uses of Thera in its myriad hues. When Tel first apprenticed, the herbalist climbed the trees and scaled the cliffs for the leaves, barks, and roots with him. As the years passed, Tel took the high places. The Yellow Master searched out the moss and fungus.

They were searching for a rare moss growing on the edge of a steep riverbank just four moons ago. Baladre lost his footing and tumbled to the bottom of the gulch. Broken and bruised, it began his decline. He let Tel ply him with tonics that should speed healing, but he refused to use the Thera stones that surely could have saved him for a time.

224

∧*∧

Zasi eh Bru'u landed on the tower facing the vent. Cloaked in invisible energy, watching. The birds chirped and insects hummed. He could sense the vibration of people in the keep, but the walkway to the vent was empty.

T‌EL NEEDED to cloak himself to be undetectable to reach the Keep doors to the vent. The sun was climbing high when he dropped to the side of the wall. This part of the plan called for a different mix of energy. Activating it would be up to him. He could sense the sun's vibration releasing the disruption energy throughout the Rift. He lifted himself to wait above the Keep doors.

The rumble of voices and fearful energy vibrated through the keep, coming closer. Szatto would come to the vent to escape and regroup. The clay balls set around the keep would disorient her and send her to the source of Thera.

The doors burst open.

∧*∧

The healer's song drifted out from the cave opening in long, full tones. Still wearing his flying leathers, Zasi eh Bru'u crouched on the rim of the entrance to the healer hall. He gazed out at the clouds obscuring the lower mountains, plains, estuaries, and finally the sea on the horizon.

He breathed in and out, letting the tone vibrations fill his chest. Behind him, his lifemate Bru'u fluffed and preened restlessly. The wave of energy surging through the rift still played across Zasi's inner vision, the clouds surrounding the mountaintop a background to his memories.

The plan worked.

Telfrombry, the sky-blue master, who could read your mind and talk in your head, taught them. He brought the secret of the energy balls. Zasi inhaled with pride. The Szatto realized the trap too late. The exaltation of success brought him back to the cave and the song that would save Telfrombry.

The Szatto had cast a disruption charge that launched Tel off the edge of the wall fully visible, his sky-blue aura incandescent. Zasi eh Bru'u swept in, catching the Blue Master before he landed, or worse in the vent, and brought him to the flyer clan home.

Zasi shifted to lean against the carved stone base of the cave mouth. The ancient guardians, both flyers and life-mates gazed down with warning expressions: their sharp features shifting with the movement of the sun.

Turning to peer into the dim cavern, Zasi could see the Thera energy glowing around the healer. It swirled and bloomed with her movements. The clear rise and fall of her healing song vibrated through every part of him as he watched.

Telfrombry, Blue Master, had earned the friendship of Zasi eh Bru'u and all flyer clans by destroying the Szatto.

The toning stopped. Zasi lurched to his feet. Bru'u chirped as he rushed to Telfrombry's side.

~♪~

Alis eh Zpo'o, the healer, turned to him. "He is not dead yet. Soon, we fear." Her voice came slow and tired, as did the play of colors that surrounded her. Other flyers gathered to hear the news.

"What more can we do?" Zasi asked, as much to Alis as to the stone-carved guardians.

"I know of a powerful singer. She lives on the mountain

island of the Warm Sea Clan. She knows the power there and has been teaching them." Alis rubbed her chin a moment considering, then continued, "It is a long way and no resting places. This walker is heavier than most flyers and Bru'u would have to carry you both."

"No," a listening flyer stepped forward, "We can put him in a carrier and trade-off during the journey. We are Faly eh Jud'I and we will show you the way."

∧*∧

Zasi eh Bru'u swept high above an endless sea. Telfrombry tied in a rough sling, rocked in Bru'u's massive talons. Faly eh Jud'i led the way on the trackless journey.

The sea colors below changed from green to blue. The wind flowing across his face became warmer. Tel, whose blue aura flickered and wavered, remained motionless in the flyer carrier, unaffected during the periodic exchange between the avians.

Faly eh Jud'i carried the color master when the speck of mountaintop first appeared. Gliding down around the mountainous island, he led the way, not to the clan home near the peaks, but to the shore.

As they dropped closer to the water, so clear that the reefs and swimmers were visible, Zasi felt a stomach-rumbling hunger. He squeezed his knees against Bru'u's neck feathers and clicked and chirped patience.

Faly eh Jud'i settled the carrier gently on the beach and then stroked the air with their large wings to lift and land in an open area. Zasi eh Bru'u landed nearby. Zasi slid down a canted wing, launching himself toward the patient. Faly tugged at Zasi's leathers, bringing him to a sudden stop.

"The Melian Master showed us this place. She kept us safe from Szatto. She only asks that we not eat the Mer." He nodded toward the shore where the large creatures, swimmers who walked on land, lounged with their young. Their bright orange vibration radiated calm and happiness.

"Bru'u can eat any of the swimmers except the Mer. There is plenty of land game." Faly's tone stressed the warning. Zasi nodded and sent the message to his lifemate. The raptors launched into the sky and curved over the bay to glide up the valley.

A GENTLE CHIME sprinkled across the air. A lush fragrance invited deep breaths. Gradually, Telfrombry noticed the song calling him awake. He blinked, but the world stayed dark. The song grew stronger. This was not where he remembered. He had been unmaking the Thera bindings used by the Szatto in the high mountains.

The song filled his thoughts and made him restless. He took a breath and shifted position.

"Yes!" Telfrombry recognized Zasi's piping voice. "He's waking up!"

This time, when he tried opening his eyes, light flooded in. The surrounding shapes swam in his vision, blurred, the colors of their energy mixed with the colors of their clothing. The song continued, ebbing and flowing.

"Where am I?"

"You are here!" Zasi's voice answered happily.

"Oh," Telfrombry wondered for a moment if Zasi had read his mind, then realized he must have spoken aloud. "Zasi, where is here?"

"You are at the home of Rashia, Melian Master. She lives at the foot of the Mountain in the Warm Sea."

"Melian?" Telfrombry whispered.

THE SONG WOVE ON. The chimes brought him back. He realized he was helpless. He still had arms and legs, but they would not respond to his conscious commands, jerking and thrashing on their own. Unfamiliar sounds came to his notice, birds, an insect chittering, the flyers' light voices, and their partner's squawks and shrieking calls. He could hear a low roar below it all. The sea, he realized, or rather the waves. Then, he remembered, Zasi had said, Melian!

With the chimes came the memory of the deadly Szatto, the transformed and corrupted Melian Order.

He struggled to understand why he was being held. He willed himself to get to his feet, yet the chimes would return, and he looked up to the ceiling of what looked like a grass house, glimpsed Zasi, then fell into the song drifting...

Sometime later, Telfrombry pondered his fate. How long had he been here? Zasi told him when he asked, but seemed to think that he'd asked before.

Visions terrified him, and then the song would surface and soothe his fears.

∧*∧

Zasi crouched beside Tel. He could see the color master's energy ebb. The normally strong blue appeared shattered and scattered. Bits and pieces of colors swirled with a sluggishness that Zasi feared foretold Telfrombry's death.

Faly's touch brought his attention to the edge of the sandy beach. Along the border, lush vines and flowering trees appeared limned with a golden light. The light floated closer and finally emerged as a golden ball. Zasi blinked, trying to make sense of the apparition. The ball of light settled beside Tel. It coalesced and resolved into a small walker child. The golden glow persisted in a corona surrounding her pale hair. Bare arms shone with a deeper, sun-darkened hue. A pale sky-colored shift covered her to her knees. Up close, she was not yet as tall as the flyers. With her soft features, pale blue eyes, and a long braid down her back, she would never be mistaken as a flyer child.

~∞~

Rashia studied the man on the litter. He was young, a warrior by his attire, though slighter than she would expect. Long white hair braided in the Askkraan style, with beads of many types woven through, almost like a helmet.

A color master, the flyers claimed, a hero. She watched as he tossed about, coming in and out of consciousness. When he opened his eyes, their dark, metal gray flashed, trying desperately to make sense of the scene around him. A damaged hero, she decided.

"Will he live?" the flyer called Zasi asked. The man looked toward them, wide-eyed but not comprehending what he saw.

"Yes, but he needs more help," Rashia answered.

"What can we do?"

"We need to place him at a vent with a sound chamber around him." Reaching out to the man, Rashia pushed on his forehead and commanded, "Sleep." He settled in a limp heap.

Turning to the flyers clustered at her back, "Faly eh Jud'i!" At the command, the flyer detached himself and dropped his head in service. "Take a party to the vent at the cave above the spire. Clear the cave of anything that will block the music." She motioned, materializing a woven litter she thrust toward the flyer. "Here, hang this in the dome. I will bring your friend."

TELFROMBRY HUNG motionless in the sling next to the vent. The pulsing power rushed out of a crack in the cavern floor. The Melian Master stood before the vent in her child form. Six flyers, with Thera sight, took positions in a circle around Telfrombry. Zasi jumped into place. The Master took the seventh point at Telfrombry's head. The flyers waited silently.

The first tone began softly. A deep red sound vibrated the floor of the cave. The colors issuing from the vent shimmered, changing from the spectrum to only red. As it filled in, the tone grew, vibrating from the walls and stone overhead. Once the energy covered Telfrombry, the room filled with the sound and a deep red glow. The girl began the healing chant. The circle of flyers matched the song, directing their voices toward the suspended figure.

Their voices moved the energy coming from the vent like a breeze on smoke. The energy flowed from the seven singers to direct the vent energy around Telfrombry. The broken splintered colors spilled out of him, consumed by the vent.

∧*∧

Zasi felt the living mother Thera in the crimson power. He felt his body and was aware of the blood coursing through his heart. He felt his place in the world. The song slowly ended, and a new tone began starting quietly and building.

This time, the vent turned orange. Zasi waited eagerly for the Melian Master to begin the chant. The Orange power showed him the connection to his clan and the clan brothers of the Mountain in the Warm Sea.

The yellow power taught the meaning of freedom. Zasi found ecstasy in the vibration of pure creativity. The green power forgave Zasi and filled him with forgiveness, kindness, and bravery. The Blue power glowed brighter because it was Tel's natural vibration. Zasi marveled at the certainty the blue power brought, the strength it gave to speak and live the truth.

The darker blue was almost invisible in the dark cavern, its power subtle and profound. This was a distance from the physicality of the red vibration. The patterns of the other powers were apparent, making their directions known both from the past and the future. The dark blue frightened Zasi and he was glad as the song ended.

The last tone was the highest and closest to the flyer's songs. The violet power flooded the vent and the flyers gladly lent their voices to the song. They belonged to Thera in this vibration, becoming the joyous ebb and flow of pure energy. Zasi hoped the song would never end and only gradually realized the Melian Master and Telfrombry were gone as the song finished.

TELFROMBRY STOOD ON A NARROW TRAIL. A dappled green light surrounded him. Endless towering trees bordered the trail, hiding its destination. Corded vines covered the tree trunks. The vines' broad leaves filled the under canopy. Flowers of radiant colors vibrated in the green walls around him. The soil on the path peeked through here and there, a rust color marking the trail.

This could be a dream, he thought. Not sure of his

purpose, he stepped down the path. Large iridescent floaters drifted across his way. Gliding down, their blue, pink, and green wings spanned a hand's breadth each, then they would pump their way back up to the roof of the forest. Whistles punctuated an insect buzzing stillness, then chirps and thrumming. The warm air, rich with jungle smells and fragrances, felt heavy. Soon, the battle leathers he still wore were wet with his sweat.

Maybe not a dream. He reconsidered as the trail circled a tree with mammoth roots. A golden glow shimmered through the foliage at the far end of the path.

The Melian Master! A tingle of fear came with the sudden realization. The glow ahead intensified. He reached the last bend in the path. The sun was lifting from the sea. He let out a breath so he could take another.

He lay there empty after the battle with Szatto. If this Melian wanted revenge, he had nothing to argue with. He hoped Zasi had escaped. The flyer had sounded so hopeful. The trail stopped at a sandy cove. Dense trees leaned over a half circle carved out of black stone. The stone walls curved perfectly. White sand covered the bottom of the grotto. The sun was still low, highlighting a low flat stone in the center and the child sitting on its edge. Telfrombry watched the small girl for a long time. She wore a shift of blue or green, depending on her movements. Her curly, unruly mass of hair now formed a thick, tawny braid down her back. Instinctively, he looked for her base color and could only see a golden hue.

Before her were seven piles of Thera stones. She examined them in the sunlight, setting out some from each section. Suddenly, she looked up at him, her small soft face glowing in the morning light. Telfrombry chewed his bottom lip as he geared up the courage to step down into the sand. He came slowly, and she went back to her gems. Finally, he reached the center platform stone. At his feet, he noticed a small leather pouch with the bottom flattened to open the mouth. Carefully, Telfrombry lowered himself to his knees on the stone. He felt somewhat foolish to have so much distrust of the small, golden child before him. She looked up into his eyes. Clear blue light shone from her gaze.

She selected a red stone and held it out to him. "You are well enough to return." The statement delivered in a child's voice stressed the power he could sense. With some resignation, he held his hand out and she set the stone in his palm. It appeared as a large bead of fresh blood.

"You need not feel guilt for killing Szatto. She is even now awaiting her return." She held his gaze as she spoke. Gently, she reached her hand out to his and took the stone, placing it in the bag. She studied her selection of the fiery orange stones. Settling on one, she set it in his palm.

"The Melian remember one another?" he asked.

"We are all related in the Melian Order. We dreamed of bringing the joy of Thera to Demia. Szatto is my sister."

"I, I'm sorry," he stammered.

"We were proud old women, gifted, with the sight. We believed we knew all the secrets of Thera then." She looked away in contemplation. "The first few lives taught us we could learn more. Eventually, master all the colors."

The orange stone glowed and seemed to throb in his hand. He looked up, startled when she took it and dropped it in the bag. A clear chime rang from the stones colliding. She smiled up at him and for a moment, Telfrombry believed he saw his daughter not yet born.

The yellow stone shone bright in the sunlight. It seemed a chip of the sun itself. Telfrombry studied the stone intently. The girl's voice just carried over the breaking waves beyond the alcove.

"You know the powers of all the colors. To master them, you must use them. To use them, you must return. You have a little time. Your disrupters have scrambled my sister's eternal memories. It may take lifetimes for her to return. You are already more powerful than she will be. By then you will have taught the Therans to resist."

Telfrombry looked up. "More powerful?"

"She grew angry and afraid when it became certain that our condition would never change. We found the first three colors the easiest to master. To move further, we need to forgive. Instead, she punishes everything and everyone."

The yellow stone chimed its entrance to the bag. The Melian Master held out the green stone. He watched her as she placed it in his palm. Before she could pull away, he closed his fingers around her hand and looked into her sky-colored eyes.

Holding her gently, he asked, "Were you my mother?"

The child's eyes widened. Then she gave him a broad smile. "Your mother was brave. I could be an aunt of sorts. Like her, green is my natural vibration."

He let her take the stone and drop it into the bag.

The blue stone felt as if it belonged. He smiled at its perfection.

"Killing Szatto only gives you some time to find her before she can destroy again. She will need to be contained. Until then, you will teach the world."

He nodded and dropped the stone into the pouch.

Telfrombry raised his palm for a closer look at the cobalt stone. It seemed to absorb the light, drawing his attention to its depths. The future appeared in his mind's eye. Not a single path, but a knowingness of countless probabilities. Despair clouded the vision. The lightest touch drew him out of the stone.

"Always remember, you are not alone." The child spoke as much in his head as aloud.

Hastily, he dropped the stone in the pouch.

The violet stone felt welcoming. He raised his eyes to the little girl and asked, "There was music. I remember, but I don't hear it now?"

The blue gaze softened. "When the spirit is about to leave the body and join Thera, you hear the music of your soul. Maybe by hearing who you are, you take that knowledge with you into the Thera. While you are in your body, the music is you," she explained, her eyes turned sad.

"You have never heard the music?" he wondered.

"That was the cost of following Szatto." She took the violet gem and dropped it in the bag. The girl climbed to her feet. Stepping over the small piles of gemstones, she stood before him, eye to eye. She continued.

"Where to send you?" she paused, after a contemplative nod, decreed, "I think back to the Askkraan Mountain flyer clan." She knelt and lifted the pouch. Drawing it closed with the leather straps, she handed it to Telfrombry.

With a last smile, she held out her hand.

Telfrombry blinked at the dark opening beyond the wind-swept ledge of the Askkraan Mountain flyer's nesting cave.

Bru'u screeched, flapping dust and feathers. Once settled, Zasi slid down his lifemate's wing.

Bowing to Tel, "Are you ready?"

"Cliick zat up um klaitt. Thank you for all your help," Tel answered. He nodded to the full herb bag secured to the harness. His bond with Zasi gave him Bru'u's trust and he crouched so that Tel could climb up to the seat. He tied down the straps across his thighs. He thought the image of the place Bru'u would take him: A tall green forest on the slope of the red-Rift valley.

His home was on the road, trading his herbs and cures. Once landed, he released the straps and ties so that he could slide down the extended wing. He stood before the hooked beak as it lowered to let him lean his forehead against the raptor's head, flowing his love and gratitude for a long moment. Then he stepped back so that Bru'u could launch up and away.

The rustle of the wind and the chirps and clicks of the forest filled his heart with green Thera.

There was still so much to learn to keep Demia safe.

THE END

BIO: Suzanne lives in Hawaii with her husband. When she's not mind-surfing paradise, she's close to finishing her book about a surfer encountering PTSD for his war experiences and dealing with his emerging psychic powers. She's been a member of Fantasy-Writers.org for sixteen and a half years.

CHAPTER 14
IT WAITS FOR US ALL
THE REWARD

by

Owen A. Wilkie

Jastin cast a wistful glance over his shoulder. The cosy hamlet, with its thatched cottages and well-tended gardens, slipped behind a rise in the road and was gone. The last tendrils of chimney smoke merged with the leaden sky. The ghost of fresh-baked morning loaves haunted his nose, lingering in the damp air. His belly rumbled in protest. A mist of fine rain soaked through his faded green cloak and stuck the brown curls of his hair to his scalp. He called ahead to his master, raising his voice above the sucking mud that pulled at the hooves of the knight's horse, "I still think we should have asked for directions, sir."

"Nonsense, boy," growled Sir Orin. "I consulted a map

before we left. South! There is no need to bother the peasants. My kingdom awaits."

"I'd rather be a dry peasant than a wet squire," muttered Jastin. "Besides, s'only half a kingdom."

The knight's ears were sharp despite the rain and his advanced years. "Tell me, boy, what do you call half a hole?"

Jastin scrunched his nose and pondered. He was fifteen summers old, or so he reckoned. Sir Orin had taught him his letters and numbers in the years he had been the old knight's squire. He considered himself to have a fine education. They had travelled together through many kingdoms, had many adventures, and the lands of his birth were now just names on a map. "I guess," Jastin said, drawing to a conclusion, "it's still a hole. Only smaller?"

"Correct," said Sir Orin. He gripped his saddle horn in a gauntleted fist and turned to regard Jastin with an arched look. The knight's lank, grey hair framed his weathered face. The ends of his moustache hung past his chin like twin spear points, and his small, dark eyes sparked with amusement. A large raindrop clung stubbornly to the tip of his hooked nose. "So, half a kingdom is ...?"

"A long, damp march away, sir?" said Jastin.

The knight frowned and turned, though his shoulders shook with silent mirth.

"Does this mean I'll have to call you 'Your Majesty' after you marry the princess?"

"Princess Tahamina is a bare handful of years older than you, boy. There won't be a wedding for a good few years. Until then, there are laws to form and taxes to levy. There'll be plenty of time for titles once we've established ourselves. But, yes, I will eventually rule the lands and name myself king."

"Does that mean I'll be a prince?" Jastin asked, guiding their mule, Thistle, around a particularly deep rut in the road. The animal shook the rain from its chestnut coat, jangling the pots and pans, and rattling Sir Orin's oilcloth-wrapped armour.

Sir Orin gave a bark of laughter. "You say the damnedest things, boy. I bought you from your mother with good silver. I didn't sire you. I could appoint you as court jester?" He turned and gave a smile at the scowl on Jastin's face. "No? How about general of my armies then? Your sword-work has been coming along."

Jastin nodded, somewhat mollified, and said, "Good enough. How will we know when we reach the southern kingdom, sir?"

"The maps I studied were old. But Princess Tahamina's father marked the boundary of her dowry. We ride south, through hill country, past the forest of Kaliana to the banks of the River Losse. And there, boy, there!" The knight spread one arm wide before him, as if conjuring a vista in the air. "Miles of good, arable land, crossed by wide rivers said to be teeming with golden trout, all the way to the coast of the Shining Sea."

"It sounds like a place to call home, sir."

"That it does, boy. That it does."

"I hope there are no more dragons to fight, sir," said Jastin. "The last one would have had us, if it hadn't been for Boku."

"Nonsense. I would have got the better of that blue wyrm eventually. Though, I won't deny, Boku's support was timely." Sir Orin reigned in his dappled warhorse, Hammer. He cast his gaze through the thick woods to either side of the road. "Where has the great beast run off to? Give her a whistle, boy. We wouldn't want her bothering the peasant's livestock."

Jastin pulled aside his neck-wrap and fished beneath his liveried tunic for the silver cylinder. He blew three short blasts, though no sound he could hear issued forth.

Within moments, the sound of snapping brush in the distance gave away Boku's position. A pair of long-tailed birds flushed up into the air, their scarlet and green plumage bright against the dark trunks of the forest. The dogwoods and bracken of the undergrowth shook wildly. Boku, the great dragonhound that had accompanied Sir Orin and Jastin on their adventures, arrowed towards them, ploughing through the sodden vegetation and sending up an explosion of rainwater. The broad wedge of her russet head burst through the foliage, a hare hanging limp from her powerful jaws. She loped through the mud to Jastin's side and dropped her kill at the squire's feet.

"Good girl," said Jastin running a hand over the drag-onhound's red bristles and stubby ears. The folds of Boku's loose skin were stuck with thornweed and stickybuds. Jastin knew he would have to spend an hour brushing her down when they camped for the night. Thistle brayed in greeting. The dog and the mule were old friends, and of a similar size. Boku lolled her tongue in reply.

"That hare will do for our lunch, once you have skinned and dressed it," said Sir Orin. "Now, come. I mean for us to see the outskirts of Kaliana Forest before we make camp for the night."

As morning passed into afternoon, the drizzle abated, and a strong, northerly wind chased the clouds from the sky. The woodland ended abruptly at the lip of a wide canyon, and the fierce red sun beat down and dried the rain from their clothes. A treacherous road of loose gravel snaked its way to the canyon floor. Boku and the horses drank from the shallow stream that crawled through the ravine, and Jastin refilled their waterskins with cool, fresh water. The canyon's far side was strewn with moss-covered rocks and boulders that gave way to verdant hills and valleys. They stopped to rest the animals in the lee of a ruined crofter's house, set back from the road which was now little more than a weathered path of earth that tracked through the taller weeds. Jastin collected what kindling he could and set to dressing the hare, while Sir Orin lit a fire and unburdened Thistle of her load. The hare was stringy and tough. Jastin brewed a pot of tea, sweetened with honey from their supplies, and they dunked road bread in the fragrant brew to soften the hard, salty biscuits. After cleaning and packing their equipment, Jastin reloaded the baggage onto Thistle. Sir Orin busied himself, grooming and resaddling Hammer and, when all was stowed and ready, they resumed their journey.

"Shouldn't it have a new name?" said Jastin.

Sir Orin stretched his back with a groan. "Boy, I am not privy to the thoughts rattling around that empty head of yours. Shouldn't what have a new name?"

"Your half of the kingdom, sir. What will people call it? It can't just be Southern Kingdom. That's boring."

"Well," Sir Orin mused, "I could name it after myself. How about Orinland? Orinia?"

Jastin pulled a face, but he caught the flash of a smile that quirked the knight's moustache and refused to be bated. "We could name it after Boku," he countered. The dragonhound huffed on hearing her name. "After all, if she hadn't bit the dragon's tail, you never would have had the opportunity to strike at its heart."

242

"I was saving Boku's name for the capital city," said Sir Orin with a laugh. "Jastinopolis will be where we send cheeky, young squires to learn how to better respect their elders."

They continued on through the hills, inventing names that grew ever more ridiculous, as the blue sky went from cerulean to marine and finally darkened to a hazy, indigo hue. Small, white flowers carpeted the land that tumbled away before them. Scattered flocks of sheep roamed the eastern slopes under the watchful eye of a lone shepherd. Jastin raised an arm in salute, but the far-off figure returned no greeting, and instead stood sentinel to their passing. A dark treeline in the distance stretched to the western horizon. Hammer's iron-shod hooves sent up an echoing clop from the ruins of an ancient road. It appeared suddenly from the grasses, its worn stones overgrown and cracked with age.

"Kaliana Forest, boy," said Sir Orin, shielding his eyes from the last rays of golden sunlight. "We'll make camp for the night in its shadow. And tomorrow we will cross the banks of the Losse to our new home."

"At least we'll have plenty of firewood, sir."

"That we will. Come, it will be good to get out of this saddle. Perhaps we can rustle up a stew and bake some apples in the fire, eh?"

Boku raced ahead of them through the long grass, sending up a cloud of butterflies; blue and copper wings filled the air. The crushed, white flowers left the scent of almonds in the dragonhound's wake.

Some recent storm had felled one of the wide-trunked oaks at the treeline. Sir Orin tethered Hammer to its branches. He removed the horse's saddle and set about brushing the animal down.

Jastin secured Thistle and removed her burden. In short-time he had a pit dug for the fire, his broad shoulders working the small shovel they carried with them through the turf with ease. Firewood lay in abundance. Soon Jastin had a stack big enough to last them the night, and he set about the business of coaxing a flame from the wood. When the fire was underway, he rose to fetch the pot for the stew.

The muted thrum of a bowstring came from the trees without warning. Death flew forth on black-fletched wings. Sir Orin staggered and gave a cry of pain. Three men burst from the treeline, each with a wild scream. They were dressed in little more than rags and mismatched armour. Their unkempt hair and beards were matted with filth, their skin streaked with dirt. Two of the men waved long knives above their heads, the blades chipped with hard use, while the third carried a wicked long-axe in both hands.

"My shield, boy!" roared Sir Orin. The old knight took up his sword from where it lay against the fallen tree. He raised it high, one hand on the hilt and the other gripping the blade still in its scabbard. Sir Orin blocked the overhead swing of his assailant's axe. Locking the blade with his own, he wrenched the snarling man sideways, stopping his accomplice from bringing his knife to bear.

Jastin pulled his master's kite shield from among the baggage. He turned to find the third man leering at him. This close, Jastin could smell the waves of sour sweat that rolled off the brigand. What few teeth the man had were brown and stained.

A second hiss flew from the trees.

Jastin grunted as the impact of an arrow nearly tore the shield from his grasp. The man before him stepped quick to strike with his knife, then disappeared screaming beneath Boku's weight, as the dragonhound leapt the fire and bore the brigand to the ground.

Sir Orin had freed his steel from his scabbard. His back was pressed to the trunk of the fallen oak. The shaft of an arrow protruded from his hip. Blood soaked through the tan cloth of his leggings. Sweat beaded his forehead. He flicked out with his scabbard, keeping the knife-man at bay, while he parried the thrusts and cuts of the other man's axe with his sword.

"Boku!" Jastin shouted, gripping the dragonhound's loose skin. He raised the shield, pointing to the treeline. "Bring down that archer. Fetch, Girl!"

The great hound shook the fallen brigand a final time and shot for the trees, punching a hole through the undergrowth.

Hammer strained at his tether and bucked, the scent of blood and clashing weapons agitating the war-trained horse. As the knife-man darted back from Sir Orin's tired swing, he passed behind the dappled horse. Hammer planted his forefeet, lowered his head, and lashed out. Iron-shod hooves caught the man in the arm and chest. The brigand spun away and collapsed, blade falling from nerveless fingers.

A high scream rose from the forest. Boku had found her prey. Jastin gave silent thanks and rounded the campfire, knowing better than to get too close to Hammer when the animal's temper was up. The axe-man was beating mercilessly down at Sir Orin's upraised sword. The old knight's face was pale with blood loss and pain. Jastin slammed the shield into the back of the brigand's legs, throwing him off balance. With a cry, Sir Orin drove his blade up through the man's chest. The last brigand crumpled to the ground and sprawled dead before the fire. Sir Orin collapsed back against the trunk of the fallen oak, breathing in short breaths through clenched teeth.

"Sir," said Jastin, coming to his master's side. The shaft of the arrow had snapped during the fight, and the knight's leggings were dark with blood. "Are you alright?"

"I've had worse," Sir Orin said, forcing a weak smile. "Fetch the kit from the baggage and get some water on to boil, boy. Did we get them all?" Jastin nodded. Boku padded from the forest and sat at her master's side. The drag-onhound gave a whine. Her muzzle was dark with blood. Sir Orin reached up to scratch her neck. "Good girl. Good girl."

"Where did they even come from?" said Jastin, as he dragged the bodies away from their camp and threw wood upon the fire. He busied himself collecting the kit of bandages and salves from the baggage, and set the cook pot on a hook above the flames.

Sir Orin groaned as he shifted his weight. "I suspect that shepherd we passed was their lookout. Must have signalled ahead somehow. It matters little now. Once we reach the border, we'll organise the locals into a militia to sweep the road and send word to Tahamina's father. King Merronjou should learn of this."

Once the pot was filled with water from their skins and had begun to steam, Jastin attended to his master's wound. He cut the cloth of Sir Orin's leggings and rolled the fabric away from the arrow shaft. The blood was dark and seeped steadily.

"We should leave this in, sir, until we find a settlement."

"Nonsense, lad. We're miles from the nearest village,"

said Sir Orin. "A field-dressing will have to do. I can't sit a horse with this sticking out of me. I've taught you your craft. Now be about it. Though I'd thank you for a skin of wine and a stick to bite on before you begin."

The arrow had lodged in the bone of the old knight's hip. Jastin tugged it free as sharply as he could, pressing boiled cloth to the wound to staunch the bleeding. Sir Orin bore the pain stoically, teeth champed around a wadded stick, knuckles white as they gripped the earth to steady himself. When the wound was cleaned and dressed, the old man sat propped near the fire. He took another pull from the wineskin and let out a sigh.

Boku sat away from the fire's edge, staring out into the night and keeping their watch, while Jastin fed Thistle and Hammer and tended to the pot of cured bacon, beans, and roots that simmered and sent up a fragrant cloud.

"Fetch me parchment and ink, lad," said Sir Orin. His voice was thick with wine, his eyes fixed on the incandescent sparks that rose into the dark sky.

"What, now?" said Jastin, stirring the pot to stop the stew from sticking to the bottom and burning. "There's barely light to see by."

"There's light enough, yet," said Sir Orin. The old knight gave a wracking cough and took another pull of wine. "I mean to write King Merronjou."

"But the brigands are dealt with, sir," said Jastin, gently. "You need your rest if we are to make it beyond the river lands, come tomorrow."

"I'll have my rest once I've written the damned letter, boy!" said Sir Orin with a sudden ferocity. "Now, bring me my quill."

Jastin scrabbled to his feet and searched among the baggage. He brought the writing materials to his master and propped up his back against Hammer's saddle. The old knight shooed away the offer of food, focusing intently on his missive through squinted eyes. Jastin ate his stew in silence. He rolled out his blankets by the fire, but not before spreading a thick woollen cover over his master's legs.

As soon as the first rays of morning caused him to shield his face from the glare of the new day, Jastin knew the old knight was gone. Heavy sobs heaved the squire's chest. He could scarce see for the tears that filmed his eyes as he crabbed to his master's side.

Boku whined and lifted her muzzle from the old knight's legs. Sir Orin's face was grey; his skin was cold. His sightless eyes stared up into the lightening sky. The knuckles of his hand stood white against the roll of yellowed parchment he clutched to his chest.

With a gentle hand, Jastin closed the eyes of the man who had been the closest thing to a father he had ever known. Through his tears, he read the words that proclaimed him son and heir, sealed with Sir Orin's signet in thick, red wax.

It was said King Jastin buried his old master under the boughs of Kaliana's broad trees. At his queen's insistence, it came to be known as Orinswood. Though, after generations of Jastin and Tahamina's children had sat the throne, its origin passed from all memory.

THE END

BIO: Owen is a British fantasy writer living in the northwest of England. He is rapidly approaching fifty, and he's not happy about it. When he is not writing, he can be found escaping reality in other ways, such as gaming, reading, or trying to entice the neighbourhood cats to come and live with him instead. He has tuna. Owen has been a member of Fantasy-Writers.org for a little over ten years.

CHAPTER 15

FISHED AND ORBED

THE ROAD BACK

by

Oruwari Ibiapuye Tom

Mt. Cameroon

I "Keep going," I said, pushing through the northerly winds of Mt. Cameroon, a blizzardy landscape of multiple snow-capped peaks, with a silvery orb in my hands. "Eylerion depends on you, Gracyn," I reminded myself, exhaling through the thin air as the cold seeped into my leather coat. Eylerion had handcrafted this gothic overcoat of a jacket, saying every archer needed a villainous cape to mask themselves.

I chuckled, and my shallow breath failed my body for a moment. My legs gave way, and I collapsed on the fresh, never-ending snow. Then curled into a ball around the orb. The energy core. One of the last magical artifacts within West Africa and Cameroon and the only hope of my home island. And the answer to my prayers, with the power to resurrect Eylerion before forty-eight hours elapsed.

White clouds escaped my lips as my mind focused on the time Eylerion and I were in South Africa—memories of unplowed roads to Lesotho, which cars couldn't travel. That was July 7, six months ago, Forest Day in my confederate state. Hence, Eylerion and I had set out to plant trees along the barren terrain of Sani Pass. Foolish, especially in such weather, but I had a tradition to uphold: planting a tree. Although the twisted, grey-mossy, rocky mountain pass made me realize my mission was to plant a forest.

"Gracyn, my legs are freezing and exhausted." Eylerion's accent always made my name sound special. Yet, I eyed him hard, not giving in to those puppy dog eyes nestled within a bevy of brown curls.

"It's barely evening." Didn't know for sure. Lost in heavy winter, the rhythm of day and night forgotten. Valleys were iced, with no phone network

"You could slump to death if you don't rest."

"So wordy and not working. For effing's sake, give me a hand!" I eye-rolled and lifted my shovel but lost my footing, sliding over snow. Then, he caught me; our eyes locked for heartbeats too long.

"Fine," he whispered, letting me freely drop into the bed of snow. "Watch and learn how the Oracle of Abonnema does things." He looked over his shoulder, a smile curving one side of his lips, and his magical aura accelerated.

He gave off a glow of green, and the snow erupted into an avalanche along the edges of the great escarpment of South Africa. Trees sprouted out of nothing and stretched tall. Wind blew against my coat, dropping the hood to my shoulder, ruffling my hair like a national flag, and my heart swirled at the sight of his dimpled cheeks.

I had fallen in love with this American-born Rivers boy, whose name twisted my tongue in failure of its correct pronunciation. I nicknamed him Rion, my Rivers affinity!

"Show off!" I had broken the awkward moment of shared stares between us and slipped an arrow out of my quiver. Channeling my energy into it, I manipulated the wind to whirl at its shimmering head, and shot a vortex of snow, burying him in it.

These memories kept me going down Mt. Cameroon, despite seeing only white, my feet sinking endlessly into this winterland. The nearby town of Buea, which ought to be my safe haven, was far east, out of my route. The sea, through which Eylerion and I would sail back to Rivers, was at the westernmost slope—the port of Limbe.

I missed the tropical winds of my island and the swaying tree branches, but if Eylerion and I didn't return with the energy core, there would be no more vegetation to admire.

Abonnema, like the rest of Africa, was dying; our magic, which made us Africans, was dying. The Channels and AIT broadcast footage of extinct tribes and nations: *Famine strikes Madagascar. Madagascar sank into the ocean. New desert discovered in Congo.* Madagascar was just the beginning. The death of a million acres of forest within West Africa was just a warning. And the Royal family only cared when the plant of Abonnema, a towering tree, the source of Abonnema's magic, was withering. Eylerion, the last plant magic user living on American soil, was brought back to his roots and installed as the Oracle of Abonnema. Yet, even when that was done his powers didn't revive the plant.

Meeting a land stretched in brown, leaves donning

cloaks of amber-bronze, and the sun bathing the island in blistering golden rays, Eylerion asked me to elope with him to Georgia in the States. What a strange fella! Persistent with the offer, even though we barely knew each other. Kept saying I was beyond any lady he had laid eyes on.

I laughed. "If you care about me, save Africa."

Three years later, six months after catching feelings in South Africa, Eylerion and I had sat under the plant of Abonnema as it shed its last set of leaves. We were the only ones left with magic in Abonnema. Eylerion's fingers knotted with mine while we both absorbed the fact each browning leaf counted down to the loss of our magic.

"I prayed to the gods and finally had a revelation. Our solution lies at the highest peak of Mt. Cameroon." I sighed and looked elsewhere.

"That's great! Have you told the Royals?" he beamed.

"This is a desperate time. Everyone wants whatever magical artifact is left. We should keep this to ourselves and go get it. That way, the Cameroonians won't suspect a thing."

Eylerion stopped listening, slipped a ring on my finger, placed a knee on the floor, and gazed into my eyes. "Once this is all done, let's get married under the radiant glow of the plant of Abonnema."

"I love you." Our lips met. The same love had to overcome the snowstorm of Mt. Cameroon and death itself.

THEN, at last, in all that snow, something stood out. I ran, and felt warmth within my heart as I spotted what I believed was his hand sticking out of the snow.

"Rion!" I dug and dug, till I had identified him. Curls

turned straw, dark-complexioned skin now white frozen, pinkish layer of snow that hinted at blood loss, icicles protruding from the edges of his coat and lining his eyelashes and lips.

Although I couldn't resurrect him here. Not with the ice-bloodied rags hanging loosely on him. Just the thought of him shivering, let alone freezing to death was daunting.

I slung him over my shoulder and moved onward, knowing I had a little over ten hours to resurrect him. Even in the coldest and darkest weather, for his sake, I had to reach the port of Limbe.

2 Limbe

After a myriad of hours, not knowing day or night, and hobbling through a lush canopy that stretched miles, I was startled by sunlight passing through the entanglement of tree branches. The forest felt asleep: no chirp, neither a chatter from swinging monkeys, nor a shriek echoing the life within the dense greenery. The temperature was warm, letting snow melt and pool on the floor. Meanwhile, something lurked within the shadows like an anaconda before the strike. Haunted by the trauma of the attack that left Rion dead and buried in the snow, my eyes followed the movement of shorter trees. Never had I heard of wind at the base of crammed trees that didn't ruffle the top leaves. The presence didn't belong to a forest god or human. Most of the gods had fled from the destruction caused by Africa's fading magic. Whatever monitored Eylerion and me felt sinister, a safe distance away from my arrows, except if I attempted to shoot flames and burn down the forest.

The faster I resurrected Eylerion, the better the odds against our adversary.

My feet sank deeper into the watery earth as I navigated my way to a river, a piece of the forest kingdom's secret. Its water held memories and the essence of life.

The energy core had enhanced my sense of magical aura, and just staring into the water, my gaze piercing through the still fog atop its surface, I felt the pulse of the forest's dwindling magic. Soon, the Biafran rainforest of Cameroon would be no more. Then again, I had less than twenty minutes to resurrect Eylerion, before his soul moved through the veil of the afterlife.

I dropped him into the water, barely thinking of unseen onlookers within the fog, and clenched the orb as if trying to burst it into smithereens. I had no idea how to tap into its abundant energy. My entire plan revolved around crossing bridges one at a time, and now I needed a ferryman.

"Connect with nature," Eylerion's voice whispered from the fog and pulled me into memory lane. My mind focused on the time we were in the Ahoadian North Woods of our confederate state, Rivers. A forest truly alive, beams of sunlight colouring the wings of diverse birds, enormous butterflies flitting from plant to plant, the native crocodiles basking in the smooth waves of their passage.

Eylerion had directed my gaze towards a dead bird— black wingspan missing a number of feathers and blood seeping through the scratches on its body, probably from non-indigenous kid leopards. I then looked at Eylerion. He was staring down at the bird like a battlefield medic, assessing whether or not the bird could be saved.

"It's gone. There's nothing we can do." I held his arm, but he didn't shift his gaze.

"The Oracle ought to have the power of resurrection, right?" Tears streaked his cheek; my eyes widened.

"It hasn't been done in thirty years. Long gone is the time anyone could learn such art."

"But you can teach me, right? Your magic takes the manifestation of your thoughts—" He held me as I shook 'no' and refused to listen. Instead, his voice grew louder, and he looked into my eyes. "I've seen you with the tomes and ancient scrolls. You gotta know something."

"Eylerion!" Mispronounced, and for the first time in two years, I called him by his actual name, not Rion. "Everything I know is, or will soon be, a myth." Sobs punctuated my voice. "Our magic, our culture, our continent will be history, just something in books."

"Gracyn?"

"Forget the damn bird!" I pulled out of his grip and left.

That wasn't something I wanted to remember. Why now, at the eleventh hour of Eylerion's resurrection? Unsureness swirled in. The fog and water felt unforgiving, awkward, and everything else a waste of time. Eylerion was gone, but I could save Abonnema, if not Africa.

"No!" I dropped to my knees. "Is the forest discouraging me from resurrecting Rion?"

I heard only the ruffling leaves and occasional crickets, like the following night after that outburst. Eylerion had been seated by a crackling woodfire. The rounded sphere of the moon had called upon the creatures of the night. My hands swatted at insects, lots of them, settling like a clump, while Eylerion focused on the full moon as if waiting for an answer. Lately, he had been engrossed in Ahoadian tales about their gods, recipes, spells against evil spirits, and the forest.

"I'm sorry." I sat beside him, embraced by the heated air.

"No, I am. It was stupid." His voice had lost its warmth

and life. "The thing is—" His red-tinted eyes darted. He had been crying before I arrived.

"Talk to me."

"My mom believed a dead black bird was an ill omen. We saw one on my eighteenth birthday, and my parents died going to fetch me a birthday present."

I gasped. Sounded inappropriate. Then instinctively held his hand, nodding with my lips pressed into a thin line as he continued.

"Seeing one earlier caused a cascade of my young adult-hood trauma... and I can't lose anyone else, especially not you." If only he had known it was his death he had foreseen.

I placed his head on my shoulder and hugged him. "I'm not dying anytime soon. Still, I owe you an apology. I keep forgetting you lived your life mostly in America, yet here you are, learning our culture."

"Don't worry about it." He whisper-talked in that way people sometimes do in American movies, where they should be talking but you have to turn the volume to the highest setting so you can hear them. And then he drifted into a slumber.

"I promise, I will perfect resurrection and be your protector." I ran my hand along his shut, teary eyes.

My determination strengthened as the memory surrendered to the current situation. Less than ten minutes to make a decision, to save Eylerion. He was my world. Without him, there was no normalcy.

Eight months of reading and attempting resurrections on cockroaches, beetles, weevils, and a bird, only to learn there were a million ways to do it, but I had to find my specific way. I'd hoped to teach Rion, too. Now I stood, knowing over three thousand ways it didn't work for me, and barely had five minutes to attempt another trial on him. Try as I might, I broke down in tears and pulled out an arrow from my quiver, placing the head atop the energy core.

"For you, our love, and our future." I kissed the feathered tail and dropped the orb into the water. "Under the radiant glow of the plant of Abonnema, I beseech the gods and goddesses that can hear my voice, grant me the power of resurrection. I don't care what toll it has on me, but I care about the one who rests upon this still water."

Unslinging my bow from my shoulder, I fitted the arrow to its string. The water swirled, rising and falling; its whitish foam shimmered. The fog lifted and vanished. The pulsed water pushed upwards and raised Eylerion and the energy core hundreds of feet above the roaring surface. There was no wind, just the speed of the water producing the illusion of wind, a towering whirlpool resembling a tornado.

The orb gave off a golden glow like an amateur sun, yet lambent. The swirling water shone green, and so did the entire forest. Branches stretched towards the orb and droplets of water levitated. Each wave, whether air, water, or leaves, accumulated life magic, and the energy core multiplied it.

Then I shot my arrow at Eylerion, and an outburst of magical energy filled the landscape. The wave probably travelled thousands of miles. In a matter of minutes, helicopters and drones would scour the area. But that didn't matter now. Eylerion floated, clad in soft, green clothing. His straw-like hair curled into a headful of voluminous puffy twists. There was my Rivers American.

"Uh!?" He groaned and halfway opened his eyes.

"The gods be praised!" I wrapped him in a tight

258

embrace and finally shed tears of joy. "Don't ever get your-self killed again. Resurrection isn't an option."

TWO HOURS LATER, out of the river, far off in a thatched shelter built from scratch by my hands, we welcomed the darkness and its rain. I lit an arrow through mental concen-tration. It gave off a rain-splattered cone of light spreading into the forest.

"Aren't you... consuming... too much magic?" Eylerion's chest heaved with each word, weak to the marrow; even his legs were jelly and couldn't carry his weight.

"There's something out there." I drew out a dagger from my boot, its blade glinting in the light. "Wriggle your toes." I smiled as he did. "Unfortunately, we can't wait for your strength to kick in. We move in ten minutes."

"Why the rush?"

"Not safe, and who knows what's happening in Abon-nema? The sooner we use what's left of the energy core for the plant, the better. Hopefully, my dad's yacht is still at the Port of Limbe." I threw the dagger, and it spun across nearby trees, slashing off a vine and some branches, and swirled its way back to my hands.

I pulled off my coat, dropping it to the floor, and stepped into the rain, carrying the medium-sized woods and vine into the shelter. There and then, I crafted a raft-like carrier.

"You gotta be kidding!" Eylerion's sudden husky voice shot over the drumming rain.

"Oh, no! This masterpiece costs more than utility bills. Be appreciative, and put on your big boy pants." I placed it beside him along with taut vines under the carrier.

"Can't you dial an emergency line?"

"And draw attention to the orb? Thankfully, our phones died in the snow. Now—" I tossed my leather coat to him. "—Put it on and roll into the carrier."

"What happened to my sweet angel?" He pouted.

I found myself smiling and eye-rolled. "You're just lucky you're cute. Resurrection isn't as easy as it sounds." I lay beside him and held his hand, my breath matching his slow, soft exhalation.

"I'm sorry."

"Don't be. Just promise not to die."

"I don't know the future." He laughed while I playfully punched his shoulder. "I love you."

"I love you, too."

He rolled over. I strapped him onto the carrier with the vines. Then raised him to his height and strapped the carrier to my back.

"Is the weight much?" Almost like a pack of cement, but this raft would be helpful when we encounter more rivers. "I could try walking."

I stepped into the rain. "Wear the hood and hold firmly to that arrow. Besides, I carried you dead for twelve hours."

After the passage of rain came the grey and grimy night sky. Moonless yet misty blue, probably midnight.

It felt easier carrying a corpse than my awakened boyfriend, who kept worrying about his weight on me. Four hours walking, and we approached the edge of the forest to where golden lights from Limbe's street lamps shone in the distance. My former pace before his resurrection would have had us at the port by now.

I shifted Eylerion's weight, slowly crouching, and slid his raft-carrier to the floor. After fumbling with my coat and asking many questions, he fell asleep. I made a fire, nudging more wood into its heart, and sparks crackled into the air and faded.

Lodging wasn't an option. In a town, our decisions would be balanced against dollars and royal cowries, and our accents would triple the price of a room.

"No." Eylerion uttered in his sleep. "Run!" Nightmares flitted into his dream, his legs and arms jittery. One of my hands ran through his hair while the other knotted with his fingers.

"It's alright. I'm here." But none of my words got through to him. Instead his fear gave me a dose of the nightmare, details I wished to erase—the encounter at Mt. Cameroon.

THE MOUNTAIN WIND howled and sprinkled us with snow from our heads to toes. I had let down my hair, bathing in the flashes of Eylerion's phone camera. After days of scouring the different peaks of Cameroon for the orb, our last spot to search was the highest summit.

Despite telling Eylerion my phone battery was flat, he drained his by taking multiple shots of us to update his Instagram, forgetting we had no solar power to recharge. Then a deeper darkness met up with us. The crystal blue sky turned stark and doomy, and the snowfall intensified.

I drew out an arrow and held the head, concentrating magic into it, and shot at the sky. It twinkled like a diamond, grew into a shimmering gemstone, and birthed a ball of light, casting golden rays on the landscape.

"Nicely done," Eylerion yelled over the winds.

"We gotta find shelter and make—" An ear-splitting screech cut me short and we both held our ears.

The snow gave way. Rock-hard ice and frozen stems splintered into flakes and filled the air with fast-moving white dust. Revealed earth was riddled with cracks, spreading toward us as if something swum underneath. A moment later, a huge creature arrowed out of the ground to spiral as a silhouette beneath my ball of light, its large fins resembled dark, ghostly wings. Fear gripped me, and I lost focus on maintaining the light. Gone, the sudden darkness revealed a glowing fish, letting off sparks of different colours. Its flat head, adorned with a pair of beady eyes, had a series of feathery, long whiskers framing its mouth.

Another shriek, and it dived toward us, erupting a wave of snow.

"Gracyn!" Eylerion wrapped an arm around me and raised the other, conjuring a wall of crammed trees to block the mini-avalanche. "What's that thing?"

"I have never seen a floating catfish. Not even in books." Its shrills drew my gaze to it, each fin rippling the snowy air with magical waves. "Right now, it's a threat and needs to be pinned down."

I drew out another arrow, my magic swelling within the tip, and shot at it. A flaring flame in the shape of a phoenix formed and enveloped the fish. But faded, leaving not a scratch on the creature.

Eylerion's whole body emitted a verdant light, silhouetting his frame, and the ground rumbled as trees sprouted and weaved into a gigantic hand, rubble sliding off in bits. Then, the tree-crafted hand swatted the fish to the ground, where more cracks surfaced.

"That should do it." He spoke too soon.

Dark mist pooled around the base of the hand, reducing it to a pile of ash. The fish rose inches above the ash-bed and drifted towards us. It shrieked, so loud this time that blood seeped out of our ears.

"Let's see you escape death from a thousand arrows," I said.

Immensely thick magical energy coated my arrows, levitating them one by one out of my quiver. Then, they spun around me, multiplying in number. Filings of twinkling dust produced the illusion of a mini tornado, and all rocketed into the sky creating a trail of sparks. A rain of a thousand arrows pierced the elongated body of the fish. Yet it shook the arrows free to scatter into smithereens, while it seemed unscathed.

The creature hovered over us, I felt my magic dwindle, and my breath became heavy. Both Eylerion and I dimmed.

"It feeds on life force." My legs gave way and Eylerion caught me, keeping me stable on my jelly legs. My eyelids rivalled the heaviness of my legs.

"Of the two of us, I have the most magical energy, which will give you time to run and find the orb, while I impede its attacks."

"Don't be stupid. You will be dead before a third attack."

"Find the orb and save Abonnema." His soothing voice and teary eyes pierced my heart; his gaze of conviction failed to hear anything else.

"No! I can't lose you. At least think about Africa. You're the last plant user."

Such bravery, yet treachery to lay down his life for me while the continent needed his ability. As the catfish extracted his magic, our world of ecstasy drowned in Eylerion's blood. The fear in his eyes was framed by bloodied brown skin streaked with tears. It was the last I saw of him before he conjured a palm tree and swung me to the topmost peak of Mt. Cameroon.

$\approx$

PULLED out of the nightmare by the crackling woodfire, I sniffed and lay beside Eylerion, skin on skin underneath the warmth of my leather coat. "Rion, I will never let anything happen to you again."

"Mom." He partly opened his eyes and tears rolled down. "I'm so glad you're here."

"Yes, baby. Mummy is here." I played along and dozed off.

An hour or two later, sunrise approached, a bright glimmer stretching over the horizon, vanquishing the darkness to the far-away ends of the forest. Soft beams warmed my skin. My eyes opened, and Eylerion wasn't beside me.

Sitting upright, my gaze met the fella flexing his teeny-weeny muscles. He leaned on a tree and tossed his hair as he noticed my stare. "Love what you see?" He smirked.

"I'm starving and could eat you."

He laughed. "Then let's head to your dad's yacht and buy something along the way." I stood, and arm in arm, we stepped into the cozy sunlight.

3 GULF OF GUINEA

With the dewy ocean wind in my hair, I walked up the bow of my dad's yacht to where Eylerion stood. The fragrance of coffee lingered, and he had a streaming mug cradled in his hand. I raised a brow.

"This is a racing yacht devoid of a coffee maker and beans, so where came the coffee?"

"Bought from a hawker." He pointed at the massive dock, brimming with life and clamour and hustling and bustling. I spotted vendor drones roving with items atop.

Eylerion and I were departing from the shores of Cameroon on a foggy day to the Port of Abonnema in the Western Isles of Rivers.

"Gracyn!" Eylerion's voice wasn't its usual soft, controlled tone, instead almost forceful, with croaks to it. "I still can't believe it."

"Eylerion, please... stop talking about it. I would choose you over any situation."

"I know." His eyes moved to the deck, then the sail; one hand held his coffee, and the other clenched the rail, lining the bow down to the stern.

"Are you ok? Do you feel different, dizzy, or anything?" A sudden tautness gripped my chest.

"I saw my parents." He pressed his lips together and bowed his head.

"I'm sorry. Don't you remember what happened to them? Does any of your memory feel blurry?"

"Gracyn, I remember, and dying, my entire life replaying before my eyes, made me realize how much I miss them."

My eyes stung, brimming with tears, and I blinked fast. "What are you saying? I don't understand a thing!"

The thought of him wanting to join them in heaven swirled in.

"Gracyn," he called softly and held my hand. "When we are done with this task, let's fly to Georgia. See my parents' grave."

My jaw dropped, and my eyes widened. "I'm lost for words," I said.

"Come on, Gracyn." His voice grew audible and stronger.

"No. The expense, the distance, the police brutality... You aren't fit for such travel yet."

"Gracyn." His cup fell off the boat slicing the water, and his sullen eyes sank my heart. "I need this."

"Ok, but after our wedding, maybe our honeymoon." I forced a smile and walked to the cockpit.

Three hours of sailing through sea fog and navigating by GPS passed by quickly. Then again, the sun felt distant, only glowing for itself while the darkness deepened, even at noon. Unlike Southern African seas, I didn't spot any whales.

"Our climate is a mess," I said.

White smoke escaped my lips; the Atlantic air was colder than Limbe. Eylerion shuddered with cold, despite wearing a trailing overcoat. If only our phones weren't dead and this damned dim boat-lighting, we would have taken pre-wedding photos in our matching outfits. Meanwhile, I womanned the left steering while Eylerion operated the right. We kept the shores of Kula in sight, the largest archipelago kingdom in the Western Isles, where Abonnema was the capital.

"Less than twenty minutes and we will be home," I said, then noticed the orb flickered.

"Oh, my God, a whale is out there!" said Eylerion.

He watched the seas with binoculars. I didn't need a pair, the orb's energy heightened my senses. I saw a pair of large, unblinking eyes and whiskers.

"No!"

My hands stretched out, trembling, and I summoned my arrows and quiver from the cabinet. At that moment, the catfish flew out of the water with a huge splash, shone

266

with a cold light rivalling that of the moon, and floated above our yacht. It must have sensed my aura.

I fell and my arrows spilled to the ground. Eylerion raised a hand but nothing happened. The energy core flared, while the fish absorbed some of its energy and perhaps mine. I could feel my energy dwindling and my arrows becoming dormant.

"I have no magic!" Eylerion fell to his knees.

I turned to the floating catfish. "You killed my boyfriend, tumbled my world, and now wanna destroy my homeland's last hope."

I ran and snatched the orb from the floor of the yacht.

The fish shrilled, bursting the windows into shards and drawing blood from my ears. Eylerion also bled from every opening: eyes, nose, ears... I had to protect him.

The orb radiated an imperial glow and my arrows levitated, rocketing skywards and multiplying. An infinite number giving the illusion of a starry night.

"Survive a million arrows, witch!" Flight after flight of arrows pierced its elongated body. After a downpour of glowing blood and the air being filled with horrifying screams of the fish, the fish retreated into the deep swells of the sea.

"Gracyn, you can't let it escape."

"You don't need to tell me."

I placed an arrow on the orb, and the glow illuminated the entire landscape, sky, and even underneath the water. The bleeding catfish dived into the dark depths.

"Go to hell," I said as I shot at the sky.

Beams of bright, blinding light descended into the roaring sea. Sizzling sounds and blistering steam replaced the fog. The monster floated to the surface along with other dead aquatic creatures.

To my horror, the orb turned pitch-dark, devoid of magical energy.

"No!" I crumbled to the floor and tears ran down my cheeks. "What have I done?"

Eylerion crawled towards me and wrapped me in an embrace. "You did your best."

"No." His words flew over my ears. Tears blurred my vision. "My people, my island. The whole journey has been pointless."

My eyes widened to see Eylerion's hand was on the orb and it glowed dimly. His hair bleached white within seconds, his skin wrinkling.

"Stop!" I kicked the orb away from him. "It is taking away your life force."

"You mean, it is taking its own energy from me. I'm dead." He whispered and shrugged his shoulders with a shy smile.

"Whatever you are thinking, trash it."

"You need to save the plant of Abonnema. Let me give back the core's energy." He squeezed my hands softly.

"How can you be so selfish? After all that I've been through to resurrect you," I yelled.

"I'm sorry."

"Let's elope to Georgia, get married there, and start a family."

"We can't. I promised, if I cared about you, I would save Africa—"

"Stop talking!" I shook my head, hands covering my ears.

"I can't save Africa, but you can save Abonnema. Your people."

"Shut up. I'm not allowing this." I said as I rose to standing.

"I appreciate everything you have done for me, but this isn't your choice." Eylerion stood up and dashed for the orb, wrapping his fragile fingers around it, brittle like dry bone.

"Why?" I whispered.

"Because we won't be able to live with ourselves." He cried, "I love you, and I pray you forgive me someday."

He faded into a cloud of glinting dust and the orb swallowed him up, leaving me alone as the coast of Abonnema loomed large.

THE END

BIO: Oruwari Ibiapuye Tom is an upcoming writer, hoping to make a difference. He majors in Biochemistry at the University of Port Harcourt and has a thing for story-crafting, particularly urban fantasy, contemporary green stories, and a slice of forbidden love, sometimes BL.

When he isn't fantasizing about a forest kingdom or advocating for a greener, cheaper world, he is on a magic carpet, experiencing some other form of life.

CHAPTER 16

THE PRINCESS OF PROPHECY

THE ROAD BACK

by

Matt Hansen

"What'm I looking at, general?" asked the President of the United States as he barged into the situation room, still knotting his tie.

"Satellite image of the west coast, Mr. President." The general indicated the wall-sized display behind him. The landmass was only distinguishable from the ocean because of the twinkling glow of city lights. A dark circle in those lights rolled northward like someone putting a coin on a projector. It cut west towards the water. "We're unsure what the phenomenon is, but something is knocking the power out in an approximately five mile radius."

The President sat down. "Is it some kind of storm?"

"Sir, it isn't moving like that. Unpredictable patterns. Potentially manmade. Causing all sorts of destruction."

The President glanced at another man, dressed in a black suit with a wire dangling from behind his right ear, and asked, "Director? Is it something of ours malfunctioning?"

"No, Sir." The man hesitated. "And it isn't the uh—object we've been tracking. That's still sitting about a quarter million miles out. Just this side of the moon's orbit."

"Is it from an enemy nation?" The President turned back to the general.

"Sir," he said, face having turned whiter than the President's house after the exchange with the suited man. "We don't even know what it is, let alone who sent it. All ground level recon we've tried is showing dark. We're scrambling the jets for a better view, with a couple of fighter escorts, but for now all we've got is the eye-in-the-sky."

"Get me some intel," said the President. "Damn near twenty million people living there, and you're telling me not a single cell phone is up and pointed at the thing?"

"We're looking," said the general.

IGNORING her older sister Samantha's scoff, Rachel pulled out her new phone as the arena lights dimmed. Received on her last birthday, the phone and the accompanying live account, @RedheadReporterRachel, were Rachel's whole life. And the account was just starting to build momentum, having received over a thousand views on the exposé about her cat Casper's ability to do backflips. Tonight, she'd ride the wave, and hopefully the show would get even more.

Placing her elbows on the yellow counter in front of her to steady the camera and checking her shot exactly like her hero, Veronica with the Local News, had taught in her latest webinar, Rachel started the live stream. She panned around the vibrant room. Shaped like a hockey rink, the sandy oblong competition area was ringed by rows of tables and benches with spectators packed shoulder to shoulder. Each section was colored to represent one of the half dozen competing champions with banners hanging on the walls behind the painted decor.

Settling on the opening at the far end of the arena, Rachel began. "Reporter Rachel here. The stage is set for what promises to be a great show. For those who didn't join this afternoon's broadcast, Sam's twelfth birthday," she swiveled the phone toward Sam, who hissed at her to be quiet, "is taking place at—"

"Stop, Rach. It's starting," said Sam as she grabbed Rachel's phone.

"Hey, give it back," said Rachel. "Veronica says, nothing should stop—"

"I don't care what Veronica thinks. Just watch the show," Sam said, though she did hand back the phone, having turned off the stream.

Rachel was about to turn it back on when the spotlight nearly blinded her as it whirled around the room before settling on a man who appeared as if by magic in the center of the sand.

"Greeks." His voice boomed around the auditorium audacious as the clashing yellows, greens, and purples of his mottled pantaloons and flopping hat. "Bah. Their myths have grown cold, their gods nothing but a dream." He spun around in a twirl of flying sand, showing his back to Rachel while addressing the crowd on the opposite side. "The far east? Stale legend of black powders and assassins." Cartwheeling to his right, he faced the spectators on the curving end. "The spirits of the new world? Weak, younglings whose thunderbirds wouldn't last a moment against one of our dragons."

His voice was so loud and deep, Rachel could feel it in her chest. It was exactly the type of voice that belonged on air. The type of voice that screamed at Rachel to pay attention.

As he found his way back to the center stage, he continued, this time whispering in a way that his words still found every ear. The wooden benches creaked as hundreds of spectators inched forward. "As everyone knows, all legends worth telling, all fantasy worthy of awe, all romance to inspire the next thousand generations of hearts,"—the man smiled and Rachel's face burned—"live solely inside the medieval times."

"The man's a genius," Rachel said to Sam. "Better even than Veroni—"

"Shut up," hissed Sam as she punched Rachel's leg.

Eyes watering at the pain spreading all the way to her knee, Rachel missed the fool's backflip and bow. The whole crowd laughed with applause that would make that thunderbird he'd mentioned proud.

"I'm sorry," said Sam. "I didn't mean to hit so hard. You okay?"

As the lights sprang back on, Sam and Rachel's mother leaned forward on the other side of Sam. "Now, girls, come togeth—Rachel, what's wrong?"

Sam's eyes were wide, pleading with Rachel not to tell on her. As annoyed as Rachel was at Sam for interrupting her report and hitting her, she didn't want to ruin her birthday. "Just banged it on the rail," she managed through the pain.

Sam sagged in relief.

"Well, then, let's get a picture of the two of you?"

Rachel didn't want a red eyed picture of her smashed together with her sister. Instead she turned back to the show.

The mottled man continued, "Now I cry to the corners of this medieval land. Here ye, hear ye, we call to arms the knights of the realm to gather for festival and perform feats of strength, daring and skill. And to maybe, just maybe,"— the man winked—"find the favor of some young princess in the crowd."

"Rachel, look here and smile."

"Mom, stop," said Sam. "The horses are coming. We'll get a picture later."

The gates opened wide and out trotted a half dozen armed and armored knights. They all wore the bold colors of their houses and rode horses that snorted and danced in anticipation. Next to each was a squire, holding a tall lance that Rachel didn't think she'd be able to lift.

"Did you know that horses can sleep standing up?" Rachel asked excitedly. "I heard about it o—"

"—on the news," both her mother and Sam said as one. Her mother with a smile, Sam with an eye roll. "We know," Sam continued on her own.

Rachel huffed and slouched back into her seat, grabbing her phone again to start another live recording. Veronica did say that even small local stories were worthy of attention.

Because it was Sam's birthday, they were seated in the

yellow section, her favorite color. Of course it was. Yellow like the summer to go with Sam's perfect blond hair and perfect everything else a twelve-year-old could be. While Rachel, just a year behind, seemed to struggle at everything. Always lost in daydreams of excitement and adventure, her grades tended to be okay, not bad, but not exactly good. And she absolutely hated Samantha's dance team and all the sparkling outfits and makeup. Mom could understand dance, but she couldn't understand Rachel's fascination with the news and news reporters. It was simple, really, they were always where all the exciting stuff happened. That, of course, was what Rachel wanted to be when she grew up, even if Sam told her she was too ugly to be on TV.

But tonight, Rachel secretly wanted the green knight to win because she didn't think any other color could possibly match the beauty of green.

"Haha, that one pooped," squealed Sam. Sure enough, the red knight's horse had dropped a few apples. Plop, straight onto the arena sand.

Enthralled by the figures, Rachel tried to ignore her family. The lights dimmed and each knight and accompanying squire stood at attention before their section. The crier leapt onto the railing dividing the arena in two for the jousting. It was an impressive jump as far as Rachel was concerned, nearly her entire height, not that it was much past four feet.

His hat sparkled under the spotlight. "Now that our court of knights is assembled, it is time to welcome Her Royal Highness, The Queen."

The spotlight moved up to the royal booth, where out walked the tallest and most beautiful woman Rachel had ever seen. Her long, flowing auburn hair made Rachel wish she had a hat on to hide her own fiery bird's nest. And the gown. Purple velvet that Rachel wished she was close enough to touch. Imagining it was as soft as Casper's belly fur, for once she was a little jealous of fancy outfits Sam's dance team got to wear.

The knights all bowed, and before long the show was in full swing, Rachel's rapt attention not missing any of it. So furiously did she watch that, when the yellow knight struck the green, to Samantha's smiling delight—of course her knight would beat Rachel's—Rachel spilled her dragon soup on her lap, burning her, just a little. Certainly not enough to miss a moment of the show. Good thing dragon soup was just lentil beans, as her mother had told her, and not made with real, scorching dragon's fire.

Falcons swooped across the arena, and the knights fought sword to sword. Even the squires displayed their skills in archery.

The lights dimmed again, as once more the master of ceremonies skipped under the spotlight.

"Rach," said Sam. "Please just put the phone down and enjoy the show. Everything's more fun if you're not worried about what Veronica would think of your angle, or whatever."

"Fine," Rachel sighed, putting it back in her pocket. "The lighting's bad anyways."

"Before the final bouts of that greatest of knightly tests, the joust, and before the champion of all realms is crowned by Her Most Glorious Majesty," the master said, bowing to the queen, who smiled back, "I have a special tale to spin you. Listen now. For once upon a time—I know, a clichéd way to start, but this story in fact took place a thousand years ago, almost to this very hour—

276

there was a kingdom living beneath the benevolent rule of a gracious queen, until it was beset by a dragon who carried thunder in its growl and lightning in each flap of his mighty wings."

At this, a burst of electricity arched between the man's fingers. Rachel wished she'd gotten that shot.

Smiling knowingly at the crowd's gasp, he continued, "It laid waste to our fair lands of peace, until the green knight himself rode against it and skewered the beast through the heart. But alas, after the dragon's demise, a prophecy was born. A thousand years hence, on a night exactly like this one, the dragon's progeny would rise. Now, harken to this hope. With it would come the Princess of Prophecy. The Lady of the Once Bitten Apple. With flaming hair crowned by a laurel of wild ivy, she would rain fire from the heavens. And so that royal court, with their wizard as guide, transported themselves into the future to find and help the one who will vanquish our legendary foe for all time. And so, I present the Green Knight of Leon, to crown tonight's prophesied lady."

Out strode the green knight.

Rachel's heart fluttered in her chest, like she imagined Veronica's did when she had to film a particularly scary event, like a wildfire. Ignoring another of Sam's sighs, Rachel brought the phone out, hoping to get a shot of whoever in the crowd the green knight chose. She had to admit, with the green knight staring at her, all thoughts of the news and danger fled, and she sort of wanted him to choose her. His beard was thick and brown and neatly cropped, and his hair fell in soft waves to his shoulders. His eyes, foresty as his tunic, seemed to pierce Rachel as they stared at her from across the arena.

So intense was it, that Rachel barely heard the master of

ceremonies' next words. "It appears Sir Leon has found our fairest maid, The Lady of the Once Bitten Apple."

The knight was marching across the arena, still staring straight at Rachel. Her cheeks burned as she shrank as far into her seat as she could without crawling down beneath the bench.

"A shy maid, at that," said the master of ceremonies.

Her face felt like a dragon had breathed on her. She tried to hide behind her phone screen.

The Green Knight smiled, washing away some small bit of Rachel's embarrassment. Bowing before her, he offered his hand, and in a gentle whisper said, "Stand up, dear."

Not knowing if her shaking knees would support her, Rachel gripped him and stood. She squinted against the spotlight as it beamed down, bathing everything in a brilliant white light.

The knight bowed again, and his voice boomed out of the loudspeakers. "We have found our Princess of Prophecy." Holding aloft the mic, he leaned in. "What's your name?"

"Umm, Rachel."

"Into the mic, dear," he said kindly.

Stooping forward, Rachel looked at Sam, who'd grabbed her phone and was filming the whole scene. She gave a thumbs up. Taking a deep breath and remembering she was live, Rachel pretended she was in front of a real news camera and said, as clearly as she could, "My name is Rachel." Her voice was loud and crisp through the sound system, cooling her cheeks. She managed to smile.

"Well, Rachel, please bow your head. I have a gift for you."

Withdrawing an emerald laurel wreath, he placed it on her brow.

"Applause for our fair maid and the Princess of Prophecy," said the master of ceremonies as the green knight held Rachel's hand up and turned to face the crowd. For a moment, just the smallest part of a second after the master made his final bow, his eyes met Rachel's. And, through the arena's applause, she could swear those eyes X-rayed her. He looked into her soul, and a faint whisper flickered through her head. "I don't know how you do it, but be ready. The crown will keep you safe. Within it, I imbibed my own magic. It will keep out any dark forces."

All the spotlight's heat and the deep blush that always showcased Rachel's emotions to the whole world disappeared. She shivered.

THE SITUATION ROOM WAS SILENT, until the President croaked. "What happened?"

On the screen, still lacking any close up shot of the darkness, the satellite image showed a flashing red bar that read LOST CONTACT.

"Whatever it is," said the general with his ear to a phone, "it appears to have knocked out the jet's guidance system."

"The pilot?" asked the President.

"We don't know. It's frying all communication in the area. We're blind."

THE REST of the evening was a whirlwind for Rachel, but even the green knight's victory couldn't warm her bones after the announcer's stare. As they sat in the car on the freeway home, Rachel looked out the window at what few stars she could see in the city's night sky. She drifted between them and the moonlit sand of the ocean to their right.

Flashing red brake lights flickered across the whole freeway, stealing Rachel's attention.

Driving their car and cursing the traffic, Rachel's father looked around at all his mirrors.

Her mother swatted him on the shoulder, "Watch your mouth with the girls." But Rachel had heard that particular word plenty of times before, so it was nothing too exciting.

"Well, it's ten at night. Why's the freeway stopped?"

"Could be construction," her mother said in that soothing voice that she used to read bedtime stories in. "Or an accident?" It was calming enough that Rachel looked back out the window as the car rocked to a stop.

In the moment since she'd turned away, clouds had moved in from the south, bathing the entire beach in fog. Rachel could practically see how the weather woman would push the low-pressure system in on the green-screen map. A flash of lightning lit the sky like the arena spotlight, stopping Rachel's heart for just a moment. The thunder boomed over the beach, and all four in the car jumped. Rachel and Sam looked at each other and laughed.

"Just a bit of thunder, girls," said her father. "No need to worry."

Smiling, Sam said, "You must have jumped a whole foot."

"Same as you," said Rachel. "But there's not supposed to be any thunderstorms this week. I saw—"

"—it on the news," interrupted Sam. "We know."

And then thunder boomed again, this time directly over

their car. Rachel squeaked, head swiveling back out the window.

The white lights of the highway lamps winked out, followed by the soft glowing red of each vehicle's brake lights. Everything was dark.

Swallowing, Rachel whipped her head around. Sam's hand clamped down on her wrist like a vice. Rachel had to admit it was comforting knowing her older sister was there.

A bright orange light billowed into the sky ahead of them, casting a strange glow on the stopped cars. A concussion shook theirs at the same moment a bird screeched overhead. It was so loud that Rachel covered her ears.

The windows shattered, and Rachel screamed.

"What was that?" asked Rachel's mother.

Her father turned around. "Are you both okay?"

"I've glass in my hair," said Sam.

Rachel couldn't peel her eyes away from the small trickle of blood rolling down her sister's forehead until another explosion sounded behind them, this one far closer than the one before. "Daddy," she said, as her heart pounded in her chest.

"Charlie?" shouted Rachel's mother.

Unlocking the doors, her father said, "Out, out of the car. Make for the beach."

Other people had the same idea as her father. They fled their vehicles. Some held small children or grasped older ones by the hand, dragging them along like that one time she'd gotten a leash for Casper. Most of them were screaming.

"Mary, grab Rach," her father said, as both parents stepped out of the car.

Even though Rachel only lost sight of them for a second, she realized that she wanted her father. Now.

Her mother opened the door. Swallowing, Rachel tried to undo her seatbelt, but her hands were shaking too violently. Her mother's face was white as vanilla ice-cream. She slapped Rachel's hands away, but her own were almost as bad. "Charlie, I can't get her belt."

Rachel's dad had already pulled Sam out of the car. "I'm coming." Putting Sam down, he reached in through the other side of the car.

"Charlie," Rachel's mom screamed.

He looked back, swore loudly, and then jumped backwards while grabbing Samantha and tugging her out of the way, collapsing to the ground just as a flaming motorcycle crashed down on their car's hood.

Tears burst in Rachel's eyes, as she couldn't see her parents anymore.

"Rachel," her mother screamed again.

Trying to look over her shoulder and chest heaving with each breath, she saw her mother limping towards the door. As she swung her head, her vision swam like she'd opened her eyes underwater. Her father appeared and grabbed her, Sam standing next to him with wide, frightened eyes.

"Daddy," Rachel yelled again.

"Baby, I'm here, I'm here." He pulled out the pocketknife he'd almost stopped carrying after his last few got confiscated by security everywhere they went. Cutting the belt away, he grabbed Rachel with arms that felt warmer and safer than any green knight could possibly have. Sam hugged her, too, and her father carried them both to the relative safety of the other side of the freeway. All around, bruised and bleeding people, who'd also fled their vehicles, stood staring at something.

With a throbbing head, Rachel glanced at her relatively unharmed family and then across the freeway at whatever they were all looking at. In the flames of the second explosion, Rachel watched as the knights from tonight's show wove through the parked cars atop their horses.

"Sam, look." Rachel pointed.

"What in the f—" Rachel's mother said.

The squires rained arrows up at an eighteen-wheeler-sized bird that was shrouded in stormy clouds. Crackles of electricity arced out as the occasional leathery wingtip broke through. Arrayed before the beast were the knights of the realm. The green knight's horse reared as he gripped its reins in one hand and his lance in the other. Rachel's heart slowed, and she began to think again. This was it, the lightning dragon and the Princess of Prophecy.

Whipping out her phone, she looked around for the princess, wondering what she would look like and how she would rain fire from the skies.

The dragon roared thunder, and the knights danced out of the way. The cement cracked under the dragon's power as the knights charged it.

Knowing she would never be a reporter if she failed to capture the moment the woman showed up, she started a live stream.

"How's your phone working?" asked Sam. "All the lights are out."

Ignoring her, Rachel turned and began providing her report. "It's Redhead Reporter Rachel, once again bringing you the local news as it happens."

The knights fought. A lance pierced a dragon wing as the beast let loose another roar.

Clapping her hands over her ears as the sound hit her like a wave, Rachel dropped her phone just as her father grabbed for her. She bent to pick it up and he missed.

In the rush of people fleeing further from the action,

Rachel almost got stepped on. She turned and her whole family had gotten swept away in the crowd. She stood almost alone now behind the metal freeway railing. Only one other man, dressed in some kind of pantsuit and helmet, stood next to her. The reflection of the flames danced in his eyes.

His radio crackled. The only other piece of electronic equipment that was working. By the man's flinch at the sound, Rachel could tell he was just as surprised as she was.

Looking around and summoning every ounce of courage she had to stay in the thick of the action and report the news, she held up her phone again and continued the live feed.

"WE'VE GOT ONE, MR. PRESIDENT."

A vertically filmed video played on the display over the general's shoulder. The sounds coming from the film echoed like bombs around the small room, and a young girl's voice sounded over the PA. "—it appears to be a giant lightning dragon."

"What in the—" exclaimed the President. "I don't want some ten-year-old's take on the situation. Somebody get me some facts, not this childish fantasy nonsense."

"Something's attacking the city, and this is the only visual we've got." The general shrugged. "Satellite corroborates it."

"Don't talk to me about dragons. Get me real info—"

The phone interrupted the president. Answering it, the General swore. "Mr. President, we've got the pilot. He bailed over the beach and is on site."

"Finally, some real intel. Patch it through."

The young girl's voice cut out and was replaced by the garbled radio transmission. "Mr. President. This is Lieutenant Carroll. I'm onsite, and I don't really know what I'm looking at."

"Just tell us the facts, lieutenant," said the President.

"There appears to be a large bird. Size of a strike jet. And fighting it is—" he hesitated.

"Some kind of costume party?" asked the general.

"Yes, sir," said the transmission. "I—I—don't know who the costumed persons are, or what manner of technology is attacking the city, but they seem to be holding it at bay. The yellow one's down, but the green one moves like—"

"You're actually telling me," the President interrupted, "there's knights fighting some kind of UFO over one of our cities? And it isn't a hoax?"

"Confirmed, sir. I'm watching it with my own eyes. I'm not alone. Some girl's got her phone out, recording the whole thing."

"How's her phone and your radio working?" asked the general. "All other electronics are out."

"I don't kno—" the radio crackled. "—some kind of glowing crown. Everytime I step too far away, my—" more crackling, "—goes dead."

"We got anything that's point and shoot? No electronics in the missles?" asked the President after a moment of silence.

Frowning in thought, the general said, "Aye, we've got rocket's aplenty."

"Call 'em in. We'll figure out what it is later."

"Yes, sir." The general saluted before picking up the phone.

"Lieutenant," the President transmitted over the radio.

285

"Find a way to get it over water, and we'll down it. That's an order." Turning to the general, he added, "I don't want to see videos of anything bad happening to this kid online. Make sure you clear it over the ocean."

"Yes, Mr. President."

THE FIGHT WAS GETTING CLOSER, but Rachel held her phone steady, still waiting for the princess.

Glancing back as a bolt of lightning arced in Rachel's direction, the green knight met her eyes and smiled. He looked up as two jets screamed through the sky. They were the small and fast ones Rachel had seen at the air show last summer. They circled far out over the ocean and weren't firing any of their guns.

"Girl," said the man in the helmet, once he'd stopped whatever conversation he'd been having over his radio. "Do you know that man? The green one?"

"Not really," said Rachel. "But I've seen him before."

"Can you get his attention?"

"I can try." Swallowing deep and taking a breath, she strode forward. She kept a nervous watch on the dragon and waved her arms over her head.

It worked. The green knight glanced back at her, shouted something to his fellow knights, and wheeled his horse around. As they clopped across the cement road to a stop before Rachel, he said, "Princess. Have you a plan?"

"Sir," said the man in the helmet. "Can you and your, um— knights get the thing to head towards the beach? Get it over the ocean?"

The green knight glanced at the sand and then back at the dragon. "I can try."

"Good. Do that. The pilots will handle it from there."

The knight nodded at them both, slammed his visor shut and then hefted his lance. Facing the dragon, he dug his heels into the horse's flanks, and it rose on its hind legs, whinnying into the darkness. They surged forward.

Dodging a claw that swiped out of the dark swirling storm clouds faster than Casper's paw at a laser pointer, the green knight speared the beast in the snout.

The resulting roar rattled Rachel's skull. When it faded, she steadied the phone. Glancing down for the briefest second, she almost dropped it. Over ten million people were tuned in. This was it. She knew she could do it. Then she noticed the top comment from @VeronicaWithThe-News stating, "This girl's got talent!" and almost froze. Forcing herself to blink, she took a deep breath and smiled. It was all coming together. "For those of you just tuning in, there is magic happening on the western coast. The dragon is shooting lightning and snapping teeth at our heroes. And a new plan is forming. The green knight, having just stabbed it in the nose, has its full attention. And here they come."

The green knight galloped across the freeway, straight for Rachel and the beach, slipping around dead cars like an acrobat.

The dragon lurched again, barreling through the debris.

Rachel stood her ground, until they were almost upon her. The man in the helmet tackled her out of the way. Managing to hold onto her phone, she pounced back up as the knight and dragon tore past them and over the highway's divider. Razor jaws snapped air just as the horse's back hooves cleared the railing.

Kicking up its own storm of sand, horse and rider raced straight for the water.

Lightning exploded from the tips of the dragon's wings as it took flight. He whooshed past Rachel with an extended neck, gaining on the green knight.

The jets screamed back around somewhere in the sky, but Rachel kept the phone trained on the scene, sure Sir Leon would turn at the last moment and spear the dragon through the eye, or something as heroic as that.

But he raced for the water without looking back.

The dragon opened its giant mouth. And, just as the horse's hooves hit the wet sand, the dragon swallowed it, swooping low out over the ocean.

Rachel's heart fell as she watched the knight and his horse get eaten. It was clean. There was no blood, as they'd been only a mouthful.

Tears welled in Rachel's eyes, and her once-steady hands shook.

The dragon turned a large circle over the water, headed back to the beach and Rachel. She held the phone up, as horse hooves of the remaining knights clopped up on either side of her.

Out over the ocean, lightning flickering with each flap of its wings, the dragon opened his mouth again. Thunder exploded around Rachel, clapping her eardrums worse than the fireworks on the Fourth of July.

The knights readied their lances.

But before the knights could attack, when the dragon was still far out over the waves, a salvo of rockets screamed down from one of the jets, and a fiery ball exploded on the beast's side. Others hailed in from the opposite direction, slamming into the dragon's head. Its wings slumped forward, and with a huge splash it hit the surface, sinking into the shallow water.

Lights flickered back on, bathing the gruesome freeway in steady warm light.

Rachel let out the breath she didn't know she'd been holding and turned as the queen whispered behind her. "He died as valiantly as anyone." She, the fool and the knights and squires, excepting the green knight, of course, stood watching the ocean waves, tears filling each eye. "And you, my dear. Almost as brave as he." The queen bent down, kissing Rachel on the brow. "The prophecy is fulfilled, and our work here, done. Master," she said to the mottled man. "Please, take us home."

The man smiled and clapped, and Rachel flinched as they disappeared with pop, leaving only a shimmering outline of where they'd stood a moment before.

The man with the helmet stared, mouth agape.

"Rachel!" Before she could even turn towards the shout, someone's arms were thrown around her, hugging her so tight, she couldn't get a full breath.

"Sam?" Rachel managed.

"I was so worried," Sam said. Rachel was surprised to feel her tears wet on her neck. "Don't ever scare me like that again." She hugged Rachel even tighter.

Rachel found herself hugging Sam back until they both were swept up by their father, who instead of berating Rachel, proceeded to kiss her face. And her mother's face swooped in and enveloped them all, until Rachel felt like she was in her own personal cocoon. They stood there for so long that they started hearing sirens in the distance. And Rachel only let them go when it was time to get back on the road home.

THE END

. . .

BIO: Matt Hansen is a fantasy author living in sunny Southern California with his wife, Rachel, surrounded by multiple pets, including the charmingly elusive cat Casper. Inspired by Rachel's unwavering tenacity, he weaves her spirit (and sometimes her name) into his characters. Casper, on the other hand, is 100% faithfully represented in all his quirky glory.

CHAPTER 17
WYRMBANE
RESURRECTION

by

Nyki Blatchley

T he blast of dragon fire envelops me in agony. My skin feels as if it's been flayed off, and flames scorch my hair. I'll be dead in a few minutes, but that's only to be expected.

It always ends that way.

I have a job to finish, though. The great wyrm, towering over my head, is staggering, green blood flowing from the many wounds I've inflicted. Just one more blow...

No time left for finesse, though. Grasping the great sword in both hands, I stagger to my feet and rush at the beast, thrusting at that place under the forearm that many battles have taught me is the most vulnerable, other than throat and eyes. There's resistance as the point meets dragon scales, but I push in.

291

As the struggle to thrust the steel through scale and sinew gives way abruptly to the softer tissue of the creature's heart, I release the hilt and fall backwards. At the same moment, the wyrm falls in ruin.

Life is flowing away from me, but I've one more task to complete. Groping around on the cave floor for my second sword, I half stagger, half crawl over to where the girl's chained to the rock. Her terrified eyes never leave me, and she screams and shrinks back as, with my last strength, I raise the sword and strike. But my aim is still true, and both chain and blade shatter at the same moment.

I fall to the ground, surrounded by an aura of agony.

I'm vaguely aware of the girl kneeling beside me. There are tears streaming from her eyes, and she's showing all the signs of panic.

"You're hurt," she says. It almost makes me laugh. "What can I do? I've got to do something."

"There's nothing." My voice comes out as a barely audible croak. "I'm dying. That's all right, though."

She swallows. She seems sweet, but perhaps not very bright. "I... I'll tell the story. I'll tell everyone what you did. What's your name?"

"Wyrmbane." I manage to whisper it before pain and consciousness and the world flee away, and I die. As I always do.

A CLEFT IN the mountain faces me, and both the smell and the psychic signature of a dragon are all over it. Of course they are. Why wouldn't there be a dragon?

My leather and mail harness is whole again, unscorched and unbloodied, and the two swords I always carry are hanging at my sides. Both the great sword that I left buried in the dead dragon and the smaller sword that smashed on the chains.

I take a while to look around and get my bearings. This is certainly a different world from the last one. That had light purple skies, and the rocks were tinted pink, whereas here the skies are a kind of burnt orange colour, with golden rock.

It makes no difference. Although it always takes a while for knowledge of each world to seep into me, as if I'd lived a life there, they all have certain things in common. Every world I find myself in contains humans. And dragons, of course.

There's certainly a dragon just beyond that cleft, probably a big one. The experience that informs my senses is the only thing, besides my memories, that doesn't reset to its original state when I'm resurrected, and each fight adds to my ability to read the signs. I've no idea how many times I've done this. Hundreds? Thousands? Maybe it's been going on forever.

It's quick, this time. I usually have a while to experience my new life, before I find the wyrm I'm meant to fight. Those are the times I love, that make the eternal cycle of fighting and dying almost worthwhile. The times I spend with the people of each world — the people I'm going to be protecting — sharing the richness of their lives, making friends, even falling in love. Sometimes for a few days, sometimes for months, before the call comes.

Not this time, though, it seems. I'll be facing the dragon right away.

I do have the option of refusing the call, of course, of turning away from the battle. Trying to live a full, normal life in this strange world. It's not a real option, though, any more than the countless strategies I've tried through the ages. The few occasions when I've tried to avoid the fight have always led to miserable lives full of misfortune. And, in the end, unexpected, unprepared and unarmed, I've found myself face to face with the dragon anyway and died helpless.

If I go to face it, at least my death will do some good, as most of them have.

The cleft runs for a long way, its golden sides towering sickeningly far above and eventually overhanging, until it's little different from a tunnel. It narrows, too, until there's not room to stretch out my arms. I lose track of how long I follow it, until eventually it opens out into a chamber. A small patch of sky is still visible impossibly far above, but this is effectively a cave.

A huge shape moves in the almost-dark on the other side of the space. I don't need to see it, though. The prickling on my skin and the vast sense of presence always tell me when I'm in a dragon's presence.

A quick scan shows no evidence of any humans other than me. That's unusual. Dragons everywhere seem to have an inexplicable taste for beautiful young maidens, though I've never quite understood why. After all, what does a human's appearance matter to a dragon?

Drawing both swords, I move carefully towards the creature. I know it's aware of me, but it remains still. Does it think I can't see it?

I'm halfway across the distance, when a voice booms around me, careering from wall to wall and growing into a cacophony. Out of the chaos, I can just make out, "No, I know you're there."

I freeze. What's going on? The voice can only come from one source, but that's impossible. Of all the countless dragons I've encountered, not a single one has had the power of speech.

I've stopped just before the shaft of light from the hole in the roof. It slices down, and the dust motes it picks out in gold flutter around in a breeze. Beyond, the rest of the cave seems even darker than before.

"Maybe," suggests the voice, sending the motes flying like the echoes, "I'm not like other dragons. Or maybe it's just that they had nothing to say to their executioner."

Panic stabs me. Can this creature read my thoughts, as well as speak? Does this mean it's going to know my plans as soon as I think of them?

"Not necessarily." Behind the booming echo, the voice sounds thoughtful. Even a little amused, perhaps. "It depends how good you are at hiding your thoughts. From everything I've heard, I have high expectations."

Have I heard correctly? "What do you mean? What could you know about me?"

There's a slight pause. My eyes are becoming accustomed to the gloom beyond the shaft of light and the flying dust. The golden rock of the cave walls gives off a slight glow, and I catch the glint of a dragon's eye, just off a little to my left.

"Oh, every dragon knows about Wyrmbane," it says at last. "We can hear each other, from world to world. I've heard every one of my kindred that you've butchered. And I've witnessed every death you've suffered. I know exactly who you are."

Well, that's more than I do, I think before I can stop myself.

"I know." There's definitely amusement in the dragon's voice now. "The dragonslayer who's fought endless battles, who's died every time, who's always brought back to fight another battle. And who has no idea why. Would you like to understand who you are, little man?"

"Are you trying to tell me you know?" I try to keep my voice urbane and indifferent, but I can't help the surge of hope and anticipation. The dragon is surely aware of it.

I'm using the conversation to plan the best line of attack. I wonder what the wyrm's using it for.

There's a long silence, so long I'm beginning to wonder whether it's going to answer at all, before it asks, "Have you ever wanted to know who's ordained that this happens to you?"

Well, of course I have, but I long ago concluded that it's a fruitless line of inquiry. There's certainly a mind driving my fate. On the few occasions I've managed to survive the battle and gone to take my reward of an ordinary life, sooner or later another dragon turns up, and I feel the call at last.

"Some god who wants to rid all worlds of the scourge of dragons, presumably," I suggest, though I don't really believe that.

"Maybe." If the beast feels insulted, it doesn't show any sign, merely shifts a little. Not preparing to attack, I think. It seems a little restless. "Or maybe there's another reason. Maybe it's not a god. Maybe it doesn't care about dragons. Maybe making you fight and die endlessly is merely for entertainment. Have you considered that?"

"Of course not," I snap. "That's a crazy notion. You're just trying to put me off from killing you."

"Well, of course I am." The dragon sounds more serious this time. "Why wouldn't I want to avoid dying? But that doesn't mean it isn't true."

I know I shouldn't listen. I know I should simply attack, feinting to the left before whirling around to the right before the beast can turn, masking my thoughts as well as I can. I know this dragon is just playing with me. But...

"Would you like to know? Would you like a way out? A way to break the cycle and finally die?"

It's only after a moment or two that I realise I've hesitated too long for a denial to be credible. "Perhaps. But why would I believe anything you say?"

"You don't need to." The dragon's voice is softer now, almost lost among the echoes. Both eyes are visible, gleaming in a myriad of colours. I fight against the hypnotic lure of the voice and the light. "If there's a chance, why wouldn't you try? If I'm lying, how would you be worse off?"

The voice sounds eminently reasonable. Or is it the voice? Can I really hear what the wyrm is saying, or am I imagining?

"Tell me how?" It will do no harm to find out what the proposition is. I'm not going to accept it. Am I?

"You must let me devour you."

The words slide over me, not seeming to touch. The meaning eludes me, even though I know perfectly well what the creature's saying. Devour me? Could I really submit to that?

No! I shake myself out of the strange spell, taking a couple of involuntary steps towards the shadowed dragon, into the centre of the shaft of light. I raise both swords — if it didn't know where I was before, it does now.

"You've never been devoured before, have you?" The voice is just a voice again, although still clothed in booming echoes, and the eyes no longer gleam. Maybe they're closed. "Of all the ways my kindred have killed you, not a single one has ever eaten you."

"No, but I've seen people devoured by dragons."

I can't always save the victims, as I saved that girl last time. I've seen some scorched to a cinder, or lacerated by teeth and claws, but somehow the ones that haunt my nightmares are those I've seen eaten in front of me. Most are dead by the time they disappear down the great gullet, but I once had to witness the largest dragon I've ever encountered swallowing a very little girl whole and alive. I sometimes catch myself wondering how long the child lived inside the dragon's belly in utter, helpless terror before she finally died.

I should reject this out of hand, but... There's no harm in finding out more, is there? "Why would that make a difference?"

"Because there'd be nothing of you to come back. Nothing to be restored to life."

That might make sense, except... "I've been burnt to ashes, too. Nothing much left there, either."

"Not much," the dragon concedes. "But something. Once you've been through me, you'll be transformed. There'll be nothing left that's you."

Nothing left. No memories, no nightmares, no endless fights. No utter weariness. That doesn't seem so bad to me.

"Will it hurt more than other ways?" My conscience is trying to find objections, but I'm aware it's not doing a very good job. If there really is a way to make an end to this eternal life, is a little extra pain really enough to stop me?

There's a slight pause before the dragon answers, as if it's considering. "Perhaps. Some say the consciousness lives on in the body for a while after death. So, if that's true... Yes, it would hurt more." A snort of fire came from the dark corner. "Are you afraid, little human?"

Yes, I suppose I am, but that's not enough to stop me. I take a step forward, beyond the shaft of light...

...and an image rises in my mind. A memory. Cottages burning in the night, yelling people, some on fire, a vast wyrm soaring overhead, screaming children clutched in each claw...

It's always like this. I've no knowledge of the new world when I arrive, but it gradually comes to me like memories, although I usually have longer for the process. I've no doubt that I'm seeing the ravages of this dragon, the atrocities that, according to those false memories, must have sent me up the mountain to put an end to the beast.

I quickly mask my thoughts — at least, I hope I manage to. No, ridding these lands of such a scourge is worth the ultimate price. For anyone else, that price would be death. For me, it's life.

I walk forward, towards where the wyrm skulks. "All right." The words are hollow in my head. "I accept."

I feel it waiting for me, feel its greed and anticipation. Schooling my mind to be blank, I approach till the shadowy head is far above me. It descends, the vast jaws opening...

My great sword flashes upwards, countless lives and countless fights guiding it straight into the dragon's throat and on up through its head. Giving a shriek of agony, it flares fire all around me, and my skin chars, my body melts in the searing heat.

As consciousness drifts away, I wonder where I'll live next. I hope I'll have more time to learn to love, before the call comes.

THE END

BIO: Nyki Blatchley is a blue dragon, cunningly disguised as an author, poet and copywriter, who lives just outside

London. He's been writing fiction since he was four, and his novel *At An Uncertain Hour* was published by StoneGarden. He also has a collection, *Eltava: A Sword for All Ages,* from Gypsy Shadow Publishing, and around ninety shorter pieces published, recently by Smoking Pen Press and Swords and Sorcery magazine.

CHAPTER 18

THE LAST VIRTUE

RESURRECTION

by

David Staiger

The golden bells rang as Miekal rode the final hundred span down the worn roadway toward town. Though he knew it only to be the regular sevenday celebration of the Sun's Day Circle, it felt like a homecoming honor intended just for him. The timing could not have been more fated.

With a flutter in his chest, he eyed the seven belfries of the town's chapel—six at each point of the large hexagonal structure and one atop the central gilded dome itself—each glinting brightly in the midday light, sending sparkles over the surrounding maze of rooftops as the bells sang. The Dome of Delight commanded the very center of Belton, a more impressive edifice than even the Lord's manse upon its low hilltop on the town's northern edge. Growing up,

Miekal had believed Belton's chapel to be the largest building in the world, but having now seen the Dome of the Doves in Whytehal and the towering presence of the Bastion itself, he more fully comprehended the extent of such childish naivety. He could only imagine from what impossible height the king's High Tower looked down upon the capital. Pondering such things made him feel small indeed. Inconsequential.

"Oh good," said Sir Tomas Aerey in a deadpan tone. "And here I was worried we might miss Circle for the day. How fortunate we?" The knight of Moonsmont offered a sardonic grin.

"'Tis God's will," chimed Sir Parris Coldwater from the group's lead without turning. "We made good time despite all your dallying efforts this morn. Come. If we canter we can still make opening prayer."

"Really, Coldwater?" Erek Elkesmein huffed in a whine not quite becoming his station nor his age. "Without a bath or a decent midmeal? I'd really just rather go home. I've a featherbed calling not seen in days."

"As well the pillows of a servingmaid, no doubt," added Tomas pokingly.

"Come, my lord," Parris continued, ignoring Sir Tomas. "What better display for the people, and to your father, than a proper show of piety? And considering you bring no honors from the tourney, the good favor could not harm. It pleases everyone."

Sir Erek made a face as if heavily weighing good favor against a featherbed, but Sir Tomas interjected once more. "Perhaps if my horse were to throw a shoe, we might all sadly arrive too late to make it matter." He patted his black destrier's shoulder with a conspiratorial smirk.

"Honesty remains a virtue, Sir," Parris said flatly, "or have you forgotten that one along with humility?"

Tomas Aerey laughed, handsome eyes sparkling. "Either way, I shall pass upon running off to prayer this day. You lot are free to do as you will. I and my squire will make for the travel-house. You may find us there cavorting with the rest of the godless. What of you, Sir? Off to Circle like a dutiful king's man, or would you care to join me for one last drink before parting ways?"

Miekal realized Sir Tomas was addressing him. *Sir* Miekal, he had to remind himself. The bells had stopped and the question hung in silence, punctured by the unremitting tromp of seven horses over loose stone.

"I think," he began slowly, still finding comfort in his own voice among such fellows, "that Sunday is God's day, no matter where we are." He rolled his left shoulder, feeling the soreness of long riding deep in his sinew. "It is the day of the First Virtue, that of Love." He looked to the blond knight riding beside him, whose reassuring smile added confidence to every new word. "Whether that is love of family, or of community, or of friends." He steadied himself further in Tomas's blue gaze. "Why should we not celebrate the love of friendship among ourselves. I see it only fitting. And besides, even if we galloped to the chapel now, our commotion would surely interrupt the reverent in his service. I don't think that would be mindfully proper at all."

Miekal sat up in his saddle, feeling a giddy surge of self-assurance. "I'll have that drink with you. I'd like that very much. I think God will understand."

Aerey laughed again, an easy, pure release of mirth. "I do believe he would."

"That settles it," chirruped Sir Erek. "The lots are in, and the nays have it. But you can bypass the travel-house,

Tom. Save your coin for better swill. You're quite welcome at the manse. Even you, Sevensons. I'll have baths drawn and good food to table for all. After that farce of a tournament, I'm due for a fortnight of relaxation. Tut." He clamped his fingers together as if shutting Parris Coldwater's lips by force of will. "Nothing more from you. I'm going home and you're all coming with me. Done is done, as the littlefolk say. Now let's get on while the streets are empty."

Littlefolk. What did Erek Elkesmein know of littlefolk, Miekal wondered. *So is so* was the proper expression. No one said *done is done* except at funerals. He wondered if Sir Parris caught the same slip. Coldwater was a shire-name undoubtedly, but Miekal could not be sure if the man was himself a common hedgeknight or an upjumped merchant's son or truly a proper bastard. The hazel eyes could point to noble parentage, but that certainly was not as sure a telling as many people rumored it to be. Not like his own eyes.

With pale brown curls and amber eyes, Miekal's heritage stood unmistakably plain to all. Like his father, and his grandsire, praise his spirit. Even his tan complexion showed always a shade or two darker than his fellows. As a dalelander with highland roots, people commonly looked down in his direction or walked to the other side of a lane. The more kindly simply ignored his presence. But now he had been knighted. In front of the Crown Prince, no less. Under the favor of the Queen-To-Be. He still maintained her pink kerchief beneath his jerkin folded upon his breast. Three tilts and one unhorsing and everything had changed. It was truly unreal.

The four knights, along with three young squires, clopped between the tumblestone pillars at the southern end of town. There, flanking the unwalled entrance into the sprawl of buildings, the bright, white banners of House Elkesmein flapped in the wind, each emblazoned with a golden sun, ostensibly in honor of God's ever-watchful spirit. The same emblem adorned Sir Erek's white shield as well as all his and his mount's trappings. A pair of comparatively grimly-clad townkeepers gave gestures of salute at the group's passing; the second son of Lord Hermon Elkesmein still demanded that much respect.

With attendance at Circle, even on a Sunday, neither mandatory by decree nor quite fully embraced by the populace, the streets through town were not exactly empty, though the usual press of bodies in the more crowded spaces appeared considerably thinned. The narrow stone bridge over the Redrush, where the muddy tributary cut a deep channel through town before emptying into the broad, brown waters of the Tawney, remained blessedly de-thronged. The fact remained, despite the chapel's large size, the Dome of Delight could never accommodate even half of Belton's population, and certainly not comfortably. So typically only the more pious residents attended service, or perhaps merely those wishing to be seen as such by others, particularly in the eyes of Lord Hermon himself. The generosity of offerings to the Circle played its role for certain.

As a boy, Miekal had been to Circle many times, gazing up in awe and amazement at the beauty and majesty of the high, ribbed dome, delighting—as the building's name implied—at the music resounding when all seven belfries played at once. "We must be seen," his father would insist. "Let them know we are one of them." As his grandfather would say it, "The old gods are sleeping now. No point in wasting prayer on them." Now, as a young man of seventeen years—and a knight—he just listened as they passed the massive structure to the muffled thrum that must have been a few hundred voices singing within.

At seventeen, he was himself maybe three summers older than the oldest of the squires, but markedly still the youngest knight of the four, the others at least three or four summers elder. Parris Coldwater seemed like the eldest among them, perhaps by a full summer, but Miekal was not truly sure. He recalled them both, Erek and Parris, as he had grown up, watching them in wonderment, admiration, envy. Sir Tomas was a son of the Lord Aerey of Moonsmont to the north, and he appeared the storynook knight in every respect—athletic, intelligent, charming. Perfect.

In short order, they all rode the gentle slope towards the white walls and yellow rooftops of the Lord's manse. The town fell away, leaving a good view of the river and the wide, wooded fields to their right. To the left, the cultivated farmlands rolled beyond the town's west end. The manse was nothing compared to the Lord Werrester's castle in Whytehal, but the hilltop commanded a glorious view nonetheless. Once through the gates and following more salutes, the squires were dispatched to the stables as the knights stretched tired limbs and walked toward the main house. Miekal dismounted both eagerly and gingerly, feeling the pierce of weariness with every movement. The twelve year old squire, in the dark blue livery of House Aerey, took the reins from his grasp.

"We'll need to get you one," Sir Tomas said, nodding in the direction of the younger boys with the mounts. "Every knight needs a squire to attend to things."

"I was a stablehand myself," Miekal admitted. "Down at the garrison mainly. But sometimes up here. It seems unnatural not to tend to my own horse."

The blond man smiled cheerily, patting an arm around Miekal's shoulder, steering him toward the bright, yellow doors of the manor. "Don't worry on it. Let the boys handle the boy things. You're one of us now. Onto the man's world. You've earned it."

As they crossed the cobbled yard in pursuit of Erek and Parris, Miekal noted a young graymaiden, wearing the plain, gray habit and white coif of her station, maybe thirteen or fourteen years in age, standing in the recess of a canopied walkway. In her cupped hands she bore a small white flame, the Sacred Fire of her order. "I have a younger brother," Tomas said. "You should come to Moonsmont to meet him." The flame lit up her pale skin, highlighting dark eyes that seemed to follow Miekal as he walked. His heart jumped a little while her gaze held him. "He's well due to begin squiring. I could speak to father. I think it could be a wonderful arrangement." The maid's lips moved as if speaking, but she stood too far away to be heard.

"What say you?" Tomas said. "Sevensons?"

"Oh. Yes." Miekal pulled his attention forward. "Yes, that would be lovely. I'd like that very much." As they stepped up through the doors, he looked back. The graymaiden had moved on. Only a single young boy darted across the yard on some errand or other. The other knight offered a bright smirk as they entered the house.

MIEKAL HAD BEEN in Whytehal for the marriage celebration of the High Prince Arran Torrey to the beautiful and elegant Lady Renna Werrester, a gathering that spanned a full fortnight with almost every House in the Rule presenting their colors. Of course, for the first sevenday, he had been in the retinue of Lord Hermon, tending steeds and running

307

errands and keeping out of foot as best he could with so many noble lords and ladies milling about, and with a host of knights and their squires all vying for notice. Naturally, as one of the 'littlefolk', Miekal had not been in attendance of the wedding itself, but he had been lucky enough to muscle into the tight press of the Lord's Plaza when the Prince and the Lady Renna had been carried on parade between the Bastion and the Dome of the Doves. Once the revelry of the wedding had passed, the second sevenday had assumed the format of a more common spring festive —three days of games and drunkenness, three set aside for the tournament proper, and one for godly reverence, last moment bargaining, and necessary farewells, fond or otherwise.

It was in the second sevenday that Miekal had decided to change his fortunes. He had entered the hedge-match, taking seven silver marks from the meager stash his father had managed to save since his mother's passing. With his father now gone as well, it seemed an appropriate tribute to spend it on, an impulsive (perhaps drunken) choice that would either turn worthwhile or leave him no far worse off than any commonborn might be in this world. Along with the entrance toll, Miekal had penned his name in the manner and spelling his grandfather had taught him, and taken to himself the shire-name in honor of his fafa, Baenen Sevensons, of which his own father, Daevod, had been the seventh.

While the true knights went about their tests of skill and feats of prowess, the lesser crowd was entertained by challenges of running and swimming and climbing and obstacles. Surviving that first day had been a matter of youthful stamina and pigheadedness more than anything else. But he had earned his position in the second day matches. He had wrestled in the morning mires, fought with fists and feet before midmeal pause, and that same afternoon had defeated six other contenders with long-sticks and cudgels, including one poor older fellow whom he had knocked the teeth from with a horseshoe on a rope.

The third and final day, in reflection of the knights themselves, came down to horsemanship, a set of skills at which, due his experience, Miekal excelled. Racing and jumping and even steering through courses had proven a challengeless effort. Totaling his marks from the prior events, his final tally rose quite high in standing. When it came time for the jousts, his marker stood proud on the board.

Miekal had already cobbled together what armor he could: mismatched leather braces and discarded greaves, dented bits of plate and rusted, bloodied mail. His helmet fit improperly, but stayed in place. His jerkin smelled of piss and vomit, his leggings of manure. But he recalled his father's words. *We must be seen.* He stepped with pride, with eager confidence, with determination. *Let them know we are one of them.* Most contestants that made it this far were either knightless squires or men-at-arms hoping to prove their worth. More than one for certain had sponsorship paying fair coin for real equipment. One may have been a stripped and disprized knight seeking reclamation of his former honor. Whatever their varied causes, those who made the final tilts were only there for good reason.

And of course, the jousts, even of the hedge-matches, always gathered an earnest crowd. They took place in a muddied field markered by hay bales. They happened in the pause while the real knights readied for their own clashes. The knights who had not earned a run themselves came to observe, perhaps from curiosity or out of boredom or maybe just to point and jest. When Miekal came to the field, he saw Parris Coldwater with Erek Elkesmein beside him. The scowl on Elkesmein's features made him want to run. He donned his helmet quickly to hide his fear as much as his face.

Miekal probably would have withdrawn at that moment, turned heel and given forfeit to any chance of winning. His nerves came unbound, afraid of what his lordship's second son might think if recognition dawned. Would he be scorned and mocked? Would he be punished for desertion of duties? But then Miekal saw Sir Tomas Aerey emerge beside Sir Erek. Elegant in blue—a blue so deep it might have been purple—with both moons embroidered on his doublet, one to each breast. And Sir Tomas was laughing, smiling, billowing with joy beside the younger knight. He turned Sir Erek's scowl into a reluctant grin with little more than a hand on one shoulder. And Miekal felt better. A knight had power. A real knight.

Following the first two contests, it had been his turn. He mounted his borrowed horse. He hoisted his shield, a paltry wooden thing he had washed in white and painted bright yellow circles upon, six in hexagon around a seventh. Seven suns for Sevensons. He had thought it most clever. Some of the suns trailed yellow streaks where the paint had run.

Erek Elkesmein pulled a face in puzzlement, exchanged words with Coldwater. Tomas Aerey was busy laughing with some other tall man who stood beside him. Then the ready shout came. Miekal gripped his breaklance in shaking fingers. The flags dropped. He spurred his mount and charged along the bale-run toward some young man named Jasper from Millstone.

. . .

His muscles rejoiced at the caress of warm water. Miekal eased himself into the broad bathpool, remembering the beating his body had undergone only a sevenday before. The healing touch of the graybrothers and -sisters ensured that contests were almost never lethal and that even the more serious injuries were provided quick recovery. The white scar beneath his left breast reminded him that jousting was not a sport to be assumed frivolously.

He was as naked as the other three men in the pool, and each had appropriated his own corner of the bath. A pair of manservants, one much older than the other, had prepared boiling pots which they added in turns to keep the water from cooling overmuch. Scented soaps and bristled brushes had been set along the pool's edge. One young boy, perhaps ten, had been sent to the kitchens a few times to return with fresh decanters of wine. Small baskets of bread and cheese and fruit had been laid out before they had entered the chamber.

"Spring is the best season to arrive if you can," Tomas was saying of his home. "The rains and snowmelt ensure the fall is at peak spectacle. But even through summer the view is beautiful. Autumn less so. Except in drought. Remember two summers back?" he asked the others. "It barely rained all season. The Clearwater was hardly a trickle."

"I wasn't there," Erek said, biting on strawberries. "Father sent me to Oldgrove that year. To teach me patience, or some such nonsense."

"I believe the intent was compassion," Parris said without opening his eyes.

"Well, it taught me boredom is all. Nothing but shriveled orchards and even more shriveled matrons, and far too many dullards and lackwits for one abbey to house."

Parris chuckled. "And I was at Highcastle that summer, taking my shot at a golden cloak. The Festive was so hot. The Field of Fire earned its name that year. But at least King Arom kept the wine flowing and the tables full. And the girls! You might not care, Aerey, but I think I fell in love with a Sorosian beauty. Eyes like onyx and skin the color of polished umberwood." His eyes opened as he smiled, then frowned. "I wish I could recall her name. Dayana? Daynet? Daya-something."

Tomas laughed. "Good for you, Coldwater. I'm sure you'll be happy. Send me an invite once you set the wedding." Parris sloshed water across to Tomas's corner, sending ripples over the whole pool. "And what of you, Sevensons?" Tomas went on. "Where were you two years back?"

Miekal's nerves skipped. He shifted down in the water a bit, then moved further into his own corner. "I was here," he admitted, "in Belton. I've never been anywhere else. Not beyond this year." He focused on the ripples in the water, ignoring the others' attention. "It was hot. Grain was expensive. Food thin at best. We got by though. Thank the Circle for its rations. Soup Sundays were a blessing." A light in the doorway pulled his attention but was gone when he looked. He rubbed the sore spot on his chest. "My father took ill from the heat," he added somberly. A servant entered with another pail of steaming water which he gently added between Erek and Parris. Another set down a basket of fresh rolls, picked up an empty platter.

Tomas filched a roll and slid along the pool's edge. Their feet touched beneath the water briefly, making Miekal's muscles jump, his pulse hop. Thin steam rolled up from the waterpots as the blue-eyed knight broke the bread and handed Miekal a warm half. "Well, now you need never hunger again. I promise." He popped the half-roll in his mouth, smiled while chewing as he lolled back to his previous space.

When finished, they were all provided clean, soft tunics and comfortable trousers. Miekal held the Lady Renna's kerchief, folded carefully. The dark, blood-red rose pattern contrasted the pale pink. It smelled too much of his own sweat. He stuffed it in a pocket.

"Does your father have a chapel in the manse?" he asked Sir Erek.

"Hmn? No. I wouldn't call it a chapel. It's more of a prayer-room really. He likes it because it's near the garden." Erek tied his sash taut. "Why? Did you change your mind on devotions?"

Miekal shook his head. "I saw a graymaiden when we came in. I just thought—"

"Here? In the manse?" Erek shrugged and Parris stood from strapping his sandals. "Probably fetching something for father. It is Sunday after all. Come," he insisted, "Dada will be coming back. Hope you all saved your appetites for a proper supper. I heard one of the cooks mention a boar my brother felled yesterday. If we hurry, we can greet them in the yard."

Tomas patted his shoulder. "I wouldn't waste your energy on a sister. Never worth the effort. Besides"—his fingers offered a gentle squeeze—"I'm sure we could find something more...agreeable...if we put ourselves to it."

Miekal followed, his heart stuttering as he rubbed his still sore ribs.

MIEKAL DEFEATED young Jasper of Millstone in two runs, earning better tallies for balance and handling and steadiness of arm. He dropped his second opponent, an older fellow up from Springdale, on the first pass. The man seemed either too weary or too drunken to hold his saddle. Whatever worked in Miekal's favor was well enough. The exhilaration of actually knocking someone from their mount was intoxicating.

His final adversary—the last remaining contestant of the Tinman Tourney besides himself—he learned was indeed a former knight, as had been rumored. Caster Leyle, sworn once to House Raen of Greygarden, stood like a somber wall in dull, gray armor draped in a charcoal tabard. Where once perhaps a sigil sat above his left breast, only the threads of fraying fabric remained. He studied Miekal briefly with empty eyes, joyless and resigned, with strings of graying hair dangling over sunken, weathered cheeks, before donning his helm and mounting up.

The final joust, in honor of the championship, was to be held in the main lists. There before a seated throng of noblemen and their ladies, before the balcony of Lord Eggard Werrester and his daughter-turned-princess, before the Crown Prince of all Eldarion, freshly wed, the two best souls of the Tinman would be given chance to prove their worth. To the loser would be granted nothing more than injury of pride if not also of body, both recoverable in time. But to the victor would be given something of far greater value than any number of silver marks paid as an entry toll. Knighthood. At the sword of Lord Eggard himself, it was stated, in festive celebration of his daughter's marriage to Prince Arran, one man, no matter how low of station or common in birth, would be given the chance to rise instantly, transformed, into a new role, a new life, all due to the charity of joy.

With his nerves and thoughts so tangled and unraveled,

Miekal barely remembered riding into the makeshift stadium, taking his lane, waiting as the heralds announced their names. The crowd sounded like a storm of voices, a cacophony of mixed emotions that could have been laughter or rage or admiration or ridicule or any combination or all at once. To him, it was the culmination of three days distress, to end at once in triumph or defeat. To them, it was no more than an opening play, comical perhaps, or diversionary, whimsical and irrelevant in the overall scheme of events. Inconsequential. To him, it represented everything. To them, no more than an appetizer to the main meal.

Caster Leyle readied at the far end, taking up his lance from some random attendant serving as squire. Another offered Miekal his own. It weighed heavy. Too solid, too real. Leyle's ecranche was black like his horse, undecorated, nearly unmarred. Far too real. Miekal had only ever unseated one man in his life, and that man had been drunk and old and tired. The horns sounded.

When the flags dropped, Miekal had been praying for succor, for escape, considering a way out of his plight. He was late in charging. But his horse knew the purpose. He found himself moving forward by circumstance more than active thought. *Let them know we are one of them.* It was all that mattered. *We must be seen.*

When the lances clacked and tip met torso, he was busy praying to all the gods he knew.

"Do you know your Virtues, boy?" Lord Hermon asked. "Tell me. I'm curious."

Miekal swallowed, nervously pulling down a last bite of

orangetart. He wiped his mouth on a sleeve without thinking. His heart thumped.

Hermon Elkesmein sat his chair, imposing in white and yellow finery even despite the small stain of drippings that marked the otherwise perfect vest. Erek lounged near his father's seat, swirling a cup in his hand disinterestedly while the older brother, Herbet, sat upright and attentive, sipping a crystal flute of some pale amber spirit. They awaited his answer.

"Of course. My grandsire taught me," he admitted. "Actually, they're quite easy to recall. For me." He tried to avoid the stern, noble brows creasing toward him. "He named his boys for them. My uncles. And my father. In...in the old tongue, of course. In Ambarrin, not Daelic." He shook his head, rushed to answer the question, heart beating even faster.

"They are Love, of course. As for today, God bless." He made a hurried gesture to show his piety, which the Lord echoed in reply, the others less precisely or committedly. "Then Charity, Humility, Honesty. Compassion, of course. Loyalty, and Kindness."

"And which was your father's?" Lord Hermon asked, seeming to squint as if not sure Miekal had impressed him or not.

"Kindness, my lord. The last one, as he was the youngest son. Daevod. *The kind one.* Or *the gentle one,* I believe. Close to that. I'm not sure, telling true. I don't know enough to say for sure. I know it's not direct, though."

"And was he?" the lord asked. "Kind?"

"He was. He was many things, my lord. But he was always kind, yes. To others as well as me. Blessed be his soul."

The lord took another sip, set down his cup. He offered

316

another gesture of respectful acknowledgment to the blessing.

"And what does Miekal mean, I wonder," asked Erek, sounding whimsically curious if not outright bored.

"*The righteous one,*" Herbet said firmly. "From the root *mykaer,* no doubt. *To be forthright.*"

"In Daelic, perhaps," Miekal cut in. "Yes. I'm certain you are correct, my lord. But in Ambarrin, I think it also means *the gift,* or *the gifted.* Or something like that. Again, I can't be certain, my lords. I apologize. We do not study language in the stables. Time does not permit." He looked at the slightly older Herbet Elkesmein, whose face seemed to struggle with whether or not he had been insulted or complimented.

Lord Hermon inhaled a deep breath and moved in his seat before sighing. "Apologies are mine, good sir." He stressed the title with deliberate surety. "Far be it from me to question our dear Lord Eggard's judgment on the matter. Nor would I ever seek to question His Highness's blessing upon the issue. From now and hence you must consider yourself welcome in this house and in all my holding, as any noble knight of the Rule should be. And with this evening as account, I see no reason why any would have cause to believe otherwise. Remain leal and devout in your virtues, and I'm certain your name will carry far."

The lord paused, sitting as if to rise. "Might I humble myself to ask, do you yet have a liege?"

Miekal squirmed slightly, shifted his head. "No, my lord. Not formally. But I had…just..assumed…"

"Curious that Lord Eggard did not take you in." Lord Hermon smiled, chuckled softly. "Then in good time I will ask for your service. But not tonight." He rose from his chair. "This night I am old and must retire. Tomorrow we shall see to any *formalities.*" He stressed the word with good humor. "Come, boys," he announced to his sons. "Your father requires your council. You as well, Coldwater. I am most interested to know, Erek, why you arrived at midday bells but did not show at Circle this Sun's Day."

"And to you, Miekal Sevensons," he said while leaving, "I wish a fond night's sleep. I will have a servant direct you to your room if you cannot recount the way."

"I should be able to take care of that, my lord," chimed in Tomas Aerey, who likewise rose with everyone.

"Oh, of course. Good for you. A pleasure to see that even a stray tom can make themselves useful. See to it." He did not, notably, bid a fond anything to the blond knight.

Aerey bowed until Miekal and he were alone in the chamber with only a pair of servants collecting things. "Shall we," he said, gesturing toward the open arch.

When they stopped at the door to Miekal's room, Tomas leaned against the frame. "Thank you," was all Miekal could think to say.

"Well, this may be it," the blond man said. "I'll be leaving for Moonsmont quite early. It's a long days ride north if I hope to reach the Luunstone Gate by nightfall. But you know...I do still have some fruits and bottle of exceptional springwine in my chamber. The servers know me here," he stated with charming cocksurety. "I could easily be convinced to stay up a bit longer than usual, with the right company."

Miekal studied the comfortable smile, certain his limbs were shaking visibly. The soreness in his chest throbbed, the thought of bed calling him more than anything else. "I don't want to sound ungracious, but..."

"It's all well," Aerey said, pulling away from the wall. "Some other time. I meant what I said. You should come visit as soon as you can. You are always welcome to knock at my gates." He smirked, stepped, then turned back. "Did you know that my ancestors were highlanders too, a long way back. Just like the Torreys. Who knows? In another world, I might have been the Prince. And then..." His hand moved as if...then retreated. "You know, regardless of what common opinion might be, I must say that some of your kind truly have the most beautiful eyes."

Tomas Aerey smiled, broadly, and offered the deepest bow. "Fair evening to you, sir." Then he walked away. Miekal heard the other door close before he sealed his own.

It took Miekal near half an hour to get out of his tunic and remove his boots. He sat on the bed, pondering, questioning, rethinking. Considering. The day—the whole past sevenday—had been beyond belief, incomprehensible. How had he come to this? What fortune had fallen him on that last pass with his opponent. He should have been torn from his own saddle, not the other way around. What world was this that the son of trinketer would rise to the station of knight, would ride before the Prince and bear the honor of the Queen Awaiting's favor. He pulled the pink cloth from his pocket. The kerchief was damp, the rose embroidery glistening. A red spot swelled in its center, as if the flower itself bled.

A stab of pain jolted his ribs. He pulled his hand to it, smearing fresh vermilion across his scar. He was bleeding! No. Not from the wound. His nose bled. More spots appeared on his wrists, his trouser. He tasted copper.

Miekal put the kerchief to his mouth and nose, looked around for a washing bowl. He had none. He waited, soaking the kerchief more than he desired. After a pause, the bleeding subsided. He was able to wipe his face and hands, but the favor sat on the bed, smeared with deep red.

He stood, went to the door. Tomas would have a washbowl, or at least know where to go in the house to find one. He stepped out.

He took two steps down the hall—still barefoot and without tunic—before a light caught his notice. A reflection really, a glow from behind him. When he turned, at the far end of the corridor, the graymaiden stood. She held the same stance as when he had first spotted her, in plain habit and coif, holding the white light in cupped hands. Young, perhaps twelve or thirteen, she moved her mouth as if talking, maybe to him, but he heard no sound beyond his own stuttered heartbeat.

She turned, walked through an open arch.

"Wait," Miekal called. "Please."

A graymaiden holding a Sacred Flame could surely help him. Nosebleeds were the simplest of injuries to mend, for certain. He looked back to Tomas's room then jogged after the maiden.

When he reached the opening, he found a turn, then a stair. She stood at the bottom, looking up at him, dark eyes intent. More silent words moved her pale lips.

"Oh. Hello," he said. "I didn't think you heard me. I'm sorry, I'm not familiar here. I was just hoping...I was in my room and...hey! Where are you going? Wait. Come back."

The girl had turned, walking away, her bright light fading with her. Most of the lamps had been snuffed at this time, and shadows enveloped the hallways. Only her small flame gave brightness to all around her. It made her easy to follow.

As quickly as possible, Miekal went down the steps. At each turn he saw little more than her white glow around a different corner, perhaps her foot or shoulder. He called but she did not pause. She could not have been running. Could she?

At last he came through a wider arch, panting, his pulse heavy. His chest ached along with his arm. He tasted metal again.

The girl stood in a small square of a room, a private altar on the wall that she faced, her back toward him. The glow outlined her gray form. He wiped at his nose, new blood on his fingers.

"I'm sorry," he breathed. "I didn't mean to frighten you. I'm a guest. I've a nosebleed. See? I was hoping you could—"

"You don't belong here," she said in a quiet, gentle voice, not turning from her devotion. The Star of Eil gleamed on the wall above her, reflecting her light.

Miekal rubbed his nose again, smeared more blood on the back of his hand.

"I know you might think that."

"You should go," she interrupted.

"Really. I was invited."

"You need to leave." Still she had not turned.

He stood shirtless, bloody. Barefoot. Maybe he should walk away. It was a wonder she had not screamed for a guard.

"Okay," he admitted. "I understand. I'll leave. But could you tell me, where might I find the baths again?"

"Do you hear them?" she asked, her words light, inquisitive. "The bells?"

He paused, listened. He did hear them. The bells were ringing from the chapel belfries. No, from somewhere upstairs, from inside the manse. But that could not be. Some trick of acoustics maybe. But why were the bells ringing at this time of evening? It made no sense.

"They are calling," the girl said. This time, she turned. Her eyes glowed like bright stars. She held her hands parted to either side, both sets of fingers burning with white flames. She shook her head. "But they aren't for you."

The young maiden stepped forward, reached out a glowing hand. Miekal retreated, confused, uncertain, heart pounding. "You should go," she repeated, a warm smile matching the tenderness in her tone. "You don't belong here."

Miekal stepped back, unsteady. He collapsed to one knee, dizzy, every breath more shallow than the last. When her finger brushed his bare skin, just below the left breast where the white scar remained, a lance of pain seared through his ribs as if the sun itself burned into his flesh.

THE FIRST PUNCH blew the wind from his lungs. Pain gripped him from navel to neck. His eyes lost focus, blurry with tears and a swirl of yellow suns.

Miekal reached the end of the list without comprehending how or why. By some miracle—perhaps no less than prayer indeed—he held his saddle. He had lost grip on his lance, but he certainly did not remember any impact jarring his arm. He had likely missed his target altogether.

Another lance was offered to his grasp. He took it, still struggling to breathe, still wracked with pain. Did he have ribs broken? His own horse spun as he tried to gain his bearings beneath the barrage of shouts and laughter. At the other end, Leyle appeared to shift from side to side, but it may have been his own vision dancing. The horns sounded. He tried to steady his mount, fought to pull air into his screaming chest. The flags dropped. Miekal had no choice.

The thunder of hooves rattled inside his helm as the

spectators fell to silence. The dark rider came at him too quickly, the blunted lance-tip racing forward like a hurled spear. His own weapon dipped and swayed erratically. As they came together, he knew he would miss, but he feared another impact with the lance would unsaddle him for sure, if not kill him outright. He batted the oncoming tip away at the last moment, flinging his shield arm while dropping his lance to clutch the saddle desperately.

Wood shattered, perhaps bone as well. Miekal clung to balance, to consciousness, as agony seized his arm from shoulder down. Tears obscured his vision as much as the helmet. At the end of the run, the horse slowed of its own accord. At least one of them maintained wits. The painted shield was no more than a ruin of splinters. His arm dangled useless at his side. The make-do squire offered another lance. Miekal blinked, squared his helmet as best as possible with one good hand. He would not survive another pass. He knew he must yield. He must forfeit.

The horns blasted. People laughed, gasped, shouted, mocked. The young man beside his horse pushed the lance up insistently, question in his face. Silence rolled over the space like a wave. The horns blared once more. He heard his father's voice. *We must be seen.* From somewhere, he heard bells. He removed and dropped his helmet to the mud. It was not serving him anyway. Wincing, he managed to unstrap the wreckage of his former shield and let the wooden bits fall.

Somehow finding the proper direction, Miekal steadied his horse toward his opponent. The dark figure barely moved, though his mount appeared impatient, stomping. Miekal's arm was surely broken, but he used the reins to bind the wrist to the saddlehorn as best he could, ignoring the pain, embracing it. He grasped the lance. Men hooted.

Ladies gasped. The distant black horse shook its head unforbearingly. Tears streamed. The final horn blew.

When the flag dropped, at least the horse knew what to do.

The stadium inhaled. Silence. Thunder. Miekal put all his good arm into holding his tip steady. *Let them know.* He screamed out before impact, in pain, elation, fury. *We. Are. One.*

FLAME EXPLODED BENEATH HIS RIBS. A white-hot withering anguish coiled around his heart, bursting his lungs. He screamed, blood misting, spitting out with each agonizing breath. The girl looked down, eyes dark, flames extinguished. The delicate, serene smile never faded.

Miekal clawed at the floor, trying to get up. His left arm would not respond, muscles locked in a rigor of seething distress. His legs barely worked, vision tilting in odd directions. Somehow he managed to move, pulling one foot beneath him and convincing the other to abide. He tumbled down the corridor, away from his assailant, desperate to command one more breath in order to shout for help.

The little maiden followed.

His ribs bled now, the white scar opened, red tissue and splintered bone poking through. Whatever she had done, whatever magic she employed, had unsealed the wound, unbound the healing he had received after the jousting.

But that was not right. It could not be. He had not received a wound that dire, not in his chest. His arm, yes, on the second run. He heard the clash, the hooves, the crowd roaring. But the third run. The third he had won. He had unhorsed—

He—

He could not remember.

He stepped out into the garden.

It was not the garden. He was not in the manse. He had never been.

He looked around at the crowd, the wood-built stadium of lords and ladies, the mud churned and torn beneath his bare feet. The crowdstands sat lit as if by sun, but above was only black. The Prince sat his royal chair, peering away from his bride. He was not even paying attention to the jousters.

At one end, Caster Leyle sat his mount, waiting, still, lance up, ecranche ready. At the other end, another man—no—Miekal himself—nearly toppled from his steed, pivoting awkwardly as if unsure which direction to look. The helmet came off, splatted in the muck. The shield—what remained—fell next, seven yellow suns lost in the mud.

He was crying now, both he and his apparition. He knew what happened. He had always known. The only outcome there could have been.

The horns sounded, and then again. Each muffled, muted like the entirety of the crowd.

The horses charged, beautiful, majestic animals.

"Do you hear them now?" the graymaiden said beside him.

The bells echoed in the muted dark, wondrous, pure, glorious. Full of delight.

Tears choked him. "Yes." He fell to his knees.

"You call to the gods," she said. "The gods listen."

He remembered his grandfather's words. *The old gods are sleeping.*

"Yes," the maiden said. "But they hear you in their dreams."

Before him, the riders came together. Miekal's break-lance glanced ineffectually off his opponent's pauldron. The other man's weapon bit square into Miekal's chest. He watched himself lifted and hurled, thrown down as the arm was jerked free of the saddle, even as the breaklance splintered into shards. When his body fell, thrown to the muck like a broken doll, he saw one of those shards, as long and strait as the shaft from a longbow, protruding from his ribs, wedged inward for that brief moment before the reins let go of his wrist.

His own body lay before him, though Miekal had not moved. Both remained as still as silence.

The crowd moved like a whisper, a slow churn like a field of grass in a gentle breeze. At least the Prince seemed to take notice, focus pivoting. Near to him, just behind Lady Renna's seat, a small figure stirred, a slip of gray surrounded by whites and blues and greens. A small young girl, perhaps thirteen summers old, dashed down the steps, erupted through the gilded cloak of a Crownsman to leap down upon the muddied floor of the arena. The default squire was approaching, but only at a hesitant walk.

"I'm with you, Miekal," the maiden beside him said. "Remember."

The other graymaiden ducked beneath the lists, ran down the dimpled field, kicking mud behind her. As she approached, Miekal toppled forward, dizzy, losing coherence. He rolled, gazing at a bright, blue sky.

"I'm always with you. Always."

The two maidens entered his vision from either side. Their dark eyes blazed with white fire as they merged above him.

"We are one."

The world vanished as the Sun came down to meet him.

QUEST

· · ·

MIEKAL OPENED HIS EYES, the lights fading. His chest hurt—
no, his whole being hurt. Muscles ached where muscles
should not exist. His heart beat, every surge of his pulse
feeling like a contest. Or a blessing.

He did not recognize the face before him, pale, dark
eyed, a veil of white around it. A graymaiden, he realized in
some abstract corner of awareness. A young one, much
younger than himself. She smiled.

"You are well," she said, lightly, soothingly. "Just
breathe, and wait a moment." She looked around, then back
to him. "Stay still. You will recover." Her small hand was on
his chest, above his heart, his armor removed, torso bare.
"You were injured. In the joust. Do you remember?"

"He lives?" Another voice interjected, gruffer, sharper.
"Blessed be it. I did not mean—" The voice stuttered. "I
would not have wanted—"

"He lives, sir," the girl said. "He will be fine. I am sure of
it. On my word."

"Thank you. Thank you. Bless you," the man insisted.

"Thanks belong to God, Sir Caster," said a woman's
voice. "We are but instruments of the Divine Fire." A figure
stood with light surrounding her—no, behind her. She
stood in a doorframe of sorts, where sunlight still poured
outside. She wore white with a gray scapular tied by a wide,
yellow belting. A white wimple beneath a gilded velum and
a string of silver medallions across her collarpiece denoted
a reverent of high station.

"Yes. Of course," the knight said. "But thank you also,
Grand Reverent. And you, Sister. Thank you for your service.
Bless you both."

The reverent nodded, but her face remained impassive,

327

blue eyes crisp. "It is both our desire and our privilege. But perhaps if you men could find a less barbarous means to prove your value to each other, it would be less taxing upon us all. Come, Emely," she said to the young sister. "Your part is done here. His Lordship requires us at the Challengers' Procession." She bowed slightly to the knight. "Blessed be you, sir. I leave this man in your charge. We will return to make certain of his health in a short time. I will send a brother to see to his comfort until then."

The girl touched a warm wrist to Miekal's brow with a last, tender smile. She wiped her red-soaked hands on a square of cloth. The graymaiden stood and curtsied to Sir Caster before trotting after the Reverent Lady, almost hopping in comparison to her superior's reserved comportment. The older man came over. His shallow cheeks and flat hair no longer grim and bitter, but simply worn and weary. His eyes glistened. Horns echoed and cheers erupted from outside.

Miekal lay on his back on a thick blanket spread over a wooden flat upon the trampled dirt. The 'room' they were in was no more than a space beneath the crowdstands, bent nails still jutting from wooden planks above. The pounding of a hundred feet sounded like thunder.

"I knew it," called a pitched voice from the opening. "I told you I recognized him."

Three figures blotted out some of the light, if not the noise. Erek Elkesmein elbowed the larger Coldwater in the rib. "He's that highland get works in our stables. Can't imagine Father gave him leave for this. Must have been stashing coins somewhere. What a waste."

"Or he stole it," suggested Tomas Aerey. "His lot's always thieving about. Surprised your father let him in the manse ever."

"You give him too much credit, Tom. Look at him. Hardly clever as all that. What were you thinking, boy?" Elkesmein scrunched his face. "Well, good luck to you. And good ridding, I say. Someone else's problem now."

"Should have hit him harder, Leyle," Sir Tomas said. "Put him out his misery. One less amberkin to stink up the Dales."

Miekal tried to sit, but his muscles protested. He fell back on the flat as if the slur had pierced him more surely than the lance.

"Leave him be," grumbled Caster Leyle. "Boy showed more courage than you pampered lot ever will."

"I'm sure you know all about that," japed the blond knight. "How's it feel to have your title back, *Sir?*" He stressed the word mockingly. "If not your honor."

Sir Caster lurched up. "You know nothing of my honor, welp. If you care to challenge it, I will be happy to defend it before Prince Arran himself." He pressed his height against Aerey with clenched teeth, one hand gripping the pommel of his blade. "No? I thought not." Sir Tomas stepped back, a faltering sneer pretending at a smile.

"Come on, Tomas," interjected Sir Erek. "It's not worth it. Don't spoil the fun. Come, Parris, get me a good place. Muscle up on them lists there. I really want to see the blood spray."

The three young knights retreated into the daylight and the loud festivities. More cheers and stomping continued.

"I'm sorry," whispered Miekal, his chest aching with each word. "You shouldn't...don't...have...to..."

"No," said Sir Caster, kneeling back down. "Nothing for it. Pretty boys like that never seen a battle in all their days. Only earned their title from their father's loins." He leaned back against the wood. "You fought well, considering. Very brave. Stupid, but brave. I figured you would yield after the first run. I honestly don't know how you kept your horse after the second. I must have lost my touch. Sure stubborn will, no doubting." He snorted.

The old man looked out to the sunlight and shouts, listening to the energized crowd. The horns, the thump of hooves, the clatter of steel and roars of delight. "I felt bad, you know. Taking advantage. All those poor souls just looking for a chance. Something different. I robbed it from them. I robbed it from you. I did what I must. I won't regret it."

He inhaled, let out a long, weary breath. "You've will, that's certain. But you'll need training. Someone to tell you when you're doing it wrong. Someone to stop you when you're being stupid." He smirked. "Lord Eggard might have granted my title back, but I've no illusions on my reputation. I'll have to earn my honor back. Every step. And I'll be needing a squire. Someone perhaps who knows a thing about earning their place." His eyes glinted, hazel and full of honest mirth.

"What say you?" Sir Caster asked, holding out his hand, palm open. "And I promise, I won't bother one wit about the color of your eyes."

Miekal might have laughed if his chest did not burn with each movement. Even a small smile hurt. He had lost. Defeat was physical, palpable. Painful. But he had been there. He had jousted in front of the Crown Prince of the Rule. For one brief moment—three entire tilts—he had been a knight. A real knight. Sir Miekal Sevensons. He had been *seen*.

With the same grueling effort he recalled using to lift the lance and hold it steady, he clasped the older man's wrist and felt the fingers close around his own.

THE END

BIO: Dave lives with his family and assorted dogs in Upstate New York. In addition to writing, he enjoys hiking, mountain biking, rollerblading, and hockey. When he's not in the classroom teaching special needs children, Dave argues with fellow FWOers about what makes a good story. Sometimes, he's right. If he could, he'd make his living writing drabbles, but he's found the scant pay-for-word won't keep the mortgage company happy. While working on his WIPs, he has been published in two anthologies, Festival of Fear by Black Ink Press and Black Hare Press' Fourth Year Anthology. He's been a member of Fantasy-Writers.org since March 2017.

CHAPTER 19

DEAD IS DEAD

RETURN WITH THE ELIXIR

by

Ingrid Thornquest

F eet heavy, head heavier still, she, he, they—the permutations of identity ran amok in the Time Warlock's head—walked toward the cliff and stopped when their toes curled over the edge. There, they lost themselves in thought's annals. Eyes unseeing, they stared into the depths below at a tiny zaffre-coloured ball of fluff hung in mid-air with its wind-ruffled fur and feathers frozen. Eventually, they decided 'they' most accurately described their amorphous self-sense. They would be they, when they returned home to Isena Anore, the seat of the Faie'Ry Queen.

And they were almost home—one more night on the road. A bath would be nice. And a real cup of tea would fix their world.

The zaffre fluff remained frozen. Inscrutable. Surely it should be falling?

Some believe home is wherever one makes it. It is a travelling notion linked to oneself. Yet, what if one has become a stranger to oneself because one had sought enlightenment about love only to lose oneself upon the receiving of that gift?

The gift!

Gaze still glazed and centred on the tiny zaffre-coloured fluff, realization dawned as different space-time continua merged and swirled in their head akin to melting ice cream. They had stopped time—for the first time, apparently.

Why?

Fatigued beyond the body, they shook their head to loose reason free. They sought extra time to consider— what? Ahh, yes, to stop the zaffre fluff's imminent death, which they could do.

After seeking enlightenment regarding life and love from a Great Oracle, which they now believed was a spurious endeavour, they had gained the ability to travel through time. Naturally, with mind-exploding Conse- quences. Perhaps they ought to use the ability to return home? To their youth? Avoid the entire traumatic pilgrimage to the Great Oracle, which cost them their iden- tity, physical and mental? End of story.

Oh, to be young and naïve, again. Even with death threatening. At thirty-ish, they were not unfamiliar with death, having been reborn into a new persona twice over.

They barked salty laughter, which went nowhere. The stillness in time-paused was absolute.

However, the zaffre fluff had fallen—err, been kicked over the cliff unequivocally by them. As a warlock of time, they could reverse this accidental kick of the fluff when scuffing the cliff track in abstracted personal torment. Yet, should they? What would be the ramifications of meddling with time? The oracle showed them the personal costs, but what about the effect on others' lives?

They withdrew their gaze from the fluff to swivel around and stare up at looming, large, lemon-lashed, lilac eyes framed by a delicate, camel face covered in turquoise fur. Similarly frozen. The creature resembled a weird assembly of animals besides camel. The head towered above them, mostly because it sat upon a long, long neck with fur coloured in scraggly, violet squares on a turquoise base. Somewhere below the neck stood two turquoise, lion-like legs and paws ending in claws lengthened to slice and hook. In contrast, the body was covered in iridescent feathers, turquoise, except for the vibrant violet wings.

The fluff's mother(?) was a statue in mid-lunge, claws foremost, targeting them.

They sighed. Everything would be so much easier without a conscience.

Consequences be damned, they would save the wee thing. By degrees, they eased time backwards, concentrating upon the ball of zaffre fluff as it retraced its descent upwards toward the cliff edge. Playing with time was all too easy. They stopped, shocked. And received another shock. There were now two of them: the them, who manipulated time in this out-of-time moment, and the them, who they now observed live through the past as they backtracked time. They shrugged and restarted the reversal of themselves walking toward the cliff. That is, they watched themselves walk backwards, from cliff-edge to cliff track, until the fluffy ball met their foot at the end of a kicking arc. Well, not 'their foot' anymore, but 'their foot' of their past self.

Contemplating this whole temporal shemozzle that they controlled made their head ache.

So, once more, they paused time to ponder the best course of action—one which minimised altering the past, and personal Consequences. Then they eased time backwards a tad more. The world juddered and their insides nauseatingly shredded apart. The fluff ball flipped sideway in space away from their foot (the one belonging to their past self). Then the spatiotemporal interregnum vanished as they edged time even further into the past and continued to watch themselves walk backwards, scuffing the path in reverse. Nothing of note occurred. No prelude to the interregnum.

Curious, they edged time forwards once more, towards the moment they kicked the fluff. And yes, there it was, that same interregnum, plus a simultaneous shift of events sideways, causing the fluff to connect with the foot that kicked. Again, and several times more, they replayed the anomalous event. They concluded that the zaffre fluff leaped sideways towards their toe. Bizarre.

Next, they ticked time forwards seeking anomalies. In temporally controlled increments, the fluff sailed in an arc up and over the cliff edge. Before the fluff landed in a heap of what promised extreme deadness (they were no voyeur of death) they reversed time to sail the fluff back up to the cliff top. Apart from the fluff's seeming involuntary spatial jump into the kick's path, they detected no other weirdness.

Still, they had ascertained the kick of the zaffre fluff occurred because of time's glitch, which jumped the fluff sideways into contact with their foot. They concluded they would not be responsible for the petite being's death if they allowed the events to play through time in the initial manner. The spatiotemporal glitch was responsible.

They could walk away free from culpability, and free from Consequences. Although, only after dodging the mother's ferocious claws.

They exhaled the swirl of tangled thoughts inside them and turned away.

However, before they re-instated time's ordinary flow, they inhaled more thought tangles, all themed on the imbecility of seeking a Great Oracle for clarification on life and love. One tangle, in particular, crystallised into an idea and refused to budge. It held that true love comes only to those with true love in their hearts. The thought fatigued and, thereby, won its argument. Therefore, they would save the fluff.

They recommenced time. Yet, methodically. At the appropriate moment, they swept downwards and plucked the fluff from its trajectory towards death.

Then, they reminded themselves that altering life's events with temporal magic should not become a habit. That way led to beastliness, which surely would deny true love.

Once the petite creature rested in their hands, they released their grip on time's flow. As time resumed, they coalesced back into one entity and concurrently stepped sideways to elude oncoming claws.

They watched the mother drive herself through the place where the kick had occurred. Then, hands extended with fluff encapsulated, they waited for the mother to register her young was safe and offered back into her protective care. She daintily pivoted on a lion-like paw, came to a one-legged halt before the dread cliff edge and fixed her regard to them.

"Krrk cll-cll ckkk? Kkkkkvvvk ckck clll-lllk e cvvvck?" uttered the creature, while simultaneously telepathing the sense of their communication: *What in Twilight's damnation just happened? You kicked my child over the edge and also somehow didn't?*

They furrowed their brow. *You sensed a duality?* they asked mentally.

Uh-huh. Not first instance time jumped today. Just first for two potential paths.

I see. That's, err, enlightening. Farewell.

Thankful no nasty repercussions had landed upon them after manipulating time, they strode off along the cliff-edge path and searched for a route down into the valley, where they were convinced would be a village with an inn, a decent repast and a night's shelter. The sun hung low, likewise contemplating rest. At least, the sun headed in the same direction as them and thus did not hide behind the cornucopia of trees on the cliff path's other side.

Ten breaths later came a thud of paws from behind.

My name, GdGna, sent the creature. *Yours?*

A sensitive issue. It was Sundara. Since entering Faie'Ry, the name no longer fits. Recently the Great Oracle conferred another upon me. That too sits on me uncomfortably.

I help? Perhaps problem name unworn. Tell, please.

Lips pressed tight, they mentally ground out, *Ruvantrill.*

Nice. Ruvantrill means soul-singer in ancient Ry'ish.

Ruvantrill—they tried donning the name. No, it still belonged to someone unfamiliar. They let it drift away, to settle back into the less confusing anonymity of 'they'.

So, you play with time? telepathed the feathered and furred creature.

Yes. Two-edged gift from a Great Oracle, they sent as they turned to doggedly trek towards 'home'.

You caused time to jump? Not good. Deadly. Birds fly into

trees, or lose updrafts, and others suffer, too. The strange beast nodded towards three dead birds littering the ground.

No! I am not responsible. Tempted though they were to ask how the bizarre creature could sense temporal fluctuations, they didn't, being too tired to listen to the answer.

The creature, plainly far from fatigued, pressed them with, *Who? Best stop them. Else death dealt injudiciously.*

Like a food morsel catching between teeth, another notion lodged in their mind. Strange, the Oracle gifted them temporal magic just before time was right royally riled. No, they would not pursue that thought, nor contemplate the nasty, prophetic games the twilight-forsaken Oracle played upon them.

The denial was on the tip of their tongue. It stayed that way. Lying was impossible here in Faie'Ry. They stomped onwards and wished they had never come to this bedamned realm. The turquoise creature padded beside them with the zaffre fluff ensconced in an exuberance of fur and feathers on its mother's back, visibly at home. They grumphed.

So, you go stop them? sent the creature, GdGna.

They attempted another denial. This, too, refused to budge from their tongue. They stopped, harrumphed and stared across the cliff edge into the horizon.

They settled for an indirect demurral. *I have no idea who is responsible or where they are located.*

Possible I help with the where.

The personal cost of time travel is prodigious.

Perhaps you stop them other ways, sent the creature as it lifted one clawed paw to scratch behind its ear. *Stopping needed. Animals died. Dead is dead, I think.*

What does that mean?

GdGna shrugged. *Hunch.*

338

Why me?

I cannot. You can. If another can, give you them cost of stopping time-influencer?

With an exhale, this time the *No* came readily. Avoiding the personal cost of their destiny might be a high priority, but so was not harming others, whether directly or indirectly. They had been brought up to serve, to care for others' wellbeing. They had been brought up as an heir to the royal throne of Atlantis on Earth. Now they existed in Faie'Ry, though coming here was one adventure they wished had never happened.

Consequences. Always damn Consequences to what seemed good ideas at the time.

Then we go wrong direction, sent the creature interrupting their doldrums. *This way better.*

The turquoise creature stepped off the cliff path and into the violet-flowered wood. They tried unsuccessfully not to sigh as they stepped over more dead birds.

The world jumped sideways. Birds fell from the sky. So did a frog or two.

Feel that? sent GdGna.

They nodded.

Fifth time, today.

Oh. "To the seventh hell with oracles!" they murmured and then sighed.

Nonetheless, they followed GdGna through the wood, loping over bluebells, dead birds, hyacinths and caved-in fox dens. They strode under jacarandas, empty upturned nests and the mournful cries of animals who had lost a loved one. Too soon, the gloam made progress tedious. Ups and downs of the terrain could no longer be distinctly discerned, and ascertaining which shrubs might be pushed past and which were too thorny or prickly to touch was a challenge.

After a particularly brier-bound patch, they sighed as they peered through the gloom, and wondered if they should halt this ridiculous task of apprehending whoever caused time to jump. How did they know that whatever they did to stop this temporal perturbation would not be worse?

They sighed once more.

You sigh a lot, sent GdGna. *Is normal?*

Perhaps we should stop for the night. I will eat some food from my backpack and climb into a tree.

If you wish, Ruvantrill. Meet me morning time at Ways Inn. Our quest end close.

They went to sigh again but stopped themselves.

Perhaps Ways Inn might be better than— "Aaaagh!"

Pain rolled through them, enormous cart loads, the sort which causes one's eyes to roll up into their sockets and awareness to be consumed till gone.

Waking was rough and eked itself out in dribs and drabs.

They lay on a grassy patch, but not the same grass they had collapsed upon. They knew this without great effort because no purple-flowered jacarandas loomed above. Agony still ran rampant through them, although a diminished sort, except for their ears, which hurt exceedingly.

Both the antecedent pain of passing out and the aftermath pain were similar to the pain that consumed them when they gained temporal magic or when they had become a 'they' after their arrival in Faie'Ry. However, they were in no hurry to discover what identity-altering change they suffered this time.

Once they levered onto an elbow, they noticed GdGna

stood behind them. Not fourteen steps further lay a crooked inn of four storeys lit with copious, magical lanterns. The inn was pink with a green thatched roof and luminous, yellow, swinging front doors. A poster board sat in front displaying the pub's menu under garish green calligraphy, informing all this inn was indeed The Ways End Inn. More copious signs randomly impaled the grass, and all attested the same.

"How—"

Carried you. Tall but light, no fat or muscle. Should exercise more.

I've been trekking for mo—never mind. Could you help me up?

Camel teeth gripped their tunic and pulled. Extended wings flitted under their arms and, without a huff or groan, GdGna had them on their feet. However, after two steps forwards, they swung an arm over GdGna's shoulder girdle for support in tottering toward the inn.

A bevy of people congregated around the inn's door, which was comprehensively plugged with a queer contraption.

After each step, more and more heads turned. All wore hard-edged stares, promising a reckoning should the newcomers prove inconvenient in any manner. The heads, and accompanying facial hair and topknots—of which there was an abundance—were adorned in bone orna-ments. The bodies that loitered under these heads belonged to dwarves whose hands held nasty, sharp and pointy instruments of warfare. Thus, the stares had no shortage of backup if a reckoning proceeded.

"GdGna," shouted a woman's voice from the other side of the wedged contraption and the knot of dwarves, thus inside the inn. "You'll have to enter via the back door. These blasted block-heads have jammed their thingummy in the doorway. Been stuck for the last five hours. What'll it be tonight for you and your cat-eared friend?"

Cat-ears? Their stomach sank towards their bowels and churned around to emphasise how unimpressed their whole gut was with the idea of precipitating personal Consequences so soon after acquiring temporal magic. At this rate, despite having time on their side, in no time at all, they would transform into a beast.

No! No way would they invoke their time magic again. Ever!

Caught in woe, they only half-listened to GdGna as her camel-like mouth uttered more bird-like clicks and chirps, while she telepathed, *Yukihiro-san, famished. Soup, house dish, cheese and dessert with tea. With friend, Ruvantrill, bed for night. Good?* GdGna finished with a head bob.

"Of course. No honorific, my dolls, just Junjii or even June. I'll meet you at—"

For the merest of moments, the door-jammed contraption, along with the dwarves, blinked out from existence. Time bucked similarly to the previous interregnums. Birds, toads and doormice fell from the sky.

GdGna's gaze flicked to them, then back to the reappearing dwarves and device.

Hands on hips, June scowled and said with raised voice, "Blasted dwarves, always scaring my customers with some new-fangled thingamajig in my inn. This time you'll pay me recompense."

"Ach lassy," said the most rotund dwarf, huffing and puffing, "keep yur knickers on. This wee beauty will gift us treasure beyond yur wildest wishes. We go to ransack a city. We'll be sure to spare yee a tevy of silver."

GdGna clicked and sent, *The time disruptor.*

They nodded and scrutinised the contraption. Wedged on its side, half in and half out of the inn, was a red velvet seat mounted upon a sleigh. Behind the chair sat a man-sized dish, while in front of the chair was a ceramic bar with exposed wires connecting four levers and four dials. One lever was lodged in the door jamb near a door hinge. They deduced, as the dwarves jiggled and finagled the contraption to try to free it, that this lever was responsible for the sleigh, its seat and hangers-on vanishing from this moment into another, then reappearing in the next moment.

The dwarves ceased pushing and pulling the contraption to argue amongst themselves.

With several pairs of spectacles caught in her beard rather than sharp instruments and what appeared to be a manual dangling from a hand, one dwarf shook her head and said, "'Tis nae ready. Thee time not be set proper-like."

"Glorigrim," said the overly round one belligerently, "we can nae dislodge it any other way,"

Hands crossed over chest, she replied, "Griftwinch, though the spatial controls now be set, thee temporal controls remain half torn out. It be nae safe. Yee cannae move it to Atlantis till the time be altered. We'll drown."

"Yee ken thee mishap be nye. If we cannae wrest it free from the doorway, best we leave this here, err, now."

They watched the interchange, yet tuned out of further dialogue.

Rip off levers, telepathed GdGna, intruding into their musings.

I'd prefer to do that without invoking time magic, nor suffering from multiple bloody wounds, they sent.

Skewer cylinder at back? Perhaps power source.

Leaves me with the same problem of avoiding personal damage.

Must stop dwarves.

They let out a groan, rather than a sigh, and tottered toward the dwarves. As one, the knot turned toward them, brandished instruments of warfare and glared.

They stood their ground, cleared their throat and said, "Allow me to help."

The rotund dwarf, Griftwinch, answered, "Yee be a master wirer or mayhap have the strength of ten? Though honest, I doonnae see that."

"I ... I am a warlock of time and might go into the past to warn you not to attempt to take the contraption through the inn door."

Not quite a lie, because they could not lie, however, most definitely a twisted truth. They indeed might go backwards in time, if they wanted. They most assuredly did not want to. The best option seemed to get close enough to damage the hellish contraption irreversibly, and then it might be dismantled to wrest it from its currently unbudgeable position.

"Bad idea," said June from the other side. "The dwarves are too thick-skulled to listen to anyone else. I tried that earlier today when they decided to bring it into the inn out of the rain."

"Then I will—"

Their words came to an abrupt halt. Four dwarves surrounded them. Pointy, sharp instruments pressed into the warlock's person. Another three surrounded GdGna, and yet another had the zaffre fluff in a weapon's direct line of slice.

"What you'll do, me laddy," said Griftwinch, "is take oos and our wee gizmo here back in time to the era of

Atlantis. Do what we say and then return us here when we say. Got that? Else yur friend gets run through all-the-way to snuffing it."

"Atlantis is on Earth. I manipulate time, not space," they said while futilely not contemplating oracular manipulation and the coincidence of the dwarves and themselves both desiring to go to Atlantis. Yet, though they did indeed wish to return to their youth, transporting the dwarves and this contraption there seemed inherently foolish.

"Let oos worry aboot portalling to Atlantis. Right lads, bring the warlock to the gizmo."

They almost laughed at the ridiculousness of threatening a temporal warlock. They could pause time—at any time—and then play it backwards or forwards at any speed and re-arrange things as they desired. If they desired.

Therein lay the problem.

Did they desire?

There was the not-so-trifling drawback of transitioning into a beast to consider. They dared not even pause time for a good think, given their cat's ears had occurred after simply pausing and rolling time back and forth an iota.

While the dwarves hustled both warlock and GdGna toward the contraption, they resorted to ruminating on the move. However, time ran out on them faster than anticipated. The world shifted. Things jumped sideways more nauseatingly than during that first interregnum when they had kicked the zaffre fluff. More birds dropped from the sky and not a few insects, plus frogs, toads, doormice and a single sock. They saw the red-seated contraption double up and push viciously at itself, along with objects and people in its vicinity. Dwarves, GdGna, Fluff and the warlock all got sucked sideways into the doubled-up contraption and squashed between doubled-up bars, power sources, levers and seats. Faces twisted. Limbs contorted. Screaming voices distorted.

Pain, of the rolling-eyes-up-into-eye-sockets-sort ricocheted through them—not quite the agony of transformation—still, unconsciousness threatened. They gritted teeth, determined not to lose awareness while the contraption attempted to inhabit the same space twice over. Flirting with death, they resisted invoking temporal magic. Untangling the contraption from itself would probably demand a heavy cost. Assuredly the agony of entanglement would be momentary. Wouldn't it?

Around them, dwarves clutched faces, bodies buckled badly and the world frayed apart as the shimmer of two contraptions fought each other. GdGna faded.

Their insides felt sheared into pieces.

No alleviation arrived. Rather, time laughed at their refusal to play and tauntingly lengthened.

Blood dribbled from the ears of those dwarves, Glorigrim and Griftwinch, in the epicentre of the spatiotemporal distortion. Both wrestled with versions of themselves. Now, not just one other version, but two, three—no, four others. As all the dwarves quintupled and vied for occupancy of limited space, GdGna and the zaffre fluff faded in equal measure. The two creatures were perilously close to being inhabited by multitudes of dwarves.

The warlock's ribs compressed and breath tightened as the contraption poured more of itself into the space. Distinct angles and edges indicated as many contraptions as versions of Griftwinch and Glorigrim. Bizarrely, the contraption's various temporal versions menaced everyone, except themselves. They neither faded nor multiplied. Yet six versions of Griftwinch and Glorigrim horrifically shredded apart before their eyes. Life became coloured red.

A new notion landed with a thud and consumed as much mental space as it could in the same manner that the contraption ate external space. They were weary of these notions; all led to temporal magic. Regardless, they examined the thought. Five contraptions existed with the lever on, while only one had the lever in the off position. They surmised there would be no end to this bizarre interregnum that imprisoned them.

Yet?

What if they temporally reversed the contraption and dwarves and GdGna far enough away from the moment when the contraptions from different times had all landed synchronously to create the anomaly? They reassured themselves they might undo this entire incident—they glanced at Glorigrim and Griftwinch's bits, looked away and hoped by Twilight's seven hells that was true.

Then they did what came way too naturally for comfort and the exact activity they had promised themselves they would not do, because it seemed precisely what the Great Oracle wanted them to do. They jumped themselves, everyone in contact and the temporally sick contraption back through time. As they did so, their sensitive ears picked up the whir of many contraptions revving up.

By duplicitous demons, all six contraptions remained entangled and rode with them. Nevertheless, to escape the interregnum, they continued to reverse through time.

To no avail.

More was required.

They lent over dwarf remains, which refused to coalesce into whole dwarves despite travelling into a past way before the deaths. Then they passed fingers over the multitude of levers until they found a green one that felt more solid than the rest and pushed it on.

Their new hyper-sensitive ears registered only one contraption had added a new hum to its voice. Then they, one set of dwarves, GdGna and Fluff travelled elsewhere as well as elsewhen. The rest of the contraptions and copies of dwarves vanished from sight. Untanglement proceeded, much to their relief, and the landscape altered to a seascape. Their chosen contraption, at their discretion, continued its backward temporal journey until the seascape morphed into the cityscape of an ancient Earth civilisation. They stopped the contraption from travelling through time and smiled as they inhaled an immense breath of briny air. Home! Atlantis.

Scents of stone-baked bread laced with dates merged with those of freshly dyed silks and fresh-caught fish. Above them, gulls spiralled and screeched warnings. Painted red and orange from a burnt sky that hovered ominously, the city had an awful beauty to it. They had calculated their exit from time's passageways to a nicety. Death loomed for thousands of Atlanteans. It was one magical device away. Yet, they could stop it, and given the oracle had tempted them here, so be it. They would stop Atlantis from sinking and then claim the reward of evading their destiny as a beast.

They smiled.

Unaware of death's imminence should the time warlock meet failure, market stallholders yelled of their wares and customers haggled for bargains, while the warlock's gaze searched for a particular person. And yes, there she stood, the one they most wanted to meet, a young, blonde woman surrounded by royal guards on a balcony of an ostentatious hotel, commandeering the entire eastern perimeter of the market square.

Beckoned by the hope of a home they had longed for

ever since leaving, they stepped off the contraption. Casually, they twisted their body to look back at the bizarre device, now attracting a crowd. Blood plastered the red velvet seat. The whole was littered with dwarf bits. All dead. Not just the central two. However, a quite solid GdGna perched on the front bar. She looked disinclined to move.

Their insides threatened to exit.

Why, they sent to the turquoise creature, *do the dwarves remain dead after travelling to a time way before their deaths?*

GdGna's large lilac eyes blinked. *Dead is dead*, she said. *Forwards nor backwards alters that.*

I rescued your child from certain death.

For you, my child never died. Death stopped before death happened.

They blinked away fear of failure. They had left Atlantis as the tidal wave approached and the buildings crumbled from the earthquake. However, they had not actually seen a dead body, so surely they might still save everyone? Gaze returned to the blonde woman, they lifted their hands to touch their ears. Too silky soft. Too pointed and too upright. Too sensitive. Definitely too much a beast's ears. They swallowed bile.

"Princess Sundara," they yelled, "accept not the Faie'Ry Queen's gift tonight. It comes with dire repercussions for Atlantis and you pers—"

Pain.

They crumpled oh-so-slowly. Knees buckled, balance disintegrated, and their head dropped back with an interminable wail. In the corner of their eyesight, they saw Sundara's own gaze spearing them. The ignominy. Their eyeballs rolled up into hiding.

Settled on something velvet and cushiony, their skin

prickled all over and nose tickled. They opened eyes to stare up into azure orbs set in a heart-shaped face with rose-bud lips. Golden ringlets dripped and itched their nose, but were not responsible for the prickles assaulting their body. However, neither the itch nor the prickles demanded attention in the same strident manner as the young woman's face.

It felt bizarre to see this face so close when not a reflection in a mirror.

Sundara sat back on her heels, thereby ceasing to drip hair over them. Her brows knit together and she flapped her hands. "About what you said earlier, I cannot not."

They blinked, bemused. What had they said earlier?

Shaking head, Sundara repeated, "I cannot not. They will not let me be rude to her."

"Who?" they asked, though with a dawning memory of asking her not to accept the Faie'Ry Queen's enchanted 'gift'.

"Neither my fiancée nor my advisers will let me refuse a gift from the Faie'Ry Queen. I'm under strict instructions to appease her."

Enormous, azure eyes gazed at them and welled with tears.

They rolled their own eyes and said, "You are your parents' representative while they are away, and therefore, you have an absolute right to spurn this advice and the gift."

"But ... I just cannot not accept the present. Everyone ignores me anyway. So what is the point of contradicting their counsel? Someone else will accept it on my behalf."

"You are the law, not them. Be strong."

Sundara still shook her head, and tears no longer threatened, but were in full play. Frustration welled inside them in equal and opposite measure to the young woman's cravenness.

With hardened jaws, they said, "Refuse, else Atlantis sinks into the ocean, and thousands die." And you will become someone you do not wish to be, kick a fluffy creature over a cliff and murder a knot of dwarves through belated action.

"I can't. I don't believe you, man-beast."

Their choler halted mid-stride. Beast? They reached up to feel their cat's ears and their face, and stopped halfway, stunned. Their arm was covered in a velvet coat of golden fur. Breath raced inside and back outside them too fast to monitor. Too fast for contemplation. Too fast for much, beyond a wild panic.

They opened their mouth and fear spewed forth, "Sundara, don't accept the Faie'Ry Queen's gift. You will become me, a beast. I am you from the future and—"

The young woman rose gracefully to standing. She wore the newly donned pity of someone grateful to have an excuse not to do what they were not brave enough to do. "You are me? From the future? Atlantis will sink? The whole of this island? Sorry, that is nonsense." She turned her back and muttered, "Crazy," as she departed.

A grating click assured them they were imprisoned here. At least, as far as the now was concerned. Yet they were not confined to the now. There would be Consequences to escaping through time. Still, if they stole the Queen's gift and hid it within some other when and elsewhere in Faie'Ry, then problems solved, including beastliness.

Why had they not considered doing this in the first place?

Sundara was always going to be an obstacle rather than support.

After considering the best 'when' to snatch the gift, a cataclysm inciter, which resembled a bejewelled music box, they squared shoulders and reversed through time to the morning's wee hours when the room was empty and the door unlocked. All lay dark and still. They stepped back into time and exited the door. Night's shadows hid them as they slid through the hotel toward the grand ballroom where the Faie'Ry Queen would host a ball during that very night and instigate a cataclysm. Once there, they allowed almost an entire day to race away.

Armed with the knowledge of when and where the Queen would present their young self, Sundara, with the cataclysm-inciting music box, they drove through time to that precise moment. Temporal manipulation was easier and easier. With a flourish of a hand and a word of power, time returned to its ordinary flow. They plucked the music box from four hands as the Queen gave and Sundara received. Then they slowed time to race out of the hotel and into the deserted market square. Their eyes strove to locate the bloodied contraption, to no avail.

Despair took them. They shook it off with a rough laugh. They remained a time warlock. At least until they altered history.

But then what?

Would they be able to return GdGna and Fluff to their home before the Ruvantrill self was annihilated or subsumed back into Sundara?

Would they remember becoming Ruvantrill? Any of Faie'Ry?

Yet, if they did not do this, they would transform into a beast.

A manic, light-headed hopelessness wrestled them.

They slumped against a market stall's empty counter, ran hands through their shoulder-length hair and then brought their hands back down to scrutinise the soft, short, amber fur over their skin. Shakily they traced fingers across their face's furred contours.

Becoming a beast was unacceptable. So, as they could still play with time, they would finish what they had started: save Atlantis and live as Princess Sundara. GdGna had to be wrong regarding 'dead is dead'. Irrefutably the dwarves had failed to return to life, but the dwarves had died in their presence. Moreover, the warlock had not yet actively manipulated events in the past to change history. They had stolen the cataclysm inciter, but historically it had not been opened till midnight, some few hours away. Technically, history had not yet been interfered with, so hopefully, they had time. They swallowed fear and reminded themselves that if the being Ruvantrill was lost to the annals of time as a little side-story, the reward was Atlantis.

A weight from their shoulders, and that freedom, somehow, enabled them to spot GdGna at the market square's other end. She stood next to a large, covered object the size of the contraption. They loped toward the creature.

GdGna bobbed her head and said, *You fade. Home first fast, please. Look!*

Once more, they inspected their arms. The fur remained, yet they saw through themselves.

No, not self, but sky!

Above them, midnight burned. A flaming, vermillion body filled the greater part of the sky and, moment by moment, more of it. It promised death within hours.

They pulled the music box from a coat pocket. Untampered, it remained closed. Locked even.

They looked at GdGna. She click-whistled, *Many ways people death-destined, die.*

They shook their head. *I have not tried enough other options. If I travel further into the past, then—or if I go to the future and return with a device to destroy the falling star, or—*

GdGna harrumphed. *When first you left Atlantis, it dying?*

They nodded acquiescence.

Best way in life is forwards not backwards.

With that thought not precisely solid enough to admit defeat, still they did the only thing their fading self could do: save GdGna and Fluff. Since they could not program the contraption to a new spatial location, that of Faie'Ry, they resorted to undoing all they had just done and reversed time. They gave the cataclysm device back to the Faie'Ry Queen and Sundara, and then kept reversing through their recently made history till they and GdGna were back in the contraption and reversing their trip into the past. In effect, they went forwards in history to when the dwarves' contraption entangled with itself six times over. Then they slipped life further back in action to that moment, just before the contraption first doubled. Once there, they stopped reversing and finagled their actions.

They began to rewrite history. Unfortunately, the dwarves' bits continued to paint the contraption red. However, they saved GdGna and Fluff by pausing time to push them from the contraption's vicinity. Next, they removed the temporal lever's wires, reached over to the green spatial lever set to Atlantis, and pushed it forward. Time still paused, they exited from the contraption and its dwarf bits to stand beside GdGna.

Finally, they released their hold on time and watched

the dwarf-splatted machine with the red velvet seat flicker out of existence. They knew it headed for the depths of an Earth ocean and the now long-buried remains of the city of Atlantis.

GdGna said, *Fixed, Ruvantrill?*

Uh-huh, they—no—he said.

Perhaps being Ruvantrill would not be so bad. After all, the Great Oracle did promise him true love. However, on no account would he invoke his temporal magic again. Adventures were over-rated; they came with Consequences.

THE END

BIO: Ingrid Thornquest has been in search of magic her whole life. She has lived in Australia, then the UK, and now France. She has experimented with science, then dance, and is now writing fiction. Currently, she is being mentored by three cats. She has stories in: Festival of Fear, Rise & Fall, and The Rabbit Hole. She is a fantasy ghost-writer. PS Magic is elusive, but clues can be found in 'the way of the cat'. Ingrid has been a member of FWO since the end of May 2016.

...

CHAPTER 20

DOING SCRIBE THINGS
RETURN WITH THE ELIXIR

by

Matt Krizan

A flurry of activity greeted our return to Rish Puello, with distant figures scurrying about the gate-house and along the palisade's wall-walk. I imagined frantic orders being shouted by guard captains as Soralain, the midnight-blue wyvern on whose back Marnél and I rode, banked gracefully overhead and landed atop a gentle rise overlooking the town. I bit back a chuckle, understanding all too well the bowel-loosening fear brought on by the sudden appearance of this creature straight out of legend. I alighted in a puff of dust onto the narrow, hard-packed dirt road serving as the main thor-oughfare into and through town, then helped Marnél do the same.

Conveniently I return, said the wyvern, the words spoken

directly into my mind, then she launched herself into the air.

"What did she say?" asked Marnél as we watched Soralain fly away.

I shook my head. Our newly-formed bond may have allowed the wyvern to communicate with me telepathically, yet that didn't make her odd, cryptic manner of speech any more comprehensible.

"C'mon, let's go..." I offered Marnél my arm, and he took it, leaning on me heavily.

We made our way down the road toward the gate, where a familiar face strode out to meet us. The guard captain planted the butt of his halberd firmly in the ground in front of him and barked, "State your business."

"Good evening, Captain Orso." I offered him a smile in return.

The guard captain blinked, then his eyes narrowed as he studied me.

Do I look that different? I wondered.

"Eshval fend..." Orso murmured finally. To someone atop the gatehouse, he called out, "Find the Magistrate! Go! And opened this Seru-damned gate."

As the gate creaked open, Marnél and I traded amused looks.

"Apologies, Master Varun." Orso bowed his head. "I'm sure Magistrate Varik will send a tukney to convey you to him promptly. Is there anything I can get you while you wait?"

I frowned, envisioning my father rousing a slave to come collect us with his three-wheeled cart. Such a thing wouldn't have merited a thought from me not all that long ago, but that was before Alaya—and just thinking about the former slave-turned-endwife left a tightness in my throat and a familiar emptiness inside me. I gripped her jade pendant through the fabric of my shirt and pushed back against sudden tears.

I glanced at Marnél, the expression on his face telling me his thoughts were travelling along similar lines. In response to my unspoken question, he steeled himself with a deep breath and nodded.

"Thanks," I said to Orso, "but we'll walk."

Ignoring the guard captain's protests, Marnél and I passed through Rish Puello's gate together, finally returning home.

WORD of our arrival spread through town like ripples in a pond, and curious passersby pointed and whispered as Marnél and I shuffled along the road. By the time we reached the square outside the assembly hall where my father waited, a crowd had gathered. Behind us, the slave my father sent pulled his empty cart, looking decidedly confused.

On the assembly hall's steps, my father stood alongside my sister, Taysh, with the three members of the town council behind him. My father's impatience was evident in his tight-lipped smile and the way he clasped his hands, although such gestures were undoubtedly lost on most of those present. His gaze went from Marnél and me to the slave then back again, the barest furrowing of his brow hinting at a mix of confusion and displeasure. My sister, for her part, stared as if she'd never seen me before, her open-mouthed expression an amusing combination of awe and disbelief.

Apparently I do look that different, I thought.

I ran my fingers through my beard, grown well past scraggly now. My hair was sun-lightened, my once fair skin sun-burnt and darkened to a nut brown. And there was the fresh scar on my forehead, of course, stretching across my temple and ending just above my left ear.

"My son!" My father's voice boomed out. A smile split his face, the big toothy one he used whenever he was among "the common folk," as he called them. He strode forward and clapped hands on my shoulders, then, much to my surprise, pulled me close for a hug. Taysh and I traded a look over his shoulder, the sky-high arching of her eyebrows indicating she was as surprised by the physical display of affection as I was. Before I could sink into the welcome embrace, however, my father released me and turned toward the crowd. He raised his arms and said, "My son has returned!"

He launched into a speech, proclaiming a night of celebration. He extolled my virtues in a way I'd never heard him do before, to the point where I began to wonder if the "my son" he talked about was really me or some hitherto unknown brother of mine. By contrast, Marnél—who was the reason I'd left in the first place—barely even merited a mention.

"I am standing here, right?" Marnél muttered, patting himself with one hand as if making sure he was real.

Whatever combination of pride, amusement, and bemusement I might've felt at my father's words became lost under the weight of fatigue as his speech turned, much as his speeches usually did, to his favorite subject: himself. *His* fear. *His* loss. *His* fortitude in pressing on, performing his "solemn duties" as Magistrate despite the "crippling absence" of his one and only son. He spoke of his faith, his daily prayers, how he beseeched Eshval for her protection and Peth for her gift of life, how he implored Seru, the Destroyer, to turn her gaze from me. By the time my father finished, you would've sworn he was responsible for my return.

As my father clasped wrists and accepted the congratulations of various people, I passed Marnél off gratefully to his mother, grandfather, and younger brother, who had, during my father's speech, pushed their way to the front where they waited impatiently for him to finish. Taysh, too, swept forward, nearly leaping into my arms. I clung to her as she murmured, "You're alive," her face buried in the crook of my neck.

"Is that joy I hear, or disappointment? I can't tell."

She swatted me playfully on the back. Then she pushed away, holding me at arms' length, giving me another onceover. "Gods above, look at you."

"Me? What about you?" I pointed at her belly. "That was a bit bigger last time I saw you." I arched an eyebrow questioningly.

"A boy," she said, a smile lighting her face. "Varun. His Name Day was two months ago."

"You named him after me?"

Her smile slipped, and while she opened her mouth, no words came out.

My brow furrowed, wondering at her hesitancy, but then I understood. "It's a memorial. You didn't think I was coming back."

The way color bloomed in her cheeks told me I was right.

I snorted in amusement, but the amusement was short-lived. *There were times I almost didn't make it back*, I nearly said.

"Come," said Taysh, into the awkward silence. "Let's get you a warm meal and a hot bath."

"And the biggest, most comfortable feather mattress there is," I added.

"Done," she said.

THAT NIGHT, after jolting awake from a nightmare for the third time, I struggled my way off that big feather mattress and onto the floor. The breeze through the open window cooled my skin, slick with sweat, as I worked to slow the beating of my heart. The moons' light left deep shadows in the corners of the room, and although I knew there was nothing in those shadows, the urge to flee was overwhelming. I tugged on the clean clothes and sandals Taysh had left, wrapped a blanket around me like a giant cloak, and shuffled from the house out into the night.

As I wound my way amid dwellings both familiar and strange, the grip of my dream loosened. I glanced up at the twin moons, the Eyes of Seru, recalling to mind my father's prayers for the goddess of death to turn her gaze from me. I snorted, wondering what he would think if he knew just how many times I'd "embraced Seru," as they said, in order to stay alive. The memory of sightless eyes staring at me from bloodied faces was one of several things making sleep difficult.

Maybe it was thinking about Seru and those I'd crossed over that made the goddess feel especially close, or maybe it was simply the light of the moons, both approaching full amid the cloudless night sky. Whatever the case, I found myself making my way across town to the goddess' shrine. I doubted that an offering to Seru or to the souls of the people I'd crossed over would ease my troubled sleep, but, then, it couldn't hurt, either.

As I passed beneath the shrine's ornately-carved arched gate, I noticed a huddled figure kneeling atop the raised platform before the altar. Six candles had been lit, their flickering light casting odd dancing shadows, and the breeze brought with it the smell of burning cedar. At the sound of my footsteps along the crushed stone path leading toward the platform, the figure turned.

"You too, eh?" said a familiar voice.

I smiled, patting Marnél on the shoulder as I knelt alongside him. He had his own blanket draped over his shoulders, and he returned my smile with one of his own. I whispered a prayer to Seru, then added my own piece of cedar to the stone bowl amid the burning candles. A sense of calm returned to me, although whether that was the goddess' doing or Marnél's presence at my side was open for debate.

We lingered in silence, and as the candles burned low, I heard Marnél sigh. He curled up in a ball, head pillowed on one arm. The rest of the night passed much as so many others had those previous months, with the two of us taking turns watching over one another as we slept.

"So," said my father the next morning as he, Taysh, and I broke our fast, "you really aren't dead."

The jovial Magistrate Varik from the square yesterday evening was gone. With none of the common folk around, he was my father again. No hugs, no extolling of my virtues, and it's funny, but in a way his stern, taciturn manner almost came as a comfort. This was familiar, this I remembered.

"Is that joy I hear," I said, "or disappointment? I can't tell."

Out of the corner of my eye, Taysh froze, a hunk of bread poised halfway toward her open mouth.

"Is that meant to be funny?" My father's eyes narrowed. "Perhaps your time gallivanting about the countryside has made you forget your manners."

Gallivanting about the countryside. Yes, that's exactly what I'd been doing. I snorted, and my father's expression darkened even further.

I caught the barest shake of Taysh's head, her imploring look telling me to let it go, and I swallowed a retort.

"What should we do with you then," said my father, "now that you're back? Are you able to resume your duties as my scribe?"

I nodded, thinking about how many nights I'd lain awake on the damp earth beneath a tree or curled up against a cliff face and imagined myself doing that very thing. The work was hardly exciting and could be downright tedious, but it was warm and dry, and the only thing I had to worry about was a quill tip breaking or ink staining the cuff of my sleeve.

"If I may," I said.

Before my father could respond, one of his slaves entered to refill our teacups. As she poured, my gaze fixed on the tattoos on the back of her left hand, the elaborate loops and swirls forming three concentric rings. The older woman—whose name, I realized, I didn't know—had been with my father's household since I was little. I'd seen her tattoos before, but had never paid them any mind, had never understood—or cared to understand—their significance. Alaya had explained it to me one night as I lay beside her, my finger tracing the arcs of ink across her skin.

The outer ring on the back of the slave's hand was the same as Alaya's had been, their respective clans sharing the same patron spirit. When she filled my cup, I thanked her and said, "Gui's blessing on your name."

The older woman started. She hesitated, clearly uncertain as to how to respond—or perhaps wondering if she should respond at all. With a fearful glance at my father, she bowed and nearly fled from the room.

"Since when do you engage with slaves?" said my father.

"It doesn't hurt to be polite." I shrugged. "They're people too, no different from the rest of us."

My father eyed me much as Taysh had done yesterday evening—much as she was doing right then, actually—as if he'd never seen me before.

"No different from the rest of us," he muttered. He scoffed and shook his head. "Yes, well. Once you've recovered from your ordeal—as you clearly need to—you may indeed resume your duties. Attend me in my office."

With that, he pushed away from the table and strode from the room.

I frowned as I watched him go. Not a single question about where I'd been or what had happened to me. He'd never been a particularly compassionate man—not when nobody was watching, anyway—but I thought he'd at least be curious. Did my "ordeal" mean nothing to him? Was all he cared about that I was back now and could resume my duties?

"Hey, you," said Taysh, snapping her fingers to get my attention.

She studied me as if I were a puzzle she couldn't quite

put together, but in her eyes and in the way the corners of her mouth twitched there was amusement, too.

"You haven't seen my brother around anywhere, have you?"

I DONNED my scribe's robes and attended my father in his office that same day, looking forward to returning to my life as it had been before I'd left. He seemed surprised to see me, and given his comment about me needing to recover from my ordeal, I half-expected him to send me away. Instead, he nodded once in approval, then gestured for me to take the table in the corner that had served as my desk.

"There was an opening for a scribe in the Grand Magistrate's office while you were away," said my father as I arranged my supplies of parchment, quills, and ink. "It was filled promptly, of course." His expression was neutral, as was his tone of voice, but I caught his chastisement nonetheless.

While my path to succeed my father as Rish Puello's magistrate had been laid out long ago, the possibility of me becoming the canton's grand magistrate was one we'd often discussed. I'd missed a great opportunity, and I fought back a familiar wave of shame at having disappointed my father. The words to justify myself were on the tip of my tongue, but my father had returned his attention to the leather-bound book on his desk.

I spent that afternoon and early-evening making copies of the dozens of judgments he'd rendered the day before. We worked in silence, save for the *skritch-skritch* of my quill on parchment and the rustle of pages as my father pored over books and scrolls, researching various legal matters.

When he finally called a halt for the day, my hand was cramping and my back ached from having been hunched over the table for so long.

As my father perused my work, I found myself holding my breath, waiting for his reaction. When he finished, he grunted once—whether with approval or disdain, I couldn't tell.

"Supper is at seventh hour, in case you've forgotten," he said, then turned and walked out.

Well, I thought, *at least no one tried to kill me today.*

I WANDERED the winding roads of Rish Puello that night, reacquainting myself with my home. A warm breeze, hinting at the coming dry season, was a welcome relief after the enclosed stuffiness of my father's office. Familiar sounds washed over me—burbling voices from the market square, the booming of the drum tower announcing the hour. Smells from Baker's Row left my stomach grumbling, and I purchased two of my favorite lemon tarts, one of which was devoured before I even left the shop. I continued my wanderings, eating the other tart at a more leisurely—and respectable—pace.

The town was smaller than I remembered. I could make my way from one end to the other in less than an hour—a far cry from Cyuda-Peth, or the seemingly endless woods Marnél, Alaya, and I had trekked through to reach the imperial capital. Rish Puello's palisade, at twice the height of any man, had always seemed so tall, so secure. Yet, after having seen—and scaled—the fifty-foot high stone walls surrounding Sun Keep, the palisade may as well have been made of matchsticks.

I stood on its wall-walk, gazing at the foothills north of town. Above them, Soralain flitted about, hunting for her supper. The wyvern's emotions were a buzz in the back of my mind—her thrill in the hunt, her simple delight in drifting along on the updrafts—so strange and alien, yet they comforted me. I didn't understand why she'd chosen me to bond with over the others, nor why she continued to stick around now that I was home, but the significance of the honor wasn't lost on me. I smiled, thinking about the terrifying joy of flying that first time, the wind howling in my ears, tears streaming along the sides of my face, and whether I was laughing or screaming, not even I could tell.

I was tempted to call Soralain, to climb on her back and go for a ride. But seeing the way nearby guardsmen muttered to one another, gripping sword hilts and spear hafts as they eyed the wyvern, made me reconsider.

Besides, I'm a scribe, I told myself. *I do scribe things. Riding wyverns is not a scribe thing.*

I watched as Soralain plunged beneath the tree-tops seeking her meal, then I made my way back to my father's house.

I DID many scribe things in the days that followed, working dutifully alongside my father. I wrote letter after letter to provincial officials on his behalf regarding the maintenance of roads or the collection and dispensation of tax revenues. I transcribed court proceedings as they happened, then made multiple copies of each one the following day. Nobody tried to kill me—although I did accidentally cut myself once while sharpening a quill—and I was, indeed, warm and dry. More and more, however, I found myself

367

struggling to focus while the various parties argued their cases.

I used to find the arguments fascinating, the bickering and the back and forth, but now it all seemed so trivial. I guess after you've cradled the head of someone you love, watching the life bleed out of them, disputes over a few shaved coins or one farmer's sheep eating another's crops just don't carry the same weight.

While my quill scribbled out words as dry and empty as the parchment on which they were written, I fiddled with Alaya's pendant. Its weight gave me comfort, made me long for the time we'd spent together.

Sure, we'd run for our lives in terror, fleeing the valghast hunters. We'd cowered in Cyuda-Peth's sewers, hands clapped over each other's mouths so we wouldn't make a sound. But we'd also danced the rings together around the fire in her village's square as her clan sister gave birth in a nearby hut. We'd lain outside beneath the Eyes that night—the first of many such nights to come—and fell asleep, limbs intertwined, the breeze cooling our naked flesh. Through it all—good and bad—I'd felt alive, more so than I'd ever been, and in ways I'd never dreamed.

I imagined what Alaya would think to see me there, berobed and ink-stained, hunched over my table.

"There's so much more to you," she'd said one morning, her hand on my chest. She planted a gentle kiss on my lips. "So much more."

A vision of her, with her oh-so-subtly arched eyebrows and her disappointed smile, left me full of longing... and more than a little bit of shame.

~

My sleep was still plagued by nightmares, although not nearly as bad as that first night. I often found myself awake well before dawn, wandering my father's house or sitting on the veranda overlooking the gardens out back. This particular morning, as the sun rose, I stood at the railing watching my father's slaves dancing an abbreviated version of the rings around a small brazier outside their quarters. There was no singing or chanting, my father having forbidden such things.

Did they have mixed feelings? I wondered. Was their joy at new life brought into the world tinged with sadness at the knowledge that the child was being born into servitude?

I clasped Alaya's pendant as an odd tightness gripped my chest.

A new life of servitude. Alaya's voice rang in my head, asking how a life as my father's scribe was any different. I argued, telling that voice—telling myself—that I wasn't a slave. This was what I'd wanted all along, the entire time I'd been gone. The voice agreed and said nothing more, but I could tell it wasn't convinced.

Soft footfalls scraped across the tiled floor behind me, and I turned to see Taysh in her dressing robe, hair tousled from sleep, the little bundle of my nephew cradled in her arms.

"Someone was hungry," she whispered as she joined me at the railing.

"I heard," I said. There was no question of my namesake having a healthy set of lungs.

We watched the rest of the ceremony in silence. Although Taysh eyed me curiously on more than one occasion, she kept whatever questions she might have had to herself.

"Have you heard about Marnél?" said Taysh when the slaves had finished.

"No, what?" A surge of concern was accompanied by a wave of guilt. I hadn't seen him since that night in the shrine. We hadn't been avoiding one another, really, but, then, we hadn't sought each other out either. If something had happened...

"He's betrothed," said Taysh, "to Savin the silversmith's daughter. Savin's taken Marnél on as his apprentice."

I opened my mouth, then shut it again. Of all the things I might've expected Taysh to say, that was not one of them. Marnél having been caught robbing Savin's shop? Sure. But becoming his apprentice and his son-in-law? I shook my head.

Marnél had always been—well, I'll be polite and say he had a wild streak. The night that sparked our journey, when the priestess of Peth fell bleeding at our feet, reaching out to give us three of the Seven Keys, Marnél had been as happy as I'd ever seen him, ready for an adventure. (I, myself, had wanted nothing to do with the Keys, but, then, Marnél always did have a way of getting me to go along with his crazy ideas.) He had never understood my desire to follow in my father's footsteps, to have a "boring life," as he'd called it. Had our journey changed him that much? Life as a silversmith might be more exciting than life as a scribe, but it wasn't that exciting.

"What happened to the two of you out there?" said Taysh, softly, speaking into my thoughts.

A part of me wanted to tell her, to let it all spill out. But just thinking about everything that happened left me overcome by a dizzying array of emotions.

"A lot," I murmured finally.

We lingered in silence for a time, my nephew dozing in

Taysh's arms, and watched as the slaves went inside to greet the newborn child.

A new life. And now a new life for Marnél.

And for me?

With a sigh, I gave my sister a hug and my nephew a kiss, then headed in to start my day.

I'm a scribe, I told myself. *I do scribe things.*

"WHAT IS WRONG WITH YOU?" said my father one evening, after the last petitioner had left. On more than one occasion that afternoon, I'd been unable to repeat to him something someone had said—something I was supposed to have transcribed but didn't because of my flagging attention. Not only that, but I'd questioned him openly after he rendered a harsh judgment against a slave who'd fought back against his owner's teenage sons. The two boys were playing a game, taking turns beating the slave with a stick for no apparent reason. The boys, of course, hadn't been punished at all.

My father gestured toward my scar. "Did that blow to your head addle you permanently?"

The shame threatening to rise at having failed my father was swamped by irritation. "No," I snapped back, thinking about how that blow had come moments before the mortal one Alaya suffered, "it's made me see clearly."

For a moment, confusion warred with anger in my father's expression, but the anger won out.

"Regardless of what may have happened to you out there, you will respect me, understand?" Then he waved a hand at the scrolls on the table in front of him. "Take care of

371

B. R. TURNAGE, EDITOR

these—assuming you're capable of performing any of your duties."

I opened my mouth, determined to prove to him just how capable I was. I would tell him about the Seven Keys and how I'd helped Marnél and Alaya find them all and bring them to Cyuda-Peth. I'd tell him how I'd freed Peth, and how I'd given the goddess part of my life force to contain the lightning storms threatening the city. I could tell him all of that and more, and—

It wouldn't matter, I realized. None of it would.

He wouldn't suddenly forgive me for having questioned him. He wouldn't be proud of me. I suspected being named Grand Magistrate wouldn't even accomplish that. Nothing I could do would ever be enough for him.

Instead, I said nothing. I was tempted to walk out, then and there, and leave my father to deal with the scrolls all by himself. But then an idea occurred to me, an idea which, for me to accomplish it, I would need to remain in my father's good graces—such as they were. So I did as he asked, then left without another word.

THAT NIGHT, I did scribe things.

I drafted several decrees on my father's behalf—making the requisite number of copies, of course—each of which I signed with a reasonable facsimile of my father's signature and stamped with his seal. I rescinded the judgment he'd rendered on the beaten slave and delivered it to the jailer. I led the confused young man back to the slave quarters behind my father's home, where I provided him the writ of freedom I'd prepared.

We were met by Raesa, the slave who'd served my

father, Taysh, and me breakfast that first morning, and I gave her a similar writ for the mother and child whose birth rite I'd watched. Judging by the expression on Raesa's face, she hadn't believed me when I'd told her what I'd planned, and she scrambled to find the young woman and get her and her child ready to leave.

While she did, I slipped into Taysh's quarters and left the letters I'd written for her and Marnél, explaining what I'd done and why, and saying goodbye.

To my father, I wrote nothing.

"May Gui's blessing carry you," said Raesa, touching the back of her left hand to her forehead. In her smile, I saw Alaya's as well, and the pang of longing I felt this time was accompanied by a sense of pride.

"I only wish I could do more," I said. "Maybe later I can—"

"Go." Raesa waved a hand. "Quickly."

Accompanied by the two disbelieving slaves, the one with her newborn in a sling across her chest, I made my way to Rish Puello's western gate. The equally disbelieving Captain Orso blinked in confusion at the writs of freedom, but he let us pass.

Once atop the rise overlooking town, I urged the now former slaves on their way and watched until they were out of sight.

Soralain? I called out to the wyvern, and she answered me promptly.

When she descended, it was like a shadow coming out of the moons. The wind from her wings buffeted me, stirring up dust from the road. I didn't know where I was going yet—back to Alaya's village or the Temple of the Sun in Cyuda-Peth, perhaps. Either way, I knew I'd be welcome. As I climbed on the wyvern's back, I glanced at Rish Puello.

The town seemed so very small.

I had barely settled myself when Soralain leapt into the air. We soared into the sky, the wind howling in my ears and tears streaming along the sides of my face. This time, there was no doubt about it.

I definitely laughed.

THE END

BIO: Matt Krizan is a former certified public accountant who writes from his home in Royal Oak, Michigan. He's been a member of Fantasy-Writers.org since January, 2020, and his short fiction has appeared or is forthcoming in various publications, including Factor Four Magazine, Daily Science Fiction, and Stupefying Stories. Find him online at mattkrizan.com, on Blue Sky as @mattkrizan.bsky.social, and on Twitter as @MattKrizan.

CHAPTER 21

ALL THAT'S LEFT

RETURN WITH THE ELIXIR

by

John Nicol

Beyond the western mountains, somewhere close to the edge of the world, a black lake inverts a yellow moon beneath hanging teeth of aspen. On the beach beside, in the lee of a boulder, lit by a dwindling candle, crouches a man: a prodigal son, a dying star, the hero of an age.

This hero tips his golden oil flask, glinting, onto a seal-skin rag as the candlelight flickers. He holds up the flask to admire it before restoring it to a padded woolen pouch—as he has never failed to do; to him, the gold of the olive is more valuable than any ingot, and so the flask has traveled with him the entire way.

And what way, that: surely a thousand-thousand lives

—not just this meager thing he now knows has nearly run its course.

How came he here? Does he recall? It all began so long ago, and the two of them barely more than children. Ah, Lucine—the beginning and the end of all.

She was never one to second-guess herself, even then, and he trusted her completely.

Of course there was a crone, a prophecy, their resistance, and their acquiescence. Their mothers grieved (foolishly, he thought), as though they saw the future—as though they saw the depth of the sacrifice that would be required. There were tears to run the rivers over.

And the rage of his father: immutable, severe. 'Do not return,' he had said, backlit by his forge.

The hero had left those memories behind, in the village of his youth, but now they returned to consume him.

So close to where it all began.

From their village they had traveled: across the Telos range; to the plains of Akaro; to the city of Col (where he was taught techniques by the swordmaster Sroth); to the haunted forest, Kyndal, where he and Lucine consummated their love beneath the crooked boughs—through it all they had persevered and grown.

And their first real test: the festering swamp Glomear. They plunged headlong in. Within its bounds, they made enemies and allies alike (Rakmar—dearest Rakmar!— stolid, inviolable, barbarian prince), and they endured. They were tempered by their trials.

Ascendant, replete with the passion of youth: it was a heady time. They were united in purpose, and nearly in strength—but in the end, the story was his and his alone. He was the one—the prophesied one—and he was courting his destiny.

At last they reached the doomy crag Allamynth, where, for the first time, they suffered defeat—where they nearly abandoned hope.

But he did not allow it. Body shattered, in the last moments, the hero rose from obsidian shards to defeat the demon-king, Gazraa—sealing within a child's marble the ancient evil that had scourged the land since time immemorial.

But at what cost: Lucine.

In that exact moment—that eternal moment, that he knows has never released him—holding the demon-marble up to the grimy sun, he was sure of but two things: he could not face their families; and the world still needed him—it must.

There was no clear course available to him, though, no evident purpose. With Lucine slain and Rakmar departed to rule the northern tribes, he was alone.

From the side of that black lake, he perceives the memories of all that followed as indistinct impressions, unmoored from precedents and antecedents, bearing no common thread and comprising no greater meaning.

He descended Allamynth and sought the acolytes of Gazraa—they were known to raise the dead. In his naivete, he hoped they could restore Lucine. But alas, less their patron, the priests' powers were void. He made of their destruction good and holy work. It was not a fitting challenge for a hero, but he routed them for the benefit of all.

He sought more good work: he captured bandits, slew monsters, stood against tyranny. Eventually all that was left was the continuation of what he had done before, as if he were a spring-toy, unwinding towards some unforeseen conclusion.

Years passed. He endured campaigns; battles; the

weight of his own vainglory—all of which led him, eventually, inevitably, to this penultimate point by a placid lake born of the slate escarpments overreaching his ancestral mount, where he now sits, poised, having reached the end of all his roads.

It is time to go home.

Morning will bring soft sun to the descending navel of fertile acreage abutting the village of his birth. He will pass the spotted fields, the hillocks, the hogs in their rangey pens, mudding on sunstruck banks, and proceed, resolute, first to the home of Lucine's mother, before even his own, to tell her that he tried, but that in the end he couldn't, and that nobody, none of them, not even Rakmar, could have saved her.

And that he is sorry, and that he will never forgive the gods' Lucine's consignment.

Which is true.

And also dust.

Dust—but still, he is afraid. He, who is afraid of nothing, who knows their families must know the story by now, and that they hardly need hear it from him, is afraid. He will tell them because it is the final thing he has to do: it is their right; it is his responsibility.

In his memory, he watches, again, as she falls to Gazraa, and he sees Rakmar's ax flashing in the flames, and he feels his own hot breath, ragged in his chest, as he runs, futile, to her side. Chaos abounding.

Here though, all is quiet. There is hardly a cricket. Nary a breeze nor a ripple riffle the surface of the water.

All behind him, all behind him. The world has long since been saved, and grown weary, and he grown weary beside it.

The candle flickers still. With his rag, he makes to shine

his old steel blade, lustrous in the light, beautiful for its imperfections: here the gap where it glanced from the hide of the wyrm Baphemeph, there the sawtooth jag where it succumbed to the ironwood trunks of Kyndal. His journey writ large upon it. Indeed, the blade recalls more, and more clearly, than does he.

The blade is the only proof his story won't be forgotten. They commune a wistful spell by the shore, the blade and he, and finally the hero slides the old thing back into its kidskin scabbard. For a while longer he strokes the supple leather, and then this too he retires, and he reclines and chews his cheek.

The moon ranges the celestial cloak above. Sleep eludes him. His candle is long since guttered, and the paleness of the sand is the only contrast to the engulfment of the night when he hears a shifting in the weird about him: bear? Rocklion?

He pulls his sword clear, and sits stark in the pitch ink within the lee of his boulder. There is a crack; sparking light; the stench of sputtering grease.

He is thrown from his boots.

Sand grinds into his back, his shoulder, his face, as he spins, out of control, splashing, choking in the shallows. He smells petrichor and murk.

Something pulls him to his feet, and then he is looking into Lucine's face. She opens her mouth—*save me*— and snakes mash out, enwrap him completely. All is darkness and pressure and peace amidst the tendrils.

As quickly as it began, it is over: the sun is shining and he is awake—alas, just a dream. This is all he has left, the only way he sees her. Nostalgia overwhelms him. He must push on.

There is soon a fire, and a smoking griddle, slick with

chucklard, and the tremulous tweeting of jays, and it all passes him by in a haze. He eats, but not enough, which is normal for him. He does not eat because he is sick in the heart.

The sun's brilliance seems good auspice, but his mood is dark. He feels impulsive and impetuous.

An old man who appears from the tree line. The stranger stands rigid and alert.

The hero calls out: Peace! I mean no harm!

The old man comes forth.

What d'ye want?

The hero motions to the coals he's nearly pissed out.

Break your fast and sit! I've a task I'd just as soon not get to, and plenty of time not to get to it.

The old man eyes the blade and the still-slick pan, weighs them.

Time, sieur? We've none of us that.

The hero eyes the old man, weighs him: grizzled and gristled, with legs and arms poking out from oiled shorts and jerkin like darkwood tree-trunks, wrinkled and perfect. Reed-wrap sandals. Piercing eyes crouched over a matted beard. Twig-strewn hair.

The hero stirs the coals, produces a pot from his satchel, fills it with water. He puts it on the coals.

The old man settles down to wait. He receives his bacon, eats it, motions to the sword.

Are ye a fighter?

You could say that.

Ye've no heraldry. Who's man're ye, then?

I've no master.

Sellsword, then?

I've been called better and worse.

Same in the end.

Yes.

The hero crumbles dried yrrba into the pot and stirs it with a stick, pushes it into the coals farther. Do you know the village over yonder ridge?

Aye.

How stand the people? I'm bound that way.

Then ye're farther bound.

Pray, tell?

It's naught but a hole in the earth, now. Sickness took 'em, and the Proctors razed it last spring.

The old man spits, and picks bacon from his teeth.

There is silence broken by the trilling of cardinals and a breeze that comes gentle off the water, stirring the reeds.

None survived?

Not a soul.

His mother; Lucine's mother. His father. The promise of time—always, more time—was as false as all the others.

Did ye have kin there, sieur?

Yes.

The old man scratches at the dirt with a stick.

I'm sorry for ye, then. They none of 'em went too easy, but I reckon they sleep sound enough now.

The hero clenches his jaw, blinks back a tear.

The world has moved on and on and on.

The old man blears at the sun through rheumy eyes.

Has it? I'd swear to all the gods that this is the only day that ever was, as regarding sunny mornings, and the only others I've known have been rain, or snow, or wind, and all of them have been just the same as ever' other like them, besides. Seems to me the world doesn't change—just the seasons do.

But it does ... what of the demon-king? Was he not defeated?

Aye, I've heard that story, too.

The old man takes the pot from the hero; puts it to his lips; brings it down, beard wet with tea.

... but I've seen enough to wonder if maybe the monsters were men, and the men, monsters, and both the same—as with the weather. Who can say?

The hero rolls the marble between his fingers.

You speak like a poet but you are wrong, father: truth is stark. What is, is, or else it is not.

Perhaps.

The old man drinks again, returns the pot.

Thank ye for yer boons, Sieur, but I've a long road ahead. I beg you, bid me pass.

Of course, father.

The old man gathers himself up, and embarks into the brush.

Alone again.

The hero brings out the marble and places it on a flat stone by the water's edge, sits in a cross-legged position. Leaning back on one arm, he eyes the thing portentously— as he is wont to do on such mood-struck mornings.

What of it, old foe?

They have squared off many times, he staring into the orb and seeing only himself reflected, or a version of himself, but this time is different. Something has awakened within him—so close to the end of his journey.

Ah, to be ascendant. To be young, and driven by purity of intent.

White motes flash across the peaks of the lake and oscillate under the caress of a breeze. He looks at the water and squints, and sees his life again, and feels the flush of his greatest success and loss commingled.

For him the elixir has always been laced; for him, the joy, ash.

He realizes, with finality, the thing that he has always known but has never allowed himself to acknowledge.

The acolytes can bring her back ... but they need the power of their master.

He eases his blade free. The world thrums. He holds the sword up in the crisp air, and sights a cloud that wisps apart on either side. A breath fills his lungs—is it yet he that breathes?—and he slams the pommel down.

The marble shatters.

Time stops, or seems to, to one untethered from its flow. He lays his palm against the shards, and drags them across the stone, streaking blood. He feels dread, guilt, and ... relief.

The demon king is free.

The hero rises and looks to the East, and imagines that he sees the smoking fingers of Allamynth reaching up to cradle the morning star, low in the sky, and he thinks of Lucine, and for the first time in a long time he feels hope.

THE END

BIO: John Nicol lives in New England with his family. He is the winner of the 2023 Weird Christmas flash fiction contest; he hopes to someday win another weird contest. In the meantime, he fixes things around the house and tries to impress his kids with his guitar playing, which sometimes even works. He has been a member of FWO for two years.

CHAPTER 22
A HERO'S WORK
ALL STAGES

by

G. J. Dunn

"Chosen One!"

The voice that woke Davan came from outside. The woman next to him murmured and rolled over, her skin unsticking from his and, in this heat, coming as something of a relief. Summers in Venteri were never cool.

"Chosen One!"

The voice called again. Davan suppressed a groan, rolling to the edge of the bed. He sat up and rubbed his eyes. How did they find him? How did they always find him?

He'd dyed his hair, picked the most rundown bar in the most rundown part of the city, and not even mentioned his name. He glanced at the woman, took in her messy, blonde hair, lack of clothes, and satisfied smile, and remembered the last vestiges of the night. Okay, he'd mentioned his name once.

"Chosen One!"

Davan sighed. They never left when he ignored them. Their problems were always far too important for them to leave without him at least telling them. He shook his head and rose, taking care not to drag the sheets with him. Three steps across the stunted excuse of a room and he was flinging the shutters open, wincing as bright sunshine streamed in.

"Wha?" the woman murmured.

Davan stared down at the speaker. A man, maybe twenty, with a full head of dark hair. His face was sallow as if he didn't get outside enough, and his purple robes were definitely not the recommended outfit for this heat. He stared at Davan with his jaw hanging, an awed look on his face, before he inclined his head.

"Chosen One," he began. "My name is Gerith of Blik. I come before you—"

"Piss off, Gerith of Blik!"

Davan shouted the words, slammed the shutters closed, and returned to bed.

"Chosen One!"

Davan groaned. Gerith of Blik's voice had a nasal quality that penetrated even the deepest sleep and it tugged Davan to waking like a fish on a hook. The brunette next to him shot upright and grabbed his arm.

"Ah?!" she asked.

"It's nothing," Davan replied, brushing her off.

Maybe he could pay the man to leave. He glanced at the bedside table, where five silver coins lay in a neat row. Wait, silver? Well, that put paying him out of the question. It might rule out tonight's mead and Keshik weed, too.

"Chosen One!"

Davan threw himself up, the strain in his abdomen reminding him he wasn't as young as he used to be, and stomped to the window, throwing open the shutters.

"Piss off, Gerith of Blik!"

The little sod bowed to him. "If only I could, Chosen One, but you see, we have a problem—"

"Then call the bloody Guild of Heroes," Davan retorted.

"We are the Guild of Heroes, Chosen One."

Davan squinted at him.

"I don't care," he said and slammed the shutters.

"Chosen One!"

That morning's woman had black hair and the voice that woke him had a further hint of desperation. Davan skipped the ritual sigh and went straight to the shutters. It didn't matter what he did. The man just kept finding him. He ran his hands over his newly-shorn head, itched at the stubble he'd grown out since last time.

"Chosen One!"

The voice called again and the woman—Daisy? Maisie? — didn't budge. Her face pressed into the pillow as if they were lovers long parted. Davan looked at the bedside table, a half-rotting thing covered in sticky residue, a solitary silver coin stuck fast on top. He swore, casting open the shutters and glaring down at Gerith.

"Cho—"

"How much are you paying?"

ONCE DAVAN HAD GOTTEN rid of the woman and rubbed the sleep from his eyes, he descended the stairs and met Gerith outside. The boy stared at him like a puppy at its master.

"By Akatar, boy, get on and show me where we're going."

Gerith nodded enthusiastically and they set off, passing through streets not fully awake. Street cleaners wandered, here or there, and some drunks hadn't quite found their way home, but other than that, it was just the sights and scents of the city. Fresh bread baking, afternoon pastries, and, occasionally, an acrid vomit stench. Though that was mostly as they approached the drunks.

Davan couldn't remember when he'd last seen a morning. For the last few years, it had been only afternoons and evenings—an endless cycle. It was fresher at this time, the sun's heat not quite burning yet, and the air tasted better as it traveled to his lungs. And had the houses always looked like this? White-washed and grubby yet still bright enough to reflect the morning sun?

Before long, they'd walked through the roughs and brought themselves out on the promenade alongside the River Ayer. Davan didn't like the Ayeri district. Far too clean, for his mind, as if the city could only look nice if there was no evidence people lived there. He rubbed his eyes, trying to come to terms with being awake.

"What's the job so tough that the Guild of Heroes can't do it themselves?" he asked.

"It's in the Guild itself, Chosen One," Gerith replied, gazing at the blue sky.

"And that means?" Davan asked.

He waited for a reply, but none was forthcoming.

"You've at least got to give me some idea what I'm up against. It'll help me prepare."

"I—" Gerith hesitated. "The Guildhead will explain, Chosen One."

"And why does it have to be me?" Davan continued.

"You're the Chosen One," Gerith replied, eyes wide. "You saved our entire world from destruction."

Davan snorted. "Twenty years ago."

"If there's a task beyond the Guild of Heroes, it must mean you're destined to defeat it, just as you did back then."

Davan gritted his teeth and thought of the money while Gerith stared at him with unconcealed awe. He was surprised the boy hadn't walked himself into the river with his lack of attention to where his feet were going.

"I used to dream I was there that day, right alongside you."

"Everyone who stood next to me that day died."

"A noble sacrifice."

"A stupid sacrifice. If they'd just listened to the prophecy, they'd have heard I was the only bugger that could win. I kept telling them, right up until that balefire—"

Davan cut himself off. There were too many memories. The good ones soured by that last awful day. They walked on in silence, Gerith unwilling to take up the thread again and Davan still shedding the previous night's mead from his head. They walked halfway down one street or another when the boy pulled up short. He gestured at a ramshackle building, cramped in the middle of two marble monstrosities.

"Here we are."

Davan squinted. The Guild was not what he remembered. When he'd been a member, the Guild of Heroes had been the envy of all. The finest artisans and architects fell over themselves to offer discounts on repairs, expansions, and decorative works. Now, the statues that adorned the lawn were gone, weeds growing in their place. Some of the lower floor windows were boarded up altogether and, as Davan stared, he realised the edges of the building pulled away from one another, making the second floor larger and wider than the first, as if someone had assembled the thing out of cheap glue that had lost its strength. Davan reckoned he could see the skyline clear through where the joints of the building met. It looked like it might collapse at any minute.

"By Akatar," he muttered, shaking his head. "What happened to the place?"

Gerith scratched the back of his head. "We've had a few rough years," he said. "It's been so long since the Guild had anything notable to fight that people have lost interest."

"So where are you getting the money to pay me?"

"Oh, you know, there's still a bit of coin coming in. We've had to downscale our operations, of course. Work on some of the less ambitious contracts. Cats in trees, directions to the nearest guard post, helping tourists find their way around. That kind of thing."

Davan raised an eyebrow but said nothing. There was nothing positive to say, after all.

"Shall we go inside then?" Gerith asked, flashing him a smile and flourishing an arm.

Davan gave the building another once-over.

"You're sure you can't brief me out here?" he asked.

"No," Gerith replied. "Time to meet the Guildhead."

~

THE INSIDE WAS NO BETTER than the outside. The paint was peeling off the walls, exposing patches of bare brick, red amongst cream. Long gone were the busts of the Guild-heads that had lined the corridor in Davan's day—sold off to pay upkeep, according to Gerith. Though by the creak and bend of the timbers beneath Davan's feet, what up they were keeping was lost on him.

Gerith steered him to a door he already knew and opened it to reveal a small office. Inside, an empty desk was crammed in, so tight against the back wall that it contacted the chair behind it yet still close enough that the door hit it as it opened. The only items on the desk were a bowl and spoon, old porridge still glued to the edges.

Davan's mouth was still agape when Gerith squeezed past him, clambering over the desk and revealing more of what was under his robes than Davan ever wanted to see. Over the next minute, he wedged himself between chair and desk, forcing the desk out a few inches. The desk forced the door semi-closed and Davan found himself staring into the room through a crack four inches wide. Gerith craned his neck to bring himself back into view.

"Ah, Chosen One. Welcome to the Guild. I am Guild-head Blik."

The boy's voice rose at the last as if he was asking Davan rather than telling him. Many thoughts flashed through Davan's mind in response to what he had just witnessed, chief among them was one on Gerith's sanity. The fact that Gerith himself was the Guildhead was worry-ing. And the fact that he'd not mentioned it sooner was more so. Only Davan's desperate financial state prevented him from leaving then and there.

"Wasn't this a storeroom?" Davan asked.

Gerith nodded enthusiastically. "So, you remember your time with the Guild. That's good to hear. You are, of course, absolutely right. Our current state of affairs and the lack of certain floorboards in certain rooms have rendered this the best office."

Davan raised an eyebrow. The way the boy spoke: the tone, the vocabulary, and even his body language, was like an entirely different person. It was as if he was playing a character.

Wait, had he said something about the lack of floorboards?

He scratched the back of his head. "I think I'm going to need the money upfront, Guildhead."

Gerith of Blik smiled and wagged a finger at him. "I see we're dealing with a wily operator here. Of course, we have your payment right—" Gerith yanked at a drawer that had no space to open. "Right—" He yanked again, frowning down at the thing. "Right—"

Davan took a deep breath. "Maybe if you came out from behind the desk..."

"No, no, no, it's okay," Gerith gave up on the drawer and reached into a pocket, producing a few silver coins and holding them out. "I have half the fee here. Half now, and half later?"

Davan nodded, content he wouldn't have to see the Guildhead's unathletic exit from behind the desk. He took the coins and slipped them into his pocket. "So, what's your problem?"

Gerith gestured at the door. "Let me show you."

He began to wriggle free from the chair and Davan winced. Begging on the streets was becoming a more attractive option by the minute.

~

AFTER GERITH HAD EXTRICATED himself from behind the desk, they climbed to the second floor. It gave Davan a further chance to wince at the dilapidated state of the building. The stairs had practically crumbled to dust and, just as he'd thought when looking from the outside, the entire floor was tilted. As they walked down the once prize-filled corridor, Davan noted several patches of brighter paint—signs that objects once hanging there had been sold to make ends meet. He was surprised when it summoned a trickle of anger, though he wasn't sure if it was at the Guild for selling, or at himself for allowing this to happen.

Gerith walked him to the end of the corridor and stopped outside a door Davan knew well. It had once been the door to the games room. Even staring summoned old memories.

"Here we are," said Gerith, gesturing.

Davan tried the door and it didn't budge. He was confused for a second, but he was beyond caring at this point. If the Guild had reached the point where they weren't even strong enough to open a stuck door, they were beyond saving. Just do the job, get the money and scram.

"You've brought me all the way here just to deal with a locked door?"

He sucked in a breath, raised a leg, exhaled, and lashed out. The door bent around his foot, and Davan suppressed a grin.

He still had it.

Davan stepped across the threshold, and then Gerith spoke.

"Actually, we wanted you to deal with what we locked in there."

"Wha—"

Something large and hairy barrelled into Davan and sent him sprawling. They rolled down the corridor a few times before stopping, the creature on top and Davan pinned underneath.

The creature had blonde hair, blue eyes, and an eager grin, showing Davan a set of over-pointed teeth. A stinger launched over its right shoulder, and Davan caught it by reflex, leaning his head away as poison dripped from the end, sizzling as it hit the floor.

The creature snarled and raised a hefty paw from Davan's chest, the claws an inch long and shining in the light. Davan punched the creature's jaw, tugging on the scorpion tail simultaneously to drive the punch even harder.

The thing yelped, lurching to the side, giving Davan time to push himself up and glare at Gerith. "You locked up a manticore?" he asked.

"W-we thought it best," Gerith stammered in response.

Davan shook his head. This was what the Guild had become? He turned his attention to the beast, waiting for it to get its bearings. All the better to show Gerith how things should be done. He studied the manticore as it turned toward him, snarling a challenge, and waited until its toes curled, claws biting into the wood. Then he acted.

"Sit!" he commanded.

The creature flinched and backed away. Davan closed the gap and pointed a finger down.

"Sit," he repeated, widening his eyes in warning.

The manticore looked away, lowering its rear to the floor.

"Good boy," Davan said, lightening his tone. "Good, Manti."

The barest whip of the manticore's scorpion tail indicated pleasure. Davan raised a hand, palm flat, and pointed out. "Stay," he commanded, waiting a second to ensure the instruction took before returning to Gerith. The boy's face was a picture.

"That thing has been attacking our members for months. How did you—"

"Manticores are pack animals. As long as you show you're the alpha, they're meek as lambs." Davan reached out a hand and scratched the beast behind one ear. "Did no one teach you this?"

Gerith scratched the back of his head and glanced away.

"I'm the oldest member of the Guild, that's why I'm in charge. When I joined, there were only five members."

Davan barked a laugh. He hadn't realised the boy had a sense of humour. "The Guild had

over a hundred members at the battle of Armad."

Gerith snarled back at him. Clearly, Davan had touched a nerve. "And how many did it have after?"

Davan's smile dropped. They both knew the answer. Too few. Enough lost that he quit the Guild from guilt in the aftermath. He'd fulfilled his prophecy, saved them from destruction, and watched his friends die as a reward. He'd always assumed the Guild had carried on, though.

"The four who were with me were the sons of some of those who died at Armad," Gerith said. "We didn't know anything about heroism aside from we should be helping people. One by one, they died. I'm just picking up the pieces."

Davan stared at the floor, the manticore's claw marks etched into the wood. He glanced at the beast, who smiled at him, tongue lolling out. A shudder ran down his spine.

He knew how to fight them, but damn if they didn't creep him out.

"Who taught you that?" Gerith asked.

Davan chuckled. "My old Guildhead, Ferran. He was the best of us. Believed you could take care of monsters without violence."

He remembered the old man like it was yesterday. The bushy moustache and wild hair that always stood on end. The way he wouldn't start eating at table until everyone had food in front of them. The stern look he'd give when he found out someone had killed instead of using their head.

"What happened to him?"

Davan's smile dropped. "Armad."

Gerith didn't reply and Davan didn't lift his gaze from the floor.

"If you're interested in a bit more pay, there are a few other issues we have here."

Davan snorted. "Gryphon in the basement?"

"No, the attic."

Davan did a double take, but it looked like the young Guildhead was serious. He sighed.

"Show me the way."

Davan hissed as Gerith applied the antiseptic to his newly-gained scratch wounds.

"You could have told me it had a nest up there," he said as the youngster sweated nervously. "There's a big difference between a Gryphon and a Gryphon mother."

He'd taken only a few paces into the refuse-laden, bone-littered attic when he'd heard the distinctive growl-squeak of the babies. Before he could react, yellow eyes had appeared from the shadows and two great paws had pounced. A Gryphon mother's only thought was to protect their young. And they were damn good at it. Davan would rather take on a dragon.

His reflexes saved him, and then his skill with a blade, in a manner of speaking. He'd thrown the thing at some loose timber in the roof and knocked a hole clean through, while the bird had contented itself scratching his arms to shreds. As soon as there was an exit, the Gryphon gathered the chicks in her paws and set flight, leaving nothing but twigs, feathers, and gashes down Davan's forearms. It was much easier to protect by fleeing than fighting, after all. Once the mission was accomplished, they'd retreated to a storage room on the second floor so Gerith could treat Davan's wounds. They stung worse than Davan remembered, but they'd heal up. And at least everyone came out alive.

"I didn't know," Gerith replied, his voice up half an octave. He was bent double, standing as Davan sat in a chair, and didn't look around as he spoke. Davan thought the youth was scared he'd attack. The cuts did sting and Davan did feel like it, but he hadn't reached that level of anger. Yet.

"What kind of hero are you?" Davan snarled.

"The kind that keeps the lights on after..." Gerith trailed off.

"After?"

This time Gerith looked up and Davan saw anger in his gaze. The reserved anger of someone who knew it was no good to release it. At least it showed there was some spirit in the lad. "Let me get the bandages."

Davan grunted as Gerith left. He could work out well

enough what the boy had wanted to say. He'd been the one to keep the light on after all the competent heroes, the ones like Davan, had left the place to fester.

Hadn't Davan given enough? He hadn't chosen the hero life. No. Destiny had picked him up and bowled him down a path with only one end. How many times did someone have to save the world before they could enjoy their life without feeling guilty?

Davan shook his head. It wasn't his problem if the Guild was falling apart. So why did he feel so bad about himself?

Gerith returned and silently bandaged Davan's arms as he brooded. If Venteri cared so much about its heroes, why hadn't they stepped in to repair the damage?

Gerith finished up the bandages, tying them off and smiling.. Davan looked over his work, which was surprisingly good. He grunted in satisfaction.

"You could be a healer."

Gerith smiled again, colour rising in his cheeks. "I was, for a time."

"Then what led you here?"

The boy shrugged. "Sometimes the best way to heal is to stop the wounds from happening in the first place."

Davan winced—the words finding the core of him. Memories flashed again. This whole job had got him remembering things he'd spent the last twenty years trying to forget. What if they'd never happened in the first place? What if they'd been able to find another way?

He sniffed and pushed himself up. "If we're done here, we can go and sort out the payment."

Gerith made a noise like a boiled kettle. "There is one more thing."

Davan sighed. "Spit it out."

"We'll pay double the other contract rates," Gerith said

in a rush. "And cover any medical treatments you need coming out the other side. We just... This one..."

Gerith stammered some more and Davan grew tired.

"Just say it!"

Gerith jumped backward. "There's a wyvern. In the basement."

Davan clenched the bridge of his nose. "How, in the name of Akatar, did you manage that?"

"It was an egg, you see," Gerith replied, looking two feet above Davan's shoulder. "An old one, turned to stone, we were holding onto it as a memento and it, well, there was a boiler problem—"

Davan raised a hand. "Okay, I get it. But there's no way I'm fighting a wyvern. I'd rather go round two with the attic Gryphon."

Gerith's eyes bulged. "There's no one else. It's not even fully grown yet."

"Oh, so it shouldn't be a problem for you," Davan replied, turning away. Not his

responsibility, he reminded himself. He made it three steps.

"I'll pay gold," Gerith blurted out.

Davan stopped and sighed. It still wasn't enough to take on a wyvern. Nowhere near enough. "Run and get it then."

CANDLES SET in brackets lit the way down the basement staircase to a closed door. Davan raised a foot and Gerith made a strangled noise. Davan glanced at the youth, and his face turned red.

"Yes?" Davan asked, more patiently than he felt.

Gerith licked his lips and moved his mouth without any sound before attempting a second time. "Can I come?" he asked. "Just to watch."

"No."

"I might learn something."

Davan rolled his eyes and huffed. "Follow my steps exactly. And stay quiet."

He turned and stepped down gingerly, testing each step for sound before moving his full weight, making it down without issue before pausing and pressing his ear to the door. There was the characteristic hum of a sleeping dragon inside. Like a cat purr, if the cat happened to be one hundred times its actual size.

He crossed his fingers for luck and eased the door open, thankful it didn't let out a sound.

The great thrum grew louder without wood separating them. Davan stuck his head inside and let his eyes adjust, squinting into the darkness.

The wyvern was curled up in the far corner, snout tucked under its tail and wings folded. Davan noted that this was a male from how they tucked onto its back, not down its sides. From the size, he was a yearling at best, which was a relief. Fire breathing became easier with age. Normally, that was a taught behaviour, and it wasn't like there was another dragon down here to teach him.

The pile of bones he slept on let Davan know how he had survived. Even for a hatchling, rodents were easy prey and, thanks to the Guild's ineptitude, there were plenty of rodents to prey on.

He moved toward the wyvern, hand dropping to his hilt. There was no way around violence this time. He'd told himself that his killing days were done, but a cornered wyvern would kill him if he weren't careful. One strike in the throat. With a yearling, he wouldn't have to worry about scales diverting the blow. One blow and his money problems were over. Easy as that.

He was two-thirds the way across the room when Gerith crunched down on bone behind him. Davan winced as a single yellow eye shot open.

"Get out of here," he shouted at Gerith, then the wyvern was across the room, barrelling into his chest and knocking him backward, arse-over-tit.

He found himself on his chest and pushed himself up, drawing his sword and swinging at the blur approaching him. The blow sent pain down his arm, and the dragon stumbled away.

Davan had caught him well, but only with the flat of the blade. The wyvern shook its head, then resumed its frenzied attack. Davan ducked and dodged more than anything, the wyvern throwing his balance off too much for him to get a decent swing.

It reared, the claws of its forelegs catching the candle-light outside. Wait. Forelegs?

A wing crunched into his side.

He was flung across the room, on the floor, staring up as the beast charged. He rolled away from its first attack and regained his feet, swinging blind and hitting something that raised a squeal. The creature's head swung around lightning fast, teeth sinking into Davan's shoulder until he screamed. It shook Davan like a pair of dice and rolled him across the floor, his vision full of his own blood.

He tried to rise, but strength failed him. Bright blood pumped from his shoulder, weakening him with every heartbeat. Heavy footsteps boomed through the floor-boards. Could be it was time to die. At least he'd do it fighting for good again. And didn't that idea feel better than any for the past twenty years? He closed his eyes and relaxed, one last time.

And nothing happened.

He opened his eyes again. The creature, dismissing him as a threat, had turned to where Gerith stood. The Guild-head was quivering, face pale. His hand hadn't even gone to his sword. A burst of anger flooded Davan's veins. How were these people supposed to help others if they couldn't even help themselves?

Davan launched himself up, stomach muscles scream-ing, and flung himself at the beast's back. He grabbed the tail and yanked it toward him, away from Gerith. The crea-ture didn't budge much, but the action made him hiss. His neck whipped around and Davan slipped off the creature's back once more. He dodged the follow-up lunge and wondered what his plan was. He hadn't got much further than 'keep it away from the kid', which was probably a mistake. He retreated, dodging another lunge, this one passing so close to his head he felt breath hot on his ear.

"Gerith!" he shouted. "This isn't a wyvern, it's a dragon."

He dodged another lunge and swung around, levelling his blade to keep the dragon distant. His shoulder roared in pain as he held his sword out, blood still oozing from the wound. The edges of his vision were darkening. He knew he was running out of time. If it was a dragon, there was a chance to end this quickly, without more death. But he only had Ferran's words, the memory of them, that it would work.

"But they told me—"

"Just look at its forelegs! Wyvern's don't have them!"

The dragon lunged again. Davan pivoted, bringing his blade around as the dragon's tail whipped and knocked it from his hand. It was possible twenty years without action hadn't done much to sharpen his reflexes.

The creature reared again, jaws wide so Davan saw the flame bud at the back of its throat, directed right at him. Davan dropped to a knee, reached into his pocket and pulled out the gold coin Gerith had given him, his pay. Before he could react, the dragon swiped a claw toward him. Miraculously, he still had a hand after, minus a gold coin.

The dragon fell onto its back, forelegs, and hind legs in the air, the gold coin gripped tight in its claws. Smoke furled from its nostrils as it looked at the thing in awe.

"Hoard!" the dragon squealed, excitement clear in his voice.

Davan rose to stand and caught Gerith's eye over the top of the dragon. Confusion was writ on his face, clear as day.

Davan smiled at him, the biggest beam he could achieve, and collapsed to the floor.

WHEN HE CAME TO, Gerith was hovering over him, chattering words Davan's mind couldn't process. For a moment, he just watched the boy's mouth move. Followed the hairs that dotted his chin as they bobbed up and down, up and down.

He was sat up against a wall, he realised, in a basement covered with blood, the sound of a happy dragon somewhere in the background. Davan looked down, his shoulder covered in bandages and bulging in places that his shoulder hadn't bulged before.

"Whassat?" he asked, his voice slurred.

Gerith shot him a look. "Healer, remember? Besides, anyone knows to treat dragon bites with Feleria bark. It's the only thing that removes the poison. Just sit. Wait. I've stuffed the wounds with bark and padded it out with moss. Give it ten minutes and you'll start feeling better. What happened there? With the dragon?"

"Something Ferran told me," Davan said. "Those old stories, the ones where the heroes go to the castle and fight the dragon. They always find the dragon's with a hoard of gold. So how do the dragon's get it in the first place?"

"I thought they stole it?" Gerith asked.

Davan shook his head. "Dragon's are smart and loyal and powerful and they love gold. So what would happen when someone made them a gift of it?"

Gerith thought it through and Davan saw he had a quick mind as his face contorted into shock. "They're tamed by it?"

Davan tilted his head. "Not tamed. It's an offer of friendship. And for them, friendship doesn't stop just because the human dies."

"They're protecting their gift."

Davan nodded. "If there's one thing you need to know about heroism, it's that a hero should reach for his brain long before he reaches for his sword."

Gerith gave him a flat look then. There was awe in there, as before, but this time, there was something else. Resolve, maybe? Davan couldn't tell. But he liked the result.

"I'll remember that," Gerith said, sitting beside him, watching the young dragon play with his new gold.

As the minutes passed, Davan was surprised to find that Gerith was right. His energy, while still low, had at least stopped decreasing.

Slowly, the initial fog in his brain cleared, and he began noticing the room.

"What's that?" Davan asked, gesturing at the hanging picture wall.

"It's a mural," Gerith said quietly. "A tribute to those we've lost. Do you want to see?"

Davan swallowed, rubbing at his eyes. "Tribute?"

"What we do isn't easy," Gerith said. "People risk their lives every time they go to fight and, with the Hero's Guild, every time they go to fight is to protect someone else. That's the reason we're here. It needs to be remembered."

Gerith's voice had grown stronger as he spoke, more confident in his opinion.

"Here," said Gerith, reaching down and pulling Davan up. He supported him as they walked to the mural until Davan could get a good look at the thing. There were faces there he recognised. People he'd known.

"Look!" he said, pointing at the face he missed most. The one with the huge moustache. "It's Ferran!"

Whoever the artist had been, they'd been talented, capturing the old Guildhead almost exactly as Davan remembered him. His gaze moved over the mural, drinking in the sight of his friends and comrades. All gone, save for him.

Davan swallowed again, his throat tight. There was a picture of him next to Ferran. Him as he had been. Before, he'd spent the last twenty years destroying what he'd spent so long building in the first place. It struck him. He'd made his decision when he'd offered the dragon its first hoard.

"Right," he said. "Do you have a bed here that won't collapse if someone sits on it?"

"I—" Gerith hesitated. "Yes, we do. Why?"

"I'll need somewhere to sleep while we sort this mess out."

The youth still looked confused. "What do you mean?"

"You just said it yourself," Davan replied, jabbing at the mural. "These people gave their lives for this Guild. They left a legacy, and we can't stand by while it crumbles to dust."

"You're staying?" Gerith asked, unable to keep the excitement from his voice. "You're returning to the Guild?"

Davan bit his lip. He'd been right all along. It wasn't his fight and it wasn't his responsibility. He could walk away right now, go back to how he'd lived for the past twenty years and no one could blame him.

Aside from himself.

He nodded. It wasn't his responsibility. He was making it his responsibility. "You did well today, but somebody needs to teach you how to fight." Davan shot him a grin. "So you can stop the dragon before it almost rips my arm off."

Gerith's mouth twitched upwards before he smothered the expression. "Today has made me realise that there's much to learn. I'd be happy to take a step back. The Guild-head job has been yours for twenty years. I've just been keeping the seat warm."

Davan nodded and placed a hand on the boy's shoulder. "You did a good job with no one here to teach you."

"You're here now," Gerith said.

"Aye," Davan agreed. He stepped closer to the mural, straightening his picture. "And I think it's about time we started setting things to right."

THE END

B. R. TURNAGE, EDITOR

. . .

The Hero's Journey in A Hero's Work:

ORDINARY WORLD: Davan is in his ordinary world, going from tavern to tavern, trying to forget the events of his past.

Call to Adventure: Gerith calls to Davan from outside the tavern, trying to explain that he needs his help.

Denial of Challenge: Davan tells Gerith where to go. Repeatedly.

Meeting with the Mentor: Gerith and Davan head to the Heroes Guild, and meet the Guildhead, who is, in fact, Gerith.

Crossing the Threshold: Gerith explains the problem further and Davan, after some difficulty with the door, crosses the threshold and finds the manticore.

Test, Allies, Enemies: Davan solves Gerith's problem with the manticore, discusses his old mentor, Ferran, and solves another problem with the Gryphon.

Approach to the Innermost Cave: Gerith tells Davan about a final problem and, after some convincing, approaches the basement containing the wyvern.

The Ordeal: Davan takes on the wyvern, discovers it's not actually a wyvern, and suffers grievous wounds.

The Reward: After correctly identifying the dragon, Davan sacrifices his own pay and is rewarded at seeing the dragon's happiness at gaining its first hoard.

The Road Back: After some recovery time, Davan and Gerith find and discuss the mural to the
fallen heroes.

Resurrection: Davan realises that he owes it to himself

406

and his fallen comrades to ensure their legacy isn't left to crumble.

Return with Elixir: Davan accepts the responsibility of restoring the Heroes Guild to its former glory.

BIO: G. J. Dunn writes from a sofa in Leyland, UK. His short fiction has been published in various magazines including Andromeda Spaceways Inflight Magazine, Fission Magazine, and the 99 Fleeting Fantasies anthology. His debut novel, Going Fourth, is now available online. You can find him online at gjdunn.co.uk or @ridicufiction on Instagram. When not writing, he develops gene therapies, runs half marathons, and attempts to tire out his border collie, Belle. So far, he's only succeeded with the first two.

About the Author
ABOUT FWO

Fantasy-Writers.org is a free website for writers of fantasy stories to meet and interact with other writers in the same genre. The site features story submission for peer review, forums, a link directory, and private messages. We welcome you even if you are not a writer and would like to discuss the fantasy genre.

Find us at https://www.fantasy-writers.org/